Photograph by Nii Okai of Lightville Photography

Boakyewaa Glover is a graduate of the University of Ghana and earned a master's degree in psychology from New York University. She has worked as a news anchor and presenter for TV3 and Metro TV; and organizational psychologist and consultant for various consulting firms in New York, Washington DC, and Atlanta.

Boakyewaa's love of writing began as early as age six, when she collected scraps of paper on which to write down her stories. This passion and dedication has led her to author three novels thus far: *Circles* (2009), *The Justice* (2013), and *Tendai* (2013). She also regularly maintains a blog displaying her short stories, poems, articles, and movie reviews. A self-professed entertainment addict, Boakyewaa considers life to be the ultimate muse.

She is currently the regional change management manager for Newmont Ghana Gold Limited; as well as the Group Director for Minds on Fire Group, a publishing, entertainment and creative lounge company.

For more author information, visit:

www.boakyewaaglover.com
www.mindsonfiregroup.com

THE
JUSTICE

THE
JUSTICE

God. Country. Family.

By
Boakyewaa Glover

Minds on Fire, Ghana

ISBN-10: 0989225208
EAN-13: 9780989225205

This book is a work of fiction. Names, characters, places
and incidents are either the product of the author's
imagination or they are used fictitiously. Any resemblance
to actual events or locations or persons, living or dead, is
entirely coincidental.

First published 2013 by
Minds on Fire Group
No. 1a Gowa Close,
Roman Ridge,
P.O. Box 9008, Accra
Ghana

Printed for Minds on Fire

To my mother Abena Otu; thank you for my life and your unconditional love. I love you more than you could ever know.

To my brothers, Nana Kofi and Nana Akuoko, you guys are the best brothers a middle sister could ever ask for.

To my extended family, I couldn't have asked to be born into a better group of people.

And to my father, James Amoako Glover (RIP), thank you for the gift of words. I love you.

Always, B

My deepest gratitude to Jonathan Hutchful, Estella Anku and Seton Nicholas for reading, enjoying and critiquing each chapter of the book as I wrote it. Your encouragement and support got me to this point and I really appreciate you all.

My warm thanks to all my friends and family who have supported the publication, launch and marketing of Circles, The Justice and Tendai. It's been fun, it's been bumpy, and there's still more to come.

Thank you.

1

*A*bby unfurled her body from its fetal position and stretched—a long, deep stretch that she felt from the tips of her fingers down to her toes. She exhaled deeply, enjoying the soothing relief her loosened muscles gave her and hating the thought of waking up. With her eyes still closed, she turned on her side and reached out to touch him. Her eyes flipped open when she grasped air. She blinked rapidly, trying to adjust her sight to the darkness in the room. The bedroom door was slightly ajar, and light from the living room filtered in softly. Muted sounds followed the light, and she guessed Reyn had woken up to catch the morning news. She shook her head and closed her eyes again. It was Saturday, why would anyone want to wake up before noon on a Saturday? A few minutes later, she got up reluctantly from the bed and strolled into the bathroom. Hopefully a hot shower would wake her up.

The water was warm, and she welcomed each drop of it as it engulfed her from head to toe. She closed her eyes and lowered her head, savoring the feel of the warmth on her back. For a moment, nothing mattered. Nothing was more important than standing there underneath the shower. It was her sanctuary, her non-negotiable morning ritual—thirty minutes of a warm shower every morning. This was the only time she felt truly at peace.

"Babe! Babe! You need to come see this, now!"

Abby snapped out of her reverie and frowned. Did she hear something? Was it the TV? She pulled back the shower curtain and waited, listening.

"Babe, did you hear me? You need to come see this, right now!"

The urgency in his voice was unmistakable. Abby turned the shower off and stepped out quickly, grabbing a towel as she walked out to her bedroom. Reyn hurried into the bedroom just as she stepped in. He grabbed the remote from the bedside table and turned on the TV sitting on top of the dresser. Abby tightened the towel around her as a feeling of dread seeped into her skin. She swallowed.

"Reyn, what's going on?"

He didn't respond as he sat on the edge of the bed and flipped rapidly through the channels. He gestured at her to come closer just as he finally settled on a channel. He turned the volume up. The voice hit her even before the images did.

"And so it is because of this genuine and sincere desire to see this country rise again as a true icon of Africa that I have finally decided to join the race to become the presidential nominee of the Democratic National Party, and eventually the next president of Ghana!"

Abby dropped onto the bed beside Reyn and she shook her head—visibly shaken and disappointed. Her father had actually done it; despite her yearlong protests, he'd gone ahead and done it.

"I can't believe this. I can't believe this," she muttered, almost inaudibly.

Reyn reached for her hands and squeezed.

She stared at the TV screen, at his smiling face. He was acting as if he'd already won. She didn't blame him for looking so smug. The crowd was going insane, chanting his name over and over. People were ripping their shirts off and beating their chests like they were ready to head into battle right then and there. The women were screaming and waving their hands wildly. How did he do this? How was he able to get people so riled up?

It had been like this for as long as she could remember. Each time he spoke, whether it was to five people or a crowd of ten thousand like today, it was the same—people reacted. He could shut up a mob or he could rally one up in seconds. He had power—power gained through his words, his tall, dominating physique, his education, his drive, his ambition, and his religion. She could never understand why he wanted more. He had everything, and yet it was never enough. Nothing was ever enough, not even family, but who was she kidding? Her father had never been there for them. Why did she expect him to start caring after thirty years? He claimed everything he did was for his family, but it'd always felt to her that God was first, country was second, and family was a distant, forgettable third.

Reyn squeezed her hand again. He leaned over and kissed her cheek.

"I have to head out now. I'll call you tonight, okay?"

She looked at him as if she was seeing him for the first time. She hadn't even noticed that he was fully dressed. When did he do that?

"You're leaving now? It's Saturday."

"I've been dealing with emails for the last hour, crazy emergency at the mill. The community protests have escalated. If I hurry, I can catch the 10 a.m. flight to Takoradi. I promise I'll be back tonight, and then we can talk about all of this."

Abby continued to stare at him, dazed and confused by both what he was saying and what was happening on the TV. She nodded absentmindedly. He leaned close and kissed her again, this time on the mouth.

"Love you," he whispered.

And then he was gone. She took a deep breath and then returned her gaze to the TV screen, watching as her father strutted up and down the stage, smiling and waving, getting the crowd more worked up.

"Damn it!" she cursed loudly. This could not be happening.

Abby grabbed the remote and switched the TV off. Her father shouldn't have. He really shouldn't have. Everything was about to change. She could feel it, and it wasn't a good feeling. She stood up, glanced at the wet circle on her bed, and cursed again as she pulled her towel off and strode off to the bathroom. She needed twenty more minutes under the shower. Maybe that would help, just maybe.

∽

Two hours later, Abby was in her car, heading to her parents' home. She wasn't sure if her father would be home yet. Why would he? He was probably doing interviews or meeting with his party supporters, strategizing and planning. All the same, she couldn't stay home. She had to go talk to her father and mother and find out what had happened. She nervously tapped the steering wheel with her fingers. What could possibly have happened? The last time she spoke with her father about his political ambitions, he agreed it wasn't the right time. He said he would focus on her mother and their family. What had changed? Did he fully grasp the implications of the decision he'd taken? Of course he did. Who was she kidding? He just didn't care.

Abby pulled up to the gate of her parents' massive, sprawling mansion at East Legon. When she was growing up, she loved every inch of the six-acre estate, but now the ostentatious spread nauseated her. It was pretentious and overbearing, just like her father. She was surprised the ruling party hadn't criticized her father about this house and his other properties. Then again, not many dared to point fingers at the former chief justice, including the current government. He was untouchable—an untouchable who had decided he wanted more: the office of the president.

The guard at the gate let her through after a cursory glance at the car, and she sped up the long, winding tiled driveway. Surprise, her father was actually home. His Mercedes S-Class was parked right in front of the Grecian-style entryway. Once inside, she walked straight to his study and barged in.

Justice Joseph Annan was sitting in the lounge area of his study, deep in conversation with his chief of staff, Caleb Osei, when his study doors were flung open. He stood up angrily and scowled at his daughter.

"How many times have I told you to knock before you come in here?" he snapped.

"How many times have I told you not to run for president?" she snapped back.

Caleb stood up quickly and took a step toward Abby, but the Justice restrained him. He looked at the Justice, frowning, wondering why he wouldn't just let him at her. Caleb was tall, incredibly so, bordering on six foot three. He took care of his body, and his lean, chiseled frame was like a work of art. He knew how to get what he wanted and he hated to be stopped, especially when it had to do with the Justice's insolent, stubborn, ungrateful, and disrespectful daughter.

"Don't even bother, Caleb. Go call Eddy and tell him I need him at the house right now. We've wasted four years, I don't have an extra minute to waste."

Caleb glanced at her and then back at the Justice. He nodded. "I'll call Stella Adams as well. If we don't give her an exclusive today, we won't hear the end of it."

Despite Joseph's caution, Caleb paused right in front of Abby and stared hard at her.

"You should really watch how you speak to your father," he said sternly.

Before she could respond, he brushed past her and left the room. Flustered, she turned her attention to her father, who had settled back into the sofa.

"How could you do this?" she wailed, anger mixed with hurt and frustration.

"I don't owe you an explanation, Abiel. I told you I was going to run, and you thought what? You thought your childish tantrums would work?"

Abby cringed at the use of her full first name—Abiel— meaning "God is my father." Each time her father used that name, she felt he was telling her that *he* was God.

"My tantrums? *My tantrums?* I have tried to discuss this with you logically. I thought you heard me. How could you do this? How can you even consider running when she isn't well? Don't you even care? She still needs you to be there for her, and this is how you want to spend the year? Trotting across the country making speeches? And what will happen after you win? Every eye will be on you, and on her!"

Annan got up and marched up to her.

"Don't even pretend that this is about your mother! More than anyone else I know what my wife needs, and she doesn't need you acting like she's deranged or something."

Abby stepped back from him, stunned. She shook her head, trying to make sense of what he was saying.

"She has a mental disorder, Daddy. She is bipolar," she said through clenched teeth.

"Those are just words and terms that doctors like to throw around. I have your mother's situation handled!" he hissed.

She shook her head again, trying to regain her composure. He was insane. He truly was.

He leaned closer to her. "You think I don't know why you've been protesting my candidacy? You're more concerned that everyone will find out about that married man you've been cavorting with for the last three years!"

Abby was stunned into silence.

He continued, motivated by the mortified look on her face.

"You think I don't know what is going on? You've been having an affair with a VP at Proctor Oil for the past three years. His name is Reyn Proctor, son of Texas oil magnate George Proctor, married to Emma Harner, daughter of another oil magnate. They have two young children together. You thought I wouldn't suspect? You live in a $3,000 a month apartment at Airport and you drive an Audi Q7."

"I make good money," Abby mumbled.

"You make $7,000 a month before taxes. It is highly unlikely you would spend that much out of your own pocket. I know because I paid for everything for you up until three years ago. So basically, you went from living off your father to living off a sugar daddy."

His words jolted her out of her mild stupor.

"He's not a sugar daddy! And this is not about him or me! This is about Mummy. She's sick. She's sick! You want to erase the whole breakdown? You want to erase the past four years? You want to pretend that your wife is completely dandy and fully functioning? Really? Is that your play? If that's the case, then you need to wake up! It is your duty to take care of her, to be there for her. How can you possibly consider running?"

Annan walked back to the sofa and sat down. He looked at her as if he was mulling over his next words before he uttered them.

"I am going to be the next president of Ghana, and that is just a fact of life you have to live with. And the other fact you have to deal with is this: today will be the last time you ever speak to me the way you just did in front of Caleb. Do you understand?"

Without waiting for a reply, he waved her off.

"Get out."

Abby turned around and walked out. She slammed the door hard behind her. Caleb was standing in the foyer to her right, pacing up and down and hissing obscenities into his cell phone. He glanced up at her and lowered the phone, ready to say something to her. She turned to her left and walked quickly up the stairs. Her father's dressing down was enough; she couldn't deal with Caleb as well.

As she walked down the long corridor to her parents' master suite, Abby felt apprehensive. She hadn't seen her mother in months. She could use work as an excuse, but that wasn't really it. Ever since what happened, her relationship with her mother had gone from not so great to pretty bad. She avoided interactions with her mother as much as she could, which was a terrible thing to say, but she really couldn't deal with her antics and her moods.

Four years ago, in early 2008, her mother's twin sister, Auntie Bertha, was brutally stabbed and killed in the living room of her home. Auntie Bertha was a widow whose only child, Joey, lived in New York. Bertha lived alone in a sizable house that the Justice had built for her years before. She had several helpers: a housekeeper, a houseboy, a gardener, and a driver. However, with the exception of the housekeeper, the rest were all day workers who were gone by 6 p.m. On the night that Bertha was killed, the housekeeper was gone visiting her children, so the only people at home were Bertha and the security guard on duty at the gate. Abby's mother discovered her sister's body when she arrived to pick her up for brunch the morning after she was killed. The security man was lying shot dead right inside the gate, and Bertha's body was on the living room floor, stabbed multiple times. Finding her twin sister's body sent Abby's mother on a downward spiral from which she still hadn't recovered.

The police concluded that it was armed robbers, considering the amount of jewelry, electronics, and other home items that were missing. The investigation was short. A few weeks later, three men were killed in a standoff with the police. Items from Bertha's home were found in a car at the scene. Knowledge that justice had been served didn't do much to stop her mother's descent into crazy land.

Abby's mother was a woman of strong faith, but unfortunately Bertha's death permanently changed her convictions, beliefs, and principles beyond repair. She avoided the church like the plague and lost all interest in the religious activities and rituals that she used to hold dear, like prayer meetings and women's fellowship. She became erratic, easily irritated, despondent, moody, angry, sullen, weepy, and needy all rolled into one. Their family doctor said that even the bravest of people would be permanently scarred finding the body of a loved one like that, and Abby knew that even before the tragedy brave definitely wasn't an adjective she'd ever use to describe her mother.

Her mother was a delicate, sensitive, prim, and proper woman who had faith and trust in life. That was all gone now. The brutality of her sister's death had wiped away any sense of goodwill toward mankind, and coexisting with people just became harder and harder. Prior to Bertha's death, Abby and her mother had a fragile relationship. Her mother disapproved of almost every choice she made, and Abby in turn just couldn't relate to the delicate ice queen. After Bertha's death, things became worse. They could hardly communicate without descending into a tense standoff. Some days were good days, when her mother seemed at peace and content with life. On those days, she was seemingly renewed, energetic, talking and chatting like normal, and even excited and eager about life. And then there were days when it seemed that she remembered what had happened, and the sorrow and anguish took over. Then she acted crazy, possessed, angry, sullen, snappy, and easily irritated. That was it, really; Abby's mother just couldn't allow herself to be happy or remotely content.

Her mood swings become frequent and severe, and it was hard for anyone to be around her. Eventually her father decided it was best for her to stay home and attempt to recuperate and come to terms with what had happened to Bertha. Abby was living in the US at the time of her aunt's death, but she moved home soon after to help her mother get through it. Her move home made no difference to her mother's state of mind. Two years after Bertha's death, her father suggested a family vacation, hoping that a change in scenery could help. They hadn't taken a vacation together as a family in years, so they left for New York not only to visit with Joey and make sure he was okay, but also to get Abby's mother away from an environment that probably reminded her of what she'd lost.

For the first two weeks, New York helped. Her father splurged and got them a spacious three-bedroom summer apartment right in the city. Her mother began to take an interest in her surroundings, and her moods stabilized. They did Broadway, shopped, and attended a couple of concerts at Madison Square Garden. And then one morning, Abby heard her parents arguing heatedly about politics. She couldn't hear their words, but she suspected that her father told her mother he was going back into politics. Joseph withdrew from the political scene after Bertha's death to help his wife through what had happened. For a while Abby respected him for that decision, until the argument that morning in New York. Whatever it was, it set her mother off, and she was back to her snappy, angry moods. Her father finally conceded that something was wrong, so he found an outpatient facility for her mother. A month later, they went from a diagnosis of PTSD to bipolar disorder, and life hadn't been the same since.

Abby slowly pushed the bedroom door open and stepped in.

Adubea Annan was seated behind her armoire in the dressing area in between the main bedroom and the master bathroom, slowly brushing her hair. Instinctively, Abby touched her own long, thick hair. Most of her friends teased her that she probably had Caucasian blood in her. She didn't know if she did or not. All she knew was that she had her mother's hair—jet black, thick, and incredibly long. Whereas Abby got her stubbornness, drive, and intellect from her father, physically she was her mother's child— well, for the most part. Adubea was of average height, slim, and elegant, with a hint of the exotic. Everything about her was ladylike, even when she was acting crazy. She wore superbly tailored clothes—almost always dresses or skirts, with high heels and pearl accessories. Her nails were never plain or chipped. Her hair always looked like she had just walked out of a hair salon, even though she only went once a week. Abby was about the same height but curvier. Her mother had lost weight in the last four years, so physically there was a bit more contrast between the two of them. All the same, Abby had her mother's quintessential beautiful features. Fashion-wise, Abby wore her hair down most of the time and preferred jeans, although she also appreciated the power and impact of a skirt suit and heels. Today she had on her favorite denim high-rise skinny jeans, with an oversized orange rocker tee and two-inch heels that felt like flats most days. She tried to look good, but she knew she hadn't yet attained her mother's level of elegance and sophistication. Maybe one day.

"Ma? Mummy?"

Adubea turned around and then she forced a smile at her daughter. Abby couldn't tell if it was a good day or a bad day. She hoped it was the former. Adubea stood up from her chair and spread her arms wide. Okay, it was a good day.

"Abby dear, when did you get here? Did you catch your father's announcement? Wasn't his speech perfect? I am not a big Caleb fan, but I have to admit that he's a really good writer, though I'm sure Jojo added the touches that made all the difference."

Abby hugged her mother cautiously. She had missed her, ramblings and all.

"I just caught a bit of the speech, but Ma, why would you let him run for office again?"

Adubea stepped back from the hug and frowned.

"Why not? Why would you think I don't want your father to run?"

"Because he needs to be home, with you, taking care of you."

"Taking care of me? Abby, you need to stop acting like I'm an invalid. This is your father's dream, our dream. I appreciate what he did four years ago, giving up his bid after Bertha died, but this is his time."

Adubea walked out of the dressing room and went to sit on the perfectly-made massive California King bed. She crossed her legs, smoothed a little wrinkle on her skirt, and smiled at her daughter.

"And Abby, I don't need any hand-holding. I am fine, so please stop acting like I am sick, dying or worse. This is what Jojo is meant to do, and we're both going to be supportive. Do you understand that?"

Abby was surprised by the sternness in her mother's voice. She went to sit beside her mother. She reached for her hands and squeezed gently.

"You look well, Ma, you really do, but I hope you understand that you still need to take your medicines and that Daddy needs to be there for you."

Adubea stood up abruptly.

"Stop it, Abby, stop it. I am fine, so stop treating me like I'm a child. I lost my twin sister! Of course I wouldn't be the same. I was bound to go through something. It's been four years! Now look at me. Do I look sick to you? I haven't taken any of the pills in four months, and nothing has happened. I have Jojo and my family, and that is all I need."

Abby closed her eyes and inhaled. This day was getting to be too much. She wasn't sure how much more she could take. She rubbed her forehead, thinking of what to say and do next. Her mother hadn't taken her medicine in four months, and even if her parents were in denial, she knew the consequences.

"So, what is new in your life? How's work? Have you met anyone?" her mother asked, smiling sweetly at her.

The mood and tone switch didn't surprise Abby anymore. She smiled back, but didn't answer. Instead, she gripped her mother's hands and stared at her long and hard, trying to convey her worry and concern. Adubea shifted uncomfortably and pulled away, standing abruptly.

"Ma..."

Adubea waved her hands absentmindedly. "The spotlight is going to be back on us again. I don't think I've bought anything new in months. I need to get some things made as soon as possible. You should think about doing the same. You can't wear jeans to every single event. It would be inappropriate. You should get more dresses. Maybe we can convince your father to let us dash off to London for some shopping, although he'll probably say this isn't the time to be extravagant. But then again, a family vacation before everything gets crazy wouldn't hurt. We could invite Joey and—"

Abby placed a finger on her mother's lips to stop the flood of words and then she hugged her close. This was getting difficult. What was she going to do? She hugged her tighter and kissed her mother's cheek, forcing back the tears.

"I love you, Ma. I love you."

2

'*H ello everyone, and welcome to this Saturday's edition of Spotlight. We're broadcasting live from Accra. My name is Paul Yartey and I have our favorite political commentators here with me, Kweku Berko, editor of Democratic Voice, and Kwesi Pianim, a self-proclaimed political watchdog and blogger.*"

"*You know Paul, the 'self-proclaimed' you often attach to my credentials usually comes across as an attempt to discredit my contributions,*" *Kwesi said.*

"*To be honest, when someone says they're a political watchdog, I am not sure what it is supposed to mean. To me, it's a self-bestowed type of role.*"

"*I beg to differ, it is not self-proclaimed, bestowed or whatever you wish to call it. I am a political watchdog. I have dedicated my life and my career to raising awareness around political and government impropriety.*"

"You mean you've dedicated your life and career to protecting the GFP {Government for the People} and maligning all other parties?" Kweku cut in.

"I resent that assertion very much. I present objective and un-biased opinions of our political landscape."

"Okay, okay, let's get into our political landscape then, and there is only one thing worth talking about today. Former Chief Justice Annan officially declares his interest in running for the presidency of Ghana in this year's elections. Comments? Thoughts? Reactions?" Paul asked.

"In my opinion, this is long overdue. There is no greater and more respected statesman than Justice Annan, and no disrespect to our current president or former presidents, but it's the truth. No greater statesman," Kweku said.

"These are some of the things wrong with Ghana politics, the way we like to treat some people like they're gods. I mean, seriously? Greatest statesman ever? Today you want to disregard Osagyefo Dr. Kwame Nkrumah?" Kwesi retorted.

"Listen, I am a lifelong member of the CPP and I have the greatest respect for Nkrumah, but I will say it again and again: no greater statesman than Justice Joseph Annan. During the eight years he was the chief justice, he did more for this country than any other politician in the history of the country. Quote me. I mean, I have all the data and the facts. We went from being number 22 on the global Corruption Perceptions Index to number 55, the crime rate in Ghana went down, and there was an incredible sense of peace in the country. He spearheaded the successful introduction of universal healthcare, introduced practical and affordable educa-tion policies and payment systems, and led the DNP {Democratic National Party} to introduce laws and policies that facilitated eco-nomic prosperity and growth. He fought for gender equality in gov-ernment and business and focused on the true needs of the country."

"And that was all one person, eh?" Kwesi said sarcastically.

"Come on, let's not pretend here, please. The best thing President Yara ever did was make Annan his chief justice."

"We really have to be careful about how we put politicians on pedestals and treat them like gods, because they're not. Annan is a mere man like you, me, or President Otoo."

"President Otoo can never be compared to Justice Annan. You can catch me and throw me in jail if you want to, but President Otoo is, by far, the weakest and worst leader we've ever had in this country. Let him walk into a room right now. Not even a single person would blink or even recognize him as the president; but, let Justice Annan walk into a room, and there you'll see the respect and attention that will be given to him," Kweku said heatedly.

"This is not a celebrity or popularity contest," Kwesi responded sarcastically.

"Aren't our elections decided by popular vote? Huh? And there is no man in Ghana right now who is more popular and more respected than Justice Annan. And if you disagree, then just name one, name one," Kweku taunted his co-commentator.

"I won't even bother to name anyone because you don't even think Nkrumah is worthy."

"Did I ever say that Nkrumah is not worthy? Paul, you're recording this, aren't you? Did I ever say that Nkrumah is not worthy? I don't appreciate such loose accusations."

"Okay, okay, gentlemen, let's move on now. Now this announcement, isn't it a little late in the day? Asenso has been committed to the DNP for over thirty years now. He took up the mantle in 2008 when Annan dropped out, and even though he didn't win the general elections, he came very close, a difference of twenty-five thousand votes," Paul said.

"Exactly! Asenso has been campaigning for three straight years and has been a strong force in opposition, and now Annan *wants to come and reap the benefits? We need to be careful and not assume that Annan's win is guaranteed."*

"For Kwesi to make that comment, it's truly laughable, pure comedy, really. I respect Asenso a great deal and he's done his best, but you just can't compare Asenso to Annan. You just can't. Asenso may have been committed to the party, but Annan has been committed to the country. Annan withdrew from the 2008 race, but he didn't just disappear. He continued to pursue health, education, and social causes and has facilitated the building of schools, hospitals, and other critical infrastructure across the country. So, my friend, let's just put comedy aside and be serious here. There is no contest with the DNP nominations, and there will be no contest in December either. The minute Annan announced his candidacy it was a done deal."

"I really want to warn my friend Kweku Berko today, and he should listen. Justice Annan is just a man, and like any other man, he can fall, and that is what I expect will happen. Let's all just watch."

"And that's what we'll be doing on Spotlight *for the rest of 2012. I can feel that this year will be an unforgettable year in Ghana politics and in the history of the country. Stay tuned, we're going for a short commercial break, and then we'll continue with the discussion."*

∽

Caleb cracked his knuckles and rolled his head from side to side. He was sore and exhausted. He hadn't slept more than four hours in days. Planning today's announcement had taken months. All the meetings, lobbying, and research didn't happen at the snap of a finger. Caleb managed a solid staff dedicated to the Justice's political, business, and social interests, but there was still a lot that required his direct attention and coordination. The Justice relied on him for everything and expected him to be on top of his entire life and obligations. His official title was chief of staff, but his role went beyond that. He was the chief of staff, managing director, CEO, and president of the Justice's entire existence. It had been that way for the last ten years.

It was 2002 when Caleb first met Justice Annan in Washington, DC at the Article One – American Grill and Lounge. Located inside the Hyatt Regency Hotel, Article One was a favorite haunt of White House staffers, journalists, foreign dignitaries, and other politicos. Caleb was a senior legislative assistant working for Senator Josh Durbin from Illinois. It was a good job—he was critical to the senator's team and had influenced the passing or blockage of more bills and policies than he could count. He knew he was making a difference, and he was building a solid reputation as "the go-to guy" in DC. He expected that, in less than a year, he would be promoted to legislative director. If he played his cards right, he would be part of the senator's presidential campaign team. He knew the senator had ambitions. The senator didn't publicly declare them, but Caleb could read it in his eyes. It was the same hunger Caleb himself had. Despite the incredible prospects that lay before him, Caleb was antsy, particularly on that day at Article One bar and grill.

"Did you see the list of guests to this year's dinner? I don't know if it's a dinner or a pop concert. 'N Sync, Britney Spears, and Matchbox Twenty—imagine that."

Caleb smiled at the exasperated senator. The fact that Josh Durbin knew who these artists were was amusing. Durbin was referring to the White House Correspondents' Dinner. Caleb had attended three times before, and it was one of his favorite events of the year. As a Senate staffer, he had multiple opportunities throughout the year to network, but the dinner was the ultimate for him.

"Well sir, I think President Leonard recognizes that he needs the young vote. He may have won the election last year, but only 30 percent of adults between eighteen and thirty-five voted for him. That's dismal. Andrew tells me it's a priority for Leonard this year. He'd rather not wait till 2006 before he begins to court the young vote."

Josh Durbin wiped his mouth with his napkin and leaned back in his chair.

"I'm glad you brought Andrew's name up. There is something I've been meaning to discuss with you."

Caleb took a deep breath. He knew there was a reason why Durbin had asked him to lunch on a Monday in March. Mondays were busy, and March was just a hellish month. In addition, Durbin didn't invite any of the other staffers. He preferred to dine in a group and only reserved one-on-one lunches or dinners for important news or occasions. When he got the invitation for the lunch, Caleb could think of only two reasons: either Andrew, the senator's current legislative director, was moving on, and the job would finally be Caleb's, or Durbin wanted to give him an off-the-books assignment for his eyes and attention only. It wouldn't be the first time. In addition to being the known "go-to guy," Caleb had also built up a reputation as a "discreet fixer," and the senator had a tendency to pass tasks to him that required a high level of discretion and tact. Caleb sincerely hoped that he'd been invited to the lunch because Andrew was moving on. He liked and respected Andrew. He was very good at his job and he taught Caleb all he knew about Washington. There'd been talk for a while now about tensions between Andrew and the senator. Caleb had his suspicions, but he had no proof. He would be sad to see Andrew leave the senator's staff, but when it was time, it was time. Andrew was brilliant. He could get work with anyone.

Caleb leaned back in his chair and looked directly at the senator. He wanted this job very badly.

"Yes sir?"

"Andrew is leaving us, probably by the end of this month."

Caleb nodded, so far so good.

"And I'm promoting Leila to his position."

Caleb froze. What? Huh? What the heck? Leila was a new staffer who joined them two years ago. She didn't have as much experience as Andrew or Caleb, but what she lacked in experience she made up in charm, guts, and ambition. Andrew and Leila had dated, but it all ended abruptly six months ago, and rumors began that Durbin had stepped in and was now involved with Leila. *Damn, so it was all true*, Caleb thought. He was stunned. He'd been warned several times about how women in DC got their way, but this was just ridiculous.

"Leila, sir? Leila?" he asked in the most respectful voice he could muster.

"She's driven, Caleb. She got us that deal with Senator Kingsley, the one you and Andrew worked on for months. She's a fast learner and she's very good at finding loopholes. She noticed half the discrepancies in last year's health bill."

Caleb looked away from the senator and glanced around the room. He had to be careful with his next words. He was

a thirty-two-year-old, up-and-coming DC staffer and ana-
lyst, and reputation was everything. He was boiling mad,
but he had to be measured and composed—to an extent.

"Leila is good, sir, but she's not better than Andrew or
me. I went to Yale, she went to Boston U. I have fourteen
years military, law, and government experience, she has three.
You're the first senator she's ever worked for, I've worked for
three, including a long-term senior senator. She's worked on
five bills, I've worked on thirty. Leila isn't qualified to be the
legislative director. Heck, she's not even qualified for my job."

Durbin flashed crimson, and his jaw tensed. The senator wasn't a big man, but he was tall and he had stature—
features that Caleb knew would serve him well in his bid
to be president. Despite that, he had a telltale face. When
he was angry, he would instantly turn red, his jaw would
tighten, and his eyes would narrow. He would have to work
on that if he wanted to be president one day.

"I know your experience, Caleb. I hired you. Leila is going to be the next legislative director, and I do hope that you
will be interested in staying on. I'll see you at the office."

With that, Durbin stood up, dropped some bills on
the table, and walked out of the restaurant. Another telltale sign of Durbin's: he couldn't carry on a conversation
if he was emotional. Caleb waited a few minutes and then
walked out. He stopped outside the hotel entrance and exhaled. On days like this when politics reared its ugly head,
he wondered if leaving the marines and the battlefield for
the treachery of Washington was even worth it. He glanced
to his right, staring at the place he'd called home for so
long—Capitol Hill. The view was spectacular; it never
ceased to amaze him. He dug into his pants, pulled out a
pack of cigarettes, and lit one up. What now?

"That's a terrible habit."

Caleb tore his gaze away from the hill ahead of him and looked at the man on his right. He looked familiar, but Caleb wasn't sure. The man was tall, six feet for sure, but slightly portly. His face, posture, and tone reeked of money or position, but Caleb didn't care.

"Who are you?" he snapped, taking a deep swig of his cig just to annoy the man further. He blew a long puff of smoke out in the intruder's direction.

The man shook his head. "I'm Joseph Annan, chief justice of Ghana, and that," he gestured at Caleb's cigarette, "that's going to kill you in twenty years."

Caleb eyed him warily. He knew who the man was now. He was known as the Justice, and he was supposedly the most powerful man in Ghana.

"You're Ghanaian, aren't you?" Annan continued.

"Every Ghanaian thinks he can spot another Ghanaian. Are we invisibly marked?" Caleb chuckled.

Annan smiled. "I suppose."

"So, I couldn't help but overhear your conversation in the restaurant," Annan added.

Caleb laughed and shook his head. "That's the beauty of DC dining."

"I want to offer you a job, with me, in Ghana."

Caleb stopped laughing. Was he serious?

"You're joking, right?"

Annan raised an eyebrow and frowned. "Why would I be joking?"

Caleb shifted his stance and looked at Annan squarely in the eye.

"Okay, listen, I don't care what you heard, but I'm not looking for a new job, and definitely not in Ghana. My family may be from Ghana originally, but my life is here, and it'll take me less than a day to find something else here. I can work for another senator, or go into consulting or private practice. So, no disrespect, sir, but I have options and they don't include Ghana."

He put out his cig, tucked his hands into his pocket defiantly, and stared at the Justice. Was this man for real? Who did he think he was?

"You may think you're on top of the world now. You may think you have it all figured out, your future all mapped out, but you're just one of hundreds here." Annan gestured at the crowds moving around them. "In Ghana, with me, you'll be one of a few. Ghana is changing. We have the most matured democracy in Africa. We have the fastest growing economy. The work you'll do with me will be impactful, life changing, history making. You'll have more influence and power than you can imagine. You're competing with people just like you here—Yale educated, hungry, and ambitious. In Ghana, you'll be in a league of your own. So, if you want to be part of the pack, suit yourself and stay. Leila will definitely need your help. But, if you want to *lead* the pack, then give me a call."

Annan handed him a business card and then strode back into the hotel. Caleb stared at the card, his mind racing. He took a deep breath, looked at the hill in front of him, and then looked back at the hotel doors. Damn it! He took off after the Justice.

Ten years later, he'd cured himself of smoking and was sitting in the Justice's study planning a presidential campaign. In retrospect, the Justice hadn't lied to him that day in DC. He had dinner with Annan and the then-president of Ghana, Samuel Yara, that night. After that, it was a whirlwind of life-changing moments. Officially, he was hired as the Justice's chief of staff and senior advisor, but, in truth, he was everything. The Justice was President Yara's best friend, confidante, and most trusted advisor, and Caleb was the Justice's only advisor. So by extension, it felt like he was running a bloody country at the time. Every recommendation, idea, proposal, or thought he had made its way back to the president through the Justice—and once it came from the Justice, the president implemented it. It was a power Caleb never had while working in DC, a power he enjoyed, but used wisely. His ultimate goal was never personal gain, although that was unavoidable, but he was primarily focused on the Justice's success first and the country's growth and prosperity second. Thankfully, the two never really conflicted with each other.

Caleb learned three very important lessons his first year in Ghana: first, don't fight the system; second, know the system intimately; and third, nothing is more important than the system. And that was exactly what he did – he adapted. When Caleb first moved to Ghana, he was stunned by the level of corruption that existed. Politicians openly inflated budgets, diverted funds to personal interests, and lived like kings while a majority of the people struggled to satisfy basic human needs. That was when he decided that the Justice's brand would be nothing like that. Sure, Caleb didn't rule out making a little off the top, but they would be extremely discreet about it. Caleb liked to think that even the CIA wouldn't be able to find any dirt on them. Caleb ran a very tight ship. They made extra money only if the opportunity was right and their tracks could be covered completely. In addition, they wouldn't take anything that would jeopardize economic development and the general well-being of Ghanaians. Choosing to go that route was laudable, because the risk of jail was minimal. Corruption was expected, but all the same, Caleb made anti-corruption and integrity the Justice's brand. He knew what the end goal was, and he wanted to be sure no one, absolutely no one, could find any possible dirt on the Justice. The only problem was his family.

Caleb paced the Justice's study, wondering how the campaign was going to survive Mrs. Annan's erratic behavior and Abby's affair. It would be easier dealing with children born out of wedlock than this. Just as corruption was expected, infidelity was a way of life in Ghana. For any other candidate, it wouldn't even matter that the daughter of a candidate was sleeping with a married man, but the Justice wasn't like any other candidate. The Justice didn't stray, not even once, at least not on Caleb's watch. The Justice had needs that surmounted all other physical needs, including sex, and that was the need to glorify his God, elevate his country, and respect his family. God, country, and family meant more to the Justice than life itself.

Caleb admired the Justice's values even if he didn't agree with them all, particularly when it came to religion. Caleb didn't subscribe to any particular doctrine, but he also didn't consider himself an atheist. The Justice, on the other hand, had very little patience for people who questioned the existence of God or Jesus Christ. Caleb learned that the hard way within months of working for him, and now they had a delicate truce. Caleb promised not to question the Justice's God or faith, and in turn the Justice wouldn't drag him to church or to the multiple other religious events that consumed his itinerary. In some ways, the Justice didn't subscribe to the humility and compassion doctrines his religion espoused, but he was at church with his wife every Sunday without fail. He was an uncompromising man in many respects. He was quick to quote the Bible when it suited him, and he publicly attributed all his success to God. He worshipped his God in his own way.

So here Caleb was, finally with a candidate who was intelligent, powerful, wealthy, charismatic, religious, and faithful to his wife, and still success wasn't guaranteed because of two people who shared the Justice's surname. Family—they could be either the backbone to your success or your downfall.

The door to the study opened, and Annan stepped in.

"Caleb? I thought you left already. Whatever you're working on now, you know it can wait, right? It's almost 3 a.m."

"I know. I just had a few things I wanted to wrap up tonight. Is everything okay? Did you need something?"

The Justice dropped onto the sofa and placed his feet on the ottoman. He sighed.

"I can't sleep. I don't know if it's the adrenaline from today or something else, but I know a gin and tonic would help."

Caleb chuckled and walked over to the bar at the other side of the room. He mixed two glasses quickly and deftly, and handed one to Annan. Then he nestled into the armchair across from the Justice. Both men sipped their drinks quietly, lost in their own thoughts. The Justice eventually broke the silence.

"It would be a lot easier if I had a bastard child somewhere, wouldn't it Caleb?"

Caleb laughed out loud, almost choking on his drink. He set his glass down and nodded at Annan.

"Yes sir, it would be," he admitted.

They had discussed his family issues extensively over the last few months, right up to this morning before Annan took the stage. In the end, they both agreed that this was the Justice's moment. They couldn't walk away from this opportunity like they did four years ago. This was it. So, they seized the moment and now they were back to reality.

"So what now? I have a daughter who's having an affair with a married man and a wife who's unstable. First Timothy 3 verse 5 says, 'but if a man does not know how to manage his own household, how will he take care of the church of God?' and by extension, how can he manage a country?" the Justice asked.

"You know where I stand, sir. We have two options with your wife. Option one would be to admit her situation and add that she is getting the best possible care. Put it out there, and eventually it becomes a non-issue. That's my recommendation. Option two, don't talk about it or admit it. We'll keep her away from everyone, which essentially means we'd have to muzzle her. No public events with you, and no events on her own, absolutely nothing. I am not exactly sure how we can achieve that without raising some suspicion. You just announced your candidacy. People would expect your wife to be by your side, especially since you're such a family man."

The Justice was silent. It didn't sound like he had any options at all. He was hesitant to put Adubea out there publicly; she wasn't ready for the scrutiny or the pressure. On the other hand, he also didn't want to admit that his wife had a problem. It could be interpreted that he was being callous and uncaring by running for office while his wife dealt with mental issues.

"And Abby? What's your recommendation there?" he asked, changing focus.

Caleb took a deep breath. *Shoot her and bury her body where no one would find it*, he wanted to say.

"Well?" the Justice probed.

"She needs to end her relationship. Our campaign won't survive it if people find out about the affair. You and I both know the importance of mining to the Ghanaian economy, but if this affair comes out, everyone will think you're soft on mining because of your daughter's relationship. They'll think Reyn Proctor has you in his back pocket and has been paying you for your support. All those environmental and international watchdog groups who've been on the DNP's case about the lax mining laws that you established during your tenure will string us up and burn us at the stake. Everyone will question your integrity and motives," Caleb said dramatically.

He paused and then continued, "Beyond that, people will question your faith. They'll think you're a hypocrite. You talk of God and morality, but your daughter is having an affair with a married man with children."

Annan gritted his teeth and looked away from Caleb. The truth stung. He took a long swig of his drink and leaned back in the sofa, staring at the ceiling.

Caleb continued, "I can end the relationship, with your permission."

The Justice stood up and walked over to the window facing the backyard. The surface of the pool appeared to be sparkling—almost as if someone had sprinkled diamonds on top of it. The lawn was immaculate, and everything else was serene and still. Why couldn't everything in his life be like this? He could never seem to find peace, not since four years ago when tragedy hit his family. He turned away from the window and looked at Caleb.

"End it."

And then he was gone from the study, as abruptly as he had entered.

Caleb finished his drink, packed up his things, and walked out of the room. One decision had been made, but there was still the issue of Mrs. Annan. His interactions with her had reduced since her erratic behavior became severe and pronounced. He knew she was still suffering and in pain after the brutal killing of her twin sister. He couldn't imagine how that felt, but he also had very little patience with how long it was taking her to get through the trauma. He knew it was ignorant on his part to expect her to simply snap out of it, but all the same, he really wished she would. In her current condition, it would be risky to put her out there in front of people. Unfortunately, for eight years, while the DNP was in government, Mrs. Annan was by the Justice's side for almost every single event. Even though she wasn't first lady then, it almost felt like she was. President Yara's wife didn't exactly exude beauty or elegance, whereas Mrs. Annan oozed it from every pore. People knew her, loved her, and would expect to see her by his side during his campaign. Her absence would be noticed immediately and questioned. But on the other hand, her presence if erratic and unpredictable could be disastrous and distracting for the campaign. Hopefully, the Justice would make a decision on what to do with his wife soon. The campaign had been launched. Every minute counted.

3

The church was packed to the brim by 7:30 a.m., a whole half an hour before the service was meant to start. It was never even that full for the December 31st service. Cars lined up from the front door down the road for at least half a mile, but Annan wasn't worried about parking. His driver Eben maneuvered the Mercedes past the throng of cars and people and pulled up into the Justice's reserved spot next to the reverend's at the side of the church. He turned off the engine and stepped out of the car. He walked over to the Justice's side to open the door, but Annan shook his head and gestured for him to give them time. Annan looked at his wife sitting next to him. He really shouldn't have brought Adubea with him to church today of all days, but after talking to Caleb a few hours earlier, he figured he wouldn't know what option to choose with regard to Adubea until he took a chance.

"So are you ready? We haven't been here in a while, but this is a very important service to me."

"I understand, Jojo. It's important for you to be here the day after your announcement. Everyone will be expecting you to show up and say something. I understand that, and I understand your reservations too, but I can handle this. I've been by your side all these years and I'm not going to let you down now. I want this as much as you do. You can't question my support now."

Annan nodded and reached for her hands. He squeezed them.

"I know you want this, but there is a lot at stake, and if you can't handle the pressure here today, I'll have to keep you away from the campaign."

"What? Jojo, this is me here. What do you think I am going to do? Embarrass you? You think I can't handle the pressure of one church service? I'm very offended that you would even say that to me, but we'll deal with this when we get back home. So right now, just open the door and let's get going," she said firmly.

Annan hesitated and started to say something, but she turned away from him and opened her door. She stepped out and straightened her kaba. Annan got out of the car quickly and followed her toward the front entrance. As he walked behind her, his heart stirred a little. His feelings for her had changed over the last four years, but he still cared deeply for her. She looked the part of a first lady in waiting today, clad in a Fatia Nkrumah design kente, form-fitting around her slim frame, with her long hair pulled back into a tight and clean ponytail. She clutched a blue purse tightly, and he wondered if her grip was because she was nervous or excited. She lived for moments like this, to shine as Mrs. Annan, but over the last few years, she hadn't had a lot of opportunities to play the role. He caught up to her and reached for her hand. She looked up at him, surprised at the gesture, but also grateful for it. She accepted his hand, and they walked into the church together.

"Matthew 20, verses 25 to 28: 'Jesus called them together and said, "You know that the rulers of the Gentiles lord it over them, and their high officials exercise authority over them. Not so with you. Instead, whoever wants to become great among you must be your servant, and whoever wants to be first must be your slave, just as the Son of Man did not come to be served, but to serve, and to give his life as a ransom for many."'" The reverend paused and looked pensively at the quiet and somber crowd.

Then he continued, "We all know the situation we live under in this country and the type of leadership we have craved but lacked for years. That is because our politicians don't know how to be servant leaders. They don't understand that to be great, they must first serve. But all is not lost for us. We have a man amongst us whom we've watched grow to be the type of leader Jesus talked about, a leader who has always put the country before himself and has selflessly given of himself more than any other politician or self-proclaimed leader in this country. So today, I am very proud to invite to the podium a man I respect very deeply, a true man of God, a true servant leader, and by God's grace, the future president of Ghana, Justice Joseph Annan!"

The church erupted into thunderous applause, and the entire congregation got up to its feet. The Justice stood up and walked slowly toward the front of the church. He paused every now and then to shake hands and hug people along the way. The applause continued even when he reached the podium and stood next to the reverend. Annan raised his hand, and everyone fell silent. He gestured for them to sit, and they did.

"I truly appreciate Reverend Douglas's kind words. The reverend has been a blessing and a mentor to me for over twenty years, and without him and the support of this church and all of you, I wouldn't have had the opportunities to serve this country that I have had. So thank you reverend, and thank you all very much."

The church stood up again and started clapping. The reverend patted Annan on the back and walked back to his seat up front with the other senior church members. Annan waited for the church to settle back down, and then he started.

"I will not take up too much of your time, because I am here to worship and listen to God's word like all of you, so this service today won't be about me. However, I did want a few minutes to say something very short to you. As most of you know, yesterday I announced my interest to run for the presidency of Ghana—"

"Amen!" someone in the congregation shouted.

Annan smiled. "Thank you, thank you. I'm here really to assure you all of one simple thing—I do this not for myself, but for my country. Philippians 2 verses 3-8 states, 'Do nothing out of selfish ambition or vain conceit, but in humility consider others better than yourselves. Each of you should look not only to your own interests, but also to the interests of others. Your attitude should be the same as that of Christ Jesus: Who, being in very nature God, did not consider equality with God something to be grasped, but made himself nothing, taking the very nature of a servant, being made in human likeness. And being found in appearance as a man, he humbled himself and became obedient to death-even death on a cross.' That is why I have put myself forward to help lead this country, not because I feel entitled, not because I feel it is my right, and never because of hidden interests or agenda. I am putting myself forward because I want to serve. I deeply, sincerely, and humbly wish to serve the people of this country. I simply want to be a vessel for God to do his work in Ghana and lead us to prosperity and growth. That is why I want to be your president."

As the congregation started to clap again, Annan glanced at his wife, seated calmly with her hands clasped in front of her, looking up at him with a blank gaze. He felt deceitful standing in front of the church assuring them that his intentions were pure while his wife, the woman who represented what was wrong in his life, sat there like that. He paused and took a deep breath. He had to keep the woes of his family out of this. This was his moment.

"Proverbs 16 verse 9 states, 'The heart of man plans his way, but the Lord establishes his steps.' So, I've asked the Lord to help establish my steps in this coming year so that I may do his work with integrity. I hope I will get your support as well. God bless Ghana, and God bless you all."

The congregation thronged around Annan as he made his way back to his seat. He took his time to shake everyone's hand and say a few words to them. These people loved, respected, and worshipped him completely, but he also knew that the love that they had was tenuous. If they ever found out that his daughter was shacking up with a married man, they wouldn't stand in front of him and weep as they did now. If they knew half of the things that had happened in his household, they wouldn't be calling him savior. As soon as Annan got to his seat, he pulled his phone out of his pocket and rapidly fired off a short, cryptic text to Caleb: "Get the Abby situation under control ASAP." This was going to be a rough year that was certain to test his limits and push him to the edge. His competitors would do everything they could to bring him down. He expected that, but he was never going to give them the fodder they needed. His daughter, family, and secrets weren't going to cost him this presidency. Not again.

ᔦ

Just a few kilometers from where Justice Annan sat in church listening to the sermon and agonizing over his family issues, Abby was lying in bed with Reyn.

"Do you have any idea how much I love you?"

Abby smiled and cupped Reyn's face in her hands. She kissed him lightly on the lips.

"Tell me," she whispered.

"I love you so much it makes my heart hurt. And when I'm away from you for too long, my dick hurts."

"Oh my God, you're so silly!" Abby burst out laughing, smacking him jokingly across the face.

"Oh you wound me! You wound me, my love," he cried out mockingly.

Abby giggled and nuzzled deeper into his chest. He instinctively wrapped his arms around her. She loved the feel and smell of him. Reyn wasn't drop-dead handsome, she knew that, but there was just something unbelievably sexy about him. He was only five foot eleven, the same height she was, but he was lean and incredibly fit. He was a gym rat, but he didn't overdo it. His muscles were hard and taut, but they didn't bulge like melons underneath his skin. And he had such beautiful skin, smooth and wonderful to touch and kiss. She loved his hair too—Christopher Reeve-type hair, distinguished yet sexy. And then there was his face. Reyn wasn't traditionally handsome, but he had the gentlest, kindest face and bluest eyes she had ever seen. It was in such contrast to his jet-black hair. Best of all was his kindness and generosity. Reyn was forty-five years old, had a lot of pressure on his shoulders, and had a lot to prove. His family owned Proctor Oil, the third largest private oil mining company in the world. Reyn could have gone straight from grad school to a VP position at the company. Instead, he chose to start from scratch. He'd been working his way up for the last twenty years and was currently VP of operations for Ghana. His older brother was the president of the North American operation, and his cousin sat on top of the Africa operations. Knowing he was several rungs down from being CEO of Proctor Oil was tough for Reyn to handle at times, but through it all he remained kind, loving, and supportive. Abby burrowed deeper into Reyn's arms. She was in love with him too.

"Are you thinking about how much you love me too?" he murmured.

She laughed and raised her head to look at him. He had a serious look in his eyes. She pulled a strand of hair away from his face. She loved doing that.

"Yes. I love you, Reyn. I'm madly and hopelessly in love with you."

Reyn cupped her face in his hands and kissed her hard. He pushed her back against the bed, pinned her body beneath him and continued kissing her. Abby slipped her hands into his hair, pulling him in closer. Her reaction spurred him on as he deftly got her t-shirt off, exposing her full naked breasts and pink boy briefs. Abby inhaled deeply. After three years together, she knew Reyn loved and appreciated her curves. All the same, it always took her a second to be comfortable naked in front of him. Before she and Reyn had started dating, she believed the myth that if a white guy would date a black girl at all it would have to be a skinny one. So Reyn's interest in her, as curvy as she was, was surprising, but the passion he had in his eyes each time he looked at her was undeniable.

Abby exhaled as Reyn dipped his head and took a nipple into his mouth. She arched her back as he slipped his fingers through her underwear and right inside her wetness while his lips remained firmly on her breast. He came up for air briefly and then went back to her other nipple, gently sucking and biting as he increased the pace of his fingers insider her.

"Babes, please," Abby begged, as she writhed uncontrollably beneath him. He took a break from her breasts and started trailing kisses from her neck slowly down to the edge of her boy briefs. She loved foreplay with Reyn, but this morning she just wanted him. Sensing her desperate need, he got her briefs off, and his own t-shirt, shorts, and boxers followed. Once they were both naked, he wrapped his right arm around her lower waist and adjusted her, lining her body against his. He was already hard and ready, and she stroked him gently, feeling him reach his full length in her hands.

"I love you," she whispered, gazing lovingly into his deep blue eyes. And then he was inside of her, all eight inches of him. Yes, she loved Reyn for his gentleness, determination, and sense of humor, but his long, thick, circumcised manhood was the icing on the cake. She groaned as he cupped her ass, burying himself deeper into her. She lifted her legs and bent them at the knee, giving him greater access and holding him in place.

Reyn buried his face against her neck, smelling her, kissing her, nibbling on her neck. She smelled like citrus from her favorite Dove shower gel. A shaky groan escaped him as she arched her pelvis upward to meet his thrusts. He could feel her thighs shaking, so he clenched his teeth and closed his eyes, forcing himself to stay in control. He was going to explode any minute, but he needed to wait for her. She was so wet and she felt so good, he knew he couldn't hold his release off much longer. And then he felt her lose control as her wet lips clenched his hardness repeatedly and her nails dug into his back. He dug deeper and harder, and she screamed out in pleasure. As soon he felt her body relax beneath him, he let go, all of it.

Abby cradled Reyn as he convulsed on top of her, emptying himself into her. A minute later, they were still intertwined, breathing heavily against each other. Reyn lifted himself up and looked down at her. She was so beautiful, stunning really. He kissed her softly, trying to convey what he felt for her. He felt her tighten on his manhood, still buried inside her, and he chuckled.

"You want some more, baby?" he murmured.

Abby nodded, her eyes sparkling mischievously. "Yes, I want more."

"Anything you want," Reyn murmured as he pulled out slowly and slipped his fingers inside her. "Anything you want."

Six hours and two rounds later, Reyn was in his land cruiser driving home. Sundays were always bittersweet for him, for both of them. He stayed with Abby most weekends, but by Sunday night he had to leave and head back to the town-house the company rented for him. Even though his family wasn't in Ghana and he lived alone, he still tried to keep up appearances. Five of his colleagues lived in the same gated community, so if he was gone from home for too long, un-wanted rumors would definitely start. Reyn knew that no matter how hard he tried to be discreet, he was sure people at work suspected he was involved with someone here in Ghana. That was because he and Abby didn't always stay indoors. They went to dinner, the movies, and other social events. They even took trips together, mostly in Ghana, but over the last three years, they'd gone to Greece, Paris, and Rome. The Rome trip, a little over a year ago, was when he knew that he'd fallen in love.

When Reyn first met Abby, he was enthralled with her looks. He couldn't stop staring at her. It was at a barbeque that he got dragged to by friends at work. The barbeque was hosted by one of the directors at UNICEF, so it was mainly an expatriate event, but she was there with some girlfriends from her work. He remembered that day like it was yesterday. She was wearing dark blue skinny jeans that fit her like a glove, with inch-high heels and a slightly baggy gray tee. Her hair was jet black and straight, falling past her shoulders. He had an immediate physical reaction to her. What he couldn't remember was what he first said to her, but they spent most of the afternoon talking together. As they talked, he realized there was more to her than just her looks. She was smart and driven, with a lot of spunk, but still sensitive and emotional, particularly when she started talking about her family and the changed dynamic between her and her mother. By early evening, she said she was leaving, heading home to watch TV. He couldn't let her go, so he offered to give her a ride since her friends weren't ready to leave. She agreed. The chemistry between them was intense. He knew she could feel it too, which was why she invited him into her apartment, and less than an hour later into her bed.

The first year they were together, Reyn knew it was mainly physical for both of them. Abby was lonely, she had issues with her family, and Reyn was a welcome distraction despite the ring on his finger. After fifteen years of marriage, this wasn't Reyn's first time stepping out on his wife, but it was the first time he actually took it that seriously. Within three months, he got Abby an apartment and a car. She pushed back, but he insisted. He could afford it. In any case, he hated the idea of visiting her at the apartment her father rented for her. Now the car— that was purely an ego thing. She was driving a Mercedes C-class, a hand-me-down from her parents, and he didn't want his girlfriend driving a ten-year-old car, even if it was something of a classic. Plus he had an Audi Q7 back home that he missed, so why not buy one for her? The words "sugar daddy" crept into his mind a few times. He was married, fifteen years older, and had gotten his mistress a car and an apartment. That was typical sugar daddy behavior. To him though, it was a lot more than just an affair, and in Rome, as they explored the incredibly beautiful city together, he knew he was hopelessly in love with her. Divorce crossed his mind a few times, but his wife's father owned 20 percent of the business. His own family owned 60 percent, but that still wasn't enough for him to risk rocking the boat. When he explained it to Abby, he knew it must have sounded like an excuse. In essence, he told her, "Hey, I can't divorce my wife because her family owns a good chunk of my family's company, and my father expects me to stay married, and oh, we have two young kids together, and if I leave her, I'll lose the kids too." Surprisingly, Abby didn't question his reasons or give him grief. She loved him, she believed him, and she was fine with the way things were—for now.

Reyn entered his empty home and walked straight into the study. He powered up his iMac and sat down behind the desk. He opened his Skype icon and glanced through his online contacts. Emma was online. He took a deep breath and hit the green call button. Her face popped up on his screen seconds later. Her long blonde hair was pulled back, but a few loose curls draped her chiseled oval face. She was smiling, her blue eyes twinkling.

"Hey," he said quietly.

"Hey back," she said, still smiling.

His heart constricted as guilt flooded him. How long could he keep this up? He sat back and started chatting with his wife, trying hard to wipe the memory of Abby's smell and taste from his mind. Sex with the mistress in the morning and then check-in with the wife in the evening. God forgive him.

"How are the boys?" he asked, still trying to shake the memory of the morning off.

Her smile broadened. "Boy, don't I have news for you. Kacey was fantastic yesterday at soccer. He scored three goals! I filmed it for you. It should be in your Dropbox. Have you checked it today? I was sitting on the bench watching Kacey and thinking: should I get an agent?"

She was laughing and talking fast, and Reyn's mind started to drift a little as he tried to listen. He missed his family, and he missed moments like his oldest son Kacey scoring three goals. Emma had strong reasons for not moving down to Ghana with him. She grew up in luxury, and she wanted to remain in luxury. Proctor Oil took really good care of its expatriate employees and their families in Ghana, but this was still a developing country. She wouldn't have access to all the amenities and facilities she was surrounded with in Dallas. She would miss their ten-acre ranch in Dallas, their New York loft, and the five-bedroom beach house in the Hamptons. Luxury living aside, she also wanted the boys to stay in school and be with their friends. Reyn felt boys could adjust easily to any environment, but Emma said the prep school they were enrolled in was one of the best in the country, and it wouldn't be fair to uproot them. And so, four years ago, Emma and the boys stayed in Dallas, Reyn moved down to Ghana, and now he was in love with someone else.

"Is that Daddy? Is that Daddy?"

Reyn sat upright in his chair at the sound of his oldest son's voice.

"Kacey? Where is he?"

Emma moved her chair backward, and Reyn caught sight of his two boys bounding through the door and up to the computer. His heart melted. Even though he spoke with them on the phone and Skype several times a week, he still had the same reaction each time. God, he missed them. He laughed as they climbed on top of their mother and leaned forward directly into the computer. He wished he could reach through and touch them. Kacey was ten years old, with a mop of golden hair like his mother. Reese was eight and more reserved, with his father's dark looks and blue eyes. Reyn touched the computer screen with his fingers, and the boys instantly reached out and touched the screen.

"Daddy, Daddy, did Mummy tell you about my goals? I scored four goals!" Kacey said excitedly.

"No you didn't. It was three," Reese said, wagging his finger at his older brother.

Reyn grinned and sat back listening to their banter. He missed his family. He missed his family very much. There was no doubt about it. What was he going to do? What the heck was he going to do?

⌒

The shrill ringing of the doorbell jolted Abby out of her daydream. She was stretched out on her sofa, with her laptop on the floor and her work papers strewn around her. She groaned and closed her eyes, willing the ringing to stop, but it didn't. This person was persistent. She got up reluctantly and walked to the door. She knew it wasn't Reyn. He left her only an hour ago, and in any case he had keys. There were only two possible options—a pesky girlfriend or her almighty father.

She yanked the door open and rolled her eyes.

"What do you want, Caleb?"

Without waiting to be invited in, he stepped past her into the living room. He glanced around, taking in the space, scrutinizing every detail.

"Modern and contemporary styles, but also traditional, that's surprising. Although I think the fifty-five-inch LED is a bit much for the room, but I guess *someone* insisted."

Abby scowled. "What do you want, Caleb? I have a lot of work to do."

He glanced at the laptop and the papers on the floor, and then turned his attention to her. His face was straight, not a glimmer of emotion or sympathy as he uttered his next words.

"You need to end your relationship with Proctor, immediately."

Abby chuckled. "Are you serious? Is that why Daddy sent you here?"

Caleb took a step toward her. His face remained unflinchingly straight.

"Tell me, how does it feel to be dating a married older man with a wife and a family?"

"It's thrilling, absolutely exciting. You should try it. Oh wait, you already are."

Abby stared at him, her eyes burrowed into his, as she tried to unnerve him with her stare. He remained composed.

"You're simply having sex with a married man who'll fuck you for as long as he can until he moves back home to his wife and family or until he gets tired of your easy ass—whichever comes first."

Abby gasped as Caleb's words sunk deep into her heart like a knife. She felt a tear at the corner of her eye and looked down, trying to hold the flood at bay.

"Get out," she muttered.

Caleb stood there a while longer, and then he leaned close and whispered.

"This isn't going to end well, so save whatever little dignity you have left and end this, before you embarrass your father, yourself, and your boyfriend, because you really don't want me getting in the middle of this. Trust me."

He smiled and then he walked out, closing the door gently behind him.

Abby closed her eyes as the tears escaped, trickling down her cheek. She cursed out loud. Why did she let Caleb get to her like that? She ran her fingers through her hair, taking quick breaths, trying to still her beating heart and stop the unruly tears. She had to be strong. She loved Reyn, and nothing or no one was going to keep them apart. All the same, she knew that Caleb's visit today was only the beginning, just a warning. Her father was running for president now. This was only going to get worse.

Abby just had no idea how much worse it was all going to be.

4

"Finally, you decided to show up for work. Mr. Anim is looking for you. He's called here three times already."

Abby rolled her eyes at her assistant and close friend Denise as she breezed past Denise's desk into her office.

"I forgot to set my alarm."

She glanced at the clock on the wall of her office: 10 a.m. She was super late, two hours to be specific. She dumped her bag on her desk and pulled her laptop quickly out of the carrier, practically shoving it onto the dock.

"Alarm excuse? Really? That's the best you can come up with?"

Abby paused and looked at Denise, who was standing in the doorway of the office with her hands on her hips. Abby shrugged.

"Busy weekend," she muttered.

"I know. I saw the announcement on TV. Wow, it's crazy. Your father is actually going to run for president?"

Abby didn't respond. She turned the computer on and dropped tiredly into her chair. She took a deep breath and rubbed her forehead, mentally trying to ward off a nagging migraine. Another Monday was here, and it hadn't started so well. Not setting the alarm last night was one reason why, but to be honest it was probably the bottle of wine she downed by herself last night, a weak attempt to drown out Caleb's harsh words. She knew dating a married man didn't present the right impression, so of course people would say mean things. She'd just kept this relationship so private that no one had ever insulted her the way Caleb had last night. It hurt a great deal.

"Anyways, you need to go see Mr. Anim now. He was really huffing and puffing."

Denise walked back to her desk. Just then, Abby's desk phone started to ring. She didn't glance at it. She knew exactly who it was and why he was calling. She shook her head at Denise and mouthed, "Don't answer." She got up and strode out of the office and down the corridor. It was best to have this conversation face to face.

"Ah, finally you decided to show up. Are we not paying you enough for you to show up on time? I could have sworn we were paying you too much, actually."

Abby sat down opposite her boss, groaning inwardly. All bosses thought they paid their employees too well. She feigned her best tired and sick expression for him. She hadn't had her usual Koko King breakfast this morning, so she hoped the lack of "kosay" translated into tiredness.

"I'm not feeling too well. I've been dealing with these migraines," she said softly. If the alarm clock excuse didn't work on Denise, it wouldn't work on her boss.

Charles Anim leaned forward across his desk and stared at her.

"You do look a little sick," he said, squinting at her. Abby nodded, letting out a slow breath. This may not be bad after all. Before Abby could enjoy the thought, Anim got up from his desk and threw his hands up in the air.

"Why didn't you tell us? Why didn't you give us any heads up? You're a senior director here for God's sake. What's the use of having you work here if you won't even give us a courtesy call and let us in on the biggest announcement of the year? Josh said he called you several times. I heard the news at the same time as everyone else. That's just not right. I mean, I have Justice Annan's daughter working for me, getting paid a lot of money to come in late, and she couldn't even pick up the phone and let us know this was coming."

Abby sighed. This was the biggest disadvantage to working for Insel Media, one of the largest media conglomerates in Ghana. The Insel Group consisted of two cinemas, two bookstores, a TV station, three radio stations, two newspapers, an online entertainment blog, and an artiste agency for musicians, actors, and models. Insel had a reputation for being in the know, hence Charles Anim's disappointment in her. Charles was the chief operating officer, and she was the senior director for corporate affairs and communications. She was actually two levels below Charles; however, since he personally interviewed her and directly offered her the job, he was on her case quite a bit. She loved her job a lot, except on days when Charles tried to use her to get to her father and his connections.

"Sir, I didn't know he was going to announce anything. Honestly, I had absolutely no idea. I heard the same time you did."

Charles frowned and raised an eyebrow.

"Really?"

"Really. So that's why you didn't get any heads up from me. I'm really sorry about that."

Abby placed her hands on the arms of the chair, preparing to lift herself up.

Charles waved her down and went back to his chair.

"Fine, you didn't know then, but now you do. So we want an exclusive."

Abby froze. Uh, what?

Charles continued talking excitedly.

"We want an exclusive, and not just an interview, but the whole shebang. Josh and I were talking this morning. He has fantastic ideas. He suggested we do something like a "Road to the Flagstaff House"—something that documents your father's journey to the presidency. Obviously, he's going to win. That's a given. And he's probably going to be one of the most iconic presidents ever, perhaps as great as Kwame Nkrumah, except more capitalist. We would be documenting history!"

Abby raised her hand like a schoolgirl with a question, but she simply needed a way to stop Charles's unrealistic and excited stream of words.

"Charles, sir, wait, slow down. What you're talking about is impossible. A documentary? My father would never do that. He's more private than the Pope."

Charles leaned forward and looked at her squarely.

"Well I expect you to convince him, Abby. We've never asked you for any favors. This is really important to me and to the company."

Abby started to correct him and then stopped. This was the hundredth time that Charles had asked her for a favor—if she could even call it that. It always came across like an ultimatum. In the last four years since she joined Insel Media, she'd gotten Charles and Insel several exclusive interviews. She hated asking her father for favors like that, but she'd done it all the same because of Charles's persistence and subtle "do it or you're gone" undertones. This time she knew getting her father to sign up for a documentary was completely impossible, but what was the use of telling Charles that?

"Okay sir, I'll see what I can do," she said, attempting to get up again.

"Perfect! No, wait. Let me get Josh. Let's talk about this right now. I am so excited."

Charles picked up his phone and started talking fast. Abby sat back and tuned out his words. She was wondering how she was going to pull this off. Giving Charles false hope was wrong, but she didn't feel like she had a choice today. Her father's bid for the presidency was definitely big news, so she had to give Insel something. It wasn't going to be a documentary, so she had to think of a suitable alternative fast.

"Abby, hello, it's been a while."

Abby snapped out of her reverie and shifted in her chair. Josh Winkler stood in the doorway of Charles's office, beaming down at her. She forced a smile as he walked in and sat down next to her. Josh was the VP of programming and content. He was responsible for everything that was written, published, aired, and broadcast. He was one of Charles's trusted advisors and an absolute pain in her side. Josh pursued Abby relentlessly when she first started at Insel. Office relationships were permissible, and Josh was relatively attractive with his smooth brown skin and slim physique. Despite what he had going for him, he rubbed her the wrong way, and so she refused to give in. When it was clear she wasn't interested, he started to make her life miserable. Josh was close with Anthony, the VP of communications, her direct boss, and between the two of them, she could never catch a break. All the same, she knew she had it good at Insel. She was paid good money and doing what she loved to do. So for now she was willing to endure whatever came her way.

"Josh, I saw you on Thursday, four days ago," she muttered dryly.

"Well it feels like it's been a while. In any case, after the announcement on Saturday, who's thinking about last week? Charles says you're going to get us exclusive access to your father—to film a documentary of his journey. That sounds incredible," he said, a hint of disbelief in his voice.

Before Abby could respond, Charles's phone rang. He looked down at it and cursed.

"I'm sorry, but I have to go. I need to take one of my boys to the doctor. You two should go ahead and talk. Maybe we can get a signed contract by the end of the week, huh? Let's make this happen, guys. Let's make this happen."

Charles grabbed his suit jacket and briefcase and then walked out quickly, barking orders at his assistant as he marched toward the elevators at the end of the hallway.

"So, you're getting us exclusive access?" Josh repeated his earlier question.

Stringing Charles along was one thing, but Josh was a like a dog with a bone. If she said yes, he would expect to meet and discuss it with her father within days. If she said no, he would probably insist they dismiss her, even if they had no grounds to do that. She couldn't win either way. She could only buy herself some time. She looked Josh squarely in the eye.

"I told Charles I'd try. I'll talk to my father and I'll try to convince him, but I can't promise or guarantee anything right now."

"That's not good enough."

"Josh, talking to my father is the best I can do. You're talking about a documentary here, cameras and people following my father everywhere. He's a very private person," she said, exasperated.

"Exactly—that's why an exclusive documentary would be perfect. Access to such a private politician would be such a coup."

"Well you can't just expect that I'd say, 'Hey Daddy, I need you to allow my company to follow you and document your run for president for the next ten months,' and he'd just say, 'Why of course my dear daughter, I welcome your film crew anytime,'" she snapped.

Josh ignored her sarcasm and stood up. He tucked his hands into his pockets and faced her with a grim, serious look on his face. She knew he was trying to intimidate her.

"This is what I expect, Abby, so listen carefully. I expect you to talk your father into this, or Insel Media just isn't the place for you. It's as simple as that."

Abby couldn't believe he would openly threaten her with dismissal like that. She stood up as well and forced a smile.

"Like I said, Josh, I'll see what I can do."

And then she walked away, shaking inwardly with anger. She needed to find a way out of this.

Caleb strode purposefully into the lobby of Proctor Oil's regional office at North Dzorwulu, just off the N1 highway. He was a supporter of sustainable mining, but he had a lot of issues with the flashiness often associated with it. The lobby of the ten-story building was massive and opulent. The dark mahogany reception desk was at least thirty feet from the high glass entry doors. To the right of the doors was a lavish seating area with dark mahogany deep-seat armchairs and original lumber circular tables. A set of four steel elevators was lined up to the left. The walls were adorned with massive original paintings that he estimated cost hundreds of thousands of dollars. He recognized pieces from van Gogh, Kandinsky, and Hogarth, and only a couple from Ablade Glover. Caleb shook his head disapprovingly; they could at least have displayed more Ghanaian art. His disappointment in Proctor Oil worsened when he stepped up to the ample-bosomed receptionist, who looked like she couldn't breathe in her tight white shirt. He stared at her strained breasts and then up to her face. She smiled and tried to adjust her shirt, but there was no extra room to shift anything around. *What a ridiculous cliché*, he thought as he looked at her long nails.

"Jeff Hunt," he said simply.

She tapped at the keyboard and glanced up at him.

"Caleb Osei?"

He nodded.

"Oh wow, you're Justice Annan's manager, right? Or is it director? What is your title anyways?"

Caleb raised an eyebrow and stared at her wordlessly. She looked away and started tapping at the keyboard again.

"Here's your guest badge. Please take the elevator up to the tenth floor. The receptionist there will take you to Mr. Hunt's office."

Caleb took the badge and walked away toward the elevators. He had very little patience for receptionists, especially ones who had ridiculously long nails and wore clothes that wouldn't even fit a thirteen-year-old pubescent girl. He stepped onto the tenth floor and rolled his eyes. Seriously?

The tenth floor had its own lavish lobby and equally inappropriately-dressed receptionist. When she stepped out from behind her desk to greet him, he noted that the problem with this one was not her upper body, but her lower half, which was ensconced in a tight, barely-there skirt.

"Mr. Osei, good morning. Mr. Hunt is expecting you. Please follow me."

At least she sounded more professional. Caleb followed her down a long corridor to the last office at the end, which resembled a mini apartment more than an office. The tenth floor receptionist handed him off to another assistant, who led him through to Jeff Hunt's inner sanctum.

Jeff Hunt was the managing director for Proctor Oil's Africa Operations, and Reyn Proctor's cousin. Jeff had complete oversight of Proctor's operations in Ghana, Nigeria, and South Africa. Caleb had met Jeff a couple of times because of business and politics, but this meeting was going to be a little different.

"Mr. Osei, welcome. Please, have a seat. Do you want something to drink? Juice, coffee, tea?"

Jeff stood up from behind his enormous mahogany desk and stretched his hand. Caleb ignored it and sat down in one of the armchairs opposite the desk. Jeff pulled his hand back, surprised.

"Is everything okay, Mr. Osei? I assumed this was a friendly visit," Jeff said, settling into his chair.

"I need you to fire your ground floor and tenth floor receptionists, and Reyn Proctor."

"What?" Jeff asked incredulously.

"I said I need you to fire your ground floor—"

"I heard you the first time, Mr. Osei, but is this some type of joke? You can't just walk in here and dictate to me like that. I welcomed your visit on short notice because I've always admired you and the Justice, but this is ridiculous."

"You need to fire both receptionists because they look like street prostitutes who've been placed in their positions simply to attract or distract investors and visitors. They're trashy, highly unprofessional, and ridiculous looking, which says a lot about the men at the helm of Proctor Oil. And you need to fire Reyn Proctor because he is having an affair with my boss's daughter, has been for the last three years, and we need it to end, today."

Jeff's mouth fell open, and he reached for the bottle of water on his table. He took a gulp and tried to breathe, but that didn't seem to work. He leaned back in his chair and glanced away from Caleb. Damn Reyn! What was he thinking? He'd always suspected Reyn was seeing someone in Ghana, but he hadn't bothered to confirm or look into it. It wasn't really his business. Reyn had been in Ghana for four years, and he only saw his wife about three times a year for less than a month each time. Even though Jeff had his own family with him in South Africa, he also had a mistress in Nigeria, and he was bedding the tenth-floor receptionist. Her ass was truly irresistible. Reyn, on the other hand, instead of just finding a random girl to keep his bed warm on occasion, had to get involved with the daughter of one of the most powerful men in Ghana—soon to be bloody president.

Jeff turned back to Caleb, who was sitting there staring quietly at him. The man unnerved him. His boldness was one thing, but it was the expressionless face that always got to Jeff.

"I'm sorry to hear about Reyn and the Justice's daughter, but there is nothing I can do about it. Two hours ago, we announced Reyn's promotion to managing director for Africa. He's taking over my job, and I'm staying on for three months to help with the transition. After that, I'm moving back to Texas as EVP for operations. Reyn is the boss now, as decided by his father, the president and CEO. He's put in the time, and he knows the business. I can't fire him."

Caleb clenched his teeth. Two hours ago? That was unfortunate, but not a deal breaker. He leaned forward.

"If Proctor Oil expects to be successful in Ghana, or anywhere else in Africa, then you need to find a way to end Reyn's relationship with Abby Annan. You know full well the influence the Justice has here, in Nigeria, and in South Africa, and you know what he's done for Proctor Oil already. Get it done."

Jeff scowled. "Fine, I'll ask Reyn to end the relationship. He has a big stake in the company now. He'll listen."

"You misunderstand me, Mr. Hunt. Get it done without bringing the Justice's name or mine into the matter."

Jeff's scowl turned into a frown. "Listen, Mr. Osei, I respect you, and I respect the Justice immensely. I do not doubt his influence, but there is nothing I can do except to ask Reyn directly, and I'm not sure I can keep your name out of it."

Caleb stood up and tapped Jeff's desk.

"This is very simple, Mr. Hunt. Get it done without bringing us into it. If the relationship isn't over by the end of this week, then you'll need to prepare for a series of unfortunate events. I understand the workers at Takoradi are agitated. Another weeklong work stoppage would set you back by how much? Five million? Not much, right? So maybe a month would be good, hmmm?"

Without waiting for a response, Caleb started to walk toward the door. He paused in the doorway and turned back to Jeff, who looked stricken and panicked.

Caleb smiled, his first of the day.

"And oh, Jeff, I'm serious about the receptionists too. End of the week."

And then he was gone.

5

The music was too loud, and the conversations even louder, but that was typical at the Regent Lounge at 9 p.m., even though it was Monday night. The lounge was lavishly decorated, with oversized cushy furniture, expensive wall art, and fragile centerpieces. The drink prices were unreasonably high as well—a way for the owners to make back what they'd sunk into the location, décor, and overhead.

The three men seated around the table in the corner obviously didn't mind—and they were probably the reason why Regent still continued to thrive. Ohene Gyawu was President Otoo's campaign director and one of his most trusted aides. He'd worked for the GFP party for twenty years now. The DNP and the GFP, Ghana's two largest political parties, had shared power almost evenly over the last fifty years. Ohene Gyawu was instrumental in getting the GFP the wins they'd gotten, but the party also blamed him for the painful defeats in 2000 and

2004. Those defeats almost crippled the GFP, but he'd stayed on course and he'd gotten them back in, and now he never wanted to leave the helm of power again. Next to him was Bedu Afari, the government's external affairs and communications director. Bedu was relatively young, only thirty-eight, and he didn't have the same long history Ohene had, but his commitment to the party was unshakable. There wasn't anything he wouldn't do or say in support of the GFP. The third man wasn't a party or government official, but his dedication was just as strong. It was Josh Winkler. Josh went to secondary school and university with Bedu. They also worked at the Ghana News Network (GNN) together for over five years. After GNN, Bedu went into politics and Josh went into the private sector, Insel, specifically. The two men had kept in touch, and through their relationship Josh got to realize the immense access and wealth government connections could provide.

"So it's only been three days, and it seems we've already been written off. I've never seen such fervor grip the nation like this. It's almost as if God opened the heavens and announced that Jesus Christ was coming back!" Bedu grumbled.

"This is why I told you guys as soon as you came into power to find something on the Justice and bring him down. You allowed his influence and power to grow right under your noses," Josh snorted.

"We tried, briefly. There wasn't anything to find. In any case, we were busy trying to deal with the cocaine shipment nonsense," Ohene replied.

Josh shook his head and took a sip of his Jack and Coke.

"There's always something to find. No man is that clean. People may react like he's Jesus, but he's just a man, a Ghanaian man for that matter. He can't be that clean."

Ohene was irritated by Josh's condescending tone. He respected Josh and appreciated the support he'd given to the party, but he'd made a fortune off them as well. He wished he wouldn't act like he knew it all.

"So what's your brilliant suggestion, Josh? You've worked with Abiel Annan for a while now, and yet you haven't been able to dig anything up yourself."

"We're working on getting an exclusive deal with the Justice for a behind-the-scenes-type of documentary," Josh said simply.

Both Ohene and Bedu laughed.

Bedu shook his head. "Behind the scenes documentary? Are you serious? The Justice would never let cameras follow him around."

"Doesn't that help him more than us? That's publicity you'd be giving to him," Ohene added.

"It's more than likely we'll get the exclusive because Abby's job is on the line. If we do get it, it's the best opportunity for us to find something on the Justice. He won't be able to hide who he really is or what he does. And we can also use the access as an opportunity to look deeper into his family and his life. There *has* to be something. The easy thing is that anything little we find would bring him down. When a man acts that clean, even a little dirt would topple his image, paint him as a hypocrite and a liar. That's all we really need—just a little dirt," Josh said confidently.

Ohene and Bedu were silent for a while. It did make sense, but they still doubted the Justice would open his life up to cameras. Four years ago, Ohene instructed two GFP stalwarts to look into the Justice's life and businesses. After months of probing, questioning, and digging, they came up with nothing. The Justice's business connections were all legal and above board. He seemed committed to his family, and it didn't seem that he had any mistresses. He went to church without fail every Sunday, and if he was ever photographed, it was usually at some charity or religious event. He granted scholarships to brilliant and deserving students out of his own pocket before he eventually teamed up with Columbia University and two other non-profit organizations to award scholarships to twenty students each year. Ohene had even looked into the selection of the scholarship recipients himself, but there was nothing fraudulent or questionable there either. The selection process was well defined, rigorous, and consistent.

A little over two years ago, one thousand kilos of cocaine were seized at the Tema ports because of an anonymous tip. It was the raid of the century, and it was the event that brought the GFP's world crashing down. The US sent down high-ranking DEA agents, followed by a number of Interpol agents. Within a week, three high-ranking government officials, two ministers, and a police commissioner were linked to the scandal, and the evidence against them was undeniable. The country wanted blood and penance, and despite the mounting accusations of corruption targeted at the entire government, it took six months before the president dismissed the then-police commissioner and asked the accused ministers to resign pending a full investigation. The Justice issued only one statement during that time, which was surprising to the GFP. He was a renowned Justice—no one knew the law better than him—and he could have used the opportunity to make media rounds and sink the GFP completely. Instead, his statement, which was issued shortly after the news of the cocaine first broke, was brief. He stated that government and public leaders must be decisive and unflinching in their commitment to finding those involved and bringing the full weight of the judicial system on the guilty. And then he was silent. Over the last four years, the Justice hadn't really gotten too involved in politics and instead chose to focus on social and philanthropic endeavors, along with running his businesses and being home with his family. Since his sister-in-law's death, the Justice had chosen to focus on his wife and family, and not even a tantalizing cocaine scandal could bring him back into the dirty world of politics. The Justice's decision to stay away from the cocaine story made Ohene believe the Justice was truly no longer interested in politics. How wrong they were. Bringing down a man who gave up a golden opportunity four years ago—and then two years ago—in order to focus on his family was going to be near impossible.

Ohene sighed and chugged his vodka and tonic.

"Fine, Josh, try this route of yours, but I still think we'll need a backup plan. It's best to bring him down now before he wins the DNP congress and becomes the party's official candidate. At that point, it'll be much harder," Ohene said.

"I agree. We've been reactive long enough. Frankly, Ohene, I think you need to dedicate resources to this. Josh can work the documentary/daughter angle, but we should start our own investigations straight away," Bedu said.

"Listen, I'm serious. I truly believe there is dirt to find, and we have to do everything we can to find it," Josh said.

He raised his half-empty glass up and nodded at his companions.

"Here's to bringing down Justice Joseph Annan," Josh said confidently, with a smug smile plastered on his face.

Ohene and Bedu raised their glasses and toasted with Josh.

"Here's to the GFP!" Bedu said excitedly.

After emptying their glasses, they ordered another round as the topic moved on to the issue of the vice president and his philandering ways.

~

Caleb grunted as he tucked a wad of cash into the bill holder. His Monday nights at the Regent were important, but they were also expensive, and he couldn't just expense the bill to the campaign or the Justice's businesses. What he was doing here was important for the campaign, but that's not something he could describe on an expense report. He glanced at the three men talking and drinking in the corner, and chuckled. They were imbeciles, meeting at the same place and same time for the past three years. And yet, they wondered why they couldn't find any dirt on the Justice. No one on the Justice's team was stupid enough to discuss sensitive matters in public like that. After two hours, their conversation had turned to their mistresses and women, and that was information Caleb wasn't particularly interested in.

Once he got inside his car, Caleb checked his missed calls. Abby had called three times, and he had missed a few from journalists, DNP officials, and irrelevant others. There was no call from the Justice because he knew exactly where Caleb was. He ignored the missed call list and went to his favorites. Everyone could wait till morning except one person. She answered on the second ring.

"Baby, I was actually thinking about you. I'm finally on season two of *24*. You were right. It's an incredible show, and I'm addicted! I've been watching episodes all day!" she said.

Caleb smiled a little.

"No classes today?"

"I skipped class. I just couldn't tear myself away from the show. I started season one last night like you insisted, and then I couldn't stop. There was just no way I would have been able to concentrate. See what you've done to me? And I have six more seasons to go! I'm going to flunk out, big time."

Caleb laughed. She was so adorable.

"Take a break from Jack Bauer and meet me at my place. I need you," he said softly.

"That's going to be really hard. Jack Bauer is incredibly sexy. The way he threatens people, absolute turn-on."

Caleb laughed again. She was super cute.

"Please?" he said, turning his sexy voice on full max.

"Okay, okay, but you have to say 'Damn it!' as soon as I walk through the door, before you get anything."

"I'll be Jack, as long as you're not Nina, then we're good. I'll see you soon, okay?"

He hung up and started his car. His pulse was racing as he drove home. It always did when he thought of Cat, his newest flame. She was funny, young, and compliant, for the most part. When Caleb joined the Justice in Ghana ten years ago, he knew from the very beginning that regular relationships would be difficult. It wasn't just the Justice he had to ensure had a clean life, he had to do the same for himself. Most of the women he met weren't genuine or sincere. They wanted the access and the power, but they didn't know how to be discreet. So for a while, he had no social or love life, but he was a young man, and abstinence just wasn't sustainable at his age. Then he and the Justice attended a fundraising function at the University of Ghana. There he discovered the perfect source of sexual partners—foreign exchange and visiting students. The university was rife with exchange students, primarily from the United States, who were in Ghana for a semester or so, maximum two semesters. These students had no interest in politics or even in their own education. They were in Ghana for the so-called experience. It was really perfect for him. They fell for his height, looks, and American accent. He'd been an American exchange student once, even spent a semester in Paris, so he could relate.

As much as the students weren't interested in politics, he was still very cautious. He never visited them at the school. Even if the American students didn't know who he was, their Ghanaian friends and other students could recognize him. So, he steered clear of campus, and all encounters happened at his home. They usually took cabs to see him, and he would insist they stay the night and leave in the morning when it was safer. He never went out with them socially, not unless a "girlfriend" was leaving the country soon and he had to find a replacement—then he'd attend some low-key event to meet the new students. There were also times he didn't find any replacements. He simply toughed it out until his needs got too bad. He was super paranoid, and so he was very selective about whom he picked. If a girl started to act needy by demanding visits, dinners, and other treats, he ended it immediately. He made it clear he wasn't going to be a typical boyfriend, and for some reason, probably his looks and prowess in bed, they stayed. His age was appealing to them too. At forty-two, he was often at least twenty years older, and that excited them. They were tired of boys, they said. To be honest, he also enjoyed his time with most of them. They were a needed distraction, and they reminded him of his former life back in the US.

He'd been with Cat Daly a little over two months now. She was from Chicago, his hometown, and was hoping to stay for two semesters. He really liked her—over the last ten years, there weren't that many he truly liked. Cat looked like a model, and she'd even tried to be one once. When it didn't work out, she went back to school. She was five foot eleven, with a short, sexy haircut, long legs, and an amazing, toned body. She was mixed: Indian, Portuguese, African American, and White. It was an undeniably sexy combination. She looked exotic, and from the minute he met her, he couldn't resist.

Keeping who he was a secret from the students wasn't really hard. He never told the girls what his job was. Director of some made up business or other always seemed to work. They never pressed him, so he had nothing to worry about. Cat was a little inquisitive and would ask random questions every now and then, but he allowed it. If he ever felt she was getting intrusive, he'd end it. For now, she was incredible in bed. She also stoked his ego and claimed his stamina and performance were far better than the kids she'd had before. He wasn't surprised, but he didn't care much, actually. He maintained a very strict diet and exercise regimen for his own sake, not because he was trying to keep up with his young girlfriends.

He wasn't really worried that anyone would find out about his dalliances with the Legon exchange students. He was single and they were legal. In any case, besides Cat and one brief event ten years ago, there was no one currently in Ghana that he'd slept with. That was the beauty of exchange students—they were no longer around. During each relationship, there were no emails, letters, or pictures. The only form of correspondence was phone—and, at his insistence, the girls destroyed their chips before they left. They enjoyed his paranoia most of the time. They were that bored.

When he got home, Cat's taxi was just leaving. His heart started to race as he walked toward her. She was leaning against his door, wearing a Printex print t-shirt, black short shorts, a KUA-designed print bag slung over her shoulder, and two-inch heels. She probably wasn't wearing that when he called, but she always dressed up for him. As she watched him walking toward her, she slipped her right hand provocatively down her shorts.

Caleb cursed.

"Damn it!"

His lips were on hers as soon as he reached her, and he slipped his hands into her shorts, cupping her hands as she touched herself. When she moaned, he pulled back, not because he was worried about neighbors, but more because he desperately needed to get her inside and onto his bed. He lived in Dworwulu on a quiet street with aging neighbors who were in bed with the lights off by 9 p.m. They weren't in close proximity to his house anyways, so that wasn't the concern. All the same, he wasn't prepared to take her right then and there. He took out his keys, opened the door, and lifted her off her feet and into the house. It was going to be a long week, and Cat was the best way to get him going.

6

Annan watched his wife silently as she sat across the dining table from him. It was only seven in the morning, and yet she looked like she was heading to a photo shoot. She wore a cream-colored short-sleeved top with a dark brown tailored skirt. Her long hair was pulled back into an immaculate bun, not a single tendril out of place. She wore pearl earrings with a matching pearl necklace. Her fingers were bare, except for the wedding and engagement rings she never took off. The Justice stared at the rings. They were meant to represent forty years together, with thirty-five years of marriage. He didn't regret marrying his wife, but he regretted how it'd all turned out. This wasn't where he expected he would be forty years later—with a woman who was struggling mentally and a daughter who was a bona fide pain. It hadn't all gone the way he planned, but there were still a lot of good memories. He loved his wife deeply, and he always would. Adubea was a beautiful woman who'd been devoted and committed to him and given him the best years of his life. Despite the fact that she'd never had any specific ambitions of her own, he still regarded her as one of the smartest women he'd ever encountered. Some may consider him chauvinistic for thinking it, but Adubea knew how to please him and keep him focused. She knew how to manage him, his home, and their daughter. Up until four years ago, she was the perfect wife.

Abby thought he didn't care about her mother's condition, and others in the house may have suspected the same, but they had no idea how much he cared about the state of his wife and his marriage. Abby could never understand what he was going through. She had no idea the utter pain and anguish he felt as he continued to watch the woman he lived with disintegrate right before his eyes. It was almost too much to bear. Of course, he'd been in denial for a while. What man would easily accept the situation he was in, accept that the woman he shared a bed with was unstable and battling demons that he couldn't help her with? However, he wasn't the type of man to wallow in self-pity and despair. That wasn't the man Adubea married. Life had to move on. He wanted to be president. There was nothing wrong with that. His wife shared the same dream with him, so he owed it to her, owed it to the woman she used to be, to pursue it.

Annan watched her as she sipped her tea slowly—Earl Grey, with a little milk but no sugar. She was conscious about her weight. Barely eating, Annan watched as Adubea slowly but gradually finished her breakfast. Watching her eat was the most important part of the day to him, because he was watching her consume her medicine as well.

Getting Adubea to take her pills voluntarily became very difficult, and to avoid pushing her over the edge, he chose a different tactic. The cook, Sylvia, blended it with her food and drink each morning. It was a way for Annan to kill two birds with one stone. Adubea got the medicines she needed while believing she was getting better all on her own, which bolstered her confidence. Abby didn't get things like this. She was all forceful action. There was nothing subtle about Abby. She wrote him off as a terrible husband and father, and that was it. She had no idea how much he loved his family and the lengths he would go through to protect them, all of them.

"You're not eating, Jojo. Don't you like the oats? Too much sugar? I can ask Sylvia to make you scrambled eggs instead, although I'd like you to try the oats. It's really good for your blood pressure. You know the next few months are going to be stressful, so you need to eat right."

Annan picked up his spoon and tried the oats.

"The oats are fine. I'm just a little distracted, but I'll definitely finish it all. Since you're done, why don't you come and sit next to me? We have things we have to talk about. Things are going to start happening. People will start looking into this family, and we need to be on the same page about everything."

She rose from her end of the table and came to sit on his left.

"You need to relax, Jojo. You really need to relax. Why are you so concerned about me? I don't understand. What do you think I'm going to do? I would never, ever jeopardize your campaign. I want this for you, for us, so why would I put all of that at risk?"

"You can be volatile," Annan said directly.

She stared at him, her eyebrows furrowed in anger.

"Trust me, I'm the last person you need to worry about. I am not going to do anything stupid. I'm behind you one hundred percent, and you should really consider involving me in the campaign. I can be an asset."

"Just keep doing what you normally do. What do you have planned for today?"

She started to talk about her planned visit to the Accra Orphanage, something she did once a week. Annan knew her itinerary better than she probably did, but he preferred to have her tell him. It was also his way of assessing her state of mind. Beginning this week, he was going to reduce the number of appearances and events she participated in, including the charity ones, but he intended to do it gradually. Sudden changes in routine could anger and derail her, so instead he was working with her assistant and driver to screen and gradually reduce her events. Interviews were a no-no, and unless critical, he had no plans of campaigning with her. She could proclaim her support all she wanted, but he knew her too well. She wasn't ready for the limelight yet.

When he finished eating, they sat together for a little while in silence. Eventually, he got up and walked her out to her car. They hugged and kissed goodbye. It was another morning ritual of theirs, whether he was the one leaving or she was. It was his way of keeping her grounded and reinforcing that they could make this situation work. On some mornings, like this one, he felt like his heart would give way. He loved her, but things were definitely different between them. Unfortunately, there was nothing he could do to have things back exactly to the way it was before, the way it was four years ago. That was really the pivotal moment. Annan took a deep breath and composed himself. He had work to do.

～

"Good morning sir, I've prepared an updated itinerary for this week and travel schedule for next week. Our first meeting is with Asenso and his team at 10 a.m., but we have a lot to discuss before he shows up."

Annan walked past Caleb and settled into his chair behind his desk. There were printouts of the itinerary on his desk, all six dailies folded neatly one of top of the other, with Post-Its summarizing the key stories, his iPad fully charged, and a steaming cup of coffee. Caleb was meticulous and organized, which Annan appreciated, but today he was feeling emotional and wasn't prepared to dive into work immediately.

"Have you had breakfast, Caleb? Sylvia outdid herself with the oats and eggs this morning."

At the mention of breakfast, an image of Cat naked in his bed flashed through Caleb's mind.

"Yes, I've had breakfast sir," he replied, his eyes twinkling mischievously.

"Okay, but before we start, we need to talk about Adubea. You asked me what the course of action is, and I've decided."

Caleb sat down opposite the Justice and placed his materials on the desk. He wanted the Justice to know he had his full attention.

"We're not going to publicly acknowledge Adubea's situation. It's off limits, and I want it to remain within these four walls. The only people in Ghana who know are you, me, Abby, Adubea, and Sylvia. And the only person outside Ghana who knows is our nephew Joey. You've done a good job with the house staff and keeping this close and tight. I need that to continue no matter what."

Caleb nodded.

"Actually, Sylvia isn't aware of the exact nature of Mrs. Annan's condition. All she knows is Mrs. Annan has to take blood pressure drugs and she's not supposed to know she's taking them. We can trust her. Sylvia is really the most loyal person on your staff."

"She's more loyal than you?" The Justice asked smiling.

"We're tied," Caleb responded, grinning.

"Good. Anyways, that's my decision. I know you check the house, office, and campaign staff regularly, so I trust that this can be contained."

"Contained for the most part, but the only loose cannon is your daughter."

"Abby won't tell the world about her mother. If she wanted to, she would have already. She may be angry at me, but even she knows better."

Caleb nodded slowly. He didn't have the same level of confidence as the Justice did in Abby. He decided he would have a separate talk with Abby as well, even though the Sunday talk didn't quite go so well.

"If she hasn't already, she's going to ask you to give Insel exclusive behind-the-scenes access for a documentary."

"What? Is that a joke?" The Justice laughed out loud and slapped the table as he tried to control himself. His heaving and laughing stopped as he realized Caleb had a serious, stern look on his face.

"You've got to be kidding me. Is she insane? She called me repeatedly yesterday, but I didn't pick up. What in the world is wrong with her? Abby must be the only one in the country who can't tell that Insel is pro-GFP! Even if they weren't, I would never, ever allow cameras to document anything! Jesus Christ!" the Justice's laughter turned to anger.

"She's getting pressured by her bosses."

"Well, that's why I give her interviews every now and then, but a documentary is outrageous."

"I agree sir, but Insel is one of the largest media houses in the country. We won't do the documentary, but we can't ignore them either. I have a plan to get us control of Insel and control of the news. I just need time to put some pieces in place. Until then, answer Abby's calls and tell her no."

"Agreed. Nothing would give me greater pleasure than telling her no. Now let's talk about work. My mood will worsen if I spend too much time thinking about Abby and her antics."

Caleb pulled out his leather organizer and leaned back in the chair. He pointed the Justice to the itinerary and started talking.

The Justice tried to listen intently, but he was irritated now. He had a volatile and unstable wife who he had to control in order to protect his campaign, and an annoying daughter who he couldn't seem to control no matter how hard he tried. Abby was going to be the end of him. He knew it.

It'd been two days, and her father hadn't answered a single one of her calls. Abby was tempted to drive over after work, but Reyn was coming over tonight, and she missed him terribly. They didn't see each other much during the week, but he'd gotten promoted the day before, and she suspected he wanted to celebrate. Monday night's celebration was with the company bigwigs, and tonight was hers. She would go and see her father in person on Wednesday and discuss the documentary with him. She knew what the answer would be, but she had to give it a shot. Her job was on the line.

When she got home, it was a little past 6 p.m., and Reyn was going to be at her end in less than an hour. She didn't cook often, but she figured he deserved a home-cooked meal on this occasion. The promotion was huge, and it was everything Reyn wanted and had worked so hard for. It would mean more travel to the US, South Africa, and Nigeria and less time with her, but she was still proud and happy for him. He deserved to have it all. She loved him and wanted only the best for him.

It took her close to an hour to get vegetable rice, corned beef, and fried plantains ready. Reyn was addicted to fried plantains. After cooking, she only had a few minutes to shower and attempt to look sexy. That part was more important than the food.

When Reyn arrived, she met him at the door wearing a short black shirtdress and lacy black underwear that was visible through the thin shirt material. She grinned as she watched his eyes narrow with need. Without saying a word, he lifted her up and carried her into the bedroom. He dropped her hard onto the bed and climbed on top of her, practically ripping her shirt off in the process. Need was one thing, but tonight she felt there was something else going on with Reyn. She loved his spontaneity and the way he acted, like he couldn't get enough of her, but all that was a hundred times amplified that night. He kissed her like he wanted to drain the life out of her. There was desperation to his touch as he dragged her panties down her thighs and off her feet. Despite the urgency to his touch, he still took his time with her. He parted her legs and devoured her like it was the first time he was tasting her. Abby gripped the sheets as she tried to hold back, but she couldn't. He knew her body inside out. Within minutes, she exploded into his mouth as her orgasm overwhelmed her. Reyn lapped it all up, and before she could even recover, he was inside her pummeling away. It was as if he'd done his duty and made her come, so now it was his turn. She gripped him, trying to match his pace, but he pressed her back against the bed and kept going. He was like a man possessed, she thought, struggling to keep up as he turned her onto her stomach.

Twenty minutes later, she'd come once more and was thoroughly spent, but Reyn showed no signs of easing up. Sweat dripped down his face and chest as he placed her on her back at the edge of the bed and placed her legs on his shoulders. Her whole body throbbed, but she wanted him to have his moment, which he seemed to want to delay inevitably.

"Reyn," she mouthed softly, her eyes fixed on his contorted face.

His breathing was ragged as he squeezed his eyes shut and continued to pound away. There was definitely something going on with him. Reyn groaned and pushed himself deeper and harder into her.

"God, I love you, I love you, I love you!" he screamed as he unloaded himself violently into her. She breathed a sigh of relief as she held his shaking body, startling herself as she came once more.

Minutes later they lay side by side on the bed, each breathing heavily. He reached for her hand and squeezed.

"Did I hurt you?"

Now he was asking? Abby shook her head. There was something definitely off about his behavior tonight, but he hadn't actually hurt her. He let go of her hand and got up from the bed.

"Is that plantains and corned beef I smell? I'm starving," he said, pulling on his briefs and pants.

She lifted herself onto her elbows and stared at him. What the heck?

"Reyn, what's going on? Is everything okay?"

He avoided looking at her as he put his shirt on.

"Let's go eat. I'm really starving. I can't believe I didn't smell the food before."

And then he left the bedroom. Abby pulled her shirt over her body. Thankfully, only one button had popped. She left her underwear on the floor and walked out after him. What was the use of underwear now? She followed him into the kitchen and watched as he lifted the lid off the stew and took a sniff. Then he opened the oven and pulled the covered plantains out. He peeled back the foil and took one plantain out. He popped it into his mouth and started pulling out plates. He was avoiding her eyes.

"Reyn, stop! Please, talk to me! What is going on with you?" she pled.

He set the plates on the kitchen island and stared straight at her. It was the first time all night he'd looked directly at her. There was pain in his eyes. Abby felt her heart constrict as she looked at him. This wasn't good.

"I may have to move to South Africa soon, probably in the next two to three weeks."

Abby's face fell. She knew his new role required more travel. He was now responsible for the Ghana, Nigeria, and South Africa operations, but she didn't expect it would require a permanent move.

"Why do you have to move? Why can't you just go back and forth? Your home is here. I am here," she asked, embarrassed about the whininess that had crept into her voice.

Reyn walked over to her, held her hand, and then led her to the sofa. He stared down at her fingers, trying to find words for whatever else he had left to say.

"Emma and the boys will be joining me."

Abby pulled her hands away.

"What? I thought she hated Ghana. I thought she never, ever wanted to live here. What happened?"

"She didn't want to live in Ghana or Nigeria, but she's more open to the idea of South Africa. Some of her friends have visited South Africa before, and the other wives who've been on assignments there have been raving about it."

Abby stood up abruptly and started pacing the room. Her mind was racing.

"I still don't get this. I really don't. You get promoted on Monday, and then on Tuesday, Emma finds a new appreciation for Africa? I don't care if it's South Africa we're talking about. How can she suddenly be ready to uproot the boys from school and move them thousands of miles to Africa? Isn't all of that strange to you?"

Reyn frowned, trying hard to follow her reasoning.

"What's strange about that? Eventually Emma would have had to consider moving here. This is a huge opportunity for me. The timing makes sense. I told her about the promotion, and she called me this afternoon and said she thinks it's time she and the boys made the move. So, she's decided to come down this weekend, and we're flying off to Pretoria."

Abby shook her head. This was too much, too fast. She sat down next to him again and held his hands.

"Reyn, think about this. It took her a day to decide that? She's been adamant about not moving for four years! And in one day, one day, she decides to consider it? In one day, she decides to fly down here for an impromptu tour of South Africa? In one day, she decides to be with her husband again?"

"What exactly are you trying to say, Abby?"

She took a deep breath. There was really only one possibility.

"My father—he must have something to do with this."

Reyn laughed and shook his head.

"Babe, your father is powerful, agreed, but he's not *that* powerful. Come on. So, you think he got to Emma? Huh? Your father somehow convinced my wife to give up everything she loves about her life and move? Your father did that?"

She ignored his laughter. He had no idea who he was dealing with.

"Who does Emma trust most? Who does she listen to? Maybe my father got to them."

Reyn was full blown laughing now.

"Babe, come on, get a grip. I know you have issues with him, but this is just impossible. First of all, I'm sure your father has a lot more to think about than our relationship. Second, my wife is in Texas, and the one person she respects more than God would be her own father. And I doubt very much that Justice Annan somehow got Victor Harner to convince his daughter to move to Africa. Third, what leverage could your father possibly have to make any of that happen? You think your father is powerful? You haven't met Victor or my own father. Trust me, this had nothing to do with the Justice."

Abby sat silently for a while, staring at their clasped hands. And then she looked up.

"Even if my father isn't involved, Emma's decision seems too sudden. You said it yourself: she's giving up everything she loves about her life."

"She's gaining something...someone she loves too," Reyn said softly.

Abby felt a lump form in her throat. She couldn't speak, so Reyn continued talking.

"Emma knew...knows our marriage wouldn't survive another four years of us apart. She's coming for me."

"File for a divorce," Abby said under her breath.

Since the day she met Reyn, she'd never uttered those words out loud to him. She'd never asked him for that. She felt that eventually he'd make that decision on his own. He was so in love with her. How could he not? Knowing that his wife had no intentions of moving to Africa, and knowing that he wanted to take over the Africa operations, she took comfort in the fact that Reyn and his wife would be apart for another three years at least. And now this. Emma Proctor was about to invade her world.

"File for a divorce," she repeated louder.

"I heard you the first time, Abby."

He touched her face, and she saw tears form in his eyes. She forced back her own tears.

"I can't, babe. I really can't. I need them. I need my kids," he said, choking.

Abby reached out and hugged him.

"You won't lose them. You'll have your kids. You'll visit them as you do now. Emma would probably be difficult in the beginning, but she would never keep them from you. You'd have me, here with you or in South Africa, but you'd have me. And you'd have your kids too, in Texas," she said, still struggling to remain composed.

Reyn pulled away from her and took a deep breath. He stared up at the ceiling. This was much harder than he thought it'd be.

"I would lose everything—my kids, the company, my wife." He said the last part softly, knowing it would cut deep.

"You would have me," she emphasized. "If you're in love with me as much as you claim, then I should be enough."

Reyn stood up, and Abby stood as well. He turned away from her, and she gripped his arm, spinning him around. He was stronger, but she was angrier. She pointed to the bedroom.

"What happened in there? What was that supposed to be, some goodbye fuck?" she snapped.

He loosened her grip and walked away toward the balcony.

"I'm talking to you, Reyn Proctor! Jesus, is that what it was? Was that your version of goodbye? Talk to me! Is this it? You came here knowing you were going to break-up with me, but you decided, heck, let me get in one last screw! Huh? Well, you know what, your last screw royally sucked!" she yelled.

He started to walk back toward her.

"Abby, please, calm down. Let's sit and talk."

She was mad, and his calm, cool demeanor wasn't helping. It was only when he was standing in front of her again that she noticed the tears in his eyes were flowing freely down his face now. It broke her heart, and she started crying. She couldn't be strong anymore. Her world was falling apart.

"Please don't leave me," she sobbed. "Please. God, I love you so much. I'm not ready for this."

He wrapped his arms around her, and she hugged him back, clinging tightly to him. He stroked her hair gently as she sobbed.

"I love you, babe. I really do, more than you'll probably ever know. I'm just not ready to walk away from my family. I just can't." He was crying too.

For minutes they stood there, holding each other tightly and crying. Reyn was the first to step back.

"I'm really sorry, but I have to go."

Abby reached for his hand, but he was buttoning his shirt and walking toward the bedroom. She followed him and watched as his slipped his shoes on.

"You should stay. Have dinner. Spend the night."

He walked past her and back to the living room, scanning the space. She followed him again.

"Reyn, look at me," she whispered.

He sighed and looked at her.

"Don't go. Stay one night. Let's talk. This doesn't have to be the end."

He ran his fingers through his hair. She could tell he was considering it, but within seconds he had a look of steely resolve. Her heart sank deeper.

"I can't. It's not fair to you. Emma will be here on Friday, and I need to see if I can make it work. I can't do that and carry on with you at the same time. I love you, baby. I swear to God I do, but I have to go right now, or I'll never leave. I'm so sorry."

He kissed her softly on the lips, and then he was gone. Abby stood motionless for a while, and then she dropped onto the floor, sobbing uncontrollably. She knew her father's announcement was going to permanently change her life. She knew she was going to have a bad week, but this, this was unexpected. She clutched her chest as the pain threatened to engulf her. She couldn't believe what had just happened. The one good thing she thought she had in her life was gone. How did that happen? She was stunned. Why wasn't she enough? Why didn't he love her enough to give it all up? They could move to California. He said he loved it there. He said he wanted to be a winemaker one day. They could do that. They could leave everything behind and make wines. She'd get on her knees and plant the grapes herself. And they could fight for his kids together. She loved him so much, and she thought he loved her more. Why wasn't that enough for him to walk away from it all? She wasn't being reasonable. She knew that. Reyn was a man in his forties with a family he obviously loved and a family business he wanted to run one day. He wasn't a boy in his twenties with nothing to lose. She pushed the logic from her mind. Love was supposed to conquer it all. What a load of bullshit. She crawled into her bedroom and lay on the bed soaked with their sweat. She could smell him, smell the intensity of their lovemaking, if she could even call it that. She held onto the pillow he'd laid his head on and continued crying. How was she going to make it? How could this truly be the end? She was thirty years old, and this was the first time she felt this gutted and heartbroken. She wanted to sleep and never wake up. If there was a God, that's what he'd give her—He'd let her sleep and never wake up.

Abby closed her eyes, crying and praying. She fell asleep an hour later.

7

A senso Arthur was riled up beyond words. He hadn't felt this insulted in a very long time. He shook his head and shifted his gaze from the Justice to Caleb. Both men were expressionless. He glanced at his aide Fred, who looked just as perplexed as he did. Asenso gritted his teeth and returned his gaze to the Justice.

"Minister of education? Really, Joseph? That is the best you can do? This was supposed to be my turn! Everyone knows that. Everyone respects that. Don't forget that Otoo only beat me by 2 percent. That's it! And everyone knows that he wouldn't have won if it wasn't for the intimidation he and his thugs pulled up north. And since then, I have remained steadfast and dedicated to bringing the GFP down! I have been the face of the DNP for a very long time. This was supposed to be my turn, so don't throw a meaningless title like minister at me and think you're doing me a damn favor!" he snapped.

Asenso stood up angrily from the sofa, and the Justice stood up immediately as well. He reached out to him.

"Asenso, calm down, please. Calm down and sit down. Let's talk. Come on, sit."

"Don't coddle me, Joseph." Asenso shrugged him off and reached for the suit jacket draped on the chair behind him.

"Asenso, wait. We've known each for too long for you to leave here angry like this. Fred, Caleb, give us a moment, okay?"

Caleb picked up his phone and organizer and walked out. This was going as planned. He and the Justice knew Asenso would be angry and implacable. This meeting, which was moved from Tuesday to Thursday, was really just a charade of some sorts. There was nothing the Justice could offer Asenso that would appease him. He had a right to feel that way. For four years, the Justice had never openly expressed an interest in running for office, and this was honestly Asenso's moment.

Asenso had campaigned twice before for the DNP ticket. The first time he lost out to former President Samuel Yara, a senior party loyalist who had also campaigned four years earlier against Isaac Mensah, but lost. And so the concept of "turn" was created. Isaac Mensah beat Samuel Otu for the DNP nomination twice, in 1992 and 1996, but lost the general presidential bid both times. So the baton was handed over to Samuel, who beat Asenso Arthur for the nomination in 2000 and went on to win the presidency. Asenso was loyal to Samuel and the DNP, and served as minister of finance for four years, and then as governor of the Bank of Ghana for the remainder of Samuel's term. The Justice put in his bid for the first time in 2008 but pulled out after his sister-in-law was killed, which was a blessing for Asenso. After the Justice pulled out, Asenso's bid for the DNP's nomination in 2008 was contested by only person, John Santini, who knew he wouldn't win—it was more to place his name as "next in line" after Asenso. Asenso lost the general election bid, but he was bolstered by the close results. For four years, he was the face of the opposition, and he knew it was still his turn—until Joseph Annan made his unexpected announcement.

The DNP organized rallies often to maintain the excitement and commitment of their base. The first rally of each year always included a "special guest." In 2011, they managed to drag Isaac Mensah to the rally. The man was eighty-four, but he was still charismatic and vibrant. He emphasized that the DNP was the only way back to economic prosperity, and he pledged his support to Asenso. This year, when Asenso heard former President Aryee was going to be there, he expected it would be the final endorsement he needed. Getting Isaac Mensah's public commitment a year earlier was essential, but getting President Aryee's endorsement would be the icing on the cake. So, Asenso showed up to the rally all fired up with a speech prepared. It was the first official rally of 2012. It was an important moment for him. And then he saw Joseph Annan seated next to President Yara at the podium, and he knew, just knew, he was about to be robbed in broad daylight.

It was unfair and disrespectful to him when all he'd done was toil for the party, yet nothing he'd done could compare to the ever noble, faithful, charismatic, and generous Justice Joseph Annan.

"So you think you can wake up one day and decide you want to be back in, huh? You practically walked away from politics, and now you think you can win just because Samuel supports you? You have no idea what you're dealing with. The people know me. The party delegates know me. Loyalty will always be important, Joseph. And more than anyone else, I have demonstrated unflinching loyalty to this party!" Asenso shouted, pointing threateningly at the Justice.

Annan walked over to the fridge just behind his office desk and pulled out two beers. He knew Asenso had a soft spot for Heineken. Asenso stared at the beer in Annan's hands for a moment, and then he turned away.

"I won't be bought by beer."

"Oh come on, I am just offering you a drink," Annan said, stretching the bottle out to Asenso again. Asenso ignored him and sat down. He was hopping mad.

Annan set the beer on the coffee table next to Asenso and sat opposite him.

"So what do you want? What can I do?" he asked.

"Pull out of this race," Asenso said, staring directly at Annan.

"I can't do that."

"Then there's nothing we have left to discuss."

Asenso got up again and put his jacket on. He glared at Annan as he buttoned up.

"You have no respect for anything or anyone. You summon me to your office like a child, and then you have the audacity to think I'll be swayed by a ministerial position and beer! No damn respect! *This is my turn*. And I will never let you take it away from me!"

Annan remained silent, and he simply stared back at Asenso. Flustered and angered, but knowing it was useless to continue, Asenso strode out, slamming the door behind him.

A few seconds later, Caleb walked in. He raised an eyebrow at the untouched beer.

"What? The Heineken didn't work? I swear, I thought he would concede just for that."

Annan laughed and leaned back in the chair.

"It went just as you said it would. He won't budge. He'll fight me right up to the congress."

"And I assume you're still adamant that we play clean with him? I have enough dirt to bring him down you know," Caleb said, settling into the seat Asenso had just vacated. He picked up the beer and took a swig.

"Not him. We leave Asenso alone. I don't mind bringing every single GFP dirty crook to their knees, but I will not touch one of our own. I will win the nomination. Asenso knows that. There is no need to further humiliate a man we just blindsided. I won't fracture the DNP just to win."

Caleb nodded. It was typical of the Justice. He could be noble like that. In any case, Caleb agreed.

"They're all coming for us now—the GFP, Asenso, Santini, and the other wannabes in the other wannabe parties," Caleb said.

Annan leaned forward and stretched his beer bottle out to Caleb.

"Are you ready?"

Caleb smiled and touched his bottle to the Justice's.

"I've been waiting for this moment for ten years."

The Justice nodded and leaned back again. They sat and drank in silence. They were confident they had this nomination *and* the general election in the bag. They were prepared.

Abby stared forlornly out her office window. Insel Media's ten-story headquarters building was located at North Airport, a few blocks away from the N1 highway. The tenth floor had a 360-degree bird's eye view of everything above five stories and within fifty kilometers. It was a breathtaking view on most days, but not today. There were very few tall buildings within that view, and one of the most prominent ones was the Proctor Oil building. It used to excite her that she could see Reyn's building from her office, but now it just made her heart ache even more. It was Friday, three days after Reyn broke up with her, and she was hurting badly, more than she thought was humanly possible. Everything happened too fast. There were some breakups people could see coming from a mile away, when it was clear one person in the relationship had obviously checked out. And then there was Tuesday's event, unexpected, out of the blue, and devastating. In a way she knew that was partly her fault. She was dating a married man. She should have been on her toes every day waiting for the axe to fall. She shouldn't have fallen in love. She shouldn't have gotten so comfortable with him, with what they had together. She shouldn't have thought it would last forever. In the end, it all came down to one thing—she shouldn't have dated him in the first place.

Abby choked back a sob and closed her eyes. The pain was too much to bear. She hadn't eaten properly in days, and she could barely pay attention to anything. Her neediness was also alarming her. She wasn't naturally weepy. She was strong and resilient. She'd survived her aunt's murder, and her mother's breakdown hadn't destroyed her. She wished she could be strong after this abandonment, grieve for one day, and then move on like nothing ever happened.

That probably only happened in the movies. Instead, when she woke up Wednesday morning and she was still alive despite her prayers, she called him immediately, hoping he'd spent the night regretting his decision. No such luck. He didn't answer her call that morning, or the three calls and four messages after that. Eventually he called her back on Thursday and pled with her to try some distance in order to make it work. Make it work? Why in the world would she try to make the breakup work? Why did people even ask for that? She was in pain, she was lost, and she was heartbroken. Why would she try to be considerate and make the breakup work? And how could he have moved on so quickly? Why wasn't he missing her every second of every day? When they were together, she was awed and floored by his love, attention, and commitment. She'd never been in a relationship with a man who was that into her, she thought, a man who seemed to worship the ground she walked on. She thought she was his best friend. She thought she knew him better than anyone. They spent hours talking, and he opened up to her about so much. And he was there for her too. They hardly spent a single weekend apart, and during the week, he'd call several times a day to chat. He'd text and email too, whatever it took to let her know he was thinking of her. So how did that man go from that type of love to asking for distance within just a day?

Abby took a deep breath and tried to still her shaking body. God, she was in pain.

"So, you're in today. I've been looking for you for days now."

"And I've been avoiding you for days now," Abby muttered without turning her chair around.

"Excuse me?" The shock was evident in his raised voice.

Abby turned around then and stared directly at Josh. She was not in the mood today. She could weep for Reyn, but she wasn't going to be a withering idiot in front of Josh.

"What do you want, Josh?"

His mouth fell open.

"What? Are you serious? Are you out of your mind? I am your boss, you know. I am a VP in this company. You should show me some respect!" he snapped, unnerved by her audacity.

Abby leaned back in her chair, crossed her legs, and stared at him.

Flustered, Josh leaned over her table and wagged a finger directly in her face.

"You're done, do you understand me? The only thing that can save you now is if you've gotten your father to sign the consent forms for the documentary."

"Then I am done. My father isn't going to do the documentary—not today, not ever," she said through clenched teeth, trying hard to restrain herself.

Josh chuckled and shook his head.

"I see it now. You're truly your father's daughter—overconfident and cocky. That's good. You'll need it for your next job because it won't be here."

Abby smiled.

"You really need to be careful with the threats, Josh. After all, as everyone says, it's more than likely my father will be the next president of Ghana. So getting on my bad side isn't very wise, is it?"

Josh stared at her dumbfounded. He'd worked with her for four years, and she'd never, ever spoken to him like that. He'd seen flashes of her fire every now and then when she was fighting for her ideas to get implemented at meetings, but she was never this direct and sarcastic.

And it appeared she wasn't even done.

"One more thing, if you plan on getting me fired, you better cross your t's and dot your i's. You better have legal grounds to dismiss me. If not, I'll sue Insel for every employee violation there is. And don't think because this is Ghana my lawsuit won't fly. It will, even if it means I have to spend every waking moment pursuing the courts to bring you down, because I've had it. I'm hoping you can tell from my voice. I will fight whatever you throw at me, remember that."

Josh took a step back from the table like he'd been slapped. He tucked his hands into his pocket, a lame attempt at defiance. Then he regained his composure as a thought crossed his mind.

"Since we're being so open today, let me lay it out for you. Your father will be brought down, Abby, very soon. I guarantee it. Tell *him* to make sure he's crossed his t's and dotted his i's, because I will find something, even if it means dedicating all of Insel's resources to it. *I will find something,*" he sneered, laying emphasis on his last statement. He chuckled again, and then he was gone.

Abby sat still for a moment. What was she thinking? Where was that from? Was that performance a symptom of heartbreak? *Damn it*, she cursed, all she'd done was insult a senior VP and painted a target on her father's back. Her family wasn't perfect, her mother was sick, and now she'd angered an obvious GFP supporter. Her father and Caleb always claimed Insel was pro-GFP, and she could see that clearly now. How could she say half the things she'd said? Yes, sure, she'd always wanted to put Josh in his place, but she hadn't for a reason. He was unpredictable.

Abby placed her head on her table and groaned. This was Reyn's fault. He'd turned her into an erratic, needy, bumbling mess. How was she going to get through this? She sat back in her chair, took a deep breath, and picked up the phone.

Caleb was sitting in the office reviewing piles of telephone bills when his cell phone rang and Abby's name and picture popped up on his iPhone. He stared it for a minute, wondering what favor she wanted now. A couple of days ago, the Justice told her he wouldn't do the documentary, so she was probably calling with another request. It was always one thing or another with her. He really wasn't in the mood to speak with her, but he answered anyways.

"Yes?" he asked, injecting as much impatience as he could muster into his voice.

"Caleb, sorry, I'm sure you're busy, but do you have a minute?" her voice was low, and he could detect some anxiety in it.

He stared at the pile in front of him. He usually dedicated the first Friday of every month to reviewing the telephone bills of all Annan family members and staffers. That's how he found out about Reyn to begin with. He wished he could trust someone enough to delegate the tedious task to, but he'd laid off three staffers in the last five years because they were repeatedly in touch with politicians, government officials, or the media when their jobs didn't require it. There was no one else he could trust to do this, but perhaps taking a minute break to listen to Abby wouldn't hurt. She sounded like she needed to talk.

"Go on, what is it?"

"It's Josh Winkler. He's a senior VP at Insel. You probably know him. I told him Daddy wouldn't do the documentary, and he threatened me."

Caleb sat upright.

"What happened? What did he say?"

"He threatened to fire me, and he assured me that he would find dirt on Daddy and bring him down, no matter what. He sounded really serious, Caleb. I don't know what he has or what he's planned, but I've never seen him like that. I have no idea what he's going to do."

Caleb rubbed his temple. He was certain Josh didn't have anything, but openly threatening Abby like that meant he was carrying a serious grudge, and men like that could be dangerous.

"He has nothing on your father, and I may not have a Ghana law license, but I'm certain he can't fire you just because we turned down Insel's request for a documentary."

"I'm not worried about the firing. He has no grounds to do that. It's the way he spoke about Daddy that has me concerned. I am not a supporter of Daddy's campaign. He shouldn't be running. He should be focused on my mother, but I don't want that creep in our business either. He sounded really determined, like he already has something in play."

"I'll handle it. You don't have to worry about Josh Winkler."

Caleb's words sent a chill down Abby's spine. He'll handle it. Was it the same way he handled Reyn's and her relationship? She needed to know.

"Caleb, did you, or Daddy, have anything to do with Reyn's wife moving back to Ghana?" she asked, praying he would tell her the truth.

"This is the first I'm hearing of that. It's been a busy week, and I haven't had the chance to pay attention to your married boyfriend's wife's travel plans."

"Just because it's the first time you're hearing about it doesn't mean you didn't have anything to do with it."

Caleb smiled. She was smart. He'd give her that.

"So let me rephrase for you, Caleb. Have you done anything at all, directly or indirectly, to end my relationship?"

"No," he said without hesitation.

Abby's heart fell. She was hoping it was Caleb or her father. That would have given her someone to blame. Now, she was back to square one. Reyn left her because his beloved wife was moving back, and her father had nothing to do with it.

"Thanks, Caleb. I'll talk to you later," she said, in a hurry to get off. She was on the verge of crying again.

"Abby, wait..."

Abby paused, what now?

"You'll be fine, you know. He doesn't deserve you. Now you can focus on yourself and start fresh. You're strong. You'll be fine."

Abby was stunned. These were the kindest words Caleb had ever said to her since she'd known him. She could actually sense the sincerity in his voice.

"Thank you," Abby said softly, feeling her throat tighten as the tears threatened to start. She hung up quickly and

turned around to face the window again. Caleb was right—
she was strong. No more crying or worrying, not over Reyn
or Josh. At least no more for today.

Back in his office, Caleb stared at his phone wondering why he'd said what he said to Abby. Was it guilt for
the way he talked to her on Sunday or for initiating her
breakup? He wasn't sure. All he knew was that she sounded
distressed and worried for the father that she was always
fighting against. That touched him in a way. No matter
how antagonistic she acted toward her father, she obviously
cared. Caleb pushed the telephone bills aside and walked
over to the office door. The door to the Justice's office,
which was right next to his, was slightly ajar, and Caleb
could hear the Justice's voice as he chatted on the phone
with his nephew Joey. The Justice called Joey a few times a
week to check in on him. Joey was an orphan now, and all
he had were the Annans. The Justice had been trying for a
while to get him to move back to Ghana, but Joey was adamant that he had nothing in Ghana. Caleb glanced around
the open office area. Everyone looked busy.

Caleb closed his door, locked it, and then walked over
to the conference area off the center of his office. He pulled
the table aside as the rug beneath it followed, and then he
kneeled and started removing the loose floorboards. What
lay beneath it was an 11" by 17" by 15" steel box. Caleb
took it out and set it on the conference table. He rolled the
correct combination numbers in place, and then the box lid
popped open. Caleb sat down and took out the single sheet
of paper that lay on top of the folders, phones, CDs, DVDs,
and external drives. There were ten names on the sheet of
paper. The first name was the current president's, followed
by his VP, the minister of defense, the governor of the Bank

of Ghana, Ohene the GFP campaign manager, Asenso, Santini, one media commentator, and Josh Winkler. This was Caleb's "hit list"—people who posed direct threats to the Justice and those who weren't necessarily threats but still had to be taken down to secure the win for the Justice. For each of the people on the list, he had a rock solid collection of dirt that could either discredit or completely obliterate them.

Originally, he was going to focus the next month on showcasing the Justice—a media blitz dedicated to highlighting the enormous contributions the Justice had made to the prosperity and well-being of the people of Ghana. Caleb hadn't just spent time gathering information to sink their opponents. He'd also amassed undeniable evidence that the Justice was the only man of honor and integrity left in the political world. He was the clearest choice.

Timing was critical here. He couldn't just start bringing people down, even if they had obviously started their own witch hunts. However, Josh Winkler was a problem. He was tenth on the list now, but Caleb knew it was time to promote the son of a bitch.

Caleb picked up the box, set it on his desk, and quickly put everything in the room back in place. Then, he picked up a phone from the box and turned it on. He hit "1" on the keypad. The call was answered on the second ring.

"Dude, its 3 a.m." The voice on the other end was deep, husky, American, and male.

"The Josh Winkler plan, I need it activated."

"So soon? I thought it wasn't time."

"He threatened the Justice and Abby. I can't let him get him away with it."

"Of course, we can't have that, can we?" his friend responded sarcastically. "Anyways, how far do you want me to go?"

"Full scale. Make it happen by Monday 8 a.m. GMT."

"Fine, it's done. I'm off to bed."

The line went dead. Caleb went into the phone's recently dialed list, deleted the only number there, and then turned off the phone. He knew he was extremely paranoid, but it gave him a sense of comfort. He placed the phone back in the box, but he didn't close it. It was all starting. He'd actually just put a plan he'd built for years into motion. The Justice was honestly the best choice for the country, but even good men needed some help, hence the box and his plan. He'd enlisted his former marine buddy, who was a technology genius, to help. The bored bloke who was now working in the private sector was happy to oblige. Caleb felt a deep thrill, one he hadn't felt in over twenty years, not since his time in the marines. He glanced at his hit list again. The poor sods really had no idea who they were dealing with, but they were all going to find out, every single one of them.

8

*A*bby lay on her bed, surrounded by a bag of ripe plantains, empty Coca-Cola cans, DVDs, and her remote controls. It was the first Saturday in a long time that she was alone, with nothing and no one. She wasn't sure what she was supposed to do now. Find a hobby? Make new friends? She left Ghana when she was sixteen and returned ten years later. She'd never had the chance to form any real lasting relationships in Ghana. Bella, the one friend she'd grown up with, was still in Ghana, but they were like two different people now. Bella was a stay-at-home wife with three kids. Even though they stayed in touch and talked every now and then, Abby couldn't call her now and tell her she was heartbroken because her married boyfriend had dumped her. Bella obviously wouldn't understand—a wife would never side with a mistress. There were also the girls she used to hang out with four years ago when she first moved back to Ghana, but she hadn't spent any time with them in years. Denise her assistant was one of them, but since she'd met Reyn she'd kept them at arm's length. Eventually they stopped asking her questions about the mystery man she was hiding, and she stopped making up excuses. Besides Denise, she hadn't seen the other three in a year. She couldn't call them now and ask to hang out either. So what now? She'd practically spent the last three years in Reyn's arms, so she had no clue what to do on her own. What did people in Ghana do on Saturdays? Abby got up from the bed and pulled on the crumpled jeans lying on the floor. If she stayed home, she'd eat everything in existence. There was one option. It wasn't her first option, but she didn't have many choices.

Half an hour later, Abby parked her Q7 behind her mother's E-Class. There were three other cars there, her father's S-Class, Caleb's Toyota Camry sport, and a Toyota Prado that she didn't recognize. She expected there would be a lot more strange cars in this driveway over the next ten months. Abby walked straight up to her parents' bedroom when she entered the house. There were voices coming from her father's study, but she decided not to pop in. The last time she barged into her father's study hadn't gone so well. She found her mother in the upstairs TV room, sitting in the sofa and surrounded by swatches of cloth. Her eyes lit up briefly when she saw Abby.

"Abby, what a nice surprise, I didn't know you were coming. Come, sit. Help me decide on colors for the house."

Abby smiled and reached down to hug her mother. She shifted the samples to create room and sat down.

"You're redecorating?" she asked, picking up the swatches.

Her mother hadn't made any changes to the house in years. She often said her original design was timeless.

"Yes, I'm going to redo the main living room, main TV room, guest room downstairs, and your father's study. We'll be getting a lot of visitors over the next year, and I think this house has been dead long enough. So, it's time to spruce up. I'm thinking beige and browns for the living room—very earthy and inviting colors. And burgundy for the guest room—that signals warmth, I think. Your dad's study, that I'm not sure. Perhaps we could do whites and grays? Anything to brighten the room, it's really too dark in there."

Abby picked up another set of swatches. She really hated Reyn right now. Listening to her mother ramble all day was not how she wanted to spend her Saturday. She needed to make friends, ASAP.

"I think whites and grays sound perfect for Daddy's study. I agree. It is too dark in there. The living room though, can we add some gold?"

Adubea beamed and picked up a goldish sample.

"This is called ochre, and it would be great for pillows and throws, don't you think? Browns, beiges, and gold, that's fantastic."

Abby nodded absentmindedly. It was going to be a long, long day.

Caleb tapped his pen on his crossed knee, hoping the Justice would get the signal and end this dreary long conversation with Reverend Douglas. He was the third visitor this morning, and he was the most talkative. Even though Caleb didn't consider himself a Christian, he respected the Justice's faith. Although on days like this, he wished his candidate was less religious. He groaned inwardly when the reverend reached for the Justice's hands and started another prayer. Caleb knew it would be rude to get up now, but he really couldn't endure another minute of this. He picked up his phone and iPad and walked out, leaving the two with their heads bowed in prayer. The reverend was the head of Ghana's largest church, the Church of Christ, which was also the Justice's church for the last twenty years, so Caleb knew that Douglas's support of the Justice would be critical in the elections. He just wasn't ready to sit through a third prayer. He walked over to the living room and paused at the door, watching as Abby and her mother walked around the room making notes. Abby looked tired and disengaged. Her t-shirt and jeans were creased and crinkled, and her hair looked like it hadn't been brushed in a day or so. She was obviously still hurting. Caleb didn't realize she was that much in love with Reyn, but he didn't feel sorry for her. Reyn was married. It would have ended eventually. He turned from the door and started to walk away.

"Caleb, wait, come in for a minute. I'd like your opinion about these colors as well."

Abby turned away from the curtain at the mention of Caleb's name. She felt strangely self-conscious, not sure how to behave around him since his unusual words of kindness to her the day before. She smiled broadly at him. He smiled back a little and then quickly turned his attention to her mother. Adubea handed him three pieces of cloth and started talking excitedly. Feeling a little snubbed, Abby turned around and walked through the side door in the living room to the sunroom. Why had she even bothered to smile? She hated it when Caleb got under her skin, which was more often than she liked. When she first met Caleb ten years ago, she thought he was unbelievably handsome with his light chocolate skin, dark eyes, muscled build, and towering height, but it was difficult to get past the expressionless eyes and cold exterior, so she didn't even try.

"Feeling better today?"

She swung around, startled by the sound of his voice. She peered past him into the living room.

"Where's my mother?"

"I mentioned that Reverend Douglas was here, so she decided to go join your father, which means another hour of prayers. Brave on her part, really. I know she's been avoiding church the last few years, but I guess she's coming around."

Abby couldn't help smiling. Caleb claimed to believe in God, but he avoided church and religious events like the plague. She was surprised he'd lasted this long as a member of the Annan household. And in the end, that's what he was, a member of her dysfunctional and disintegrating household.

"You are really like the son my father never had."

Caleb frowned and stared at her.

"Where is that from?"

Abby shrugged and leaned against the glass door that overlooked the lawn.

"I thought of it, so I said it. My father worships you. You're not religious, you don't go to church, and you're not very sociable, but he still adores you, because you're a guy. Same with Joey. When his father died, he was really young, and my father sort of adopted him. I was born a year later, but I couldn't compete. There was always Joey," she said, gesturing at the pictures around the room.

Caleb's gaze followed her eyes, and he picked up a framed picture of the Annans on the center table.

"And then along came Caleb," she added wistfully. "That sealed my fate."

Caleb almost didn't hear her. His gaze was fixed on the picture, and a shocking, unbelievable thought hit him. Jesus, why hadn't he seen this before? A chill ran down his spine as he studied the picture he'd looked at a thousand times before. There were five people in the shot. The Justice was in the middle, Adubea was on his left, and Bertha was on his right. He could tell the difference only because Adubea was wearing her engagement and wedding rings—she never took those off. Bertha was also skinnier. In front of the adults were Joey and Abby. Abby must have been ten, and Joey sixteen. The Justice had his right hand on Joey's shoulder, and Bertha's left hand was on her son's other shoulder. Adubea had both hands on her daughter.

Caleb inhaled sharply and stared. How had he missed this? How the heck had he missed this?

"Are you okay?" Abby asked, stepping toward him.

He peeled his eyes away from the picture and looked at her as if he was seeing her for the first time. He nodded and set the picture down.

"I'm fine," he muttered, trying to regain his composure.

His heart was pounding. He could barely breathe. Abby stepped closer, a worried look on her face.

"Is it something I said? I'm not insinuating that you're usurping my position or anything like that. I don't really care anymore. My father wanted a boy, and he got a girl. No one can tell me my sex didn't matter. I've lived with his disappointment all my life. So it's not you. I never meant to imply that it was. You have no control over how my father feels about me, so—"

Caleb reached out and touched her arm, interrupting her speech. She stopped talking, startled by the touch as well as the look of kindness on his face. Caleb wasn't sure why he touched her like that. She had a lot of spunk and fire when she was dealing with her father, but he could tell she was carrying a lot of hurt as well. All the same, Caleb felt she could try to be a bit more understanding of her father. The Justice did his best.

"I'm sorry you feel the way you do, Abby, but your father loves you very much. You need to give him a chance and stop fighting him."

She pulled away and tucked her hands into the pockets of her jeans.

"Stop fighting him? You think this is all me? Are you that blinded by him? The only thing I've been fighting for is his attention and affection, which I've never had," she said, years of hurt evident in her tone.

"He sent you to one of the best schools in the US. And while you were there, he bought you a car, rented an apartment for you, and made sure there wasn't anything you lacked."

"You think that's what affection looks like? An apartment and a car? Joey also had an apartment and a car, but Joey also had the weekly phone calls and extra visits!" she retorted.

"You know what, I don't expect you to understand. Why am I even talking to you? He's your God, and heaven forbid I insinuate anything negative about him. When my parents are done praying, tell them I left," she continued.

Caleb watched her stride off angrily, but he didn't follow her. He needed to calm his hyperactive thoughts. He sat down in the wicker chair next to the center table and picked up the picture again. He wasn't sure why it was so glaring today, but the resemblance between the Justice and Joey was as clear as day. Joey, short for Joseph, the Justice's namesake, and potentially his biological son? What else could explain it? Bertha and Adubea were related, sure, but the Justice had no blood connection to the boy, and yet there they were in the picture, same eyes, same nose, same jaw, same bone structure, and same damn face.

Caleb walked around the room looking for a more recent picture, and he found one hanging above the mantle. It was taken four years ago, after Bertha was killed and Abby and Joey came down for the funeral. The picture was taken a few weeks before the funeral. Joey had thick facial hair then, and he wore glasses, so the resemblance wasn't as obvious. The body structure was the same though, and in the picture, he stood very close to the Justice, who was holding him close. Abby and Adubea were to the Justice's left, and although Annan had one arm around Abby, his body was leaning toward Joey.

Caleb cursed out loud. He was astute, observant, and thorough. As a marine, he was trained to catch every single detail, so how could he have missed this? Abby was right. Was he that blind when it came to the Justice? He needed to think. He needed to analyze. He'd been around them for ten years. He'd studied them all like a hawk. He'd watched the Justice's every move. He knew it all. How in the world could he have missed that Joey was the Justice's son? It appeared obvious now, but he had to confirm it. He had to find out, because if it was true, then everything he'd built was in jeopardy. Worse of all, if it was true, then the man he'd worshipped, the man he'd believed in, the man he'd sacrificed ten years for was a fraud. If that was the case, he had some decisions to make before it was too late.

9

Reyn glanced at his watch and then back up at the arriving passengers. Emma's flight arrived thirty minutes ago, but she hadn't emerged yet. He shifted anxiously from one foot to the other, wishing he'd gone up to the immigration section to meet her. It didn't matter how many times a traveler came through Kotoka International Airport. It could still be daunting. He took a step to head up the arrival doorway to check on her when he saw her. His heart skipped a beat. She looked beautiful. Emma had her mountain of golden hair pulled back into a casual ponytail. She wore light pink lip gloss and a hint of eye makeup that accentuated her blue eyes. She looked a bit tanner since the last the last time he saw her, and the pink dress she wore highlighted her olive skin. She really looked stunning, he thought, smiling as he stepped out to greet her. Her face lit up when she saw him, and Reyn thought his heart was going to burst. How was this even possible? He truly loved his wife, and he loved Abby too, more than his heart could handle.

"Hey honey," she said excitedly, dropping her purse and hand luggage to hug him.

Reyn held on tight, drinking in her smell and feel. It'd only been three months, but it felt different this time. Everything was different this time. She could be staying for good, and that changed everything. He stepped back and looked at her.

"I'm really glad you came," he whispered, kissing her cheek.

She smiled and touched his face.

"I'm glad I came too," she whispered back.

Surprisingly, Emma wasn't jetlagged, so they spent the rest of the day catching up. They had lunch with a group of executives from Proctor Oil and their spouses. Emma knew almost all of them, and the spouses tried to sell her on the merits of Ghana vs. South Africa. Reyn knew South Africa was the better choice because that's where Proctor's biggest operations were. And maybe moving to SA would help him get over Abby, if that was even possible. If he and Emma remained in Ghana, he wouldn't be able to resist starting things up with Abby again. After lunch, he and Emma discussed their upcoming South Africa trip. They were leaving Sunday afternoon, and a tour of Pretoria, the drill sites, and possible homes had been arranged. Then they would be back on Friday in time for the Investor Awards in Accra. Nigeria was out of consideration. Emma didn't want to consider it or even visit because of all the negative press that floated around in the US about Nigeria and the violence plaguing the country. Reyn didn't really mind that

Emma wouldn't consider Nigeria. Proctor Oil had a very capable team there, so he didn't have to spend too much time in Nigeria. After discussing their trip and calling the kids, who were with their grandparents, Reyn and Emma cuddled up in bed and made love. It felt a little stiff and obligatory to Reyn, but he decided to cut her some slack. She'd just spent more than twenty-four hours traveling. She was tired. He couldn't expect fireworks.

Hours later, Reyn lay in bed staring at the silhouette of Emma lying curled up in the bed next to him. It was 3 a.m., and Reyn was the one acting like he had jetlag. He hadn't slept a wink all day. Staring at her sleeping form, Reyn felt a deep sense of loss. It had been a relatively good day, but he still felt empty. He usually spent Saturdays with Abby. God, he missed her, he really did. Reyn turned onto his back and stared at the ceiling. He hated how he'd handled the breakup with Abby. He hated what he'd done to her. He hated being so cold when she called him a few days later. He hated it because he was still so in love with her. He was in a shitty place, and he had no idea how he was going to deal with it.

An hour later, Reyn got up from bed and went downstairs. He had to call her. He went into his study and closed the door behind him. He picked up his cell phone and stared at it. It was 4 a.m. He knew he shouldn't call, but he had to. He had to hear her voice. He had to apologize. He had to tell her he loved her.

Abby answered on the third ring.

"Reyn? Is everything okay? Did something happen?"

She was startled. Of course she was. It was 4 a.m.

"No, no, sorry, I didn't mean to alarm you. I just…" he paused, struggling to find the right words.

"You just what, Reyn?"

She sounded irritated. That surprised him. Was she over him already?

"I wanted to apologize for what happened on Tuesday. I didn't mean for it to be that way. This has been difficult for me and—"

"Reyn, what is it? What do you want? It's 4 a.m." Abby interrupted.

Reyn sighed. This was going to be much harder than he thought.

"I just wanted to say I'm sorry, and I miss you and I love you. I really do, babe."

There was dead silence on the phone, and he wondered if she'd hung up on him. He wouldn't blame her.

"Then pick me, Reyn. If you love me, pick me. Come back to me. That's all," she said, a hint of a sob in her voice.

"Babe—"

She interrupted him again. "No more words. It's your call, so decide. I need to go back to bed. It's been a long day."

Then she hung up.

Reyn placed the cell phone on his desk and sat back. That hadn't gone as he'd expected. He'd hoped she'd say she loved him too, and be willing to try something. That's what it came down to. He wasn't sure he was ready to give her up after all. He needed Abby, Emma, the boys, and his work. He needed it all. He couldn't choose, but he also knew he couldn't ask Abby to be the other woman forever. So what now?

Caleb sat cross-legged on the floor of his living room, staring up at his wall. He'd pulled all the wall art down and spent the last twenty-four hours creating a visual chronology of the Annans. When he first moved to Ghana, he spent a great deal of time learning about Joseph and his family. He spoke with other family members, friends, staff, anybody at all, and documented everything. Back then his conclusion was that Joseph Annan was a man committed to his God, country, and family. There was nothing shady or questionable about the Justice, so Caleb built the Justice's brand and image on that. Integrity. Honor. Family.

Now he realized he might have made a mistake. Everything he'd learned and discovered over the last ten years was documented and up on his wall. It also included pictures he'd taken from the Annans' home on Saturday. Caleb stood, walked to the far left of the wall, and started reviewing the pictures, newspaper clippings, and handwritten notes.

Joseph Annan met the twins Adubea and Bertha Gideon when he was in his second year at Mfanstipim School and they were at Wesley Girls' High School. They met at an inter-school event, and Adubea stole his heart with her beauty and innocent smile. Bertha was the feisty one, and she had three other boys hanging onto her every word. Three months later, Joseph and Adubea were going "steady"—Joseph's words to Caleb when he described how he met his wife. The twins and Joseph ended up at the University of Ghana together. Joseph and Adubea got married their second year. Caleb stared at the three wedding pictures he'd put up. The wedding was simple and small, no more than fifty people. The twins had no siblings, and came from a very small family. Their parents were at the wedding, along with a handful of uncles, aunts, cousins, and school friends. Joseph was from a bigger family, but he also kept it small on his end—parents, three siblings, and some uncles, aunts, cousins, and friends. There was nothing telling in Joseph and Adubea's wedding pictures. They looked happy and in love, and they were holding hands, hugging, or kissing in each picture. A year later, Bertha got married to a professor from the school who was almost twenty years older and the father of her unborn child. She was about nine months pregnant on her wedding day, and her wedding pictures did not depict love and happiness. Professor Richard Amissah, Bertha's husband, was short, stout, balding, and looked nothing like Joey, but that wasn't the only telltale sign. Bertha and Richard were married for almost five years, but Caleb could only find two pictures of the prof, and both were from the wedding day. Caleb knew that finding only two pictures wasn't particularly conclusive. Bertha could have stored her husband's pictures away after he died, but it was questionable that none of his pictures could be found in the Annan household. He was supposed to be Joey's father, after all. Caleb unpinned a picture from the wall and stared at it. It was from the prof's funeral. Joseph was holding Adubea's hand with his right hand, and his left arm was around Bertha's waist. Bertha was carrying Joey, her head was hanging low, and she was leaning into Joseph. That picture was the first of many that captured the permanently changed Annan/Gideon family dynamic.

After the prof's death, Bertha and Joey were practically Annans, and even though it was a drain on Joseph initially, he bore the responsibility. Joseph started his own law firm with two other law school friends right after graduation. They made headlines and hit the jackpot with their third case, a land dispute and lawsuit against the government that earned the firm millions. After that they were on a roll, and Joseph was the star. He knew how to pick the cases, and he knew how to win. Soon Joseph was involved in politics, which wasn't unusual. He was the Student Representative Council (SRC) president at Legon during his final year, and he was also an instigator of most of the student demonstrations. In addition to the law and politics, Joseph branched into land acquisitions and started buying up residential and commercial properties across Accra. That's where his actual fortune came from. He built the mansion he and Adubea lived in now at East Legon, and got Bertha and Joey a smaller but still comfortable and luxurious home at Ridge. He also set Bertha up with a boutique and sent Joey to school in the US.

Caleb stepped back and scratched his head. He was torn. On one hand, Joseph could just be a dedicated and highly committed uncle and brother-in-law. He had the means, so why not take care of his wife's widowed twin sister and nephew? In a lot of traditional families, uncles had primary responsibility for their nephews or nieces, particularly when a father was absent. Maybe that's all Joseph was—a generous and loving person. Yet, there were the pictures. He saw it over and over again. The Justice's body language toward Bertha and Joey was too familiar and intimate. Caleb was surprised he hadn't noticed it before. He'd had several interactions with all of them, either with the Five—Joseph, Adubea, Bertha, Joey, and Abby—or with the Three—Joseph, Adubea, and Bertha—and none of those interactions had raised any red flags. They were a close-knit family, and they supported each other. That was all he thought back then.

The bond the Five had was more apparent when Bertha was killed tragically and senselessly. Armed robbers broke in and slaughtered Bertha in her living room, making away with jewelry, clothes, and electronics. Initially, Caleb suspected the GFP, but the murder-robbery was extensively investigated by the police and the Bureau of National Investigations (BNI), and it seemed there were no ties to politics. Two weeks later, the police killed three suspects in a shootout at another robbery site. The suspects had several items from Bertha's home with them, and it was obvious they committed the crime. Even after the murder was solved, the Annan family still struggled to deal with their loss. Adubea's devastation was obvious, and although the Justice wore his grief well, Caleb sensed that he was in deep pain. It was a pain that Caleb suspected the Justice still bore. Two years after Bertha's death, Caleb and the Justice initiated the cocaine debacle that was supposed to end the GFP once and for all. It was an incredible coup on their part to discover that high-ranking members of the GFP were involved in the drug trade. Caleb and the Justice had a plan to tear the GFP apart from the inside out. It would have been brilliant. They tipped off the police and got the ball rolling, but the Justice had second thoughts and pulled back again from the limelight. He was concerned about the impact all of it would have on his family. He wasn't sure they were ready to be under the microscope again. Caleb desperately wanted to pursue the cocaine scandal, but the Justice shut it down. Mentally and emotionally, he was inaccessible, and politics was the furthest thing from his mind. The entire family was really never the same after Bertha's death.

Caleb picked up another picture. It was also from Bertha's funeral. That was the last time Joey was in Ghana.

The Justice and Joey were standing side by side in the front pew of the church. The resemblance was just undeniable. With the pair wearing matching suits and standing shoulder to shoulder with similar deep, grim expressions in their eyes, it seemed so obvious that they were related by blood.

Caleb turned away from his wall. He could speculate forever. He could stare at pictures all day, but that wouldn't get him anywhere. There was one thing he could do that would confirm whether Joseph Amissah was Joseph Annan's son.

⌇

Caleb glanced at his watch as he strode purposefully into the Justice's home and study. It was almost 2 p.m. The Justice and his wife would be returning from church any minute. He didn't have much time. He glanced around the empty room, and his eyes settled on the half-empty bourbon glass on the desk. He set the satchel he was carrying on the desk and pulled out a set of gloves, cotton swabs, sterile containers, and brown envelopes. Caleb slipped the gloves on and picked up the glass. He was certain this was the Justice's drink. He took out two cotton swabs and passed one over the inside rim and the other over the outside rim, then he snipped the untouched end off and slipped both swabs into separate containers. Caleb then stood over the Justice's chair and examined it. There were several short hair strands on the headrest that would be perfect. You could never have enough samples. Caleb picked the hair follicles up one by one and gently deposited the strands into the brown envelopes. He packed up his stuff and walked out of the house. One down, two to go.

Caleb pressed Abby's doorbell for the second time and then bent down to peer through the cubbyhole. He couldn't see a thing. He knew she was home though: her Q7 was parked in front of her apartment complex. If she wasn't home, he would have broken in, but his only option was to keep ringing the bell. He pressed it repeatedly.

"Geez, hold your horses. I'll be right there!"

The door was flung open, and Caleb stared down at Abby, dumbfounded at the state in which she chose to open the door. She had nothing on but a towel wrapped around her body, with another wrapped around her hair. The parts of her body that weren't covered were wet, and she was practically dripping onto the floor.

"You're dripping," he muttered and walked past her into the living room.

She slammed the door behind him.

"I was in the shower and I thought it was an emergency. Do you know how many times you rang the bell?"

"Ten," he said flippantly, scanning the room quickly at the same time.

"That was a rhetorical question, Caleb. What do you want? Is this going to be a recurring thing? Are you going to show up unannounced every Sunday?" she demanded, her hands on her hips.

Caleb glanced at her and then deliberately stared at her feet. A wet circle was forming on the carpet. Abby followed his gaze, and then she scowled at him.

"Seriously, Caleb, what do you want?" she repeated, ignoring her wet state.

"I just stopped by to check on you. You were pretty angry when you left yesterday, so I just wanted to make sure you were okay. First, you should go dry up and put some clothes on. I'll wait."

Abby cocked her head to one side, what was going on with him? She couldn't discern anything from that blank stare. What the heck was this guy's deal? She gestured to the kitchen.

"I don't have a fancy bar like my father, but I do have some wine, juice, Coca-Cola, and some decent vodka. I don't know what you drink, but you can help yourself. I'll be back."

As soon as she walked into her bedroom, Caleb pulled out tweezers and envelopes from his back pocket. He walked over to the sofa and leaned over. There were tons of hair strands. That was the thing about women—they shed like crazy. Caleb picked up several pieces and deposited them into the envelopes. He sealed and tucked them into his back pocket. He walked over to the kitchen and popped a can of Coke open. He considered mixing it up with the vodka but opted not to. He had a lot on his mind, and alcohol wouldn't help. He walked out to the balcony and leaned against the banister, hoping the fresh air would help clear his mind.

Abby reappeared ten minutes later, wearing a loose, long Woodin print sleeveless dress. He recognized the print because he'd considered buying it for his mother for Christmas. Abby's hair was still damp, and she'd pulled it into a messy ponytail. Caleb took a deep breath. She looked adorable. He rubbed his eyes and looked away. What was wrong with him? Why was he reacting to her like this?

"A week ago you demanded that I break up with my boyfriend, and now you're stopping by to check on me? I wasn't that angry yesterday, just in a mood. So what's really going on? Did my father send you?"

"Well, you seemed pretty angry to me, and to be honest, I feel bad about what I said to you the last time I was here. It was hurtful and unnecessary. I can tell now that you really cared about your boy, just as you care about your father," he said, trying his best to look sincere.

Abby nodded, not sure how to react. Caleb's random acts and words of kindness were confusing.

"I didn't mean to snap at you the way I did yesterday either. I just feel like everyone thinks I'm difficult, but I'm coming from a place of hurt too. Sure, I had material things, but I didn't really have my father," she said, leaning against the banister next to him.

"You think he loved Joey more?"

"Oh it's not Joey's fault. Honestly, I think it's a sex thing. Men like my father, men who thrive on power and influence, they want sons. It's everything to them. That's all. I don't really want to talk about it anyways."

Caleb smiled and nodded. Abby shifted uncomfortably. His gaze was unnerving, and the silence felt awkward. Finally, he stepped away and walked back into the living room. She hurried after him.

"I have to go. We have a busy week ahead of us," he said without looking at her as he continued toward the door.

"Uh, okay, sure. Thanks for the visit," she muttered.

Caleb paused at the door and turned around. He wanted to reach out and touch her damp hair and pull her close, but he restrained himself. He had to get a grip. Where did that thought even come from? This was the Justice's daughter.

"Take care," he said softly, and then he hurried away.

Caleb opened his glove compartment and pulled out one of many spare cell phones he kept in there. He knew it would have been best to wait till he got to his scrambler phone at the office, but he couldn't wait. This Nokia would have to do.

The call was answered on the third ring.

"Hey, I need a favor, nothing to do with the list, but still important."

"At your service," the voice said dryly.

"I'm going to send you some DNA samples by FedEx tomorrow. You should get them by Wednesday, latest Friday. They'll be labeled. Test Abby Annan against Joseph Annan for paternity."

"Wow, is that where we are now? You're questioning your beloved Justice's integrity now?"

"It's just a suspicion. I could be wrong, but it's not just Abby's paternity I'm questioning. There's actually something else I need you to do besides the DNA test. I need you to get a third sample from someone in New York, and I want you to test the third sample against Joseph Annan."

"Uh geez, are you serious? Willing donor?"

"No, this has to be a ghost extraction. Do you have something handy to write with? Let me get you the name and address."

"This is going to take at least a week, bro, and it'll cost, so I'll use our account. We just became richer this weekend, thanks to public enemy number one, also known as victim number one."

"Yes, I saw the balance this morning. Good work, as always. So use the money, do whatever you need to do, just do it. This is priority."

Caleb rattled off Joey's address and then waited for the voice on the other end to repeat it.

"Call me back in a week," the voice said, and then the line went dead.

Caleb deleted the number and chucked the phone back into his glove compartment. He picked up his regular phone and dialed.

"Hey, Cat, babe, can you come over? In about an hour?"

"Sure, but can we make it two hours? I just need to wrap up this paper I'm working on, and then I'll be there, okay?"

"Okay, see you in two."

Caleb hung up and started his car. Two hours would give him enough time to remove the pictures and postings on his wall, clean up the house, and shower. It would also give him time to clear the images of Abby in a towel and a yellow dress out of his mind. God, he was losing it.

10

Charles Anim was seething. This was the most angry he'd ever been in his entire fifty-plus life. He wasn't even this angry when his son crashed and totaled his day-old Mercedes years ago. He wasn't this angry when his first wife cheated and left him for another man. This, what he'd just learned today, took the cake. He was fuming. He shook his head, stunned by the information that lay before him.

"Are you a hundred percent certain of all of this?"

"I am more than certain, Charles. I've spent two days reviewing this over and over again. There is no doubt about what happened. Josh Winkler has stolen $5 million from Insel Media. "

Charles stared at the CFO in disbelief.

"How could he take that much without anyone knowing, without *you* knowing? How is this even possible? I don't understand."

Abe Nsiah took a breath. He was willing to take some blame, but this was not his fault, and he had to help Charles understand that, despite his blind fury.

"Five years ago, Insel, well, specifically you, made Josh a member of our investment council and co-signatory on almost all our accounts. At the time, you said it was important to have at least one non-finance executive serve on the council, just as additional oversight. Josh was put in charge of real estate and property investments, and as far as we all knew, he managed it pretty well. I mean, I checked our investment portfolio each month, and it didn't look like there was anything off."

Abe paused and picked up one of the manila folders he had brought in with him. He opened the folder and placed it in front of Charles.

Charles glanced through it, shook his head, and pushed the folder toward Abe.

"I don't understand any of this, Abe, so just explain it to me."

"For starters, Josh overvalued almost all of the properties he recommended we invest in, including this building we're in. He was working with the appraisers and the property owners. We pay the full inflated amount, and the property owner takes the actual value and then transfers the rest to Josh, who pays off the appraisers and keeps the balance. He did this on every deal, and, worst of all, Josh was the actual owner of some of these properties, just under a different name, including this building. We bought it for two million from Densu Properties, and it turns out Densu is simply a middleman firm for the real owners, Josh and two other friends of his. I hired a new set of appraisers to review all our properties, and it turns out we've overpaid on all of them by at least 80 percent. This building, excluding the modifications we've made, would have been valued at $1.2m."

Charles swore and stood up from his desk. This was unbelievable.

"Why did you decide to get independent assessors? How did you find out about all of this?"

Abe pulled out a thick, large brown envelope from his briefcase and dropped it on Charles's desk. The envelope had Josh's name and office address written across it. At the top left corner was the address of Provident Investment Bank.

"The messenger left this on my desk Monday morning. The new messenger we have makes mistakes with offices all the time. I know I shouldn't have opened it, but Provident is a competitor to our own investment bankers. Anyways, Provident sent Josh a summary list of all his investments and properties. And that's when I realized what he'd been doing. It was all there, all the transfers from the property owners into his account and from him to the appraisers. Over the last five years, Josh has played the role of buyer, seller, and appraiser, and he's made $5 million through his scheme."

Charles grabbed his desk phone and dialed rapidly.

"Get Josh in here, now!" he barked at his assistant.

He hung up and pointed angrily at Abe.

"You better be sure about this, because, trust me, there will be an investigation. Josh will pay for this, but we will also look into how this was possible in the first place. You're the head of finance. You should have noticed something!"

Abe started to speak and then stopped. Charles had given Josh too much access and power, and now he was looking for someone to blame. Abe had warned Charles and the rest of the executives several times, but Charles always defended Josh's capabilities and integrity. Now Charles would probably deny he'd ever done that.

Five minutes later, Josh Winkler strode into Charles's office, a quizzical look on his face. He frowned a little when he saw Abe and turned to Charles.

"Is everything okay? I have a meeting with the NhyiraFM guys in thirty minutes, and it takes at least that much time to get to Accra."

"You're not going anywhere. Close the door and sit down," Charles snapped.

"What?" Josh alternated his gaze between Abe and Charles.

"I said close the door and sit!" Charles shouted.

Josh finally moved. He closed the door quietly and then sat down next to Abe, whose gaze was fixed on a brown envelope on Charles's desk. Josh craned his neck, trying to read the address, but he didn't have to. Charles picked the envelope up and dropped it right onto his lap. Josh swallowed and stared at it for a full minute. Then he pulled the papers out. He sifted through them quietly.

"Five million dollars, Josh! You stole $5 million from us! I pay you $13,000 a month plus generous benefits, and this is how you repay me? I gave you everything! Anything you want, I approve! Extra vacation days, access to company apartments, facilities, cars, everything! And then you steal from me?!"

Josh shifted uncomfortably and glanced behind him. Even with the door closed, voices carried through to the hallway. Charles's assistant was staring through the glass windows, and a couple of people were loitering in the hallway trying to figure out what the shouting was about.

Josh's mind was racing. Denial was his first instinct, but he knew that what was in the envelope was undeniable. A denial would buy him some time, but an investigation was inevitable. His second thought was anger—they shouldn't have opened his private mail—but he'd stolen their money, who was he to talk about invasion of privacy? His third option would be to admit it and offer to return the money, but that wouldn't solve anything either. He had no intention of returning the $7 million—the actual amount he'd siphoned. What he needed was time to figure out how to get out of this mess.

"I have no idea what you're talking about. Five million dollars? What $5 million? All that is in this envelope is legitimate, personal financial information. There's nothing in here that shows I have taken any money from Insel. Is this from Abe? Huh? Abe, is this from you? Well, you guys can go ahead and look into it, but I've never taken a penny from Insel. Nothing!" Josh said, with as much confidence as he could muster.

Charles was taken aback, but he didn't lose his composure. Abe started to speak, but Charles shook his head at him. He knew Josh well enough to know he was bluffing.

"You're fired, Josh. Don't bother to go back to your office. I want you to leave with exactly what you have on you now. I'll let you have the cell phone, but everything else in your office is ours. Abe, alert the senior leadership team, and get me Agyari, the police commissioner. Whatever happened, whatever's been stolen, you'll pay for it, Josh."

Josh stood up quickly and walked toward Charles.

"Charles, wait, listen. I'm telling you I haven't stolen anything. This is me, *me*, Josh. Why would I steal from you? You haven't told me anything concrete. You're just accusing me of theft out of the blue, and you won't even give me a chance? You're firing me based on what? On personal information that was addressed to me? Come on, you know me better than that," Josh pled, reaching out to his friend.

Charles stepped back. His anger was strong and real. With each word Josh spoke, he knew the bastard was lying. Even if this was a mistake, he'd rather fire him and then make apologies later than have Josh return to his office and hide any evidence or incriminating information.

"Get out, Josh. Now. Abe, make sure he doesn't head to his office. Call Security if you have to. And call the police commissioner immediately. No matter what, we'll get every penny back," Charles barked, his eyes focused on Josh.

Josh dropped his hands to his side. This was unbelievable. How did this happen? Why would Provident send him all this information? He didn't even ask them for it. This couldn't be happening.

"Charles, you have to listen," he begged again, genuine fear in his voice.

Charles gestured to the door. "Out, Josh, out now or I'll drag you out of here myself!"

Josh nodded and picked up the brown envelope.

"This is addressed to me, so this is mine. Make sure you find evidence, Charles, because I'm heading to my lawyers from here. And if you think I've taken money now, wait till I file my lawsuit," he said, attempting to sound threatening and failing miserably.

Clutching the envelope tightly, Josh walked out the door and made his way toward the elevators. His mind was all over the place. This shouldn't have happened. He'd never requested all of this information from Provident. They sent practically everything! Why would they mail years of information to his office?

He pulled his cell phone out of his pocket as he slid into his car. His first call was to his personal banker at Provident.

"James, it's Josh. What is going on? Why did you send me everything on my accounts? I never asked you for it, and I've never had anything sent to my office before!"

"But you emailed me a note on Friday and asked that I pull everything from 2007 and send it ASAP to your office. Wait, let me open the email. Yes, you emailed on Friday, 12:48 p.m., said it was urgent. It's from your Gmail address, the one you use for all our correspondence."

Josh's hand stilled on the keys in the ignition, and his blood turned cold. He'd never sent any emails to Provident in the last week. None. Someone had done this to him. Someone had actually hacked into this account and done this to him!

"James, I'll call you back."

He hung up and drove quickly out of the Insel parking lot toward his home. His phone rang all the way home, but he didn't answer. He couldn't think. His heart was pounding, and a million and one thoughts were flooding his mind. As soon as he got home, he grabbed his laptop from the living room coffee table and signed on quickly to his Provident customer account. The account balance hit him like a ton of bricks. His fingers were dialing even before his mind thought it. "Jesus, James! What else did you do? There is nothing left in my dollar checking account! Fifty thousand dollars transferred on Monday! And I can't even see to whom. What the heck is going on? What are you people doing?"

"Josh, we haven't authorized any transfers. The transfer was done online from your account. You signed up for the platinum package three years ago, and it includes unlimited online transfers. From what I can tell, you also transferred $10 million from your main dollar savings account on Monday to an offshore account. There's no more information on the recipient account."

Josh closed his eyes and cursed out loud.

"Check everything else, James. Check and call me back!"

"I already checked, Josh. The cedi accounts are empty too, well, one of them has ¢10,000 left in it, but everything else is gone."

"Jesus Christ!! Find out what happened, do you hear me? Find out now, or I'll sue Provident for everything! Every damn thing!"

Josh hung up and stared at the computer screen. This was a dream, a very bad dream. Who could have done this? Who could have gained access to his accounts and wiped him clean? This wasn't child's play. Whoever did this had everything. And to think, he'd sold the last two of his properties and deposited the money into Provident just a week before. Provident was his everything. He had four accounts with them. Two were Ghana cedi accounts, one for regular checking with close to ¢50,000, and the other was for legitimate savings and had around ¢250,000. Then he had two dollar accounts, one as a holding pen for all the investments and property sales—that one had the $10 million—and the other dollar account was for discriminate spending, mostly when he traveled, with around $50,000. The $10 million was supposed to be his nest egg, the fund to support his early retirement. All he had now was the home he stood in, the house he built for his parents in Cape Coast, his Range Rover, and ¢10,000. He couldn't even report that over $10 million had been stolen from him. He'd embezzled $7 million from Insel, $1 million from Ghana News Network during his time there, and another $2 million from deals with the GFP.

Josh sat in shock for an hour as he triple-checked all his accounts. He truly had nothing. It was all gone, disappeared into some cyber black hole. How was that even possible? This was a well thought out, carefully planned and orchestrated attack. How could anyone gain access to this much information? How could anyone manipulate events as closely and as tightly as this? And then it struck him. There was only one possible answer.

Bedu answered his phone immediately.

"Josh, I called you several times before. I just got a call from Agyari, and he said Charles is accusing you of theft, $5 million. What happened? What is going on?"

"Caleb Osei."

"Caleb? What are you talking about?"

"Caleb, Caleb, Caleb! He did this. There's no other explanation."

"You're not making any sense, Josh. What is going on?"

"I took money from Insel. Yes, I did. Everyone does it. We've all done it. Insel makes millions each year. It's a moneymaking beast with $20 million in profits. They own the damn media world. So I took a little. I made money off some investment deals, but honestly it was nothing until someone hacked into my accounts and transferred every single penny out, leaving a paper trail in my direction."

"What? How? You stole from Insel, and now you're saying someone somehow got your passwords and others details and transferred the money? To where? How is it possible?"

Josh stood up from his sofa and paced the living room.

"It's possible, if you're Caleb Osei. I know it's him. I threatened Abby Annan last week. She must have told her father. They did this, Bedu. You need to check your accounts too. They're wiping us out!"

"The Justice wants to win the election, yes, but why would he go to this extreme? What's there to gain? You threaten his daughter, big deal. He's seasoned enough to expect that. You're not even GFP. Fine, you're a sympathizer, but you're not in government and you're not an official. It makes no sense."

Josh took a deep breath. Yes, it sounded far-fetched, but he was certain it was Caleb. He could feel it.

"They did this. Caleb Osei did this! Listen Bedu, you guys have underestimated them long enough! You need to listen to me."

"This is Ghana politics, Josh. People don't hack into computers, get passwords, and transfer millions. It just doesn't happen like that. I mean, you have two girlfriends and a son with a married woman whose husband thinks the boy is his. There are other ways they could come after you. This, what you're suggesting, that's just something else. This is not the US," Bedu said, exasperated.

"You need to go to your bank and sort this out. The money is there somewhere. I'm sure it's all a mistake, but you need to figure it out. Agyari says Charles is fuming and getting all the top police folks involved," Bedu added.

Josh cringed and buried his face in his left hand. He still couldn't believe this was happening. And then he had a thought.

"Caleb is the answer to everything. How much will you guys pay me to make that problem go away?"

"What? Josh, you need to be careful, seriously."

Josh sat back down in his sofa. A new wave of resolve and determination washed over him. He was certain of the perpetrator, and that gave him some confidence.

"Without Caleb, the Justice will not even get the party nomination. Without Caleb, the Justice is done. So, I'm making you an offer. I'll get Caleb out of your way, and I'll get my money back. I just want to know how much you'll give me for my troubles."

Bedu was silent for a while, and then he spoke.

"Meet me at Jacintha's in thirty minutes. It'll be empty at this time. We'll talk there, and I'll ask Ohene to join, but I'm not making any promises."

"I'll see you."

Josh hung up and exhaled. There was hope after all. He gritted his teeth and clenched his fists. Caleb Osei was about to get a hard lesson in politics—the Ghana way. Online hacking wouldn't be able to save him.

11

Abby glanced at her watch and groaned. She was going to be late for the Ghana Investor Awards if the traffic didn't let up soon. The Investor Awards was an annual dinner event organized by the Ministry of Trade and Industry, with sponsorship support from Insel, her father's law firm, and other businesses. The event was actually an idea her father proposed to the DNP government twelve years ago when the party was in power and her father was chief justice. Her father believed firmly in encouraging commerce, trade, and investment. So, the DNP instituted the event to award local and foreign businesses that invested in the economy, created jobs and wealth, and contributed to the overall prosperity and growth of the communities in which they operated. It was a very successful event, so successful and popular that the GFP couldn't scrap it like they'd attempted to do with other DNP programs. All earnings from the expensive dinner ticket sales were also donated to universities to support scholarships and expansion of infrastructure. The Justice, and the DNP overall, were big advocates of quality education, although she thought it was ironic that her father had flown both her and Joey out to the US to continue their educations. Politicians.

Abby had been torn all week, not sure if she was ready to attend the dinner and possibly run into Reyn. She hadn't heard from him since his call Saturday night, or rather Sunday morning. The call had taken her by surprise, and she'd almost caved in and admitted she loved him too, but she stayed strong. She missed him more than she could handle at times, but she was also disappointed and annoyed. She suspected that his wife had arrived and was in the house with him when he called. He either wanted to have his cake and eat it, or the reunion hadn't gone so well. Either way, she wasn't going to let him back into her life that easily. He could have her. He just had to choose.

It'd just been a very weird and difficult week.

Caleb showing up at her apartment was another weird event. She really couldn't figure Caleb out. He was so closed off and cold, and yet she could detect that he had a heart and a soul somewhere underneath that stone exterior. There was also the possibility that she was reading too much into it. So he showed up to check on her, but maybe he had another motive. Maybe he wanted to make sure Reyn wasn't with her. She doubted that though. She saw something in his eyes that looked a lot like genuine concern. But then again, this was Caleb. What looked like concern could be something else entirely.

What really took the cake this week was the firing of Josh Winkler and subsequent investigation into his alleged embezzlement. When she heard about it, her conversation with Caleb snuck into her head. He said he'd take care of it. Was this what he meant? Did Caleb have anything to do with Josh's situation? The rumor was that Josh had stolen five million dollars from Insel, and somehow all of his bank documents ended up on Abe's desk. Others were also saying that more documents turned up after Josh was let go. It was all too neat, Abby thought. It had to be Caleb. The timing couldn't be a coincidence. She wasn't sure how she felt about it, though. Josh was an egotistical slimeball, and a thief apparently, but knowing how fast Caleb had done this scared her. Was he just sitting on incriminating information, waiting for the right moment to bring someone down? She remembered that her father had known about her relationship with Reyn for years, but he'd never brought it up until she confronted him a couple of weeks ago. What else did they know? Abby shook her head to clear her mind. She didn't even want to think about it.

Abby glanced at her watch again. She had less than an hour to get home, shower, dress up, and drive to the conference center for the event. There was no doubt that she was going to be late, and this was one event that required her to take her time and get dressed. Reyn would probably be there with his wife, and she didn't want to look shabby. She had to impress, and this traffic wasn't just reducing her dress-up time, it was also affecting her mood. She looked at her watch for the third time in ten minutes. Finally, she hit the horn and left her hand there.

∽

Reyn glanced through his speaking points as he half-listened to both the conversation at his table and the MC, who was telling lame jokes on the podium. He felt nervous. It was his first time accepting the Best Mining Company award on behalf of Proctor Oil. The company had won the award five years in a row, but Jeff Hunt had been the recipient and speaker each time. He was also nervous because he'd spotted Justice Annan. He'd met the Justice on different occasions, but today was different since he knew the Justice was aware of his relationship with Abby. Reyn and Jeff said hello to him earlier, but Reyn could barely look the Justice in the eyes. What could he say? "Sorry I slept with your daughter, but I hope you won't hold a grudge when you become president." It was already thirty minutes into the dinner event now, and he hadn't spotted Abby yet. A part of him hoped she wasn't going to show up. This night was already awkward enough, but another part of him desperately wanted to see her again. It'd been almost two weeks now, and he missed her. He was zoned out during most of the South Africa trip because he couldn't get Abby out of his head.

"Are you okay, dear?"

Reyn looked up at his wife. He smiled.

"Yes, I just want to get this over and done with."

She squeezed his hand, just as the MC started to talk about Proctor Oil and the great work they'd done for Ghana and their communities of operation.

"So everyone, please join me in welcoming Reyn Proctor, the new managing director for Proctor Oil Africa!"

Reyn stood up, pearly whites on display as he stepped back from the table, turned around, and raised his hand in acknowledgement of the applause. That's when he saw her.

He stood there, frozen as he drank her in. God, she looked beautiful, absolutely stunning. She was wearing an incredibly short, silky, and loose black shirtdress with gold sleeve cuffs and gold two-inch heels. Her long, thick black hair was styled straight, with a middle part that framed her oval face. Reyn could barely breathe. She looked incredible.

Wow, she was beautiful, Abby thought. Her eyes strayed from Reyn's penetrating gaze to the woman who was standing beside him. She was wearing an incredibly tight, figure-hugging mid-length white dress with red heels. She had the body of a goddess, Abby thought, suddenly feeling self-conscious of her thick thighs. The woman's hair was blonde, long, and wavy, and cascaded softly around a face that looked like God himself molded it. Abby exhaled. Wow, wow, wow! Who was she kidding, thinking she'd show up and make him swoon because she was showing major leg and wearing heels? He was married to a Charlize Theron lookalike! Abby watched as Reyn and his wife walked toward the stage. His wife kissed him on the cheek, and then he walked up the stairs of the stage to a standing ovation. Abby wasn't surprised. Proctor Oil had definitely done a lot in terms of education, health, small business investments, and technology. Proctor made billions, and unlike most of the leeches in town, they also gave back.

Standing in the back of the room, Abby watched as Reyn stepped up to the mike on the podium. Their eyes met, and her heart skipped a beat. She didn't want to smile, but she could tell he was nervous, so she nodded at him and smiled. He nodded back and began his speech. Abby's gaze went back to his wife. She was smiling and gazing lovingly at him. Abby looked away and started searching for a familiar face. She'd secretly hoped that Reyn's wife would look old, boring, and miserable, but she was absolutely nothing like that. She saw her father sitting with Caleb, and she walked toward them. She didn't really want to join her father, but she didn't want to sit with the Insel guys and listen to the exaggerated rumors about Josh, and she couldn't walk up to Reyn's table and sit with him, so that left her father.

"Abby, I guess you just couldn't make it on here on time, could you? And are you missing part of your dress?" her father asked disapprovingly as she pulled up a chair next to Caleb at the table.

Abby rolled her eyes at her father and ignored him. She focused on the other guests at the table. She knew Caleb and Albert, the former a senior lawyer at her father's law firm and the latter a member of the campaign team, but the other three guests, two men and a woman, were strangers to her, and she didn't want to exchange words with her father in front of them. Caleb placed his arm on the backrest of her chair and leaned close.

"You look beautiful," he whispered.

Abby's heart fluttered, and she smiled at him. Caleb was strange, she thought, as he held her gaze. She just couldn't figure him out, and that was unnerving. His eyes looked softer tonight, and she wondered if it was because of the white dress shirt he wore, or perhaps maybe it was just the lighting. Either way, he looked relaxed, open, and human, and he was still looking at her.

"Aren't you going to listen, Abby?" her father interrupted her thoughts.

Abby turned away from Caleb and glared at her father. She knew he was just baiting her and being an asshole. She wasn't going to get into it with her father tonight. She stared at her clutched hands, trying hard not to listen to Reyn's speech, which sounded like it was finally coming to an end. It was hard enough being in the same space as his wife, but if she looked at Reyn, if she listened to him, she would be a mess. Everyone started to clap, so she naturally turned to look. Reyn was waving and walking off the stage. His wife, beaming broadly, walked over to the podium to meet him, just as she'd walked him there for his acceptance speech. Abby shook her head. This woman was impossibly perfect. Feeling rejected and self-conscious all over again, Abby stood up abruptly from her father's table and walked away.

She started walking quickly toward the back of the conference hall, where the bathrooms, storage, and offices were lined up. She slipped through a side door and entered the main auditorium. The dinner was set up in the lobby, so the auditorium was empty. She sat down in a chair, crossed her legs, and sat back, trying hard to still her rapidly beating heart.

"Hey beautiful."

Abby jumped up quickly and exhaled with relief and surprise when she saw who it was.

"How did you know I was in here?" she asked, folding her arms across her chest, trying to appear irritated.

"I saw you walk away, so I excused myself from my table and followed you," Reyn said, stepping close up to her.

Abby tried to step back, but the seat behind her prevented her from going any further. She tried not to pay attention to how blue his eyes looked in the dark, how his jet-black hair was nicely tousled, and how inviting his lips looked.

As if he was reading her mind, he cupped her face and kissed her. Abby didn't resist at first. His lips felt like heaven on hers, and she eagerly kissed him back. She'd missed this so much. As the kiss deepened, she tried to step back, but Reyn was holding onto her tight, and her back was pressed against the chair. It was only when his hands snaked underneath her dress that she pulled away.

"Reyn, I can't do this. I just can't. You can't just come in here and think I'll fall back willingly into your arms. God, you have a wife who looks like a supermodel out there. You picked Ms. Perfect over me, and I get it. I look nothing like her, skin color aside and all. I get it, okay? So let's not do this."

Reyn sighed and tucked his hands into his pockets.

"You just don't know how beautiful you are, do you?"

"Don't patronize me, Reyn, just don't. I can't believe you right now. She looks like a frigging goddess!"

"Geez, Abby, cut it out. You're so beautiful. It's crazy. My heart tightens each time I look at you. You take my breath away, and that's the truth."

"Then why didn't you pick me?" Abby whispered, struggling to maintain control of her emotions.

Reyn reached for her again and pulled her close. She placed her head on his shoulder and wrapped her arms around him, soaking in his smell and warmth.

"I'm sorry. I really am, but I need to give my marriage a try, for my kids' sake."

His words jolted her, and she pushed him away, anger replacing pain and hurt.

"So what do you want with me, huh? What? Why did you follow me in here? If you've made up your mind, then just leave me alone!" she snapped, pushing him away again for good measure.

"Babe..." he started.

"Don't! Don't call me that. You have no right to call me that! I'm done. Seriously, this is it. I'm done. I swear, I can't do this anymore. Don't call me at dawn when you're home with your wife. Don't approach me in dark places when your wife is around the corner. Just leave me alone!" Abby yelled, not caring who heard or walked in.

Abby ignored Reyn's stunned face and walked past him and back out into the lobby. It seemed like they'd gotten to the musical interlude part of the dinner. The space felt crowded and overwhelming. She hurried out through the front doors and down to the parking lot. The bravado she'd exhibited with Reyn had ebbed away, and the anguish, abandonment, and pain were back. She needed a quiet place to bawl her eyes out, and her car was the only place she could think of.

She barely made it to her car when the tears started flowing. She leaned against the door and cried.

"Abby."

Abby kept her head down. She knew who it was, and she didn't want him to see her like this.

"Abby," he said again, softly.

Abby turned and looked at Caleb. It wasn't the lighting, she realized. He looked genuinely concerned. He handed her a hanky and she took it, wiping her tears and mascara at the same time. She blew her nose and tried to look decent.

"Keys?" he asked, his hand stretched out to her.

She dug into her clutch, pulled it out, and handed it to him wordlessly. He led her to the passenger side, opened it, and helped her in. Then he got into the driver's side.

"What about your car?" she asked.

He shrugged. "I'll come back for it after I drop you home."

"I don't want to go home," she said, staring out the window as the tears threatened to fall again.

"Okay," Caleb said simply.

He started the car and drove off.

Fifteen minutes later, they pulled up to his house. Neither one of them had said a word on the way.

"Do you want some coffee, tea, or something stronger?" he asked as they stood awkwardly in his living room.

"Water would be great," Abby said, staring around at her surroundings.

So this was the home of the mysterious Caleb, she thought. It was unusually homey and cozy, with a lush cream-colored, L-shaped sectional, and a light gray, thick, soft carpet. Abby stepped out of her heels and rubbed her feet on the carpet. It felt soft and warm. The walls were adorned with African paintings depicting different facets of life, and there were pictures of a couple she assumed were his parents. He never spoke about them, she thought as she stood in front of a small picture of the three of them.

"Here you go," he said from behind her.

She turned around and took the bottle of water he had in his hand, then she set it down on the coffee table closest to where she was standing. They stood there silently.

"I know it hurts a lot now, but you'll be fine, trust me," he said, breaking the silence.

She nodded, but remained silent.

Caleb felt slightly guilty, hence his concern for her over the past two weeks. He'd spoken to Jeff Hunt and gotten confirmation that Reyn's wife would be moving to Ghana to be with him. Jeff said he emphasized with Emma and her father that she needed to be with her husband or risk losing him for good. Caleb didn't ask for further details.

He was sure that that wasn't all Jeff said to Emma, but he didn't need to know more. The relationship between Reyn and Abby was over. That was all that mattered, although he didn't expect it would hurt Abby this much. Why did married men have such appeal?

"It's his loss, Abby, his loss," Caleb added.

Something shifted within her when he said that. It wasn't just the words. It was the way he said it, so softly, yet so firmly. And the way he looked at her. She reached out and touched his face.

Caleb felt himself unravel when she touched him. His years of self-control and professionalism came undone. He placed his hand over hers and closed his eyes, soaking in the warmth of her touch on his face. There was no way he could hold himself back and fight what was about to happen.

Standing on tiptoe, Abby slipped her hands around his neck and brought his lips down to hers. A jolt went through her body as she kissed him. She stood back, shaken and alarmed, her heart beating rapidly. What was happening?

Caleb inhaled sharply. Her lips on his, it was electrifying. They stared at each other for what felt like a lifetime, and then they moved at the same time. Caleb kissed her hard, and she kissed him back with equal ferociousness. He wrapped his arms around her waist and pulled her close and tight as they kissed as if their lives depended on it. He slipped his hands into her hair and pulled her head up, trying to gain greater access to her lips and body as his hands roamed her curves. Eventually, with his lips still on hers, he grabbed her legs, picked her up, and walked into his bedroom. He deposited her gently onto the bed and continued kissing her. He could kiss her forever. She tasted so sweet, and her body felt so soft beneath his touch. His mind, heart, and whole body were on fire.

Somehow, he managed to disentangle himself from her embrace and peel off his shirt. He leaned over and stared down at her. Her hair was tousled, her lips were swollen, and her eyes were wide and inviting.

"Abby, are you sure?" he whispered against her cheek.

Less than an hour ago, she was crying over another man, and now she was here in his arms, and in his bed. If this was any other girl, he wouldn't even ask, but this was Abby, his boss's daughter, and the girl who'd slowly crept into his mind over the last two weeks.

Abby placed her palms flat against his chest. He was so cut and muscled, with just a little patch of hair down the middle of his chest. She slipped her right fingers through the hairs and placed her palm flat over the area where she assumed his heart was. She could feel his heart beating hard against his chest. She moved her fingers further to the right and gently rubbed her thumb over his nipple.

Caleb groaned and pulled her face right up to his. His breathing was ragged, and he looked like he was in pain.

"I need to hear you say it. I need you to say you want this," he said hoarsely.

"I need you," Abby murmured.

That was all the invitation Caleb needed. He slipped his hands underneath her dress and pulled her panties off. Then he lifted the hem of her dress slowly upward, drinking in her naked body as he got the shirt up and over her head. Her bra followed right after, and then she was completely naked in front of him. God, she was beautiful. He kissed her neck, and then moved down to her collarbone. Then he moved down to her ample but firm breasts. His tongue lapped gently at her nipple, and then he sucked it hard, caressing the other nipple simultaneously with his hand. Abby moaned and reached for his belt buckle, but he grabbed her hand and pinned it beneath her body. Without taking his lips off her breasts, he placed his right knee in between her legs, parted them open, and then slipped his fingers deep inside her. Abby closed her eyes and groaned. She instinctively gripped his arm with her free hand, and her inner thighs tightened on his fingers. Abby writhed beneath him, but Caleb kept her pinned as his lips worked on her breasts and his fingers drove her to the edge. Within minutes, she was screaming and exploding, and her body convulsed uncontrollably underneath him.

When she was still again, Caleb stepped off the bed and switched the light on. Then, he pulled the rest of his clothes off slowly. Abby was stunned at how perfect he looked naked. He looked like he didn't have an ounce of fat on him. His upper torso was lean and cut, and his six-pack dovetailed into a chiseled waist. And if she thought Reyn was sizable, then Caleb was something else. His erect manhood was thick, long, and glorious. Abby felt herself getting wet and excited again, hoping she wouldn't have to wait long.

Caleb pulled a pack of condoms from his side table and ripped one open.

"Wait," Abby whispered.

She sat up on the bed and placed her feet on the floor. Then she pulled him toward her, his manhood inches from her face. She glanced up at his face, and, without taking her eyes off his, she circled his shaft with her hands and took him in her mouth. Caleb grabbed her shoulders and groaned. He gripped her hard as her lips worked on him, and he watched in awe as she took him in.

He was stunned—stunned that she could even take all of him in her mouth and stunned by her effect on him. A jolt went through his legs, and he knew he wouldn't last if she kept going. He tore himself away and pushed her back on the bed. He climbed on top of her, and faster than he thought possible, he slipped on the condom and slid into her wetness.

Abby's inner lips tightened hard on him, and for a moment he thought she was resisting, but she opened up again and he slipped in deeper, and then she tightened. Caleb groaned and wrapped his arms around her waist. She was killing him, and he was trying so hard not to lose it.

"Are you okay?" he asked, once he was all the way inside her. The last thing he wanted was to hurt her.

Abby nodded, and to prove it she wrapped her legs around his thighs and sucked him in deeper.

Caleb almost came undone then, but he grabbed her ass, lifted her slightly off the bed, and started thrusting hard. His lips were on hers. His hands were on her ass, thighs, and all over her body as he dug in deeper and deeper.

Abby didn't consider herself a screamer, but Caleb was tearing her apart in a crazy and delicious way, and she couldn't get enough of him.

"Don't stop. Please don't stop," she screamed as her hands roamed his back and her nails dug into his flesh.

Caleb heeded her wishes, and he increased his pace. There was a lot of moaning and screaming, and he wasn't sure if it was just her. He doubted it though. She was driving him insane, and he could barely control himself.

"I love you. God, I love you," Abby whispered into his ear as she came a second time.

Her words unraveled him. He kissed her hard and gripped her tight as he exploded inside her. When her shaking subsided and he had emptied all he had, he withdraw from her and lay on his back staring at the ceiling, trying to catch his breath and calm his thoughts.

"I shouldn't have said what I said. I don't know where that came from," Abby said softly.

Caleb turned on his side and pulled her close to him, her back against his chest. He kissed the nape of her neck, and a shiver went down her spine.

"It's okay," he said against her ear.

Caleb wanted to tell her he loved her too, but he knew she'd said what she said because she was having an orgasm. Sex did that to people. She couldn't be in love with him, and as much as this was incredible, mind-blowing sex, he wasn't in love either, but he was definitely in lust.

Caleb slipped his hands over her belly, down below her waist, and right inside her. Abby moaned and rubbed her ass provocatively against him. He slipped his hands out of her briefly and reached for a new condom. Without wasting any time, he got the condom on, pressed her face down on the bed, and took her from behind. Abby lifted herself onto her hands and knees and arched her back. Caleb moaned as she backed her ass against him. He closed his eyes and gripped her waist. It was going to be a long night.

12

Caleb woke up with a start. He looked around the room, blinking rapidly as his sight adjusted to the darkness. Abby was lying half on top of him, her right arm draped across his waist. He lay still for a moment, trying to figure out what had woken him up. And then he heard it—the unmistakable sound of footsteps in the house.

Caleb gently shifted Abby off his body and got up from the bed. He slipped his hand underneath the mattress and pulled out the .45 Magnum and silencer he kept there. He pulled on his pants and walked quietly toward the door. He placed his ear against it and listened. It was tough to hear much because of the thickness of his bedroom door and the length of the hallway, which separated the master bedroom from the living room. All the same, he could discern that there were at least three people in the house. They were congregated in the living room, walking and whispering.

He knew it was only a matter of seconds before they reached the bedroom door. He glanced back at Abby. She was still fast asleep. He turned the safety off on the gun, cocked it, and then opened his door quietly. Holding the gun firmly in his right hand, Caleb tiptoed down the dark hallway toward the living room, which was also bathed in darkness. He leaned against the edge of the wall and listened.

"Walla, check the kitchen and the back. Amidu, you wait here. I'm going to check the bedroom," a deep, surly voice said.

Caleb took a few steps back down the hallway and waited. A few seconds later, a short stocky man stepped into his view. Even in the darkness, he could see the outline of an AK-47. These guys weren't here for a friendly visit at 3 a.m. Without wasting a moment, Caleb pulled the trigger and fired off two shots. The man went down and hit the floor hard.

"Jesus! Walla, come back! He's in the hallway!"

Caleb hurried down the hallway and swung to his left. The second man was standing in the middle of the living room, gripping his AK-47. He raised the gun to fire, but Caleb's gun was already up and ready. He squeezed his trigger twice, and without even waiting to see if he hit his target, he swung sharply to his right, toward the kitchen. As the second man fell behind him, the third walked out of the kitchen, gun aimed high with bullets flying. Caleb swore and dove back into the hallway. He ran down fast toward the bedroom as he thought of Abby in his room, unprotected. Bullets whizzed past him as he stepped into the bedroom and slammed the door shut. Abby was sitting up on the bed, her eyes wide, a scream on her lips, but before she could let it out, Caleb grabbed her off the bed and practically threw her into the bathroom.

"Lock the door and stay inside!"

Without waiting for a response, he closed the bathroom door and walked up close to the bedroom door, his gun up and ready. The door was purposely thick, so the rain of bullets barely made it through. Eventually the man would have to come in, and if he did there was no way Caleb would miss from his position. A few seconds later, the gunfire stopped and the house was silent. Caleb closed his eyes and listened intently. The man was somewhere in the hallway, Caleb could hear him breathing heavily. Caleb calculated quickly. The man had been firing in bursts of three for close to a minute. He was definitely out of ammo. Caleb pulled the door open quickly and, without pausing to aim, pulled his trigger successively, getting off more than four bullets before he realized the man was on the floor. He stepped over him and the first man and walked back into the living room. The second body was still lying there. He scanned the room quickly and then walked into the kitchen. He went back into the living room and opened the front door, gun stretched out and ready to fire. He swung to his left and right quickly. There was no one there, but there was a black Nissan parked right behind Abby's car. He walked toward it slowly, but there was no one in it. Caleb looked around the street, but it was dead, nothing in sight. He walked back into the house and to the bodies lying in there. He crouched over the first man he shot and searched his pockets. He had a wallet on him with money, ATM cards, and his voter's ID. His name was Abdul Mukhtari. Caleb didn't recognize the name, but that wasn't surprising. They were obviously hired guns. He checked the other two—same thing: wallets with IDs and names he didn't recognize, but he intended to find out who they were and who hired them.

Caleb walked into his bedroom and opened the bathroom door. Abby was curled up next to the tub. She was shaking badly, even with the big, thick towel she'd wrapped around her body. She looked up at him, and her eyes bulged at the sight of the gun in his hands. Caleb flicked the safety on and set it in the sink. He knelt in front of her and pulled her into his arms. She pulled back and looked at him.

"What happened? Who were those men? God, Caleb, what is going on? I'm so scared."

He pulled her onto her feet and held her close.

"It's okay. Everything is okay now."

"Everything is okay? Someone was just shooting at you! Talk to me, what is going?"

"I need you to get dressed and go home, Abby," Caleb said leading her into the bedroom.

Abby looked at him incredulously. "What?"

"Abby, I need to call the police, and I need to call your father. I don't want them to find you here."

"I'm not leaving. I can't go home by myself. I'm terrified. I can't leave."

Caleb sighed and held her.

"Okay, it's okay. You don't have to leave, but you need to get dressed, and I need to make some calls, okay?"

Abby nodded meekly. Caleb tilted her head and kissed her long and softly.

"It's okay. Trust me, it's okay," he lied. It wasn't okay at all. Shit was about to hit the fan.

The Justice was the first to arrive. He showed up with his driver. Eben lived in the boys' quarters of the house, so he was on call 24/7. Caleb was sitting in the living room with Abby, who was still shaking in his arms. The bodies were lying where he'd shot them.

"Jesus Christ! What in God's name happened in here?"

Caleb scrambled up at the sound of Annan's voice. Abby got up slowly.

"Jesus Christ!" the Justice swore again when he saw her. He glared at Caleb.

"What is this? What is she doing here? Was she here when this happened?" he bellowed, gesturing at the dead bodies.

"Daddy..." Abby started to say.

"Don't say a word, Abiel Annan! I am speaking to Caleb!" the Justice snapped.

He fixed his glare back on Caleb.

"I asked you a question. What the heck is this? What is she doing here?"

Caleb gestured at Abby to sit back down, and he stepped up toward the Justice.

"I know what this looks like, and I will explain, but not right now. She needs to go home. Agyari will be here any minute, and we know it's best if she's not here. Can Eben take her home?"

The Justice glared at them both, and then he turned to Eben.

"Eben, drive Abby home. Use her car and then take a taxi home. I'll drive myself back."

Abby stood up and looked questioningly at Caleb. He smiled and nodded at her.

"Go with Eben. I'll call you later."

He knew it would be disrespectful to touch her intimately in front of her father, but she was still quivering like a leaf. The ordeal had shaken her up badly. So, against his better judgment, he pulled her in for a hug and kissed her forehead.

"Jesus Christ! Don't you have any respect?" the Justice snapped.

Caleb stepped aside and watched as Abby walked past her father and out of the house with the driver. The Justice turned around and followed her. He grabbed her on the porch and shook her.

"What are you doing here? What the heck are you doing here?"

"Stop it, Daddy, stop it! Yes, I was here. I was upset at the dinner, and I didn't want to go home. Caleb brought me here. That is all you need to know."

The Justice tightened his grip.

"Stay away from him. Do you understand me? Whatever this is, end it! Caleb is not the type of person you should be around. He's very dangerous. Are you listening to me, Abby? I'm very serious. Look at what happened in there. You could have been killed. You could have been killed because you were with him!"

He let her go abruptly, and she stumbled backward. She'd never seen him this angry, so she shut up and started walking away.

He followed her and swung her around again.

"I'm dead serious. This is over. I don't want you near him ever again!" he hissed.

Abby looked past her father and saw Caleb on the porch. He stepped down toward them. The Justice let her go, and she hurried away into her car. Eben was already in the driver's seat. Caleb waited until they'd driven off, and then he turned to the Justice.

"It won't happen again."

"It better not!" the Justice snapped. He strode past Caleb and walked into the house.

Caleb stood there and stared out into the darkness. He dug his hands into his pockets and looked up and down the road. He was going to find whoever did this and make them pay. They could count on it.

13

'*I*ve been waiting for two hours! Where have you guys been?"

Josh jumped up from his sofa and screamed at Bedu and Ohene as they walked into his house.

"Where have you been?" he yelled again.

"Are you serious, Josh? You think you can just say jump, and we'll say how high? You're under investigation. And thanks to your stupidity, Caleb Osei survived that lame attempt you pulled last night. We had to make sure it was safe to show up here," Ohene screamed back.

Bedu was calmer, but the anxiety in his voice couldn't be masked.

"What happened? You said you had this under control, and I told you that you shouldn't underestimate Caleb Osei. I told you. Now look at this mess."

"We're in this together," Josh muttered. "And I need the $1 million you promised."

Ohene snickered. "Are you insane? You failed! What do you want to be paid for?"

Josh took out a recorder from his pocket and hit play.

Ohene's voice could be heard distinctly on the recorder: "We'll pay you $1 million on two conditions. One, you better make sure you get rid of Caleb Osei, and two, you need to leave town and stay out."

Bedu's voice chimed in: "That's the best we can do. One millions dollars and this is done, but you need to be sure you can do this."

Josh's voice was the third: "Trust me, he's only a man. Caleb Osei will be dead by the end of this weekend."

Josh turned the recorder off and stared at Ohene and Bedu's stunned faces. Ohene was the first to speak.

"You idiot! Stupid fool! What do you think you can do with that? Your voice is on there! If you release that, you go down as well!"

Josh shrugged.

"I have nothing to lose, but you two do. So, I want the money now."

He picked up his laptop from the center table and flipped it open.

"Sign into your accounts now and do the transfer. I know you have the money, so let's skip the useless objections. If you don't do the transfer, I'll get on a flight tonight and have this released by Monday morning. I'm very serious. Pay me now, and I'll leave."

Ohene turned to Bedu.

"Talk some sense into him. He's the one who's your friend!"

Josh shook his head at Bedu.

"Are we really going to discuss this? It's $1 million. You have more than $20 million between the two of you. Didn't you make about $3 million each from the Sankara deal? Huh? You're lucky I'm not asking for more. Just transfer the money and let's be done. My bags are packed. Once I have the money, I'll be gone, tonight."

Bedu turned to Ohene.

"Let's just do it. I'll transfer $500,000, and then you can do the rest. I want this over with."

Josh handed Bedu a piece of paper with his account information.

"Send it here. It's a new account I set up a few days ago after I got hacked. This should be safe. The computer is new and I've changed my Internet provider and password details."

Bedu took the laptop and paper from Josh and opened up the browser to his offshore account. He completed the transfer within minutes and then handed the laptop to Ohene. Ohene grumbled inaudibly as he logged onto his account to complete his portion. When he was done, he handed the laptop back to Josh.

"What about the tape?" he asked.

Josh took the laptop and checked his balance. A smile crept onto his face. He closed the laptop and looked at Bedu and Ohene.

"The tape is collateral. I won't give it to you, but I won't ask for more money either. Think of it as a gentleman's agreement. And honestly, I still think Caleb Osei is just a man. He can be killed. The idiots I hired botched it last night, but I recommend that you try again. Caleb is the key. You get him out of the way, and it's over for the Justice."

Ohene stepped up close to Josh.

"You better be out of here by Sunday night. Do you understand?"

Then he turned and walked out. Bedu shook his head at Josh and then followed Ohene.

Josh stuffed the laptop into the carrier and hurried off to his bedroom. He wasn't lying about one thing, at least. Two suitcases were packed and sitting by the door. He picked them up and dragged them to the living room.

"Jesus Christ!" he screamed, dropping the bags onto his feet.

"Hello Josh," Caleb said.

Josh stared at the gun pointed right at him.

"What is this? Are you crazy?"

Caleb chuckled. "Am I crazy? You sent three men into my home to kill me, and you're asking if *I'm* crazy? You need to look into the mirror more often, Josh."

"What? That wasn't me. I swear it. That wasn't me. Please," Josh begged.

Caleb dug his left hand into this pocket and pulled out his phone. He hit play.

Josh: "And honestly, I still think Caleb Osei is just a man. He can be killed. The idiots I hired botched it last night but I recommend that you try again. Caleb is the key. You get him out of the way, and it's over for the Justice."

"You see, you're not the only one with a recording device."

Josh closed his eyes and cursed.

"What do you want? You have all my money already. I know you do. All I have is $1 million. Is that what you want? The $1 million? You can have it."

"You tried to kill me," Caleb said, stepping closer with the gun still pointed directly at Josh's head.

"Jesus Christ, please, listen to me! That was a mistake. I swear that was a mistake."

"Yes, it was," Caleb muttered under his breath.

He pulled the trigger once, and Josh crumbled to the floor immediately, a gaping bullet hole between his wide-open eyes. Caleb bent over the body and pulled out the recorder from Josh's pocket. He rewound the tape, hit play, recorded the conversation with his phone, and then tucked the device back into Josh's pocket. Once he was done, he walked over to the living room and dug Josh's laptop out of the carrier. He hooked up his phone to the computer and uploaded the audio file. Then he signed into Josh's email and typed an email to multiple recipients: the DNP headquarters email address, Insel's main contact email, and other smaller media houses: "I am fearful for my life, so I am leaving the country. The GFP is corrupt, and they are willing to murder people to get their way. I hope this will help bring them to justice."

Caleb hit the send button, and then he shut down the computer. He stood still in the room for a moment. He was waiting for the guilt or remorse to kick in, but nothing happened. He'd killed four people in twenty-four hours, and yet he felt absolutely nothing. He was angry, but calm.

Caleb walked back to Josh's body and stared at it.

"Stupid bastard," he muttered.

Josh was a stupid fool who bit off more than he could chew. The idiot tried to kill him, on the one night Caleb had Abby in his home. Yes, Josh had definitely made a mistake, and some mistakes were just very costly.

Abby hit "end call" on her phone and sighed. She'd called Caleb five times already, but he wasn't answering. It was almost 6 p.m. on Saturday, and she was worried. He hadn't called to check up on her since she left his house with Eben. She'd spent most of the day in bed, confused, scared, and in shock. Her father hadn't even called her. No one had bothered to check up on her to see if she was okay. That was just plain disappointing and rude. The only calls she received were from Denise, Charles, and a couple of other people who didn't know she was there, though they'd heard about the attempted robbery attack on the news and wanted more information. That was what the police and the media were calling it—an attempted robbery attack on Caleb Osei, chief of staff and campaign director for Justice Joseph Annan. The story was on every single news channel, and even though the Justice's campaign office released a brief statement, speculations and exaggerations were still rife. According to the statement, "Caleb Osei had been attacked by three armed men, but he'd overpowered them in self-defense and wasn't injured during the attack. The police were investigating the incident, and the Justice trusted them to find out the truth." Despite the press statement, the stories on the news were all over the place. Some said Caleb was badly shot and wounded, others said five men had attacked Caleb, and others attributed "Rambo-like" characteristics to the incident, calling it an all-out gunfight between Caleb and over ten men.

Then there were those who focused on the two key questions on Abby's mind: One, was it really just a robbery, or was it a politically motivated attack? And two, how did Caleb kill three heavily armed men without sustaining a single injury? Abby couldn't stop thinking about that. There was something eerily efficient and focused about how Caleb dealt with the situation. She'd seen the dead bodies, and they were shot either right between the eyes or in the chest. Caleb couldn't have done that randomly. When Caleb first joined her father in Ghana, she briefly remembered her father mentioning that Caleb used to be in the military, a former US marine, but that wasn't something anyone talked about. If he was military, it would explain a lot—his cold, steely, calculating demeanor, and the efficient, methodical approach he embodied. It would also explain her father's words: "Caleb is not the type of person you should be around. He's very dangerous."

There was no doubt that there was more to Caleb Osei, but there was also no doubt that something emotionally and physically significant happened to her when she was with him Friday night. Being with him that night, making love with him, was incredible. She'd never felt anything like that before, and as much as she loved Reyn, as much as she enjoyed what they had, Caleb rocked her senses in a way she'd never experienced before. She didn't think it was possible to fall for someone like that, so dramatically, after only one night, but she had. Abby couldn't describe what she felt, but her heart and tummy were in knots just thinking about him, which is why his silence today was so painful. She picked up her phone and dialed his number again, and again, but no answer. After five minutes, she turned her phone off and lay exasperated on her bed. Men!

An hour later, Abby's doorbell rang multiple times in a succession, and she rushed to it eagerly.

"Where the heck have you been?"

Caleb stepped past her and walked into the living room. He looked tired, like he hadn't slept all day. He probably hadn't.

"Caleb, where have you been? I've been calling you all day," she asked again.

Caleb walked over to her sofa and sat down. He placed his feet on her center table and leaned back with his eyes closed. Then he finally looked at her. He looked tired, but there was something else going on in his eyes.

"I saw your calls, but I couldn't talk. I had some things to sort out."

"Some things to sort out, I see, that's great. Then I'm really glad you managed to find time today to check up on me. That was very thoughtful of you," she snapped sarcastically.

Caleb stretched his hand to her and gestured for her to come over to him. Despite the anger she felt, she really couldn't stay away from him. She sat in the sofa next to him and placed her head on his shoulder. Caleb wrapped his arms around her and drew her in closer. He kissed her forehead and lips lightly.

"I'm sorry. I should have called you. No excuses," he murmured, rubbing her back and her arms.

Abby wrapped her arms tighter around him. She loved the feel of his body. Since he was bigger and taller, it made her feel small and protected.

"What happened, Caleb? Who were they? What did they want?"

"I didn't get to ask them what they wanted. It's a bit difficult to have a conversation with bullets flying over your head," he murmured, as his lips trailed kisses from her cheek to her neck.

Abby pulled back and glared at him.

"You're very sarcastic."

"I know," he replied, a little gleam in his eyes.

He reached for her again, but she shook her head, sliding away from him a little.

"I want to talk. Tell me what happened."

Caleb sighed and closed his eyes. Women! This was why he wasn't into girlfriends. He opened his eyes and looked at her. She was serious.

"You were there, Abby. What more is there to say? Three men I've never seen before in my life came into my house and attempted to kill me. I shot and killed them, and now the police are looking into it."

She ignored the irritation in his voice.

"You have absolutely no idea who they are?" she probed.

"No."

"Were you in the military?" she asked, trying a different angle.

Caleb leaned forward and slipped his right hand under his shirt and into the back of his pants. He pulled out his .45 Magnum.

"Oh my God! Caleb! What is that doing here?" Abby jumped up from the sofa and stood away from him.

Caleb double-checked that the safety was on, and then he pulled the cartridge out and laid it on the table.

"It's a .45 Winchester Magnum, my preferred gun of choice. It can fire up to twelve shots a minute. The trigger is easy to pull, and it hardly jams. Very handy and serves its purpose, always."

Abby was stunned and speechless.

"So yes, I was in the military, US marines. I joined when I was seventeen and served for five years. It was my life for a while, but it isn't anymore. That doesn't mean I don't know how to defend myself. I can, and I will do whatever I need to do to protect myself and the people that I care about."

Abby was still standing there quietly.

Caleb slipped the cartridge back into the gun and tucked it behind his shirt. He stood up and walked over to Abby.

"I know you have questions. I get that, but all I want is to hold you and be with you. I'm sorry I didn't call you earlier. I'm sorry I left you here scared and worried. I'm really sorry, but I'm here now, so just let me be with you," he said softly.

Abby nodded and reached for his hand. Caleb pulled her into his arms and held on tight. Everything had changed in the last twenty-four hours. He'd killed for the first time in twenty years, and he was falling for the last person on earth he thought he would ever have feelings for. He couldn't fight it even if he tried. Somehow, Abiel Annan had snuck into his head and heart, and she was creating some chaos in there. What he felt for her wasn't something he could plan out and control. He just had to go with the flow.

"I'll never, ever hurt you, Abby. And I'll never let anyone hurt you," he whispered.

Abby wrapped her arms around his neck and kissed him deeply. She felt him stiffen, and her heart raced.

"I love you," she said, with more conviction than she had the previous night.

Caleb felt his pulse quicken. He wanted to tell her he loved her too, but saying it would sink him for good. It would be too much for twenty-four hours. He lifted her off her feet and started walking toward the bedroom. If he couldn't say it, the least he could do was show her how he felt. That much he could do.

14

*A*bby lay on her back and stared up at the ceiling. If someone ever said to her a month ago that she'd ever be in this situation with Caleb Osei, she'd say they were crazy. Two weeks ago, she was in this bed with Reyn having a lazy Sunday morning, and now it was Caleb who was lying next to her. It was probably 10 a.m., and they hadn't left the bed much since the night before. She couldn't get enough of him, and he was equally insatiable. In between sex, she tried to ask him more questions, but he deftly turned the conversation back to her each time. He was so closed off that it seemed impossible to penetrate the walls he had up around him. She wanted to know so much more, but Caleb wasn't the sharing kind. He was so different from Reyn, she thought. She and Reyn talked like girlfriends all the time. She knew everything there was to know. Reyn spoke about his parents, his kids, his work, his ambitions, his frustrations, his love for her. Everything on Reyn's mind he let it out. With Caleb on the other hand, talking definitely wasn't his strong suit. She turned slightly on her side and looked at him. He was lying on his back and his eyes were closed, but she was sure he wasn't completely asleep. She glanced at the gun lying on the bedside table and then looked away. At first, she'd objected to him bringing it into the bedroom, but he insisted, and after Friday night she knew it was probably wise. Abby inched closer to him and draped her body onto his. How was this even possible? How could she love someone so quickly?

The doorbell rang, and Caleb's eyes flew open. The gun was in his hands, and his pants were on before she could even react.

"Wait! What the heck are you doing?" she yelled after him as he walked out of the bedroom.

Abby quickly pulled on a t-shirt and hurried after him. Caleb was already at the front door, peering through the cubbyhole. He looked back at her, a frown on his face.

"What?" Abby mouthed, concerned by the look on his face.

"I thought this was over?" he asked, opening the door at the same time.

Reyn Proctor stepped through the doorway, and Abby's mouth fell open. Perfect. Absolutely perfect.

Reyn looked at Abby, and his heart sunk. She had bed-hair and was half-dressed in a skimpy t-shirt. He could tell she had nothing else on, since he could see the shape of her uninhibited breasts. He glanced at Caleb, and his heart sunk further. He was shirtless, and with his pants hanging so low, Reyn could tell he was briefless as well.

"I guess I should have called," he said, a little under his breath, but still loud enough.

"Yes, you should have," Abby muttered, attempting to tug down her t-shirt, but knowing that it was hopeless.

Caleb tucked the gun back into his pants, but not before Reyn caught a glimpse.

"Jesus! Is that a gun?"

Caleb ignored him and walked past Abby and into the bedroom.

"Reyn, you should have called. What are you doing here?" Abby asked, stepping closer to him.

"Abby, how long has this been going on? I thought you hated him. What is this? Seriously, I don't understand. You've never said anything nice about him," Reyn asked, raising his voice a little.

Abby glanced nervously at the bedroom door, which was slightly open. The last thing she wanted was for Caleb to hear any of what Reyn was saying. She turned back to Reyn.

"You need to leave," she said firmly.

"No, he doesn't."

Abby swung around. Caleb was standing behind her, fully dressed. She took a step toward him, but he turned away from her and walked toward the front door.

"Caleb, wait, he's leaving," Abby said. She hated the whine in her voice, but she didn't want Caleb to leave like this.

Caleb paused in front of Reyn and stared down at him. The four-inch height difference was one thing, but Caleb was also bulkier, and the cold, dead look in his eyes was enough to make any grown man cower. Reyn shifted nervously.

"Step aside," Caleb hissed, deliberately emphasizing each word.

Reyn stepped away from the door quickly and watched with his mouth open as Caleb strode through and slammed the door behind him. He leaned against the wall and tried to breathe, and then he turned to Abby.

"Are you kidding me? Are you serious, Abby? I get that I hurt you pretty badly, but rebounding with your father's Jason Statham look-alike assistant? That's your play?"

"Jason Statham is shorter," Abby sniped.

Reyn gritted his teeth and walked right up to her.

"What are you doing?" he asked angrily.

"This is none of your business, Reyn. Nothing I do should concern you anymore. I told you that on Friday," she snapped and turned away from him.

She walked into the bedroom, and Reyn followed.

"I still have a right to care and to be concerned. We had three years, Abby. Three damn years and you think I can just shut it off and forget everything?"

"Are you high, Reyn? You *did* shut it off. You dumped me. Remember?" Abby yelled as she pulled her t-shirt off and searched for her underwear, not caring that he was standing there.

The sight of her completely naked body unnerved Reyn for a minute, and his body instinctively reacted. He hated the way she made him feel. He hated that he missed her so much and loved her more than he could handle. He hated that she was screwing Caleb Osei. The thought of her with another man, that man in particular, infuriated him.

"You're a fucking tease, you know that?" he yelled.

Abby placed her hands on her hips and looked at him.

"And you're a fucking idiot," she said with less volume, but no less anger than him.

Reyn clenched his fists and took a step toward her. Then he stopped midway, distracted by her still naked body.

"Yeah, I'm an idiot, but an idiot who'll love you for a very long time, probably till the day I die. I really hope you know what you're doing with him. Goodbye, Abby."

Then he turned around and walked out. A few seconds later, the front door was slammed for the second time that morning.

Abby dropped onto the floor and choked back tears. She was falling hard for Caleb, but he was cold and emotionally inaccessible. Further, she still loved Reyn, who was physically inaccessible and confusing her. Everything was a mess. She dragged her bedspread down onto the floor, curled up in it, and cried for the hundredth time in two weeks.

⌇

Caleb checked his missed calls and messages as he drove away from Abby's apartment. There were two calls from the Justice; three from Agyari, the police commissioner; five from Albert, the assistant campaign director; and twenty more from various media personalities and DNP officials. It was barely past 10 a.m., and the whole world was looking for him. He knew why, though. He had killed Josh around 5 p.m. the day before, sent the emails right after, and then went straight to Abby's. He was sure that between then and now Josh's body had been found and the story had broken. There was really no time to waste. They had to take advantage of the situation now. Media personalities had a way of twisting things, so it was best to stay on top of it and control the commentators and the story. The GFP was going down regardless, but he was definitely going to speed their demise along.

Caleb dialed Albert first.

"Caleb, where have you been? I've been calling you all morning. Have you heard?"

"What's going on?" Caleb asked, feeling no need to explain his whereabouts.

"It's chaotic, completely chaotic. Josh sent an email with a recording of Ohene Gyawu and Bedu Afari making arrangements to kill you. They're the ones who sent the men, Caleb. Stella Asiedu got the email as well, and she insisted that the police had to look into it, but they didn't check on Josh until this morning. He's dead, Caleb. The police suspect Ohene and Bedu killed him after the attempt on your life failed. The police have witnesses who claim they saw Ohene and Bedu leaving Josh's house yesterday. Can you believe this, Caleb? I can't believe they would go this far."

Yes, he believed it, because he'd directed the whole story himself. He was also glad Stella Asiedu was on the story. She was one of the few truly objective and unbiased investigative journalists left in the country. She was currently the head of news at iTV, Insel's flagship TV station. Caleb knew that a few years ago, Charles had considered her for Josh's role, and it was more than likely that she would get it now.

"I'm surprised they would go this far too. I'm heading over to the Justice's place now. Draft a press release and send it to me now. Make it strong, no holds barred, and no niceties. We want Ohene and Bedu's heads on a damn silver platter, do you understand?"

"Yes, of course. You'll get it within the next half hour."

Caleb hung up and scrolled through his missed calls again. Stella had called him a few times as well. He would call her back, but the next call had to be to the Justice.

"Where have you been, Caleb?" the Justice sounded irritated.

"Albert just debriefed me. I'm on my way to your place. No church today for you. We need to milk this, and we need to do it fast. This won't be another lost opportunity. I'll see you in twenty."

He hung up quickly before the Justice could ask him where he was again. Where he'd been was irrelevant—what was going to happen next was the key. He needed to focus on work again. He had allowed himself to get emotional both the night before and this morning. He hated that the sight of Reyn this morning got under his skin. He knew it shouldn't have, but it did. He'd only been with Abby two nights, but Reyn was her boyfriend for three years. Seeing Reyn at the door this morning reminded Caleb that Friday night and Saturday night shouldn't have happened. She may have said that she loved him, but she was obviously rebounding. He was angry—angry at the darn Proctor man who had such a strong hold on her, angry at her for getting to him like that, and angry at himself for falling.

Caleb's phone beeped, and he glanced at it. It was Abby. He hit "decline call" and focused on the road. He was done. He would find a way to tell her that. He couldn't deal with the way he felt, and he needed to be in control again. He also knew she needed to be completely over Reyn before he could even consider being with her. The way she stood crying by her car Friday night and the way she looked when she saw Reyn this morning were indicative that there was definitely something still there between them, and Caleb didn't have the patience or the heart to be the other man.

15

Three hours later, the Justice and Caleb were at iTV filming a live interview with Stella. iTV had the second largest viewership in the country. GNN was the national TV station and had the widest reach, but the GFP cronies who ran the station were notoriously incompetent and corrupt. It didn't matter anyways. Stella's *News Now* show was the most watched news show on any network. She'd been on air discussing the situation almost all morning and afternoon. When something out of the norm happened, her show was often put on air to run for hours. She dubbed the unplanned broadcasts *Breaking News Now*, and it could run for hours with different guests. This was the only interview the Justice was going to do that day, but Caleb knew it would be the most impactful.

Caleb wasn't on air, and that was his preference. The Justice was the candidate, and even though the attack had happened against Caleb, it was by extension an attack on the Justice himself.

"You know, Stella, you'll have to forgive me because I'm not going to mince words with you today. I am outraged, completely outraged by the sheer audacity of this crime. I was hoping that the elections would be about serious issues like education, health, infrastructure, and economic growth. I thought we would be able to focus the conversation and the people on what matters most, but I suppose that was too much to ask of a party with a history steeped in violence and corruption."

"So you believe this was a GFP-orchestrated attempt, and not a move by some desperate party individuals?" Stella asked.

"Individuals? What is a political party, Stella? A political party is driven and managed by individuals. The decisions the individuals make are representative of the party. Bedu Afari is the government communications director. Ohene Gyawu is the campaign director for President Otoo's re-election and one of the president's closest friends. You think Ohene Gyawu would do anything without the knowledge and blessing of the president?" the Justice responded tensely.

"That's a serious accusation, Justice Annan. Why would the president or any member of his government sanction this attack on Caleb Osei? Why not direct it at you?"

"They did direct it at me. Caleb is my chief of staff and campaign director. Everyone knows Caleb plays a critical role in my campaign, and he's like family. This was a desperate, miscalculated attempt by a failing government that will stop at nothing to retain power."

"So the attack on Caleb wasn't actually directed at your daughter?"

Caleb froze and looked up sharply at the Justice seated on the set a few feet away from him. Their eyes met, and Caleb tried to mouth a response, but the Justice turned away too quickly.

"What do you mean, Stella?"

"Your daughter Abiel, or Abby as you call her, we're told she was there with Caleb the night of the attack. Was she?"

Caleb cursed softly under his breath, and he rose from his seat behind the cameramen and crew. He glanced around the room looking for the producer, but he was nowhere in sight. This was the downside of dealing with someone like Stella. She was thorough and knew how to dig deep. Caleb took a step toward the set, fully prepared to intervene and end the interview.

"Yes, Abby was with Caleb when it happened, but this wasn't about her. Her name wasn't mentioned on the tape. She wasn't their target. It was Caleb they wanted. But whether or not my daughter was there is irrelevant. A few days ago, Ohene Gyawu and Bedu Afari contracted their friend and GFP supporter Josh Winkler, Insel's very own VP, to kill and get rid of my campaign director, Caleb Osei. When that failed, Ohene and Bedu killed Josh. Those are the facts. This is 2012, and we have GFP officials prepared to pay for murder. That is the story. You can choose to focus on that, or you can stoop low and continue to ask about Caleb and my daughter's relationship. Your choice."

Caleb almost clapped right then and there. He smiled and nodded at the Justice. That was a perfect response. He'd taught the Justice well. Rule number one for interviews was never tell a lie on live TV. You can bend the truth if it's recorded because there were ways for Caleb to find and destroy recordings, but live TV lying was a no-no. The Justice was also a very smart man, Caleb acknowledged. He was one of the most intelligent people he'd ever known or worked for.

Stella cleared her throat and glanced at her questions.

"So, the GFP has issued no statement yet, and no arrests have been made. What is your reaction to that?"

"I refuse to let this become like the cocaine situation. I respect the police commissioner a great deal, and since he's been in this role for the last two years, he's demonstrated that he is more objective and devoted to this profession than the last one, who's in jail for his involvement in the cocaine debacle. So, I expect that Agyari will do the right thing and investigate this properly. I also still have some respect for the president, but if his past actions are anything to go by, then I know he may not be decisive. So let me say this now: if those responsible aren't held accountable according to the law, I'll take them both to task myself. That's a promise."

Caleb smiled again. The Justice was on fire. He walked off the set and out to the iTV parking lot. It wasn't necessary for him to be there for the rest of the interview. There was something else he needed to do now.

Caleb found Eben leaning against the Justice's Mercedes and chatting on his phone. He hung up immediately when he saw Caleb walking toward him.

"Is the Justice ready? Should I bring the car to the front?"

"Give me the keys. You're fired."

Eben's face fell. He glanced behind Caleb, obviously looking for the Justice.

"What? What happened? What did I do? I don't understand."

"Who did you talk to about what happened at my house? Who did you tell that Abby was in my house?"

Eben froze. His mouth started to move, but no words came out.

Caleb stepped up close to him, and Eben backed up against the car.

"No one, I spoke to no one," Eben muttered.

"You were in my house. You saw the bodies. You saw what I did. Do you think it's wise for you to lie to me right now?" Caleb snapped.

"I'm sorry. I'm very sorry, sir. I only told my wife. I swear, just my wife and my daughter. It was just them, no one else! And I made them promise they wouldn't go and talk to people. They promised me, but you know women, sir. I swear it will never happen again. I've worked for the Justice for fifteen years. I am very loyal. I swear! Please!" Eben wailed.

"Give me the keys, Eben. Don't make me ask you twice," Caleb said coldly.

"Oh Bra Caleb, please oh, Bra Caleb," Eben begged.

"Don't 'bra' me right now, Eben. If you make me ask for the keys again, you're going to be very sorry."

Eben reached into his pocket and handed the keys over slowly.

"Go home, pack up your things, and be gone by nightfall. Your last pay will be deposited into your account as always. And if you reveal anything, and I mean anything, about the Justice or his family, I will find you and you'll be very sorry," Caleb hissed.

Eben started sobbing, but Caleb ignored him. He got into the car and started it. Eben was a difficult driver he'd tolerated for years. There had been several leaks from him before, but Caleb had let it slide because he'd been with the family for so long. In some cases, he thought it was best to keep an eye on folks like Eben while they still worked for the Justice, but not this time, not today. The Justice had handled Stella's questions well, but the story was still out there. Amateurish propaganda journalists supportive of the GFP could latch onto it and make him and Abby the news. That's the last thing he wanted. Caleb didn't crave the limelight. He preferred his role as the puppet master, and now the idiot Eben had brought a personal situation into a story that should have been completely focused on the crime. A few minutes later, a still sobbing Eben was gone, and then thirty minutes later the Justice texted that he was done. Caleb drove up to the front of the station building to pick him up. He'd caught a ride with the Justice to the station, so at least he didn't have to return for his car.

"You fired Eben?" the Justice asked as soon as he got into the car.

"Yes."

"Should I fire you too for sleeping with my daughter?"

Caleb gripped the steering wheel harder, his eyes fixed on the road. They hadn't talked about Friday night much since the Justice found Abby in his living room. He'd promised the Justice an explanation, but he'd never given him one. What was he supposed to say?

"It was a mistake. It won't happen again, I assure you."

"Of course it was a mistake. Getting involved with my daughter was stupid, foolish, and reckless. You should have known better. I am your boss. She is my daughter. I don't care how important you are to the campaign or to me, but if you get together with her again, you're done."

Caleb swallowed. He wasn't intimidated by the Justice, but he was embarrassed because what the Justice said was true. Hooking up with Abby was a mistake, not only because it was unprofessional, but also because it undermined everything he'd worked for and believed in.

Nothing else was said during the ride home. Caleb was mentally mapping out the coming week's strategy. Their original itinerary had the Justice scheduled to make appearances along the coast—a five-city tour from Axim to Keta, meeting with delegates and winning the populace. He would have to change that plan. The Justice was a powerful orator and lawyer, so it would be important to have him beating the drums and calling for justice himself against the men who had sanctioned the hit on Caleb. They had a communications and PR team that usually made the rounds on radio and TV, but not this week. This week, he wanted the Justice himself to call for blood. That would be the most effective way of bringing the GFP down quickly and swiftly, although he still had a few trump cards left to play, if necessary.

"Are you coming in? We still have a few things to talk about, right?" the Justice asked when Caleb pulled up to the house.

"I'll be right there, just need to make a few calls first."

As soon as the Justice was gone, Caleb picked up his phone from the cup holder. During the drive, he'd seen an unknown number pop up several times. It could be anyone, but he also knew today was Sunday, and his marine buddy had promised him DNA results by Sunday. Against his better judgment, he called him from his cell.

"I've been calling you. I thought you wanted this information immediately?" the voice quipped.

"You called my personal cell phone. I thought we agreed you'd never call me on my personal cell phone."

"Crikes, Caleb, you know how to wipe a phone, and I used a scrambler on my end, so calm down. I have news."

"Go on."

"He's the father of both of them."

Caleb closed his eyes as the words sunk in. He muttered thanks, hung up, and slammed his palms repeatedly against the steering wheel. Shit, shit, shit! The fucking liar! The Justice had the nerve to lecture him about Abby when he'd screwed his wife's twin sister and fathered a child with her. Hypocritical bastard! Caleb was boiling mad for a lot of reasons. First, he'd been made to look like a fool. He'd bought into the whole man of integrity, principles, and faith persona. He'd fallen for it hook, line, and sinker, and over the last ten years, he'd built on that persona and taken it to a different level. He'd taken a man who was apostle-like and turned him into a god. And now with this Josh situation, he'd more or less handed him the election. It was a lock, a damn done deal. The second thing that bothered him was, if the Justice could hide the affair so well from him, from everyone, then what else could he be hiding?

Caleb got out of the car and strode into the house. He was done speculating. The Justice was on the phone when Caleb entered the study. He raised his hand, asking Caleb to give him a minute. Caleb wasn't that patient.

"How long did you have an affair with Bertha?" he asked straight away, his steely eyes fixed on Annan. It was interesting watching Annan's face. His mouth dropped mid-sentence, and his eyes widened in shock. Then within seconds, his face was composed.

"Eben, I support Caleb's decision on this. I'll add a little extra to your pay, but I'm afraid that's it. I'll talk to you later."

The Justice hung up and slowly placed his cell on his desk. He cocked his head to the side and looked squarely at Caleb. Neither man said anything for minutes. And then the Justice broke the silence.

"I've been waiting for you to ask me that question for the last ten years. I've had answers prepared for a while, but hearing you ask now, I can't seem to remember what those answers were," the Justice chuckled.

He didn't deny it; Caleb thought that was a good start. Now he needed details. He sat in the chair opposite the desk and crossed his legs.

"When did it happen? For how long? And why did you keep this from me? What else don't I know?" he fired off.

The Justice chuckled again. "The 'Caleb Inquisition'—I haven't sat through one in a while."

"I'm waiting," Caleb said, unamused.

The Justice nodded.

"Okay then, I'll get to it. Bertha and I, it was a mistake that happened once, absolute lapse in judgment on my part. It was shortly after her husband died. She was vulnerable, alone with a child, and deeply devastated. I checked in on her a couple of times after work, and it just happened. Once, and that was it. We both knew it was a mistake, and it never happened again."

"So you had sex with her once after her husband died, but somehow your sperm managed to impregnate her five years before then?"

Caleb watched as the blood literally drained from the Justice's face. He clenched and unclenched his fists several times and gritted his teeth. He stared at the picture on his desk and picked it up. It was one of many pictures of his "family" that he had in his study—Adubea, Bertha, Joey, and Abby. He set it back on the table and looked at Caleb.

"I'm not going to ask how you know all this, and I'm also not going to make any excuses, but there is something about twins, you know. They're like two sides of the same coin. Adubea was...is sweet, kind, gentle, loving. Her love was so deep and so genuine. It was exactly what I needed. Bertha, on the other hand, was a firebrand, feisty and outspoken, just like me. She excited me. She challenged me. I loved Adubea, but Bertha got to me on a different level. It happened at Legon. We both fought it for a while, but it happened, and when it did I felt complete. Between the two women, I had my perfect woman. And when the kids were born, I had my perfect family. The affair ended eventually, around the time you moved here. Bertha just wasn't the kind to be the other woman forever. She moved on and quietly started seeing other people."

How convenient for him to say the relationship ended when Caleb joined them.

"Don't lie to me."

The Justice shook his head. "I am not lying to you. You know, Caleb, when I hired you ten years ago, I knew it was a risk. You had the intelligence, real-world smarts, and dedication to authority that could help me get to the presidency, which was always my goal. I also knew you had the potential to dig up my mistakes and sink me into oblivion. But I weighed the risks. I had one secret, just one: I had an affair and fathered a child. I could survive that if it ever potentially came out. I knew I could, but without you I knew my chances at being the president I was destined to be were limited. That's why I didn't tell you, because I wanted your absolute commitment."

Caleb stared at him silently, trying to read the Justice's body language. Something was off. The Justice admitted that he'd prepared his responses in anticipation of this, so was that what he was getting, a carefully crafted response?

"Here's the thing about absolute commitment—it's based on an ideal, a strong premise that invokes passion and dedication. You had it—integrity, family commitment, and Christian values. I am not a Christian, but you got me on that. You sold me on your mantra: God, country, and family. I believed in you because that was what you believed. I'd never met a man who was that committed to his faith, country, and family. That's why I bought into it. That's why you had my absolute commitment. So now tell me, what do you think happens to that type of dedication when the foundation turns out to be false and a lie?"

"That's the basic question, isn't it, Caleb? Will you stay or will you go? Will you still fight for me, or will you fight against me? Where do you stand? Isn't that the wrap-up to this conversation?"

Caleb stood up from the chair.

"I've basically handed you the presidency. The GFP will crumble, and Asenso won't be able to show any leadership, so the people will look to you. The election is yours. What you wanted me to do is done. I'll see you through this week, and then I'll hand everything over to you and the team. I don't see any need to keep up the charade, because you're not the man I thought you were."

The Justice nodded. "I'm truly sorry you feel that way, Caleb. I made a mistake, but you should know that I do stand for those things. I love my wife and my family dearly.

I love my country wholeheartedly. I *am* the man you believed in."

"You may think it was just an affair, but that's not all there is to it. By hiding this from me, you were deliberate and calculating. You manipulated me. You lied to me and millions of others. You're a cheat, a liar, and a hypocrite. That's the man you are. I am done."

"In Hebrews 10 verse 17, God says, 'I will remember their sins and their lawless deeds no more.' My God has forgiven me, and my yoke is now his. He shall remember what I did no more. We've had ten years together. Why can't you forgive me?"

"I'm not God, Justice, not even close."

Caleb turned and walked out of the study.

The Justice waited for ten minutes, and then he picked up his cell phone.

"It's me. He found out about the affair and about my boy....No, I don't know how he did. This is Caleb— who knows how?...No, that's all he knows, but I'm concerned that he could piece it all together. He could start digging into things, and then who knows what he can find?...Yes, he could be a liability, but he's also like family. I'd rather not do anything rash. There's too much heat and visibility on him anyways....Again, this is Caleb. It would be stupid to do something against him....We should be good for now, but I just hope he doesn't go to her.....Yes, I know that would be catastrophic for me and the campaign....I insist, do nothing for now. Let's see how it all plays out, and I'll keep you updated."

The Justice hung up and leaned back in his chair. He picked up the glass of scotch on his desk and took a sip. It was unfortunate it had come to this, but Caleb was right:

it wasn't just an affair. There was a whole lot more he needed to protect, and now everything was at risk. When Caleb was working for him, he could keep an eye on him, to a degree. Now, if Caleb was out there, how would he know what he was up to? There was so much at stake, but he also wasn't sure what his options were. Since the GFP had already made an attempt on Caleb's life, it wouldn't be shocking if something unfortunate happened again. Beyond that, in the past ten years, Caleb had become like a son to him. Caleb was his right-hand man, his confidante, and his trusted advisor. He deeply respected Caleb. He was astute, incredibly intelligent, and focused. He knew that there was no way he could have achieved what he had in the last ten years without Caleb. Caleb helped him soar to heights he thought weren't possible. He was now untouchable, mostly thanks to Caleb. But now he was at a difficult decision point. There was no way Caleb would just walk away. Caleb would start looking deeper into the Justice's relationships and past, and inevitably he would find something. The Justice could either stop Caleb now, permanently, or he could just wait and watch. Unfortunately, he'd waited four years for this moment. He'd put his political career on hold to take care of his family, and now that he had another opportunity, he had to be smart and protect it. He was meant to be president, and being president meant taking difficult, unpopular, and distasteful decisions, even if it was against people you loved.

The Justice stared at the ceiling and sighed. God forgive him.

16

Caleb closed his eyes, leaned forward under the shower, and allowed the hot spray to soak his body. He was tired, drained, and dejected. Everything was haywire, and it was all because Josh threatened Abby, causing Caleb to initiate the chain reaction to Josh's downfall early. In two short weeks, he'd gone from being a disciplined, methodical campaign director to killing four people, sleeping with his boss's daughter, and resigning from a job to which he'd dedicated ten years. How did that happen?

Caleb slammed his fist against the wall and gritted his teeth as pain ripped through his hand. He was annoyed with himself. This wasn't supposed to happen, and he had no clue what to do next. Obviously, he had to clear up everything and hand it over to the Justice and the campaign team. The Justice already had access to his offshore accounts and all campaign funds. Albert was also very capable, and he could lead the campaign for the rest of the year if he stayed on message and continued to beat the GFP on corruption and the economy. The only thing the Justice didn't have was all the dirt Caleb had amassed on potential competitors. Caleb wasn't sure he wanted to hand that over. He'd done enough for the Justice. It was time for Annan to win this election on his own.

Caleb stepped out of the shower and grabbed a towel from the rack. He could have stayed under the shower forever, but he needed to lie down and de-stress. It'd been a hectic weekend, he'd barely had a moment to himself since the awards dinner on Friday, and now it was Sunday. He just wanted to shut down for a while and give himself a moment to regroup. He wished he was home instead of at a hotel, but after the police took the bodies from his home, he'd hired a crew to clean the blood, and that was going to take days. So, he'd gone home, packed some stuff, and checked himself into a hotel. He'd had only about six hours of sleep over the last two days. So now, all he wanted was a moment to close his eyes and sleep.

He toweled himself dry, dressed up in a t-shirt and track bottoms, and lay on the bed. After a few minutes, he picked up his phone and checked his messages. As usual, he'd missed a million and one calls. Abby had called over ten times, but he didn't feel like calling her back. Sure, he didn't work for her father anymore, so he could technically date her, but if he no longer worked for Annan then he was going to pack up and head back to the US. So why start a relationship? Cat had called him several times in the last hour, and she'd sent several texts saying she needed to see him. He didn't feel like company now, but her texts sounded panicked, so he called her back.

"Caleb, I've been trying to reach you. Are you home? I'm in a cab on my way."

He frowned. "Why would you just take a cab and come to my place?"

"Because I need to see you. Two men came to see me this afternoon, and they threatened me, Caleb. They said you work for a presidential candidate and they wanted details about our relationship. They said they would revoke my visa and have me deported. I would lose my credits and my scholarship. What is going on, Caleb? What are they talking about?"

Caleb shook his head and rubbed his temples. Was this ever going to end?

"I'm not home right now. I'm at the City Hotel, room 598. Call me when you get here."

He hung up and lay back on the bed. He was truly tired of all of this. Who was threatening Cat? What was going on? How did they even know about their relationship? He'd been extra careful. He was sure of that. He just needed to wait for Cat so he could get more information. Speculation just wasn't going to get him anywhere.

Twenty minutes later, there was a knock on the door, and Caleb got up reluctantly. He'd dozed off for a little while, and he wished he could have continued. He peered through the cubbyhole to make sure it was Cat. Considering the weekend he'd had, he had to check. He opened the door, and she hugged him straight away.

"Oh my God, Caleb, what is going on?"

Caleb hugged her back briefly and then stepped back. She looked so scared and vulnerable that he felt sorry for what her association with him had put her through. He led her to the sofa in the living area of the suite and sat down, holding her hands in his. He squeezed her and tried his best to convey concern.

"Do you want to tell me what happened?"

Cat nodded. "Two men showed up at the hostel today. They came up to my room and said they needed to talk to me about my boyfriend. I was confused at first, and then they showed me your picture. They said you'd killed some people, and they were looking into what happened. They threatened me, told me they'd have me detained at some secluded place if I didn't cooperate, BNI or something. I said I was a US citizen, but they wouldn't listen. They were threatening to take me with them, but a couple of my neighbors stepped in…"

Cat paused, choking back tears. Caleb pulled her into his arms and hugged her. She started crying then, so he hugged her tighter.

"I'm really sorry, babe," he said, kissing the side of her head as she cried into his shoulder.

"I'm sorry too, Caleb," Cat said.

The suddenly cool and calm tone of her voice sent a shiver down his spine. Caleb tried to pull back, but Cat held on a little longer, and within a second he felt a sharp stab in his neck. He pushed her away and touched his neck.

"Jesus, Cat, what did you do?"

Caleb stared at the syringe she'd just pulled from his neck. He raised his eyebrows at her, stunned and shocked.

"What did you do?" he repeated, stretching his hand toward Cat.

"It's a poison called strychnine. It's already in your blood stream. First it'll weaken your muscles, shut down your lungs, and then within thirty minutes you'll be brain dead."

Caleb lunged at her, but she was faster and he'd already started to weaken. She stood up and stared down at him.

"Relax, don't fight it. Isn't that what Jack Bauer would say?"

"Cat, don't do this. Please, don't do this," he pled, ironically recalling how Josh begged him for his life just the day before.

Cat stared at him for a minute, almost as if she was considering his plea, and then she opened the door and was gone. Caleb groaned out loud as sharp, excruciating pain gripped his entire body. He knew what dying felt like. He'd been shot twice before, but the pain zipping through his body now was more physically and mentally crippling than anything he'd ever felt before. Caleb struggled to stand up from the sofa, but his legs buckled immediately and he fell hard, hitting his head on the center table on his way down. He lay there for a moment, his fists and teeth clenched as another bout of pain coursed through his body. When it subsided, he grabbed the desk line and hit the "0" button.

"Reception, this is Adwoa. How may I help you?"

"I've been poisoned. I need you to get an ambulance or a car to take me to the hospital now," he mumbled.

"What?"

"I need to get to the hospital now. I'm dying. I've been poisoned," he repeated, trying to inject more force into his voice.

"Sir, I don't understand. You've been poisoned? Are you sure? What happened?"

"God damn it! I'm in room 598. Get me to the god damn hospital now!" he screamed out of both pain and frustration. He closed his eyes and grimaced.

"Okay, okay, I'll get the manager. I'll get someone. We have an onsite clinic, and the doctor is already here on call. Did you say room 548?"

"Jesus Christ! Don't you have caller ID? Isn't this a five-star hotel? It's 598!" he snapped, although it sounded more like a whimper.

He hung up and lay back on the floor, trying to catch his breath as his lungs constricted painfully. He dug his hands into his pocket and pulled out his cell phone. He dialed frantically.

"Calling from your personal cell twice in one day?"

"Strychnine," he muttered.

"Jesus, man, have you been poisoned?"

"Yes, Strychnine, two minutes now, twenty-eight minutes left. Find me an antidote now. And call Abby as soon as you have it, you have her number. Tell her I'm at the City Hotel. Hurry."

"I'm on it. Hang in there, okay? Hang in there."

Caleb hung up and tried to pull himself up. His legs felt like lead, and he could barely move, but he knew he had to try. It could take the incompetent hotel staff a while to get up to him, so he had to get down there somehow. He grabbed onto the sofa and reached for the door, but his body betrayed him and he collapsed onto the floor. Caleb closed his eyes and lay there gasping for air. When he was nineteen, he was shot twice in the chest and left for dead until reinforcement troops found him two hours later. At the time, he thought getting shot was the most painful experience a human being could ever experience. This pain tearing repeatedly through him and ripping his muscles and organs apart was excruciating beyond words. He was dying, and he knew it. The hotel staff wouldn't get to him on time, and even if his friend got the antidote, the clinic probably wouldn't have the ingredients, or the clueless doctor would mess it up. This was Ghana—his chances were not great. The poison was a rare drug that probably didn't exist in Ghana. He was going to die. If this was it, he had several more calls to make.

He dialed his parents' numbers, but neither one of them answered. He kept his voice messages simple, hoping his near wheezing voice wouldn't give anything away: "Mom, dad, just checking in on you. I'll call again. Love you."

With barely any energy left, he dialed Abby's number, prepared to tell her how he felt, prepared to lay it all on the line. He heard her answer and opened his mouth, but no words came out. His throat was constricted, and his fingers could barely hold onto the phone.

"Caleb? Caleb? Hang in there. We're coming. They're coming up to get you, and I'll be there soon. Hang in there, okay? Please. Talk to me, Caleb, please. Caleb!"

He dropped the phone and allowed the pain to wash over him. He closed his eyes and unfurled his clenched fingers. There was nothing left to do. He just had to let it happen.

⌒

Abby stared at Caleb's still body forlornly, mentally willing him to wake up, but he'd been in a coma for three days, and there'd been no physical movement from him the entire time. She crossed her legs beneath her, picked up her iPad from her bag, and leaned back in the chair. She tried to read, but she couldn't focus. The events of the past week, the last two weeks to be honest, weighed heavily on her mind. She couldn't even begin to make sense of it all, no matter how hard she tried. It was all too surreal. She looked up from her iPad and glanced at Caleb's body. Only his chest moved up and down. The rest of him was eerily still. The only activity was from the multiple tubes and beeping machines.

She closed her eyes and tried to think. None of this made any sense. Two attempts on Caleb's life over one weekend? And what about the man who called her with ingredients to an antidote for a poison she could barely pronounce? Who was he? He didn't even give his name. His voice, tone, and accent sounded a lot like Caleb's—straight to the point, cold, and precise, even as he asked her to rush and get to Caleb. Thankfully, City Hotel had a state-of-the-art onsite clinic with a Swiss doctor who was apparently familiar with the poison. Unfortunately, almost thirty minutes had passed between when Caleb called the front desk to when the doctor got to him, so the doctor induced a coma before mixing and applying the antidote. He said Caleb's vitals were good and he would wake any minute, but it'd been three days, and Abby was worried. She didn't understand why or how any of this had happened, but she suspected it couldn't all be a coincidence. There was something going on, and Caleb was right in the middle of it. She just couldn't figure out if he was the perpetrator, victim, or both. What had she gotten herself into by falling for such a person? Abby closed her eyes and tried to sleep. She hoped this was it, because she wasn't sure how much more craziness she could take.

"Ughhh…"

Abby's eyes flew open, and she jumped up. Caleb was awake and struggling to sit up. She rushed to his side and grabbed his hands.

"Don't move. Don't move, okay? I'll get the doctor."

She ran out through the open glass door and down the corridor. It was a moderate-sized clinic, with one operating theater, three recovery rooms, x-ray facilities, lab, and reception. On the night Caleb was brought in, the clinic was empty—and was still empty, which wasn't surprising. Use of the clinic was free for hotel guests while they were staying there, but extremely expensive for any other visitors, so it was rarely busy. Abby hurried to the reception. Two nurses were lounging around, watching TV.

"He's awake. Get the doctor now."

One of the nurses got up slowly and walked to the phone.

"I think the doctor is out, but I'll call him and see."

Abby rolled her eyes. Even money and good intent couldn't buy competence.

"You'll call him and see? Are you serious? You better call him now and tell him it's urgent. His *only* patient is awake. And then one of you needs to come with me and check in on Caleb."

The nurses exchanged looks, and Abby stepped forward.

"I mean now," she repeated, quietly but firmly.

The seated nurse got up and followed Abby, and the other got on the phone. When they got back to the room, Caleb's eyes were open, but barely. Abby gripped his hands and smiled down at him while the nurse checked his vitals. He gripped her hands back and blinked rapidly at her. She leaned forward and kissed his forehead.

"Everything is going to be okay. Just relax and get some rest."

He nodded slowly, and then he closed his eyes. Abby kissed his forehead again. She prayed this was the end. She prayed it was all over, but she had no idea what was yet to come.

17

"I'm going to cut right to the chase and ask the question that I know is on everyone's minds. What the heck is going on in Ghana?"

"That is the million dollar question, Paul. Every time I turn on the news, I feel like I'm watching a movie of some other country. It is amazing the lengths people will go to just to bring down one man—one man that these same people have always claimed is nothing but a man. So, why the fear? Why the need to terrorize and attack him and his family like this?"

"Kweku, Kweku, Kweku, I know you like to be dramatic, but please, what are you talking about? Who is terrorizing whom? A handful of GFP loyalists on their own and without direct government or presidential sanction attempted to take out Justice Annan's chief of staff in order to derail the Justice's campaign. That we know, and that is all we know."

"Kwesi, come on now, that is all we know? Are you serious right now? Two days later, when another attempt is made, you don't think that is suspicious? And you think this isn't terrorism? And how can anyone know for sure that Ohene and Bedu acted without presidential knowledge or sanction? Obviously, nothing would be written on paper, and if Josh hadn't recorded his fellow conspirators, we wouldn't know about this at all! The GFP is creating a very dangerous situation in our country with these antics, and it needs to stop!"

"Okay, okay, let me just step in here and ask the questions on our viewers' minds. An attack in the middle of the night by armed men, that isn't so far-fetched or hard to believe, but a rare poison attack? That's very strange, isn't it? Is that something the GFP is capable of pulling off? From what I understand, it was a very sophisticated poison and extremely rare. Does it seem logical that the GFP would go that route?"

"Exactly, Paul, exactly!" Kwesi said emphatically.

"Paul, you can't put limits on how far corrupt and evil people would go to get their way. These are modern times we're in, and the crimes will obviously evolve to suit the times. I don't think it's far-fetched at all. Honestly, I don't. Caleb was staying in a hotel, so obviously they couldn't go in there guns blazing. So, they adapted to the situation and sent in an unknown woman to seduce and poison him."

"Let's look at the facts here, Paul. Let's take this from the beginning. Friday night, three armed men attack Caleb Osei in his home. By Saturday, evidence is discovered that indicates that Josh Winkler was contracted by Ohene Gyawu and Bedu to kill Caleb Osei. I won't argue too much about that. And then just a day later on Sunday, a mysterious woman in dark clothes and dark sunglasses bypasses the City Hotel reception and heads right up to Caleb's room. According to the police, they have footage from

the hotel cameras that she knocked on his room door and entered without breaking in. He let her in! A few minutes later, she walks out and disappears. Just like that. How can any logical man not question all of that? Who is she? Why did he let her in? How did Abiel Annan end up at the hotel just a short moment later with an antidote? Why is the family refusing to comment? Caleb is now awake, but he's refusing to cooperate with the police…"

"Because he doesn't trust the police!" Kweku interjected.

"Oh for God's sake, get off your agenda and open your eyes!" Kwesi snapped.

"Gentlemen, please, let's be civil here or I'll have to mute both of you and do this show by myself. Kweku, let's look at this as objectively as we can. Don't you think Caleb and the Annan family are hiding something? I haven't seen this hotel tape, but according to my sources, Caleb let the woman in. Don't you think that is suspicious?"

"Everything that has happened over the last week is suspicious. I haven't seen the tape, and neither has Kwesi. This whole tape thing was leaked by someone in the police commissioner's office. We don't know what really happened. The official statement from the police is that Caleb Osei was poisoned in his room. The hotel staff found him and rushed him to the clinic, and the doctor treated him. That is it. It's only a rumor that Abiel Annan had an antidote on her. No one has confirmed this. So look, all I am saying is I won't put anything, and I mean anything, past a desperate, decaying party that wants to remain in power at all cost. I just won't."

"Your lack of objectivity really affects your credibility, Kweku. You need to think about that, because you're becoming very obvious with your rants and rhetoric. It's very disappointing, unprofessional, and not worthy of any seasoned journalist."

"If that's the case, then I guess it took too long for me to follow your lead. I am now officially just like you."

"Okay, Kweku, I don't want to come across as biased in any way, but I have to press you a bit more. Yes, we don't have a lot of facts or evidence around what happened in the City Hotel, but doesn't the lack of information flow say something too? After Caleb's first attack, the Justice was on TV with Stella calling for blood. But after the poisoning, there've been no TV appearances or even radio interviews. Just one statement that just said that a second attempt was made on Caleb's life and the family would leave it to the police to investigate. That was it."

"But Paul, what more do you want them to say? Imagine if you were them and it is obvious that desperate people are trying to bring you down. You may also be hesitant about what to share. There have been two attempts on Caleb Osei's life. That is a fact no one can deny. And I am saying that I have no doubt in my mind that both attempts were orchestrated and planned by GFP officials in order to derail the Justice's campaign. Everyone knows that Caleb Osei is the engine behind the Justice's success. Everyone knows that that man is a maverick, and if you want to bring the Justice down, you go through him. Everyone knows that. The GFP knows that."

"There you go again with your broken record. Blame it all on the GFP," Kwesi quipped.

"Oh, I will blame it on them. We need to stop the tyrants before they destroy our country."

"If you're looking for a tyrant, perhaps you should start by looking at the man you worship so much," Kwesi retorted.

"I think that is my cue to go for a commercial. This is Spotlight and we'll be right back."

"So, are you ready?"

"Actually, Abby, I need some time."

Abby frowned at Caleb.

"You agreed you'd come away with me for a few days to rest. You promised."

Caleb sighed. He'd promised because he was sick, weak, and emotional. He'd spent three days in a coma and another two days strapped to a bed pumped with fluids and all kinds of drugs. Of course, he'd promised to take a break and go out of town with her, but now that he was up and on his feet, he knew he couldn't leave just yet. He was being discharged today, and it was the perfect opportunity to get some answers. He'd been evading the police's questions and pretending that he couldn't remember much, couldn't even remember the woman he'd willfully let in after she came to his door. He could lie to the police, but he couldn't lie to himself. Cat tried to kill him, and he had to find out why. He simply couldn't leave town yet. He'd wasted enough time.

"I'm not taking no for an answer, Caleb. You're coming with me for a few days, and that's it," Abby insisted.

"Okay, I will go with you, Abby," Caleb said, conceding a little. "But I need to get a couple of things done. Drop me off at home and I'll meet you back at your place in two hours."

"You promise you'll show up?" she asked, concern in her voice.

Caleb wrapped his arms around her waist and kissed her.

"I'll show up, unless someone tries to kill me again," he said, smiling.

Abby pinched him lightly and kissed him back.

"That's not funny at all. I almost lost you."

Caleb hugged her tight and whispered, "I'm never, ever going anywhere."

Thirty minutes later, Caleb walked out of his house with a duffel bag full of essentials—clothes, toiletries, passport, money, the contents of his box that he picked up from the office, a lock picking kit, and two .45 Magnum pistols with four cartridges. His first stop was Legon campus. He knew Cat wouldn't have stuck around, but there was no harm in checking. People made stupid mistakes all the time. He pulled up to the International Students' Hostel and stepped out of the car, his gun loaded and concealed in the back of his jeans. He walked through the reception, ignored the man behind the desk, and hurried up the stairs to the third floor. He'd never visited Cat at school before, but he knew her room number and he knew the complex. He walked up to the door and turned the handle. It was locked. He looked around the floor. There were people milling about, but no one was looking directly at him. He pulled the kit from his back pocket and selected an instrument. Then he leaned close, inserted the pin, and popped the door open. Caleb glanced around the floor. No eyes on him. He turned the handle and stepped in; his right hand was under his shirt on the gun, prepared for anything.

As his eyes adjusted to the darkness of the room, he realized there was nothing to prepare for. The room was completely empty and bare. You couldn't even tell that it'd been lived in a week ago. All the same, he searched it thoroughly, but there was nothing. Caleb stepped out and closed the door. He walked up to a group of students leaning against the balcony a few hundred feet from him.

"Hey, I'm looking for Cat Daly. Do you guys know where she is?"

"Oh, Cat had a family emergency. She packed up everything and left on Monday. I think it's really bad. It's her mom or something," one of them said.

Caleb nodded, mumbled thanks, and walked away. He knew she wouldn't be here, but he didn't like to leave anything to chance. He dialed as he walked toward his car.

"So, you're alive. You could have called me."

"Sorry about that. I wanted to get out of the hospital first. I really appreciate what you did. I didn't think I'd make it. I owe you, bro."

"Come on, brothers for life. You know that. So, who did this? What happened?"

"Cat Daly, the recent student I was with."

"Huh? The hot American student?"

"Yes, obviously there's more to it, so I need you to find her. She's a Chicago native, lived there all her life, final year University of Chicago student. Her passport number is 871440023, and Social Security is 987-65-4328. I should have had you run a background check on her when I first met her, but I assumed she was just another clueless student. Find her and call me as soon as you have details."

"Got it. Glad to hear your voice, bro."

"I'm glad to hear my own voice too."

Caleb hung up. He had one more stop to make.

⌣

"Hello, Justice."

Annan looked up from his newspaper and jumped at the sight of the gun fixed on him.

"Good God, Caleb, are you crazy?"

"Funny, people always ask me that when I point guns at them," Caleb said, stepping closer to the Justice. Annan stepped backward, but he really had nowhere to go. The windows were directly behind him, and his desk was right in front. He glanced around his study, but there was no other exit except for the one Caleb had just walked through. He glanced down at his desk, but there was also nothing with which he could fight back. Caleb could shoot him dead in seconds.

"What is this, Caleb? You think I had something to do with what happened to you? Abby called me. I came over that night they found you, and I was there again the next day. I personally wrote the statement that was released to the press. I've been talking to Agyari all week about what happened. I've been trying to get to the bottom of this! How can you stand there and think I did this? Obviously, it was the GFP."

Caleb inched closer.

"The GFP didn't hire a girl I've been dating for three months to poison me with a sophisticated and deadly poison. They're too reckless and small-minded for that. This was orchestrated by someone smart, careful, and thorough."

"Gyedu and Bedu were only arrested on Tuesday. They could have done this. You have no idea how far these guys will go. They're desperate, and it shows. In any case, it wasn't me either. Why would I try to have you killed, huh? You think it's because you confronted me about the affair? You think I'd actually risk everything because I got caught cheating? An affair won't bring me down. You and I both know that. I have nothing to gain by killing you."

Caleb switched the safety off and stretched the gun closer to the Justice.

"People do unpredictable things," he said.

"Caleb, I didn't do this. You've known me for ten years. You've been like a son to me. I didn't do this."

"I want you to listen to me very carefully, sir. I am not very...what's the word? Ah yes, I'm not very forgiving with people who try to kill me. That's an absolute no-no. Josh Winkler can attest to that."

Caleb lowered the gun and stared at the now silent Justice.

"So consider this a courtesy chat, because if you did this, if you tried to kill me, trust me, there won't be a conversation next time."

Then Caleb turned and walked away. He was over an hour late, and he didn't want Abby to think he'd stood her up.

⌐

"So, are you ready to talk?" Abby asked, staring at Caleb, who was slouched in her passenger seat. His eyes were closed, but she knew he was awake. They'd only been driving for about twenty minutes.

Caleb's eyelids fluttered open, but he didn't look at her straightaway. He was surprised it'd taken her two days to ask him what was going on. She'd quietly and patiently nursed him back to his feet, but he knew the inquisition would come eventually. He sat upright and nodded.

"What do you want to know?"

"Let's start with Josh Winkler. I told you he threatened my father, and you said you'd handle it. What did you do?"

Caleb was silent. He thought she'd ask about the poisoning.

"Caleb, did you kill Josh? Did you frame him?"

He took a deep breath. He was on a dangerous precipice, and even though jumping was unwise, it was also unsafe to stay on the ledge.

"I didn't frame him. He stole millions of dollars from Insel and made millions more through deals with the government. I didn't frame him, but yes, I killed him because he hired men to come and kill me."

Abby sucked in her breath and gasped like she'd been punched. She briefly lifted her hands off the steering wheel and then grabbed it again. Tears flooded her eyes, and she blinked rapidly.

"He was unarmed, and you shot him. You just shot him."

"Yes, I did," Caleb replied.

Abby slowed down and pulled off to the side of the road. She got out of the car quickly, gasping for air as his words hit home hard. He'd actually killed Josh. Caleb stepped out of the car and walked over to her.

"What do you want to do?" he asked quietly.

Abby dropped down to her knees on the gravel and buried her face in her hands. Eventually, she looked up at him.

"I don't know what to say. I feel responsible. I'm the one who told you he threatened Daddy."

"Josh was unarmed, yes, but he tried to kill me. I don't take that very lightly."

"And who poisoned you? Did you handle that too? Is that why you asked for two hours? Did you go kill someone?"

"I haven't handled that yet," he replied calmly.

Abby cussed and lowered her head directly into her hands.

"You need to make a choice, Abby. We can turn around and go back, and you can do whatever you want to do, or we can keep driving to Ada like planned. Frankly, I'd rather be in Accra hunting down whoever tried to kill me, but you wanted to be away together, and I do want to be away with you. So, I'm willing to postpone my retribution for a few days. The choice is yours."

Abby remained on the ground with her face buried in her arms as she rocked back and forth. Caleb stood quietly over her. She stood up after five minutes and stared directly at him. He could see the tears glistening in her eyes.

"No more killing, please," she said softly, staring into his eyes.

"I can't promise you that," he murmured, maintaining her gaze.

"Caleb—"

He interrupted her. "There was a girl I was seeing, from Legon. She came to my hotel room Sunday and stabbed me with a syringe full of Strychnine, a very deadly poison. We dated for over three months, and she stabbed me without a flicker of remorse. Someone very smart, resourceful, and determined either hired her before I knew her or got to her while we were dating. Either way, I need to find them."

"So, you invited her up to your hotel room Sunday night, when you were with me Sunday morning?"

Caleb allowed himself to smile.

"That's the part you heard? You have nothing to worry about. Obviously that relationship is over," he chuckled.

"I'm not worried about some psychotic girl you were sleeping with. And yes, I heard everything else too. You need to know that this is Ghana. You can't just go about killing people. We don't do things like that here. This isn't Chicago, or some war front in Iraq or wherever you've been. You need to let the police handle this. I told you to talk to them after you woke up, but you said you didn't remember how any of this happened. "

"You want me to talk to who? The Ghana police? That's the police you're referring to, right? Okay, let me call them now and tell them my ex-girlfriend stabbed me with poison. I'm sure they'll find her and whoever's behind it soon," he said sarcastically.

"Caleb—"

"Damn it, Abby! Are you hearing me? She used a poison! She didn't stab me with a knife or shoot me with a gun because she knew I could overpower her if she tried that. She planned this to a T. She used a fucking poison. Do you have any idea what thinking and planning goes into that? So I'm sorry, Abby, I can't promise you anything. Decide now: back to Accra or continue to Ada?"

Abby got into the driver's seat and started the car. Caleb climbed in next to her and stared out the window as she got back on the road. The Tema highway exit was ten minutes away. Whatever decision she made was entirely up to her now.

⤷

Justice Annan paced up and down the room, wringing his hands as he walked. He'd been waiting for over thirty minutes. Where was Samuel? Unfortunately, the former president's living room didn't have a bar or a fridge, so Annan couldn't even make himself a drink. The assistant who led him into the room to wait for Samuel only gave him a bottle of water, and he desperately needed something stronger than Voltic. He knew where the bar was—just a few steps away in the main dining room—but he didn't feel like making the thirty-second journey. His head was spinning, and his heart was beating fast. He needed to talk to Samuel now.

"Kofi, bring some drinks in here. I'm sure the Justice would appreciate a cold beer."

Annan swung around at the sound of the former president's voice.

"What were you doing? I've been waiting for thirty minutes! You know better than to keep me waiting like this."

The former president and Annan had known each for over forty years and were very close, so rank and title didn't matter so much in private. As such, Samuel didn't even blink at Annan's raised voice and tone. "What would you like to drink? Actually, you know what, I know what would be good for you. I received a shipment of Dos Equis a few days ago. Kofi, bring some bottles into my office, okay?" Samuel said to the assistant hanging around the doorway. Then Samuel walked off in the direction of his office. Annan followed quickly.

Annan wasn't impressed easily, but he was always impressed by Samuel's style and taste. Samuel was one of the few men in Ghana with comparable wealth to his. It was wealth both men amassed before Samuel won the presidential ticket in the 2000 elections. Although to be fair, it was wealth that slowly, but obviously, got multiplied during the eight years they were in power. For Samuel, it was hard to tell that he'd been out of the limelight for four years. He'd expanded his home recently, and his office alone looked like a sizable studio apartment. The sitting area of the office was lavish and plush, with imported high-end pieces from the B&B Italia Home collection. He'd mentioned once that his sofa cost $20,000. Beyond the sitting area was the actual office, completely furnished with pieces from Baker Furniture. The office area had two distinct spaces: the main desk and chairs, and a conference table with chairs. There were also floor-to-ceiling bookshelves, paintings, high-end rugs, and art deco pieces.

Annan sat in one of the armchairs in the sitting area, and Samuel dropped into the other. Annan started to speak, but Samuel raised his hand.

"Drinks first."

A few minutes later, Kofi, the assistant, brought in four Dos Equis bottles. He set two up on the center table and then deposited the other two in the fridge in the corner of the room. As soon as Kofi was gone and the door was closed, Samuel spoke.

"So, you created a monster."

"I didn't create him. He was probably born that way," Annan responded heatedly.

"You basically brought a lion into the den of zebras. I told you that hiring someone with his military background could be risky. A marine of all people, Joseph."

"I didn't know about his military background when I first made the offer. It was a good decision. I stand by that. We needed someone with his drive, smarts, tenacity, discipline, and commitment. How many people in your staff would you say exhibit half of his qualities?"

Samuel shrugged. "None of the people on my staff have pulled a gun on me, either."

Annan grimaced. "He felt betrayed, so he was suspicious. I'm not too concerned about Caleb. I just want to know if you were stupid and reckless enough to do what I forbid you to do. Tell me the truth, now."

"Forbid me? Joseph, I know you. You may have told me to hold off on the phone, but I could hear the panic in your office. In any case, it wasn't your decision to make alone. I have a stake in this too. I have a lot to lose if this man of yours starts to poke his nose in places he shouldn't. We really need to figure out what to do about your ticking time bomb, because that's what he is, a ticking time bomb. I don't know Caleb as well as you do, but I've worked with him to a large extent, and we both know he's not going to give up. He's probably concluded that this second attempt wasn't GFP, no matter how much we spin that story in the media."

Annan drank his beer and tried to think. Samuel kept talking.

"We do need to find another way to get rid of Caleb."

Annan shook his head vehemently.

"We? There is no 'we' here. I told you not to do anything! What were you thinking? It's too soon. It doesn't make any sense that the GFP would try multiple times to kill one man. That won't fly with anyone. This is Ghana, and we're not in the middle of a coup. Plus, Caleb will see any other attempt coming from a mile away. We just need to lie low, and you need to help me win this election."

Samuel paused. He was reluctant to agree with Annan.

"I hope you're not suggesting we leave him alone because he's with your daughter."

Annan's nostrils flared, and he leaned forward.

"My daughter has nothing to do with this. If I knew we'd be successful, I'd say go ahead, send someone to shoot him, or stab him, or whatever else you can think of, but I know it won't work. His awareness is probably heightened now. He'll be on guard. But if you really want to know, yes, I don't want to put my daughter in harm's way either. He found out about the affair, and I panicked. I shouldn't have, and you shouldn't have either. Caleb is off limits now, do you understand? I just want to focus on the elections. That's it."

"Fine, we'll do it your way. But Joseph, remember that there's $300 million at stake here. That is our endgame. We have to protect this deal at all costs. You need to be president, and we need to get this money. We've come too far to have your rogue chief of staff derail us. I'm not prepared to have anyone come between me and that money, and that includes your boy Caleb," Samuel said sternly.

"You know, Caleb would have been the best person to help us with that deal. We've been able to make and keep over $20 million thanks to him."

"We decided together that this was too big a deal to include him. For God's sake, he quit working for you because he found out you had an affair. You think he'd go ahead and let us make a deal with a company he detests for $300 million? I would rather get the money and then figure out how to stash it than lose it altogether. So stay on top of this. If Caleb comes close to finding out, I will walk up to him and put a bullet in his head myself."

Annan ignored Samuel's comment and continued drinking his beer. He wished they had involved Caleb from the beginning, but he also knew there was sense in what Samuel said. Maybe he shouldn't have called Samuel that

Sunday night and told him that Caleb had found out about his affair. He and Samuel both knew that the minute Caleb found out about the affair and lost faith in Annan, he was likely to find out more. Even though Caleb had lived in Ghana for ten years now, his thinking and methods were deeply rooted in his upbringing in Chicago and his military background. After this second botched attempt on his life, there was no way he would stop digging. And knowing Caleb, it was likely he'd find a whole lot more, like the business deal Annan and Samuel had been working on and nursing for three years. It was only a matter of time before everything came crumbling down. Caleb would do everything to find out who tried to kill him, and most likely he'd succeed. They'd poked a damn sleeping bear, and it was about to get ugly.

18

Soft sunlight drifted into the room and bathed them in a warm glow. Caleb stretched lazily and turned from lying on his back to his side. Abby's naked back was to him, and he leaned forward and kissed her on the nape of her neck. She stirred a little, but continued sleeping. He gently stroked her arm, trying not to wake her up. An overwhelming feeling of content washed over him, and he kissed her neck again. The last three days had been bliss and more peaceful than he thought possible. Once Abby decided to continue on to Ada with him, she was committed, and so was he. They switched their phones off as soon as they arrived at the Annan's massive lakefront home. Caleb had been there several times over the last ten years, but it felt different being there alone with Abby.

The first night they were there, he used the outdoor grill and cooked some meats she'd asked the housekeeper to stockpile before they'd arrived. Then they sat on the lakefront deck, ate, and talked, with the water lapping softly underneath their feet. Caleb's confession fever had subsided, and he was more cautious about what he shared. He told her a little about his marine buddy back in the US who called her with the antidote, but he didn't reveal names, and he didn't talk about the other ways his friend had helped. Then he spoke about his parents and how they were initially against him getting involved in Ghana politics. Discussing his family was safer, so he stayed on that topic for a while. Eventually Abby asked about women, but he was reluctant to discuss his cycle of sleeping with students. He was oddly embarrassed by it, and he didn't want to come across as a dog. Weirdly enough, it was easier to confess that he had killed Josh than it was for him to talk about women. Abby tried to bring up the topic of Reyn, but he avoided that too. She obviously still cared for him, and knowing that was hard for Caleb to deal with. After dinner and talking, they went for a late night swim in the pool and then made love with a passion that threatened to engulf them both.

The next three days were just as idyllic as the first night. They talked, cooked, ate, swam, took the speed boat out for rides, went on long walks, and spent extended periods in bed making love or just lazying about. Each day he spent with her helped him peel back the layers that sheathed Abiel Annan. She was incredibly strong and defiant, a true firecracker like her father. Yet, she was also extremely caring and sensitive. She was like a medley of unpredictable emotions. It kept him on his toes, and he enjoyed it. It still surprised him that he could shut everything out and just be with her. He was one hundred percent focused on her, and it made him feel human and complete.

After staring at Abby lying next to him for minutes, Caleb got up from bed, pulled his pants on, and walked out of the house to the lakefront deck, his cell phone tucked into his pocket. He'd kept his promise of no phone, but after three days, he was antsy. He really needed to find out who'd tried to kill him. He was content spending time alone with Abby, but he couldn't get the picture of Cat stabbing him with a needle out of his mind. He'd come close to dying, and he was only alive out of pure luck. It was luck that he was staying at the City, a hotel with an onsite clinic. It was even greater luck that the clinic had a doctor on call that night with experience in infectious diseases and poisons. Pure luck was the only reason he was still alive, and he hated that thought. Someone very resourceful and smart had tried to kill him, and had almost succeeded. He had to find out whom.

Caleb leaned against one of the pillars supporting the lakefront deck and dialed. He'd used his personal cell phone more than he would have liked, but he had no choice. His extreme paranoia hadn't helped him much in the past two weeks or prevented Cat from getting to him, so who cared if he made one more call from his cell?

"I hate to tell you this, but I don't have much to report on. I have her on security cameras leaving JFK Tuesday morning, but that's it. A man in a black Ford picked her up, but there's no trace of them or the car after that. Not even a ping on any credit cards in her name."

"It's only been a week. She may pop up somewhere," Caleb said.

"She's not going to. Cat Daly didn't exist until four months ago."

"What?" Caleb stepped away from the pillar.

"I think she's a professional, Caleb. The name and social security didn't exist up until four months ago when she just popped up in Chicago. Within a span of one month, she got a Chicago state driver's license, a passport, and a University of Chicago student ID. There's no trace of her prior to that. You really shouldn't have stopped me from running background checks on the girls."

Caleb grimaced. It was difficult staying on top of everything all the time, and after screening several of the other American students with whom he'd been involved, he decided it wasn't necessary anymore. They were exactly who he thought they were: young students who just wanted to have mindless foreign experiences. So over the last two years, he hadn't done any background checks on them. It was tough for him to process what he was hearing. The implication was just too much. If Cat didn't exist up until four months ago, then there was something big going on. Someone hired her, created the Cat Daly persona, and sent her down to date Caleb and, when the time was right, kill him. And why would anyone plan all of that four months ago? The Justice only announced his intentions to run for president three weeks ago. Who could he have been a threat to months ago? Caleb closed his eyes. How was any of this possible? This was Ghana. Politicians didn't go that far to win elections. A worrying thought crossed his mind.

"Maybe this is Company?" his friend asked, voicing what was on Caleb's mind.

"The CIA was involved in Ghana politics over forty years ago, so I guess anything is feasible, but it doesn't really make sense. Why would they be back now? The Justice is nothing like Kwame Nkrumah, and he's not a threat to any American ideals or interests. It doesn't make any sense at all."

They were both silent for a while, and then his friend spoke.

"I'll send you the picture of the man who picked her up. I'm trying to track the license plate, but I suspect that was forged."

Caleb cringed. This was too much.

"Find me something. Cross-reference Cat's name with everyone on our list, including the Justice and every single damn prominent person in Ghana. And then check with your contacts. Find out if this could be Company, but be careful on that. I don't want us to get into something above us. I know my limits, but try and find her. She's the key to figuring this whole thing out."

❧

Abby yawned and stretched lazily in bed. She turned to her side and frowned, disappointed Caleb wasn't next to her. She lay back on the bed and allowed her mind to wander. She'd made the decision to continue to Ada with Caleb because she was undeniably in love with him, which thrilled and scared her at the same time. She couldn't quite get over the fact that he'd killed Josh, but she was too in love to stay away from him. She was a goner the minute he kissed her that Friday night in his house, and there was no fighting it, no matter how hard she tried. It took several months after she and Reyn first hooked up for her to fall in love with him, but with Caleb it took only one night. She found his mysterious persona sexy and exhilarating. He was definitely cold, stoic, and dangerous, but over the last few weeks he'd displayed a caring, sensitive layer that touched her very core. Knowing that there was more to him excited her.

Abby knew she was in a hopeless situation. Caleb admitted a couple of days ago that he had quit working for her father. He jokingly said the job was hazardous to his health. They hadn't really discussed what was next for him, and Abby was afraid to ask. Would he even want to stay and be with her? And if he decided to leave and asked her to come along, would she be able to leave with him? She'd dreamt about leaving Ghana with Reyn to start the vineyard he'd always talked about, but there was something about Caleb that made her wonder if they could truly be together.

She had to admit that the past three days were near perfect. Caleb was incredibly attentive and loving. He never spoke the three words she ached to hear, but his actions spoke volumes. He was hugging, holding, and kissing her every chance he got. And each time they made love, she could feel the intensity of his love through his touch and his eyes. She didn't pressure him to say it out loud. It was really enough that he was with her. God, she loved him with an intensity that really scared her. Someone had tried to kill him. That was a fact, and since he had no idea who was behind it, she knew it could happen again. What would she do if she lost Caleb for good? If losing Reyn to his wife was painful, then losing Caleb in any way would be devastating. She doubted she could survive it.

Abby sighed and got up from the bed. She pulled on a shirt and then walked out to the deck. Caleb was sitting there staring intently at his phone. As she drew close, she could make out the profile of a man and a woman. The structure of the man looked familiar, but before Abby could get more details, Caleb slipped the phone into his pocket and stood up. His eyes were dark and pensive.

"I need to leave," he said.

Abby paused mid-step and then continued walking toward him.

"Did something happen? Any news on who tried to kill you?"

"No," Caleb lied. "I just have a lot I need to sort out. I can't just stay here."

Abby reached for his hand.

"Talk to me, Caleb. Something has happened. I can see it on your face. I saw the way you were looking at the picture on your phone. Who are they?"

Caleb pulled his hand away and sat back down.

"I just need to leave, okay?"

"Suit yourself, don't talk to me, but you need to remember what I said before. This is Ghana. You honestly can't go around killing people, no matter what. If you know something, you need to talk to the police. I won't deal with it, honestly. If you take matters into your own hands and you kill one more person, I'm through," Abby said firmly.

"So, I know where you stand, and you know where I stand," Caleb's voice was equally firm and cold.

"Fine, whatever, it's early. I'll go fix us breakfast, and then we can leave later in the morning."

Caleb waited until she was gone, and then he took his phone out and stared at the picture again. It had been four years since Bertha got killed, but he remembered the morning after it happened like it was yesterday. It was Sunday, and he was asleep in bed with one of his girls when the Justice called him. The Justice could barely speak, but eventually he managed to get the words out. Bertha had been killed, and Adubea was the one who found her sister. It took Caleb less than five minutes to get to Bertha's house. The Justice and Adubea were in the house, bundled together in the living room, and the two of them were sobbing. The police were on the scene, and a crowd had already gathered outside. What had happened was unusual for the relatively calm, upper-middle-class neighborhood, so the neighbors had all poured outside to watch. As Caleb drove past the crowd, one face stood out to him, a dark, tall muscled man who stood on the street outside Bertha's house. He was wearing some type of security uniform, but he wasn't with G4S, the firm that the Justice used for both his home and Bertha's. The man had his hands in his pockets and was observing the scene calmly and quietly. Caleb noticed him because he just seemed out of place. It was around 9 a.m., but the man was fully dressed and had on dark sunglasses. He also didn't look like a curious spectator. He looked unusually calm and composed. He was not chatting or gossiping like the other onlookers. He simply stood there. Caleb went back out as soon as he parked his car in Bertha's driveway, but when he stepped back out onto the street, the man was gone. Caleb's paranoid mind had pondered this detail for a few days afterward, but once the police found the robbers and the stash, he'd let it go until today.

Caleb gripped the phone tightly. This couldn't be a coincidence. The mysterious man who was outside Bertha's house was the same man who picked up Cat from the airport. What were the odds that that could be pure coincidence? This didn't start with the Justice's announcement, and it didn't start when Cat appeared out of nowhere in Chicago. Whatever was going on had been in play for a long time. Abby could repeat a hundred times that this was Ghana, but what was happening was happening here and now. He was also certain that the Justice was the key, which was why he couldn't tell Abby or hand this over to the police. If his mentor and idol was behind all of this and involved in something more sinister than an affair and an illegitimate child, then Caleb would have to keep the promise he'd made to the Justice: next time he pointed a gun at him, there would be no conversation.

19

The smell of bleach, soap and a host of other detergents overwhelmed Caleb the minute he stepped into his house. The cleaning crew had cleaned thoroughly, no doubt about that, but they'd also closed and locked every window and door. And in the week and a half that Caleb had been gone, the smell had taken on a life of its own. Caleb dropped his bags on the floor in the foyer and walked around opening his windows and doors. Thirty minutes later, the whole house was bathed in sunlight, and the smell had abated. The damage was also even more glaring in the sunlight. Caleb's walls, living room furniture, and bedroom door were riddled with bullets from the AK-47 as the third gunman made his way from the kitchen door to the bedroom. The cream-colored carpets lining his foyer, living room, and hallway, though clean, were also discolored and distorted beyond repair.

He bought the house six years ago, and he'd carefully and lovingly renovated, decorated, and modified it to suit his style and needs. It was a modest, but modern, three-bedroom house, no more than three thousand square feet. He'd done a great deal of work and ended up with a full modern kitchen with an island, a sunroom furnished with cozy wicker pieces, a welcoming foyer and living room, and a man-cave where he kept up with American sports, usually by himself. It'd been his sanctuary for a long time, and even though he brought his girlfriends home, it was still a place he regarded as his private space. This was where his parents stayed when they visited, although they hadn't visited in a long while. He preferred to have them removed from his life and work in Ghana. Now, his sanctuary had been desecrated.

Caleb sat quietly in his bullet-riddled sofa and placed his feet on the center table as feelings of tiredness, frustration, and loss washed over him. He wasn't just grieving the destruction and invasion of his home, he was grieving the unexpected and unwelcome changes in his life. The loss he felt was also compounded by the way he'd left things with Abby. Their drive back to Accra was silent, with only the sounds from the radio filling the void between them in the car. She was upset he wouldn't open up and share, and upset that he couldn't promise he wouldn't kill someone else. He understood how she felt, and he wished he could just let it all go and leave the country with her. He'd always wanted to live on an exotic, semi-private island, and he could picture himself doing that with Abby. They could relocate to the Maldives, Bali, or the Seychelles. He'd never been to any of those islands. He could afford to go, but it was a trip he wanted to do with someone special, and he just hadn't met someone who even came close, except for Abby. He deeply wanted to give her what she wanted, what she deserved, but he couldn't. Someone tried to kill him, and that wasn't something he could easily let go. He'd been in Ghana for ten years, and he'd never felt this incompetent and incapable before. He felt as if he'd lived in a bubble for the last ten years—a bubble where he erroneously thought he knew everything that was going on in the political world, a bubble where he thought he was the master of the world he governed. And in three short weeks, that bubble had come crashing down. He was the master of nothing.

Caleb knew he was being hard on himself, but he felt he deserved it. The Justice had an affair with his wife's sister and fathered a son, and Caleb, the supposedly ever-astute chief of staff, had absolutely no clue. A girl he'd dated for three months had tried to kill him with a sophisticated poison, and he had no clue who she was, who sent her, or why his death mattered to this person. If he couldn't figure out who tried to kill him, his ego would never recover. It would haunt him till the day he died, and so he couldn't just walk away, even if he cared very deeply for Abby. He owed it to both himself and his sanity to finish this, and he hoped that Abby would still love him through it all. He just had to try not to kill anyone.

❧

"Nancy Schaffer?"

The short, petite blond girl swung around and squinted up at him. She wrinkled her nose defiantly.

"Who's asking?"

"I'm Caleb, with the US Embassy. We're looking for Cat Daly. Her parents have reported her missing."

The girl's eyes widened, and she gripped his arm tightly as she looked fearfully up at him. Caleb winced slightly. For a small-sized person, she was surprisingly strong. She let go of his arm and dropped down onto the bench behind her. Caleb sat down next to her, held her hands, and started to talk, trying hard to maintain the fake concern in his voice.

"We have you listed as one of her friends at the school, but we don't have much more to go on. So we need you to help us. Tell us everything you can about everyone she interacted with here, at the school and off campus. We need to find her."

"Oh my God, of course I'll help. I'm just so stunned. Cat left over a week ago, or maybe it's been two weeks already. She said her mother was really sick and she had to go. The weird thing is she packed up everything, you know. I figured she'd go and come back, but I went to her room the next day and everything was gone. I didn't expect that. The whole room was bare. She didn't even leave her sheets behind, you know. And I don't even know when or how she did all that. She was out this one day, I think it was a Sunday, and when she came back, she just told me and a couple of other folks that she had to leave. That was it. The next day I was on my balcony, and I saw her get into a black SUV. I think it was a Ford Explorer. There're not many Fords here, so I kinda notice, you know?"

Caleb listened intently, trying to pick up useful bits of information from the rambling. The good part was she wasn't asking him a lot of questions.

Nancy continued, becoming more animated as she talked.

"I never saw who was driving or anything. And she was only carrying a duffel bag when she got into the car, that's why I was so surprised when I went to her room later that day and everything was gone. She had a single room. I have a single room too. Some folks think the single rooms in these hostels are expensive, but they're not. I'd rather have my privacy than share a room with three other girls, you know. It's only about a hundred dollars more a month. I mean, that's peanuts, right?"

Caleb smiled a little and nodded. This was going to be painful.

"Well, so anyways, I don't know when she got everything packed. She must have done it in the night. I was out partying, not doing anything crazy, mind you. Cat didn't really like to party, which is fine; she would have stolen all the attention. She was super hot. I think she had a boyfriend though, but I suspect she had two of them somewhere."

"Two?" Caleb interrupted.

"Well, that's just my thinking. There was this one I saw around here just a couple of times. He was tall, really dark, burly looking. My balcony overlooks the car park you know, so I see a lot. Not like I'm spying or anything, but I like people watching."

Caleb smiled. A people watcher who couldn't stop talking—maybe this would yield something after all.

"I like people watching too," he said and winked at her, trying to establish a common bond.

Nancy's face lit up.

"It's fascinating, isn't it? You get a sense of who people really are when you watch them without them knowing that you're watching. Anyways, I saw him here at the car park about twice or so. They didn't look particularly intimate, but she acted all mysterious when I asked her later, so I figured there was more to it. The second time was a couple of days before she left. She was really quiet after that visit. Thoughtful, I think."

"So she never told you anything about this guy?"

"I'm sorry, but she didn't say anything, and I'm only guessing about the second guy because she was out quite a bit. It felt like she had someone else somewhere, but like I said, I am only guessing. Cat was very private, you know. We were barely even friends. Hey, so how did you get my name?"

First question from her, but he was already prepared for that.

"She mentioned you to her parents. They gave us your name, but they didn't have anything else," he lied.

Truthfully, Caleb remembered Nancy Schaffer from Cat's Facebook. There was one night at his place when Cat spent an hour on Facebook tagging pictures from a trip to the Western Region and rambling on about the people she'd gone with. He remembered Nancy's name because one of his best friends from the Marines was called Schaffer. And he remembered telling Cat that Nancy was the opposite of a buddy he knew who was six foot two and dark-haired. Cat joked that they should do a Facebook introduction, and Caleb declined. Once again, he wished he'd done a background check on Cat and paid more attention to her life. Her Facebook and Twitter pages had been deactivated, and he had nothing to go on. Nancy was a chatterbox, but she hadn't really given him much. He dug into his pocket and pulled out the picture of the mystery man from the airport. He showed it to Nancy.

"Oh my God, that's him! The man in the car park! What's going on here? Isn't that JFK airport? Did Cat run away with him or something?"

Caleb tucked the picture back into his pocket.

"We don't know. All we know is there's nothing wrong with her parents. She didn't show up at home, and the police can't find her. She's disappeared, so her parents asked the embassy to look into it on this end. They're very worried and desperate, so Nancy, anything at all you can share, trust me, it could help. We need a name. We need something to help us find him, and her."

"Oh my God, I don't know. I really don't know, but Page might."

Caleb frowned. "Page?"

"Honestly, I wasn't that close to Cat. We hung out a couple of times and we went on one trip or so, but Page Affleck was her friend. They had the same classes, and their rooms were next to each other. Page is in the study room now. Give me five minutes, and I'll get her."

Before Caleb could respond, Nancy was up and off, running across the grass toward the hostel. Caleb leaned back against the bench and glanced around the little park. He'd dated countless American students who lived in this hostel, but this was the first time he'd spent more than five minutes on campus. The University had tried to make the hostel resemble an American campus, with the little park area off to the side of the car park. A couple of students were throwing Frisbees, and there were some others lying on blankets spread on the grass. There was a fountain right in the center of the park, and a couple of girls had their heads stuck under the flowing water. It was a serene sight, but he also knew this serene environment had harbored a cold-blooded contract killer. Cat had probably lounged in this very same park, played Frisbee, hung out with friends, and then gotten up and gone to his hotel room with a syringe full of poison.

"You're looking for Cat?"

Caleb stood and stared at the girl before him. A few months ago, he would have been weak in the knees for her. She was breathtakingly stunning. She was tall, close to six feet for sure, with a body that should be on a pedestal and worshipped. She had on really short shorts that displayed long, muscled yet soft-looking thighs and legs. The wife beater she had on accentuated her full breasts and flat abs.

Caleb swallowed.

"I'm Caleb, from the US Embassy. We're looking for Cat," he delivered the words absentmindedly as he struggled to keep his eyes from her body and on her face, a flawless face that was framed by her cascading black hair.

"I don't know where Cat is. She left to go see her mother a couple of weeks ago, but she took everything with her. I've emailed her, but my messages keep bouncing back. Her Facebook and Twitter accounts are down too."

Caleb nodded. "We know that. This man was with her at JFK the day she arrived in the US. Nancy says he was here at the hostel a couple of times as well. We think he may have her."

Page took the picture and nodded.

"That's Linc. He's American. Well, at least that's what she told me. I saw them in the car park once, and I asked

her about him. She said she met him at the mall or something, and he gave her a ride. I thought it was the mysterious boyfriend she was seeing. She had someone in town.
She never told me his name. She was very private. Anyways,
this wasn't the boyfriend. She just said his name was Linc
and that he gave her a ride. I thought he looked army or
something. My dad was in the army, so I notice types like
that. You look army too, but then since you're from the embassy and investigating the disappearance of an American,
it's not surprising. I'm thinking ex-Marine? FBI? CIA?"

Caleb smiled. This girl was astute and fascinating.
Where was she when he met Cat? He could have hooked
up with her instead of the psycho killer he ended up with.

"Do you remember anything else about Linc, or anything you can share about where Cat could be? Trust me,
any little detail you have could help," he said, ignoring her
last questions.

"Actually, I'm not surprised she's with Linc. She seemed
like she was into him, even though she denied that it was
her mystery boyfriend. It was strange. They were standing
next to some dark car, can't remember what model it was.
She had her head down, and he was talking. He looked serious, and surly. I watched them for just a couple of minutes
to make sure she was okay. They weren't there for long. He
got into his car, and then he was gone. All she said was that
he was an American she met at the mall, his name was Linc,
and he gave her a ride back, nothing more to it. I'm sorry,
but I have no idea where she is."

Caleb nodded. At least he had a name. Whether it was
a real name or not, he didn't know.

"Do you have a card? In case I remember something?"
Page asked.

"Why don't I take your number instead?"

Page smiled, and Caleb took a deep breath again. No wonder Page and Cat were friends. Beautiful girls tended to hang out together. He just hoped this one wasn't a hired gun as well. He dug into his pocket and pulled out a note-pad and a pen. Page rambled some numbers off, including her US cell, Facebook name, and Twitter handle.

"Hey, take my numbers too," Nancy quipped.

Caleb politely took hers as well. He doubted he'd have a need to call either one of them. They'd given him all they had. Sure, Page was stunning, but it would be extremely foolish on his part to hook up with her even if Abby wasn't talking to him. He had a singular purpose: to find Linc and Cat and find out what the heck was going on. He couldn't allow himself to get distracted, not even by an Amazon-like goddess.

"Call me," Page said, her eyes twinkling at him, the first signs of flirting since she had started talking.

Caleb couldn't help flirting back. He leaned close and whispered in her ear.

"You can count on it."

Then he walked away without glancing back. He had a name. Now what?

20

*A*bby threw her handbag and computer case onto the floor of her living room and walked into the bedroom. She pulled back the covers and crawled into bed. It was only 6 p.m., but she wanted to lie in her bed and allow the tears to flow. She'd held them back for the last two days. She'd restrained herself throughout the drive back to Accra with Caleb, and even though she almost lost it when she dropped him home and watched him walk away, she'd kept it together. She'd kept it together at work today, and it was probably one of her most productive days in a while. Now, she couldn't hold anything back any longer. When the tears started, Abby felt no relief, only aching pain. Was this what her life had been reduced to? Daily crying? That's all she'd done for the last few weeks, and it made her feel weak and helpless. This wasn't her at all. She used to have a good life.

At least, that's what she thought. She had a good job that paid well, even if her bosses always wanted favors. Even more, she had a man who loved and worshipped her, even if he technically belonged to someone else. Now what did she have? She'd taken a two-week leave of absence from work when Caleb got poisoned, and even though she'd returned to work today, she wasn't even sure she wanted to go back. Her work suddenly had no meaning anymore. She'd lost Reyn, the first true love of her life, and before she could even recover from that, she'd fallen hard for Caleb, a man who'd killed four people recently and couldn't promise that they were his last. She didn't want to belittle what had happened to him, but his methods were wrong. Sure, the Ghana police weren't as well-trained or resourced as the police force in the US, but they'd still found the men responsible for Auntie Bertha's murder. If Caleb told them what he knew, and if he helped them, they could find who tried to kill him, too. It was a long shot, but it was the right thing to do, except Caleb wanted to go off and be like a lone ranger.

The doorbell rang, startling Abby out of her self-pity daydream. She hoped it was Caleb. He was aggravating and annoying, but she still loved him intensely. If he was there to apologize, she was willing to welcome him back with open arms. Abby hurried toward the door, holding back the smile that was threatening to burst on her face. She couldn't let him know she was that eager to have him back.

"Jesus, Mother? What are you doing here?"

Abby stared in shock at the sight of her mother standing in her doorway. She'd been living in this apartment for almost three years, and her mother hadn't been to visit once. That wasn't really unusual—since her breakdown, her mother's movements were restricted and pre-approved by her father. Even her father hadn't been to her apartment before, so she didn't expect he'd encourage her mother to visit. Abby opened the door wider and stepped aside to let her mother step in. It was Monday, but her mother was dressed like she was heading to church. She wore a tailored light green skirt suit, two-inch white heels, and white pearls around her neck. Her long hair was braided into a loose French twist and accessorized with a costume jewelry hair broach. She looked beautiful and dignified, despite the mental struggles underneath the surface. Abby wondered how long before someone noticed that Adubea Annan was noticeably absent from her husband's campaign, but she also knew her father probably had a reason for her absence prepared and ready for distribution.

"So, this is your apartment. It's very…modern? Or is the word contemporary? What style were you aiming for?" Adubea asked as she walked past Abby and into the living room. Abby's eyes followed her mother's as she stood in the center of the living room and looked around. Abby took a deep breath. *Here we go again,* she thought, as the feelings and inadequacy she felt around her mother started to bubble up.

"I didn't have a particular style in mind, Ma, but let's call it contemporary. I think that works. Do you want something to drink?" Abby started walking toward the kitchen.

"Water is fine," Adubea said as she sat down slowly and cautiously. She straightened her skirt and brushed invisible lint off it. Abby smiled a little as she watched her from the corner of her eye. She pulled a bottle of cold water out of the fridge, got a glass and coasters, and set it all on the center table in front of her mother. Abby sat in the armchair across from her and waited for her mother to pour a glass and take a sip before she started with the questions again.

"What's going on, Ma? Is Daddy okay? How did you know I'd be home?"

Adubea finished the glass of water and then leaned back. Her eyes started to scan the room, and then she focused on Abby.

"Can't I just visit with my own daughter?"

"You've never been here before. Did Darko bring you?"

Adubea looked away from Abby and settled her gaze on the fifty-five-inch LED TV, the same one that Caleb detested.

"Yes, Darko is waiting downstairs in the car. This is a really nice apartment. The building looks very secure, the lobby is impressive, and the doorman is very professional. He told me the property has a full gym and swimming pool. It must be very expensive then. This is a two-bedroom, right?"

Abby sighed. Now she knew for sure her mother's visit wasn't random, but she decided not to press her to talk. She would get to the point eventually.

"Yes, it's a two-bedroom. The door to your right is the main bedroom, and the guest room is over to the left here, just down that short corridor. I set it up as a study, but I hardly use it anyways. I'm always in my bedroom, this living room, or the balcony. That's it."

Adubea was silent, and Abby knew she was trying to find something mundane and safe to talk about before she got to her real purpose. After a two-minute silence, she looked at Abby, a serious look on her face.

"You need to end things with Caleb."

Abby shook her head. This was a new low, even for her father. He was obviously the one who'd told her mother about her relationship with Caleb, and since Darko, her mother's driver, basically reported to her father, then this visit was all orchestrated.

"What did Daddy say, huh? I am a grown woman, Ma, and I can make my own decisions. I understand that Caleb works for Daddy. Well, he said he quit, so honestly, it's my business only."

"It doesn't matter if he doesn't work for your father anymore. They worked together for ten years. Your father knows him better than he knows anyone else, and he's very troubled that you're with Caleb. I'm concerned too. What are you expecting out of this relationship? Caleb isn't the settle-down-and-raise-a-family type."

Abby stood up from her armchair and went to sit next to her mother on the sofa. Her mother's interest in her relationship actually wasn't so bad. Before Auntie Bertha's death, her mother used to check in on her all the time, and the topic of conversation was almost always about the men in her life, or lack thereof. However, since the incident, her mother stopped showing interest in anything except for her father, maintaining her appearance and other OCD behaviors like decorating. She reached for her mother's hands and squeezed.

"I'm not expecting anything, Ma, and it's too early to be thinking along those lines. I'm not in a hurry."

"You're thirty. You're not a child. You can't keep making bad decisions."

Abby frowned. "Bad decisions?"

Adubea pulled her hands away from her daughter and reached for the bottle to refill her glass. Abby waited patiently for a reply.

"What are you talking about, Ma? What bad decisions?"

"You were with a married man," her mother said simply.

Abby cursed out loud. She could kill her father right now. Was this necessary?

"Don't use that language around me," Adubea said firmly.

Abby stood up and threw her hands up in the air, agitated and annoyed.

"Well, I make bad decisions, so why don't you chalk my swearing up to that as well?"

"Abiel Annan, don't you dare talk to me like that. Your father has warned you about that insolent behavior of yours."

Abby stood still, stunned. Adubea stood up and picked up her clutch. She looked directly at her daughter.

"You need to think about what I've said. Caleb isn't the type of person you should be around. I know everything that happened at his house, and the poison attempt afterward. He's dangerous. The life he lives is dangerous. He attracts dangerous people. Abby, you need to listen to us. I've never seen your father this concerned, and you need to take that seriously. End the relationship and encourage Caleb to go back to the US. There is no need for him to still be here."

Abby remained silent. She had no words for how she was feeling. She'd just been blindsided by her mother, but all the words that came out of Adubea's mouth were her father's. She was sure of that.

"Fine, don't respond. Just think about everything I've said and end the relationship. Now."

Abby waited until her mother had left the apartment, and then she dropped into the sofa and pulled her knees up to her chin. What just happened? Had her father no shame? How could he send her mother here to do his dirty work? How could he tell her mother about Reyn, Caleb, and all that had happened? What was he thinking? Did he think at all? He obviously had no concern for her or her mother. If they weren't towing the Joseph Annan line, they were dealt with. Abby buried her face in her hands and sat there. She was so tired. And then the tears that had been interrupted by the doorbell started again. Maybe someday the crying would stop, but until then she was okay sitting on her sofa, crying and wallowing in her pain.

∽

"Darling, you seem distracted. Is everything okay?"

Reyn looked up from his drink and stared at his wife. She looked irritated, and he knew she had a right to be.

"I don't want to be here," he muttered.

"What? Jesus, Reyn, I wanted to stay home and catch up with the boys and my family, remember? You said we had to attend this. You insisted. Now you don't want to be here?" she asked, her voice rising higher than normal.

Reyn glanced around the ballroom, wondering if anyone was looking at him or her, but they were all busy drinking, dancing, or eating. It was Proctor Oil's one-hundredth anniversary dinner party, the first in a series of events planned for the year. He had no choice but to be there. He was the managing director for Africa now. He couldn't skip company events like this, even if they were really unnecessary and wasteful. What he wondered, though, was whose idea it was to have a dinner party on a Tuesday. He had to talk to someone about that, and about the five champagne bottles given to each of the thirty tables. That totaled 150 bottles, and that excluded the liquor flowing from the open bar. Why were they spending so much?

"Reyn?"

Reyn sighed and looked at his wife. Her eyes were narrowed with concern, anger, and irritation, all mixed up and rolling around in her blue pupils. The past few weeks had been mixed for him. There were moments when he was glad to have her around and on his arm—his beloved, beautiful wife and mother of his children. She was such a sport, following him to South Africa and numerous company events and activities. She'd gone with him to check out drill sites and potential homes across South Africa and Ghana. Her preference was still SA, but she assured him Ghana was a strong contender too. He loved her for her efforts, for being here in the first place. And yet, he knew he didn't love her enough. He just didn't. If he did, he wouldn't go to bed each night and wake up each morning with Abby on his mind. If he loved his wife enough, he wouldn't be sitting there, wishing he was in Abby's arms right now, kissing and making love to her. His breath got caught in his throat as the thought of Abby in his arms hit him. How was this possible? How could he love someone this much? It didn't make any sense, especially when he had someone like Emma, the perfect wife. He gripped Emma's hand and walked away from the party. She followed him silently out of the ballroom, through the lobby, and out to the poolside. They settled into a loveseat nestled under a couple of palm trees. Reyn looked down at their intertwined hands, struggling to find words to convey what he was feeling and thinking.

"What is this, Reyn? Talk to me. What is going on?" Emma pressed.

Reyn nodded and started talking.

"I'm not sure this is what I want anymore, Emma."

"This? What does this mean? Can you just talk straight? No meanderings, just talk."

"This—my work, Proctor Oil, my marriage, all of it. It's what I've always wanted all my life, but now that it's happening, it doesn't feel right, or complete. I just feel like I'm a robot, going through some motions laid out before I was born."

"God, Reyn, stop this, stop right now. Did you feel like a robot when you said you loved me, when you swore it would be us until death? Did you feel like a robot when we had our boys, huh? You don't want them anymore either?"

"Emma, I never said that. I'm just struggling here."

"Struggling with what? You have it all. You're destined to run your family's company. You know that, don't you? You're the goddamn managing director of Africa now, and you're what, forty-five? You have me. You have two beautiful boys. You have everything! So what in God's name are you struggling with?" Emma countered.

Reyn was silent. He ran his fingers through his hair and stared out at the ocean before them.

"You're overwhelmed. I get that. You just got promoted, I'm moving back, and we're looking at houses. All of that can be a bit much for you. I get that, but you need to man up and deal with the changes that are happening, because they're good changes."

Reyn remained silent. He wanted a divorce. The words were on his lips, but he couldn't get them out. He needed to be with Abby, and he couldn't win her back if he was still married. A divorce would be his ultimate declaration of love.

"Look at me, baby."

Reyn obeyed and looked at his wife. Her face had gone soft, and she had tears in her eyes.

"I love you, Reyn—"

"I want a divorce," he said quickly, before she could finish.

Emma inhaled sharply. Her eyes widened, and she stared at him, stunned.

"I want a divorce," he repeated, with more conviction than the first time.

"Fine," Emma said quietly.

Reyn was surprised. He'd expected a fight, but he also realized she probably thought he had no idea what he was talking about, and she was willing to entertain him for a little bit. Emma often treated him like a child who was into Superman one minute and then Batman the next. She didn't take him seriously, and so he felt a need to shock her, force her to acknowledge what was happening.

"I had an affair, for three years. And I'm in love with her."

Emma's eyes glistened with tears, and she nodded, a weak smile on her face.

"I suspected. You're a man. I didn't expect you to be twiddling your thumbs down here. Plus, Jeff Hunt told my father that if I wanted to save my marriage then I had to move down here immediately. I figured he suspected you were seeing someone. He sounded serious."

Reyn frowned. "Jeff did what?"

"Does it matter?"

"No, I guess it doesn't. I really want a divorce, Emma."

"I'm going home. You should stay at this hotel for a few days. Think things through. If you want a divorce in a week, I'll give it to you."

She leaned forward and kissed him softly on the cheek. Then she got up and walked away. Reyn looked down at his hands. They were shaking. This was the hardest thing he'd done in a very long time, probably second to the day he broke up with Abby and walked away from her. Most of his friends and colleagues were on their second or third marriages, but he wasn't that type. He couldn't believe this was happening. What if Abby didn't want him? What if this thing with Caleb Osei was serious? What if she was lost to him forever, and he'd asked for a divorce for nothing? Reyn dug his phone out of his pocket and dialed.

⤷

Abby placed the kitchen knife down as she tried to figure out where her ringing cell phone was. Then she remembered it was still tucked into the handbag she'd dumped on the floor of her hallway. She got it out of the bag quickly, hoping it was Caleb. She needed him so desperately, needed some reassurance after the visit from her mother. She glanced at the caller ID and took a deep breath. Reyn. She was aching for one man who just wouldn't call her, but instead she gets the other one who just couldn't let it go.

"What is it, Reyn? I'm not having a good day."

"I love you, Abby. God, I love you so much. I'm sorry about everything, but I can't be without you. I just can't. I asked Emma for a divorce, Abby. I did, because I love you and you're all I want. I don't give a shit about Proctor or about anything, because I know if I'm with you, I'll be okay. That's all that matters to me."

Abby sat cross-legged on her floor and closed her eyes. He asked for a divorce. That was unexpected.

"Baby, please talk to me. Please. I need to see you. I need to talk to you and tell you how I feel. Please let me see you. I can be at your end in ten minutes."

"No, no, you can't come here," Abby said quickly. The last thing she needed was for Caleb to show up unexpectedly and find Reyn in her apartment.

"I'll meet you somewhere," she said.

"I'm at the Crystal Resort, you know the new one off the Labadi beach road?"

"I know it."

"I'll be in the lobby. Thank you, Abby."

Abby hung up and groaned. This was probably a bad idea, but after her mother's visit and Caleb's abandonment, she could do with some words of love tonight. In any case, she was with Reyn for three years. He deserved some face time if he'd finally managed to walk away from his marriage. That was all she was going to do. She was going to listen to him and get some closure on that front. They both needed closure.

⁓

Reyn knew it was risky meeting Abby in the lobby with a Proctor event happening in the ballroom just a few meters away. Anyone could walk out and see them. Everyone knew who she was, and since Reyn and Abby had no professional affiliation, people could assume things. And he wasn't even sure if Emma had left the hotel. What if she'd gone back to the ballroom? He hadn't even asked her how she was going to get home. He had the car keys. Reyn shook his head and tried to clear his mind. He needed to stop caring. It didn't matter if anyone from Proctor saw them. They could gossip. He didn't care. Although out of respect for Emma, he wouldn't want her to see them together. That would be rude. Ask for a divorce one minute and then run into the arms of your mistress less than thirty minutes later? Reyn left the lobby and walked back out to the poolside and toward the beach. It was quiet and private out there. There was a lot of light out there too, but it was still better than the lobby. He texted Abby and told her where he was, and then he waited nervously. What would he do if she turned him down?

"So, you really asked for a divorce?"

Reyn turned around and stared at her. Her hair was pulled back into a loose braid with some tendrils floating around her face. Even with no makeup on, she looked beautiful. He wanted to kiss her, but he also knew he couldn't push his luck and ruin his chances.

"Yeah, I asked for a divorce. I love you, Abby," he said simply.

Abby stepped up and stood next to him. She gripped the railing in front of them and stared out at the rough waves slapping against the rocks in front of her. Her heart felt like that, like it was being pounded and pulled in different directions. She loved Reyn. She wasn't going to deny that. They'd spent three wonderful years together, and she thought she could never love someone as much as she loved him. That was until Caleb somehow got into her heart that night after the awards show. She couldn't explain how she could fall for Caleb so quickly. The sex was unbelievable, yes, but it wasn't just that. Caleb was...Caleb was just it for her.

"I love you too, Reyn, but I don't know if I can do this with you. I'm..." Abby paused as she saw pain flash across his face. She felt her heart constrict. She reached out and touched his face.

"I'm in love with him," she continued.

Reyn grimaced.

"I don't understand it. You detested him for years. You've never said anything nice about him. How did it happen? We broke up less than a month ago, Abby."

"I can't explain it. I really can't, but I know what I feel."

Reyn reached for her hands, brought them to his lips, and kissed them.

"I love you, and I know you love me too. I know it. I can't believe it's all gone. Not so quickly. I just can't accept that."

Abby was silent. She could barely breathe when Reyn kissed her hands. She felt something very strong for him, but she was afraid to give in because she wasn't ready to let Caleb go, even if he was being a vigilante idiot. Abby opened her mouth to say something, but before she could get any words out, Reyn's lips came down on hers. Buried feelings washed over her as his lips pressed down and his arms snuck around her waist, drawing her close to him. There was no way she could fight it. She wrapped her arms around his neck, opened her mouth, and kissed him back. He pressed her against the railing and kissed her harder and deeper. Abby felt herself getting weaker and weaker as they kissed. This was her baby, her boo, the love of her life. She dug her fingers into his hair and kissed him back fiercely and hungrily.

And then she felt him growing against her. She pulled back.

"I can't do this. I really can't do this back and forth. I just can't. I love you, Reyn. Yes, I do, but I love him too, so much more. I can't do this. I'm so sorry," she mumbled as her trusted friend Mr. Tears started to flow again.

"Let me go, okay?" she said, almost under her breath.

Reyn heard her.

"I can't, baby," he replied hoarsely.

They stared at each other silently, and then Abby straightened her shoulders.

"I have to go. Please don't call me, or email, or anything. Let's give it time. Let's move on. Go back to Emma. Let this die, baby, let this die."

"He's not right for you, Abby. I know that. I feel it, just as I know that you love me, more than you'd like to admit to yourself. So, I'll wait, because eventually he's going to fuck up. He's going to fuck up because he doesn't deserve you and he couldn't possibly love you as much as I do. So I'll wait."

Abby shook her head at him.

"Goodbye, Reyn."

She walked away, relieved and somewhat disappointed that he didn't follow. This didn't quite feel like closure, but it would have to do.

⌐

Asenso grinned excitedly as he scrolled through the pictures on his phone. Even from over five hundred meters away, he'd gotten some really good shots. The zoom on his camera phone was fantastic, and the quality of the pictures was crisp and clear. His heart was beating fast with excitement about what he'd witnessed and captured. Annan's daughter and Reyn Proctor, the married managing director of Proctor Oil, kissing heatedly right there, just a short distance from where he himself was cozied up with a young girl he'd been dating for a short while. The girl he was with didn't get why he was taking pictures of another couple, but he knew how monumental this was. Annan was notoriously easy on mining companies, particularly oil mining companies. Proctor Oil was the biggest, and Annan always spoke openly about why mining was important to the economy. Of course he would. His daughter was sleeping with their top executive. Who knew what other benefits Reyn had kicked Annan's way? However, Asenso knew that Annan's stance on oil companies wasn't the worst part. It was his moral stance that made this encounter even more delicious. Abiel Annan, daughter of Mr. Righteous, was sleeping with a married man. No one would care if Asenso or someone from his family was caught cheating, but Annan acted like he was God himself, blemish-free. He acted like he had zero tolerance for infidelity and what he referred to as the continued decay of the institution of marriage. Asenso was giddy as he selected the most compromising picture out of his collection and typed the email. He kept the message simple. Whoever said that a picture represented a thousand words was right. The subject line said it all: "Drop out of the race by morning or this will hit all news outlets by 10 a.m." He hit send and then tucked the phone into his pocket. He turned to the girl curled up next to him.

"Where were we?"

21

Caleb closed his laptop and leaned back in the chair. He was tired and frustrated. He'd spent the last few hours scanning Page Affleck's Facebook, searching for clues or signs of this Linc character, but he'd found nothing. There were some pictures of Cat, but they were not revealing either. He'd also asked his partner to look into Page, but he wasn't expecting anything out of the ordinary to come back. He doubted whoever Cat was working for would have planted two girls, but he also knew that anything was possible. He was frustrated that he was at a dead end. He had no idea what to do next. The systems and infrastructure in Ghana made this worse and difficult. The hostel had no cameras, so there was nothing for him to hack into to even try and get a license plate of the car this Linc guy was driving. And what would a license plate do for him anyway? Ghana license plates weren't automatically connected to valid addresses, so that was useless. The mall where Cat supposedly met Linc had cameras, but the footage wasn't hosted on any central database that he could hack into. The mall's security system was managed by Ghana's biggest security firm, G4S, but their size didn't indicate sophistication. The footage was pulled, scanned, and erased daily. That was because G4S had too much on their plates and couldn't store footage from over thirty complexes and businesses as well as over three million homes. So, that was a dead end too. The airport security was practically useless too. There was just no way for him to hack into anything to track passengers departing or arriving. He didn't even want to get started on the cameras there. He'd called the main security desk and pretended to be part of the US Homeland Security, doing a check on a sample of international airports. The clueless supervisor he spoke to admitted that their cameras had been down for three weeks and they were waiting for funding from the aviation authority. He had no shame in saying that. It was just life.

Caleb stood up from his chair and walked out to the porch. He couldn't figure out a way forward. He'd gone through all the scenarios, but there was nothing. The men who'd allegedly robbed and killed Bertha were all shot dead during the police gunfight, so he obviously couldn't go and interview them. He knew this Linc was on Bertha's street for a reason. He refused to believe it was a coincidence. This same person picked up Cat at JFK. There was more to the story. He just needed a break.

Caleb turned around at the sound of his ringing cell. He suspected it was Abby again. Perhaps he should pick up this time. At this pace, it wasn't likely that he was going to be killing anyone, so he might as well get back with her.

He glanced at the phone and frowned. It was the Justice. He answered quickly.

"Yes?"

"Caleb, I need your help. It's important."

"I don't work for you anymore, Joseph. You have an able team. You should call them."

"I'll try and ignore the fact that you just called me by first name."

Caleb couldn't help chuckling. "You're something else, you know that? Seriously."

"It's about Abby, and it's important. Be here in ten minutes."

Before Caleb could respond, the Justice had hung up. Caleb stared at the phone. What now?

⌒

"He wants me to pull out of the race or he'll release these pictures to the media by 10 a.m. tomorrow."

Caleb scrolled quietly through the pictures on the Justice's phone. He felt his heart breaking as he looked at each one. He tried to control the emotions that threatened to escape as he studied the pictures. He was in pain, a great deal of pain. He could barely speak or breathe. His reaction surprised him. He'd practically walked away from her and ignored her attempts to reach him. All the same, he felt incredibly betrayed. He was with her less than three days ago, and now she was back with him? He looked at the fingers that had touched him, which were now buried in another man's hair. They were holding each other so tightly, kissing like their lives depended on it. He placed the phone down on the Justice's desk and closed his eyes for a second. Then he focused on the Justice, who was sitting in his chair, looking disturbed, but Caleb knew they had different reasons for their reactions.

"What do you want me to do?" he muttered.

"Deal with Asenso. These pictures wouldn't just hurt my campaign, but they would ruin Abby too. Any other person would be forgiven for having an affair, but not my daughter. These pictures can't be released."

Caleb sat down in the chair opposite the Justice and tried to still his rapidly beating heart. A part of him wanted Abby to be duly embarrassed and punished for creeping around on him, but he knew the Justice was right. These pictures would ruin her because she was the daughter of a man who appeared to have no patience for people who didn't honor God, family, and life.

"You said before that Asenso was off limits, so what exactly are you asking right now? What do you want? Do you want the pictures to be gone or do you want me to end his campaign?"

"End his campaign, for her."

"For her? Is that your hook? Is that your way to get me to jump up and do your bidding? Huh? Technically, your daughter is cheating on me, but that shouldn't surprise me because she's your damn daughter and the apple truly doesn't fall far from the tree, does it?" Caleb shouted.

The Justice jumped up from his chair and glared at Caleb.

"Don't you dare speak to me like that! I know you're angry at me, and now at her, but none of that gives you the right to speak to me like that. If you truly want to hurt me, fine, don't do anything. Let him release the pictures. Who cares, right? Except you know damn well that Asenso doesn't have the spine, intellect, or leadership to lead this country. You know damn well that idiot will run this country into the ground. That's the consequence, Caleb. If he releases the pictures, he wins, my reputation will be shot to hell, my daughter will be branded a harlot and a home wrecker, and *he will win*. If that is what you really want to happen, walk out now," the Justice hissed.

Caleb rubbed his temples and sat silently in the chair. He was falling apart. The man he'd worshipped for years had cheated on his wife and lied to millions about the type of person he truly was, and the girl he'd started to fall for was back with her married boyfriend, just days after they had parted. And last but not least, someone had tried to kill him, and he had no idea how he was going to find him or her. Of course he was angry, but worse of all, he was coming apart. He needed to get a grip. He needed focus.

"Fine, I'll do this, because yes, Asenso is the last person on earth who deserves to be president. So, this is not for you or for Abby. It's for this country, because you know what, it's my home too."

The Justice settled back in his chair and looked intently at Caleb.

"I'm not a bad person, Caleb. I really hope one day you believe me. I cheated on my wife. I fathered a child. I broke my vows and I broke promises, I know, but it doesn't change what is in my heart. I love my God, my family, and my country. Nothing can take that away from me. You know that is true. You know it. It's always been about my God, my family and my country."

Caleb stood up and looked down at the Justice.

"I said I'll do it, so stop selling whatever it is that you're trying to sell."

"I'm not giving you a pitch. I mean every word of it. Abby and I, we've hurt you. I see it. I let you down. She's done the same. I'm sorry about that, but one day I hope you'll believe that you're like a son to me, and I wish more than anything that I was honest with you from the beginning. That's all I have to say."

Caleb forced back tears and clenched his fists. This family was going to drain him dry. Yes, they'd hurt him. They'd broken his heart, a heart he thought couldn't love, but he'd loved them both. There was really no denying it. He was angry with the Justice for lying to him and deceiving him because he loved him as he would his own father. He'd never adored anyone more than he adored the Justice. Finding out about Bertha and Joseph was heartbreaking. His idol was human after all, but worse of all his idol hadn't shared that humanity with him. And somehow his daughter had wormed her way into his heart and was tearing it apart. Caleb swallowed hard. It hurt like a damn motha...

Caleb reached for the Justice's phone and deleted the email from Asenso. Then he stood up and walked out.

∽

Asenso sat behind his desk at his campaign office, scrolling through the pictures on his phone for the hundredth time. There was just no way Annan was going to get out of this situation. He was either going to step down or face certain ruin. He felt like David, poised and ready to bring Goliath down. Asenso laughed out loud. He wished he could have seen the look on Annan's face when he got the email. The egotistical idiot had underestimated him, and now he was going to pay for it.

"Isn't it a little premature for that gloat plastered on your face?"

Asenso dropped the phone onto his desk, startled by the sound of Caleb's voice. For a moment, fear crept up his spine. Everyone knew that Annan's chief of staff was not a man to be trifled with. He was calculating, cold, and dangerous—nothing was beyond him. And since he single-handedly killed three armed men in his house, his reputation as a deadly viper had been cemented. Asenso knew Annan could set his rabid dog on him, but he also knew that Caleb would never do anything to endanger Annan. That would have to be his saving grace now.

"I figured he would send you, but I don't care. You have nothing on me, and anything you think you have would implicate your master as well. So you can stand there and look threatening, but I am not moved. He's going down. Do you understand? He's going down and there is nothing you can do about it."

Caleb smiled and clapped his hands at Asenso's attempt at bravado.

Asenso frowned.

"I'm serious. I'm not afraid of you. You have nothing, *nothing* on me," he hissed.

Caleb laughed and sat down opposite Asenso.

"Let me be honest, I really respect your confidence. It's refreshing. I didn't expect it, but I'm pleasantly surprised."

Asenso slammed his fist on the table.

"I'm going to send the pictures and then I'm going to be president! You and your boss will just have to accept it. It's over."

"You will never, ever be president," Caleb said quietly.

He pulled a brown manila envelope from his pocket and dropped it on the table in front of him. Asenso stared at it, and then his gaze went up to meet Caleb's eye.

"You're just bluffing. There is nothing in there. You think I'm not used to intimidation tactics? You think you're the first person to threaten me? I've had macho men harass me and smash my windscreen just to prevent me from casting my ballot. I've been robbed two times. I've led protests and survived teargas. You can never scare me. Do you understand that?"

"Okay, your misplaced confidence is getting old, so please shut up and listen to me or I'll break your fucking neck right now and be done with it," Caleb snapped.

Asenso's mouth dropped open as the fear crept back in. Before he could respond, Caleb continued talking.

"You're never going to be president, and it's not because of the Justice or me, or anyone else. Even if you'd never taken those pictures, there was no way you were going to be president. You know why? You know why, you stupid, damn fool? Do you?"

Asenso started to talk, but Caleb wasn't done.

"You know, back in the US, there's one particular type of criminal no one can stand. Axe murderers and serial killers have easier prison lives than these criminals. Do you know what I'm talking about?"

Asenso swallowed and started to cry.

"Jesus, please, it happened once. It was eight years ago. I was weak. I was drunk. It happened once. I swear it. Please."

Caleb ignored his crying and continued.

"Pedophiles. They're the most detested criminals on the planet, hands down. I could shoot you in the head right now, point blank, broad daylight, and it wouldn't be as bad as pedophilia. And do you know that within pedophilia there is a subset that is detested more than the devil himself?"

Caleb paused and glared at Asenso.

"Incestuous pedophilia, that's the worst of the worst. What do you think?"

Asenso couldn't control the crying now.

"I was drunk," he repeated.

"I think the most abused excuse in history is alcohol. It's amazing. It's the go-to excuse for every single vile and detestable human behavior. Insanity is the second most abused excuse, but I think that works better for you than alcohol, although honestly, who cares what excuse you give? Hmmm? You raped your twelve-year-old granddaughter and left her in her bedroom, bleeding and bruised. And then when your wife found her, battered and permanently scarred, you automatically blamed it on the houseboy. House staff, they can never catch a break. They're blamed for every single shit that happens. And if a minister of state says his houseboy raped his granddaughter to the point of near death, then of course it's the houseboy. Who else could it be? Poor child is traumatized, can't speak, and can't remember, so yes, it's the houseboy."

Caleb watched as Asenso disintegrated before his eyes. Determined to punish him further, he pointed to the envelope before him.

"When I joined Annan, we identified people we needed to keep an eye on and planted cameras in their homes. I've sat on this evidence all these years because my master, as you call him, wanted to spare the party the humiliation. I should admit that there've been times I've wanted to kill you. Like now."

"Jesus, please, I beg of you. I've prayed to God so many times for forgiveness. I have repented. I truly have. My heart is clean. My soul is clean. If you've been watching me, you should know this."

"Of course your soul is clean. You simply upgraded to prostitutes and barely legal women. Absolutely you're clean," Caleb said sarcastically.

"The man you protect, do you think he's any better than me? Everyone has demons. You know everyone else's, but do you know his? He's a hypocrite. If his daughter is involved with a married man, then I wouldn't put anything past him. I see through that lie he projects. You're just a blind dog who fetches without questioning anything," Asenso retorted, getting a bit of his confidence back.

Caleb leaned forward and snarled, "I'm trying very hard not to end your miserable life right now. Push me, and I'll lose control."

Asenso pressed back against the chair. Caleb leaned back and glanced around the office. He had a couple of options for bringing Asenso down, but this wild card was the riskiest. He also he knew it would have the biggest impact. Unfortunately, he only had blank pieces of paper in the envelope.

Eight years ago, when Caleb heard Asenso's granddaughter had been raped, he knew instantly. He could never explain it properly, but he just knew. Maybe it was the way Asenso spoke about the incident during the press conference, maybe it was the way the little girl clung to her

grandmother for dear life and couldn't look at her grand-
father, or maybe it was the fact that the houseboy vehemently denied the crime even as he was whipped, beaten,
and dragged around in public. He died two days later at the
police station from injuries sustained during the mob beating. In the week that followed, the Justice spoke strongly
against rape and child violence, and Asenso tried to tout
the same horn, but it was weak. This whole thing could
have backfired, but Caleb had two things going for him.
First, he had a reputation as an enforcer, someone to be
feared, someone who had access and could bring anyone
down. If he said he had evidence, Asenso would believe it.
Second, he had observed Asenso for years after that, and
he'd seen how he handled women, particularly very young
women. There was no doubt in his mind that Asenso
raped his granddaughter, and even though he could have
brought him down just as easily with some orgy pictures
he'd snapped of Asenso and some women from the streets,
he wanted Asenso to know that someone else knew about
what he'd done.

"What do you want me to do?" Asenso whimpered.

"Unlock your phone and give it to me."

Asenso complied. Caleb wiped the phone clean. All
pictures, emails, contacts, and every single bit of data were
wiped. Then he gestured to the computer on Asenso's desk.

"Log into your email account and hand it over."

Asenso logged on quickly and then turned the monitor
and keyboard over to Caleb. Caleb checked Asenso's inbox.
He only sent the email once, to Annan. No other emails
since then, but to be safe, he proceeded to wipe the entire
email account clean. After that, he opened up the pictures
folder. The stupid man had tons of pornographic pictures

in there, some downloaded from the web, he suspected, but some of them also looked like they were from women Asenso knew or had had relationships with. And then his fingers stopped and clenched the mouse tightly as his eyes fell on him—Linc.

Caleb swung the monitor back toward Asenso. He pointed to the picture of Asenso and his wife, with Linc standing off in the background. He tapped on Linc's face.

"Who is this?"

Asenso frowned and squinted at the picture.

"Oh, that's Lincoln Jackson. He's with SecuriCorp. It was when we first came into power in 2000. SecuriCorp supported the Ghana army on the Liberia mission. When that was successful, we struck a deal with them to supplement our protocol detail. Lincoln, or Linc I think he was called, was assigned to Samuel. He did about two years and that was it."

Caleb tried to restrain himself. He remembered now. SecuriCorp was a $20 billion security and technology contractor firm based in the US. When he was in the Marines, they had SecuriCorp soldiers deployed with them. Supplemental support, they were told, but the SecuriCorp guys were simply ruthless mercenaries. They had no code of ethics and no moral grounding. All the same, the US was dependent on SecuriCorp and a ton of similar contractor firms. They provided weapons and manpower, and they helped to win missions, even if their methods were questionable. When he first moved down to Ghana, Annan spoke briefly about SecuriCorp. They supported the Ghana troops in Liberia, and they provided some men for executive protection, specifically for the president, VP, chief justice, and select other ministers. Caleb spoke openly against SecuriCorp and told

Annan it was a bad idea to have them around. When the contract expired, the government didn't renew it, and as far as he knew, SecuriCorp was gone. He didn't remember Linc from Samuel's security detail, but Samuel had over twenty men who rotated through his detail. It would have been tough for him to remember them all. So Linc was part of SecuriCorp, and somehow he was connected to Samuel, Bertha, and Cat. Now he had something to follow up on.

"Is something wrong?"

Caleb looked absentmindedly at Asenso. Then he shook his head.

"Nothing, mistaken identity."

Caleb closed the pictures folder and wiped the computer clean. Then he got up and stared down at Asenso.

"Release a press statement today announcing that you're withdrawing from the campaign because, after deep thought, you know Justice Annan is the man for the role, and you want to focus on supporting him to win this election."

"You want me to sell my soul," Asenso murmured.

"You sold your soul when you raped your granddaughter!" Caleb snapped.

Asenso nodded quickly as tears flooded his eyes once more.

"Now pull yourself together. Your people outside must be anxious. I told them I had a deal from the Justice. So tell them you've agreed that the Justice needs your support and you're willing to support him in whatever capacity he decides. I've drafted a statement for you," Caleb said as he pulled a sheet of paper out of his pocket. "That's all. And remember, I'm watching you. One false move, and I swear to God, I will kill you. I swear it."

Caleb meant every word of the threat he'd just issued. He was sick and tired of the vile, repugnant men who wanted to rule this country. They were all corrupt hypocrites who should be locked up instead of directing the affairs of innocent millions. If the Justice turned out to be a murderer and a liar too, then he would put him down too, without hesitation.

22

Abby placed her feet on the windowsill and leaned back in the chair, staring out at the silhouette of the Proctor Oil building. Despite her feelings of hopelessness the day before, she'd decided to return to work. She needed the distraction because she was still reeling from her kiss with Reyn, and each time she thought about it, she had goose bumps on her arms. She closed her eyes as the memories of the night before assailed her. She clasped her thighs tightly together, and her arms instinctively cradled her upper body, remembering the way Reyn held her, his body pressed hard against her. She moaned.

"Heads you're thinking of Reyn, tails you're thinking of me."

"Oh my God!" Abby jumped up from her seat and looked at Caleb, her mouth open. If she were white, she would be beetroot red.

"What are you doing here?" she asked weakly.

"Do tell me, which one of us got you moaning like that, in your office of all places?"

"No one," she said quietly.

"I doubt that. Has to be one of us. If we go by most memorable lovemaking, then I think it would be me, but if we use recency effect, then it would be Reyn. You can probably still taste his lips, can't you?"

"Jesus, Caleb, are you following me? Is that what you're up to now?"

"Dear Abby, if I was following you, the kiss would never have happened."

Caleb lowered himself into the chair opposite her desk and smiled at her. He was enjoying the stricken look on her face. She straightened her skirt, sat back in her chair, and looked at him.

"So how do you know?"

"Asenso Okyere was there last night. He took pictures of you and your beloved making out for dear life."

"Oh my God, is he going to release them? Is that why you're here? To warn me?"

"No, he's not going to release them."

Abby shook her head. "What did you do, Caleb?"

"Have some faith in me, dear. I didn't kill him, if that's what you're thinking."

She sighed with relief, although she was disappointed that Caleb was so cavalier about the whole thing. He'd seen pictures of her kissing her old boyfriend passionately. Didn't he care?

"You don't seem too fazed. I guess the thought of me kissing Reyn doesn't bother you much, does it?"

274

"You have no idea what it did to me," Caleb said softly, his eyes fixed on hers.

Abby swallowed as her eyes misted over. God, would these tears ever end?

"It was only a kiss. He wanted to talk, and I wanted to give him and myself some closure. I let the kiss happen because I had missed him, and I was pained because you let me go, but I'm so in love with you and I just wish you could see that."

Caleb had her in his arms within seconds. He kissed her hard and deep. It wasn't an attempt to erase the memory of Reyn, but it was his attempt to put into action what he was feeling. And he felt a lot.

He pulled apart from her and stared down at her face. She had tears in her eyes. He guessed he'd hurt her as much as he'd felt hurt. He knew he could keep hiding behind his actions, but eventually the words had to come out.

"I love you, Abiel Annan. I can't explain it, and I don't know how it happened, but God, I love you."

Abby let out a sob, and he cradled her face in his hands.

"And I'll kill you if you hurt me or hook up with that other one again."

Abby stepped back from him, her eyes wide and fearful.

Caleb chuckled. "Jesus, can't you take a joke?"

"Jesus, can't you not threaten to kill someone?"

"Touché. I'll try not to threaten you again, but honestly, if you're ever, ever with him again..." he paused deliberately, a serious look in his eyes.

"What does that mean? You want this to be monogamous? You want to be in a committed relationship with me?" Abby asked, smiling.

"Till the day that I die," Caleb murmured against her cheek, shocked by his admission but knowing that he meant it all. He was in love with her, and the realization hit him hard when he saw the pictures. There was no turning back from there. He wasn't just going to walk away and let her be with Reyn. He loved her, and he was going to be with her. As he hugged her tight, he prayed he wouldn't be forced to take her father down. He really hoped he wouldn't have to. Their fragile love and relationship wouldn't survive that.

∽

The Justice read Asenso's press release for the tenth time. He hadn't planned on eliminating Asenso from the race, but the man had forced his hand by bringing his daughter into this.

He wasn't sure what Caleb had used, but he knew it would work. He knew there were the women, but for a known womanizer like Asenso, it was unlikely that alone could topple him. He'd simply trusted that Caleb would have something more, and it turned out that he did. Asenso's press release was contrite. It stated that he'd thought through it a lot and had come to the conclusion that the Justice was the right person for the country, and he was completely ready and willing to lend his support. The statement also added that one of the characteristics of a good leader was being reflective, honest, and accepting when there was someone more capable to accomplish a common goal. He and the Justice wanted one thing—the economic and social prosperity of Ghana—and he knew the Justice would get them there.

The Justice wondered if Caleb had written the statement. His fingerprints were all over it. Asenso competing against him would have given his eventual win more legitimacy, but now he was the only titan amongst weaklings. He would have preferred to stand toe to toe against Asenso to prove that he'd won fair and square. Asenso's withdrawal diminished that. And even though the statement was good, the Justice was sure some people would still question the true reasoning behind Asenso's withdrawal. Asenso had been campaigning nonstop for three years, and now a little over a month after Annan announces his campaign he withdraws? That was suspicious. Annan hated that it had to be this way, but there was just no way he could let the pictures be released, and Asenso's cheap and unnecessary attempt at getting at him had angered him. Stopping the release of the pictures wouldn't have been enough. Sometimes errant kids needed to be taught difficult lessons. Proverbs 22 verse 15 states, "Folly is bound up in the heart of a child, but the rod of discipline drives it far from him." That was what he did—Asenso behaved like a child, so the Justice had disciplined him.

The door to his office opened, and Caleb stepped in. The Justice raised an eyebrow, surprised.

"I didn't expect to see you here today. I was just reading the press statement that was released this morning. Thank you for doing this, and I won't even ask how you did it."

"I'd like to lead the campaign again."

The Justice's eyebrow arched higher, and he gestured to Caleb to sit down.

"Obviously, I'm happy you want to come back, but are you sure you want to?"

Caleb nodded at the Justice.

"I'm very sure."

Today was his day for reconciliation with the two people most important to him—besides his parents, of course. His reunion with Abby was sincere and heart-felt. He loved that girl more than he could express in this lifetime. On the other hand, his reunion with her father was mixed. He needed to be back in the fold in order to investigate the SecuriCorp connection properly. He also wanted to give the Justice the benefit of the doubt. Despite his cheating, he believed the Justice was the right person to be president, unless of course he was somehow connected to the death of his sister-in-law and the attempt on Caleb's life. That would be a different story altogether.

"I'm surprised, but pleased. You built this campaign, and despite the way you've paved for the team, there's no one better to see us to the end," the Justice said, beaming.

"I have to be honest with you, Justice. I am still hurt by what you did, and I mean the affair with Bertha, but a part of me believes you're meant to be president, so I'm here to get you there. Just don't lie to me again. If there is anything I don't know, you should tell me now."

"I love you like a son, Caleb. I hope you know that," the Justice said sincerely and truthfully.

"And I love you like a father, too. I mean that," Caleb said, equally sincere.

"So believe me when I tell you this: there is nothing more. At this point, you know it all," the Justice lied.

"Then believe me when I also say I'm here to support you. I'm with you one hundred percent," Caleb lied back.

The two men smiled and nodded at each other, each lost in his own thought about what he hoped to gain from the fragile and tenuous alliance.

⌒

"What are you thinking, Joseph? What in God's name are you thinking? What do you hope to gain from letting him back in?"

Annan took a sip of his cognac and relaxed back in his chair. He shook his head at Samuel, who was standing before him, looking agitated and concerned.

"I think it's important for him to be in the fold where I can keep an eye on him, instead of out there, doing God knows what. This way, he's busy with the campaign. He's at the office now, reviving our Ghana tour, getting interviews set up and getting posters and billboards done. I know where he is and what he's doing."

"How can you trust him? Forget that, how can you even be sure that he trusts you?"

"I could see it in his eyes. He believes me, and he'll stand by me like before. I'm certain of that."

"You better be certain, because you've told me several times that Caleb doesn't trust SecuriCorp, and it was because of him that we killed the deal years ago. If we're going to do this now, then you need to be sure he's not going to find out."

"This is Caleb. He'll find out eventually, but by then I'll be president and there will be nothing can do about it."

Samuel picked up two thick stacks of paper from his desk and dropped them onto Annan's lap.

"The draft contract was hand delivered today. There are two versions, and I made only one copy of each for you. No soft copies, no trails. Read and provide your comments. The first set is the real contract, the one that we, or should I say you, will have to sell to parliament next year. The second outlines our cut. I know you didn't want that on paper, but we can't just go by their word alone. We're months away from signing, but the discussions can't wait. Read, pencil in your comments, and let's discuss on Friday."

"I'll read them both now. I'm not taking these back to the office or home with me."

Samuel shrugged. "Make yourself comfortable. My office is yours for the day. Margaret is in the house somewhere, and if you ring that bell over there, Kofi will come running. I had it installed last week. It's very nifty. I have some meetings in town, so I'll be a while. At least, I'm the last person on Caleb's mind right now, so I can go about my business."

"Tei Q, what's going on? It's Caleb."

Tei Quartey was the head of protocol for the office of the president. He was in charge of security and all protocol-related matters, and had been in the role for fifteen years. Tei was honest, efficient, and uncompromising. Caleb trusted him, and he knew Tei trusted him too. He would speak freely.

"Caleb! Where have you been hiding? I tried to call you a couple of weeks ago, but it just wasn't going through. You know the phone lines in this country are useless. I read about what those GFP idiots tried to do. They had no idea who they were dealing with, did they? Caleb, my man!"

Caleb joined in Tei Q's laughter. Even after ten years, he was still getting used to the fact that, in Ghana, when you call people or meet them somewhere, you have to allow them to ramble on till they remembered who called whom. You could never rush to your point.

"I mean seriously, I was telling my old lady that they sent only three men to get you? They should have asked me. I would have told them about Caleb my man. You should come train some of the boys, Caleb. Share your skills."

Caleb saw his in and he took it.

"I want to talk about the boys, Tei. I'm trying to find Lincoln Jackson. He's with SecuriCorp, and he was on President Arthur's detail during his first term. He's tall, pretty big guy."

"Oh, you don't have to describe him. Of course I remember Linc. He was officially on the detail for the first term, and then we got him back as a suit for the second term."

Caleb frowned as he scribbled. He knew what a "suit" was. Once a SecuriCorp soldier finished his contract and no immediate extension was available, his status was changed to that of a suit, a glorified, highly trained handyman. In the spy world, they were also called fixers.

"Why did Linc come back as a suit? Why did the president need one?"

"Well, I think the president really trusted Linc, but after the SecuriCorp deal died, we couldn't have him on the detail full time, so the company offered him up as a suit. I think he came down a couple of times during the second term, but I didn't keep track of him. Ahiable handled that. It was no longer a Protocol matter."

Caleb nodded, even though Tei couldn't see him. Ahiable was Samuel's chief of staff and had served with the president for years.

"Is everything okay? Why are you looking for Linc?"

Caleb had his story prepared.

"I caught a glimpse of him at the airport a couple of weeks ago, but we couldn't chat. With this attempt on my life, I figured it wouldn't hurt to talk to him, see if he's freelancing or something."

"Those SecuriCorp guys are bad news, Caleb. I was glad we killed the deal. If you need security, just let me know. I know some guys, okay?"

Caleb grinned. At least he and Tei were on the same page.

"I hear you, Tei, but do you have any contact info for Linc?"

"Just what was submitted when he joined the detail. If you saw him recently, then Ahiable will have his information. Check with him, but make sure you don't sign any deals, Caleb. Those SecuriCorp boys have no morals, and Linc was the worst of them all. I never told you this, but I feel like I can tell you now. Linc cracked a woman's skull open six months into the assignment. It was at the President's private home. She worked in the kitchen, and God knows why, but around 2 a.m. she snuck into the president's room. She startled him, and he screamed. Linc was in there in seconds, and he smashed her head against the wall just like that. Can you imagine? Just like that. The president called me in to sort it out. Linc and his boys got rid of the body. I don't even know how. They cleaned her room, packed up some items from the house, and the story was she stole from the First Lady and then ran away. No one asked any questions. That's SecuriCorp, Caleb."

This sounded like Bertha's story, Caleb thought. Fake robbery, and those men who were shot down by the police were probably set up. Why would a robber shoot a security man and then stab the woman in the house? Why use two different weapons? It meant Linc was simply a fixer. Caleb was almost certain that someone else killed Bertha and called in Linc to clean it up.

"This has to stay between you and me, Caleb. You know I took an oath, and I could be sentenced to life if this gets out. I just want you to know who you're dealing with."

"Trust me, Tei, this is between us. I appreciate you sharing, and I am not going to pursue Linc. I wanted to have a chat, but that's not necessary anymore," Caleb lied. He meant the part that he'd keep this story secret, but he was still bent on tracking Linc down. He had a name and a history now. He just needed to find him. And no matter where he was, he was going to find Linc and find out who set the crazed dog on him. He had two guesses—Samuel or Annan. It had to be one of them, and Caleb was now a step closer to finding out whom.

Caleb hung up the phone and stared at the papers strewn on his desk. Under the guise of working, he'd stayed behind closed doors in his office and spent almost all day researching SecuriCorp. The company had grown exponentially over the last few years. Contract soldiers were big business now, and while he was tucked in his bubble in Ghana, they'd grown like a virus across Africa, with some countries adopting full privatization of their armies using SecuriCorp technology and manpower. The national armies were offered two options—join SecuriCorp as private soldiers to be trained and deployed in their home countries and elsewhere, or retire. In these struggling African countries, retirement wasn't an option.

If Linc was a suit or a fixer for either Samuel or Annan, then what was happening here wasn't about privatization. It was about using Linc to hide or execute personal atrocities. Caleb was determined to find out who had hired Linc, and as much as he loved Abby and had promised no more killing, he knew someone, maybe more than one person, was going to go down. It was unavoidable.

23

"*D*o I look demure enough in this? Or is it showy? It's showy, isn't it?"

Caleb glanced up and stared at Abby standing in the doorway of her study. She was wearing a simple, floral colored strapless mid-length dress with a slightly cinched waist and billowy skirt. It looked like a GTP print, or maybe it was Woodin. Caleb had noticed that Abby had a thing for African print materials. He was assaulted by the colors each time he opened her closet.

"You look like a choir girl with boobs dying to escape and sing Hallelujah!"

Abby giggled and walked up to him.

"The bust is rather tight, isn't it? I feel fine, but it does look like my breasts are imprisoned, doesn't it?"

Caleb laughed and pulled her onto his lap. He kissed her softly.

"You look beautiful, baby, and I was kidding about the breasts. Throw a shawl over it and it'll be perfect. Even your mother would approve."

"You should come with me. Please change your mind."

"Dinner with your parents? Uh, no, thanks. I know you've told your father about us, but I'd rather not flaunt the relationship in their faces. You should go, enjoy yourself, and then come and tell me about it."

"I still think you should come. They need to accept this," Abby insisted.

"They will, in time. You have to see it from their perspective too, okay? I've been working for your father for ten years, and now I'm dating his baby girl. It can't be easy. I'd like to give them time and space."

Abby stroked his cheek with her fingers and kissed him.

"You're such a wise man," she murmured against his lips.

"It's called age," he murmured back.

"Whatever," Abby said chuckling.

She got up and glanced down at his papers.

"Don't work too late, okay? I'll be back in a couple of hours."

"And I'll be in bed waiting for you."

Abby winked at him and then left the room. She grabbed her handbag and a multi-colored shawl from the closet in the hallway, and walked quickly out of the apartment. She was already thirty minutes late.

She was surprised her parents were hosting a dinner party together. They hadn't done much entertaining over the last four years, but since her father was running for president, he couldn't hide in his home with his wife forever.

They had to emerge together eventually, and a small dinner party for twenty close family and guests seemed appropriate enough. Abby wished Caleb was coming with her, but she understood his reasoning. If she showed up at her parents' dinner party with him on her arm, it would set tongues wagging, and her relationship would be the center of attention. It would also remind her parents that they weren't keen on the pairing. So he was right, they had to give her parents time to adjust.

When Caleb declared his love for her earlier that week, she couldn't believe it, and she was ecstatic beyond words. He also rejoined her father, which was fine with her. Her father needed Caleb if he wanted to win the elections. Reyn also called a few days after she met with him. He was still getting a divorce, but he'd decided to quit his job as well and move back to Texas to fight for his boys. Abby was stunned. She thought Reyn would go back to his wife once she turned him down, but it looked like he was serious. She was sorry to hear that he was leaving Ghana. It was very likely she would never see him again, but she was also reluctant to say goodbye in person. She couldn't risk that. Caleb would never understand. So instead she said her goodbyes on the phone and wished him well. Reyn would always be dear to her, but she had to focus on Caleb now. Caleb actually loved her, and that was more important to her than anything else.

They'd spent every night together since he'd said those three words, and even though he left in the mornings, he was back each night. She'd wanted to suggest that he move in, but he needed time and space too. She didn't want to throw a ball and chain at him so early. She was going to be extra careful with this relationship. No psycho needy girlfriend stuff. For instance, she didn't like the fact that he spent hours on the computer and on the phone each night, but she wasn't going to complain, because each time he crawled into bed, he woke her up and made love to her like it was the end of the world. She really hoped she wasn't dreaming, because if this ended, she would never survive. Reyn was wrong on this one. Caleb wasn't going to fuck up, and neither was she.

～

"So I heard the GFP is scrambling, trying to figure out how to recover from the hit they put on your man Caleb."

Annan handed a drink to Boadi Agyeman, the current chancellor at the University of Ghana. Boadi was also one of Annan's long-time friends and supporters. Next to him was Etse Adzaho, president of the Ghana Medical Board, and another dedicated supporter.

"I don't see a way for the GFP to recover. The evidence is too damning. They hired thugs to bring down an innocent man. I'm not sure what they were hoping to achieve though. Was Caleb onto them? Did he have something on them? I'm hearing that Caleb has the ability to end everything for them, including the president himself," Etse chimed in.

Annan forced a smile and handed Etse a drink as well. This was the problem with pinning Josh's murder and the attempt on Caleb on the GFP—motive. Sure, they'd said in interviews that the GFP wanted to get to Annan and derail his campaign through Caleb, but how strong was that? Another problem was that the scandal made Caleb seem like some type of indestructible legend, with the secrets of the most powerful tucked into his back pocket. Annan didn't like that at all. Caleb was supposed to be his secret weapon; now, unfortunately, if any competitor of his went down, all fingers would point to Caleb.

"Look, Caleb isn't some spy who's amassed shaming or criminal evidence on everyone. He's just very good at what he does. We all know he helped Samuel win his second term, and we wouldn't have gotten 54 percent of the votes in 2004 if it wasn't for him. That's just a fact. That's what Caleb does. So the GFP was worried, that's it. If Caleb remains in the game, they lose. No other reason," Annan said, regurgitating words he'd said several times over the past few weeks.

"So this Asenso withdrawal, Caleb had nothing to do with it? I heard a rumor that he was in Asenso's office the morning he released the press statement," Etse said.

Annan expected the question at some point during the evening, so he had his response prepared for that as well.

"We've been talking to Asenso for a while. He was doubtful of his chances as soon as I announced, so we've been talking, trying to figure out the best way forward for the party, for our success. Caleb went over to discuss some ideas. Look, we know Asenso just wasn't the man for this, and he realized it."

Boadi and Etse nodded in agreement. Annan took a deep breath. Thankfully, there was no one else Caleb needed to take down. From now until the elections, they had to run a clean race, and he had to ensure Caleb stayed above aboard. He couldn't spend the next six months explaining why things that didn't typically happen in Ghana politics, like attempted murder on a politician's staff, were happening repeatedly now. He also knew it wasn't Caleb's fault. Josh tried to take him out, and Caleb took advantage of the situation Josh had created. He just needed to make sure that that was it. His campaign wouldn't survive any more Caleb-related occurrences.

"So Boadi, let's talk education for a minute. I still think education is one of the biggest challenges the country is facing today. Caleb and I have been discussing a really radical idea that I'd appreciate your feedback on."

"Of course. So how's the wife? I feel like I haven't seen her much in the last four years."

Annan sighed. Discussing Caleb was no better than discussing Adubea. He just wasn't having any luck focusing the conversation on safe topics. He glanced at Adubea, who was talking to Samuel and a couple of other guests. He looked back at Boadi and Etse, and began to lie again. It seemed like that was going to be the theme of the night.

"It was a good dinner, wasn't it? You did a fantastic job, dear," Annan said, staring lovingly at his wife.

Annan, Adubea, and Abby were sitting in the family room, relaxing a little after the last guest, the Honorable Mrs. Obeng, left. Abby wanted to get home to Caleb, but she knew she couldn't just act like a stranger and up and leave. She could spare her parents ten more minutes.

Adubea smiled at her husband and then turned her gaze to her daughter.

"Abby, did you talk to Andrew at all? I seated him next to you, and you barely said five words."

"I honestly think it was ten words, Ma."

"Abby! Don't be cheeky. Andrew is the new managing director at Choice Bank. It's incredible, really, managing director at forty-two. I'm surprised he's not married, but I asked him and he said he's just waiting for the right woman."

"You asked him? Geez, Ma, I am with Caleb now. You need to stop flinging these prospects at me."

Adubea turned to look at her husband, her eyes flaring.

"Are we really entertaining this? Caleb? Are you really not going to do anything about it?"

Annan sighed and turned to Abby.

"Do you really care about Caleb, Abby?"

"I told you a couple of days ago, Daddy. This is it for me. I have never, ever felt like this before. I don't expect you to jump up and down with excitement, but I'd like you to respect my decision."

"Respect your decision? All you ever do is make bad decisions!" her mother snapped.

Annan stepped in before Abby could respond.

"We'll respect your decision, Abby. I already told Caleb that. He's been very busy in the office, and we haven't really had the chance to have a personal chat, but I will let him know soon that I'm fine with it as long as he doesn't hurt you. Then we'll have a serious problem."

Abby stared at her father, surprised at his tone and words. What was going on here? Her mother was on the verge of losing it, and on the other hand, her father was respecting her wishes? Her mother's hands were shaking, and Abby couldn't understand where all the anger was coming from.

"Do you have any idea how much Caleb cares about me and both of you? There isn't anything he wouldn't do for you or for me. He's been working like a dog all week. Gosh, he's even researching security firms. I'm sure it's because of the attempts on his life. And now that he's with me, he wants me to be safe. So Ma, he's thinking about me."

The Justice's right hand tightened on his glass, and he could barely get his words out.

"Researching security firms? He could use the same one we use for the home and the office."

Abby shrugged. "I don't know, maybe he wants options. I saw some files with SecuriCorp on them. I haven't heard of them, but maybe they're new and better. Caleb is particular about those things."

The Justice winced and grasped his chest as if the wind had been knocked out of him. Both Adubea and Abby were by his side in seconds.

"What is wrong, Daddy?"

"Nothing, nothing, please. I think the drink went down the wrong tube." He forced a smile and stood up weakly.

Abby reached for his hand and squeezed.

"Are you sure?"

"I'm positive. Why don't you get going now? It's getting late and Caleb isn't the only one who wants you to be safe."

Abby nodded and kissed her father on the cheek. It was the first time she'd done that in years. She reached for her mother and hugged her, even though her mother barely lifted her arms in response. Abby sighed and picked up her bag and shawl from the sofa.

"I'll call and check in tomorrow. Goodnight."
She blew them a kiss and walked out.

⤸

"Jesus Christ, did you hear that? Did you hear her? He's looking into SecuriCorp!"

Annan gripped his wife's arm and hissed at her.

"Calm down, will you? Just calm down!"

She yanked her arm away and glared at him.

"Calm down? I am tired of being told to calm down! He's looking into SecuriCorp! The deal that's going to give you, us, our financial freedom is at risk, and you want me to calm down?"

"So he's looking into it, but there's nothing to find."

"Can you be sure, Joseph? We missed an opportunity four years ago, and if you don't control this, we're going to lose it again. So you need to step up!"

"Don't you dare tell me to step up! What do you think I do every single day of my life? I tell you things because you're my wife and I can't do this without your support, but don't disrespect me again. Don't tell me to step up!"

Adubea cowered and stepped back.

"I just want you to have everything you've worked so hard for. I don't want anything, or anyone, to come between you and your dreams."

Annan softened his tone.

"I have it under control. Everything just needs to be put in perspective. Even if Caleb finds out that we have a deal in the works with SecuriCorp, what is he going to do? What can he do? He'll come and talk to me about it, and I'll convince him it's what we need—it's what this country needs."

"You said he hates that company more than anything. You said he was the one who forced you and Samuel to end the deal the last time. You're not taking this seriously enough, Joseph. How much did you say you were going to get out of that deal? Three hundred million dollars between you and Samuel, right? Do you know what that money could do for us? We would never have to worry about anything again for the rest of our lives."

"What do you worry about now? Do you worry about having food on the table? Do you worry about having clothes on your back? Do you worry about not having money to buy pearls? Is that it? What do you need that you don't have? Tell me!" Annan shouted, getting angry again.

Adubea scowled at him.

"I'm going to bed now. Sit down here and do nothing, but you need to remember something. Caleb isn't your son. He's not our family. You owe it to your family to secure your future, our future. That's your responsibility. So whatever is holding you back from facing the reality of this situation, deal with it."

Annan dropped into his armchair and picked up his scotch. He had to talk to Sylvia about Adubea's meds. She was getting loud and excitable again. This was his situation, and as much as Caleb's investigation into SecuriCorp was worrying, it wasn't the end of the world. There was one thing troubling him, though. Why was Caleb looking into SecuriCorp in the first place? Why now? What happened to trigger it? If Caleb was onto something, there was no stopping him. Someone on Samuel's side had probably slipped up, and he needed to figure out who, how, or why before he could do anything else. He would call Samuel in the morning. For now, he just wanted to sit in his chair, drink, and pretend all was right in his kingdom.

24

"*A*n interview together on the *News First* show, yes, I like that. Thankfully, Samuel is as charismatic as the Justice, and they have similar ideals and philosophies. Samuel has the best track record of any president. Closely tying him with Annan will definitely help the Justice, especially since it was Samuel who more or less presented him during the announcement."

Caleb forced back an eye roll, irritated by Ahiable's overinflated perception of Samuel's reputation and capabilities. Fine, Samuel had the best record so far, but he struggled during his first couple of years until Caleb came along and cleaned his camp. Whatever ideals and philosophies people thought Samuel had, all came from Caleb. It was widely known and accepted that Caleb won Samuel his second term, even though he wasn't the campaign manager, a fact that Ahiable, Samuel's chief of staff, tried to ignore. The Justice didn't need Samuel—not even close. The two men had history and a bond, so during Samuel's tenure as president, Caleb made an effort to mold Samuel to reflect some of the tenements the Justice held dear. And now, Samuel and the rest of his minions thought he was as great as the Justice.

"All we're trying to do is take advantage of an already existing friendship and bond. Since Asenso has withdrawn, we need to demonstrate that the leadership of the party remains strong and behind the Justice," Caleb said.

"Of course, of course, I understand that. How about Santini, Osei, and Fusi? Should we add them to the interviews? That could be historic, the president with the leading party contenders. It would also demonstrate that our election process will be fair. No favoritism here."

Caleb looked down and scribbled in his notepad. He'd been with Ahiable for only twenty minutes, but he wasn't sure how much of this he could endure. He came to see Ahiable in his home today because he wanted information on Linc, that was it, but it wasn't something he could just ask for outright. So, he drew up a media plan involving Samuel and Annan, and figured he could start from there. The downside was that his patience was wearing thin.

"Sure, that could work. We could start with the interviews and then stage DNP party debates."

"That's fantastic! Yes, absolutely. Samuel would love the idea. I'll call Insel and make the arrangements," Ahiable said excitedly.

Of course, because you want to take the credit, Caleb thought to himself.

"We have to be careful about security though, especially with the recent attacks on me. It would be all four candidates together in one building, plus Samuel. One bold, but stupid, move by the GFP, and our party would be crippled," Caleb said, taking advantage of an in to discuss security.

Ahiable frowned. "They can't be that stupid. It would be too obvious. It still doesn't make sense why they tried to kill you."

"Has the GFP ever been smart? I think we need to be cautious. Does Samuel have any trusted security?"

"There's G4S. They're reliable, but they're also paid for by the government, so I don't know if you think they could be compromised."

"They could be, but we may have to start from there. The Justice uses G4S too. So...oh wait, does Lincoln Jackson still do some work for Samuel? I think I caught a glimpse of him at the airport a couple of weeks ago, but I'm not sure. He was really good, wasn't he?"

Ahiable paused, and Caleb could tell that he was carefully thinking about his response.

"Linc comes and goes. He's just supplemental, you know. He gives the Justice a sense of security."

"So can we ask him to be around for the next couple of months? You know what, do you have his contact information? I'd like to ask him if he has other colleagues who can spend the next six months or so down with us. I would feel much better if we had some extra SecuriCorp help."

Ahiable frowned again. "I thought you didn't like SecuriCorp?"

"These are unusual times we're in, Ahiable. I had my reservations about SecuriCorp before, but I know with everything going on, I would feel more confident about the Justice's safety if we have them around. A couple of them at least, you know. Let's say Linc and maybe a few others."

Ahiable shrugged. "I guess that couldn't hurt, if you're sure. I remember how much you spoke against renewing our contract with them. Let me get you Linc's Ghana information. Samuel often calls him directly when he's abroad, but I arranged for a house for him some years ago. I think he still uses it when he's in town. Give me a second."

Caleb let out a slow breath as Ahiable left the porch and entered into his house. He was close. Finally, he was close to finding Linc and getting to the bottom of this. Ahiable returned a few minutes later and handed Caleb a piece of paper.

"That's the address, and rough directions. It's easy to find. And I added a couple of phone numbers too. I'll talk to Samuel about our media and security ideas tonight. He may want to talk to Linc first, so let's see what Samuel says, and then you can follow up with Linc."

"Of course, I have to talk to the Justice too. So let's catch up tomorrow then."

As he walked away, Caleb knew that there was no way he could ask Ahiable not to talk to Samuel. That would raise suspicions, and Ahiable wouldn't understand, so he just had to let this play out. A couple of things were bound to happen. If Samuel was the one behind Bertha's murder and the attempted attack on Caleb, he would immediately ask Linc to return and finish the job once and for all. There was no way he'd do nothing if he heard Caleb was asking about Linc. He wasn't incredibly smart, but he wasn't a fool either. Alternatively, he could warn Linc to stay away and cut all ties to him. The downside to the second scenario was that Samuel had no idea how much Caleb knew so far. He probably wouldn't take chances and have Caleb walking around looking into things. If killing him weeks ago was important, then getting him out of the way now was going to be even more important. The only catch was that Caleb had no idea when or how Linc would come at him. Cat was unexpected, and if that was Linc's MO, then the next attack would be unexpected too. Thankfully, he had an address. He could be prepared.

❧

Ahiable tapped his feet rapidly against the carpet as he skimmed his notes and waited for the ex-president in Samuel's study. He was brimming with excitement. He always relished any chance he could get to meet with Samuel and discuss opportunities that would help the president shine. Ahiable knew that people thought he was incompetent, and that was mainly because of Caleb. Caleb's sharp business acumen, penchant for details, efficiency, creative thinking, and general attitude were tough to compete against. Caleb managed the Justice incredibly well, and he also played a critical role in Samuel's second term campaign. Ahiable had tried over the last four years to ensure Samuel remained relevant and in the limelight, but it was nothing compared to the buzz Caleb managed to build and sustain for the Justice. In the last four years, the Justice had appeared on over fifty magazine covers and given twenty interviews to the BBC, fifteen to CNN, and ten to Al-Jazeera. He was extensively profiled on CNN International, and he was also one of *Newsweek's* "Top 10 Powerful People in Africa." To be honest, he'd never left that list since he got included fifteen years ago, and the person who kept him there was Caleb. The Justice had a strong, formidable reputation before Caleb came along, but it was Caleb who kept him at the top. On the other hand, Ahiable hadn't been able to do much for Samuel since he left office. There were a couple of interviews and speaking events here and there, but nothing significant that he could be proud of. He also wasn't sure Samuel actually cared about his public status anymore, so Ahiable never felt pushed to do more. This election, however, could be his opportunity to let Samuel shine. Caleb's visit today was a godsend. Initially, Ahiable knew that after the announcement of the Justice's candidacy, Samuel would be required to make some public appearances after the party selected a candidate. However, participating in the process before the congress was going to be perfect. It would position Samuel further as the leader and shepherd of the party and its candidates. This could be a new opportunity for him to shine and be part of a process that could change the course of the country. This could be it, for both him and Samuel.

"Ahiable, I thought we'd discussed that after dinner isn't a good time for these meetings."

Ahiable stood up quickly as Samuel entered the study. The former president looked irritated and annoyed. Ahiable glanced down at the printed Outlook calendar in his folder.

"I'm sorry, sir, I don't remember that. I have this as a standing meeting every Tuesday at 8 p.m."

"Change it."

Samuel walked over to his desk and sat down. He motioned to the chair opposite the desk, and Ahiable scuttled over to sit.

"Make this quick. I have things to do."

"Yes, of course, sir. Well, Caleb came over to see me today."

Samuel tried not to react, but his eyes betrayed him and narrowed anxiously. This was the second time someone had brought up Caleb's name today, and the first time it was bad news—news he was trying hard not to think about.

"Caleb?"

"Yes, yes, we discussed a couple of things, particularly how we can involve you more in the campaign process. Since you and the Justice share similar ideals, he wants to capitalize on that. I did remind him that you can't appear to be supporting one candidate over the others, so perhaps we can do a series of internal party events with you and all the candidates, like interviews, debates, forums, things like that. Basically, I'm thinking events that position you as the leader of the party."

Samuel let out his breath, unaware that he was even holding it in. He shrugged at Ahiable.

"Sounds fine, work it out."

"Okay, okay, but he's also concerned about security, which is reasonable considering the recent attacks on him. If the GFP is desperate enough, who knows what they could do? So, he asked about Linc. I think he ran into him at the airport, and just wants to know if we could get Linc and a couple of other SecuriCorp guys around for the next six months or so. I don't think that could hurt, but I want your opinion of course."

Samuel gripped the handles of his seat and stared blankly at Ahiable as he struggled not to react. Earlier today, Annan called him and told him Caleb was digging around into SecuriCorp, but he didn't know what could have sent Caleb in that direction. They both agreed that the likelihood of Caleb finding out more was inevitable, but this was worse than Samuel thought.

"Sir?"

Ahiable's voice was like a mouse's, but it got Samuel out of the dense fog clouding his thoughts.

"Did he mention Linc directly by name, or did he just ask for SecuriCorp?"

Ahiable paused, sensing that something was amiss. He probably shouldn't have given Caleb Linc's address, but that was information he wasn't going to share.

"He mentioned Linc's name, sir. He said he saw him briefly at the airport, which just got him thinking about beefing up the candidates' security."

Samuel closed his eyes briefly as his heart skipped a beat. If Caleb had Linc's name, then Caleb was definitely on to something. He didn't know how this was possible, but somehow Caleb had probably connected Linc to his recent attacks. Why else would he be looking into SecuriCorp and asking Ahiable about Linc? Why else?

"Did he give you any other specifics? Why Linc or SecuriCorp?"

Ahiable's nervousness increased. The president was trying hard to mask his true reactions, but it was obvious that he was concerned that Caleb was asking about Linc. Ahiable couldn't understand why. He didn't know that the president kept his association with Linc a secret. The man was his bodyguard for a couple of years and then came in every now and then to escort him around. Was all of that supposed to be a secret?

Ahiable took a deep breath. "No specifics, sir. He said it's because of the attacks on him, but I think Caleb is actually afraid. I know that's surprising, but what the GFP did must have really shaken him up. He says he wouldn't put anything past them and he'd feel more confident if we had the extra hands."

"We have G4S."

"They're paid for by the government, so they can be compromised."

Samuel squinted at Ahiable. "Compromised? Is that your word or his?"

"Uh…his words, not mine," Ahiable stuttered, eager to distance himself from this whole situation. Samuel didn't look happy at all.

"Okay, I need to think about it. When do you need to get back to him?"

"I told him tomorrow."

"Stall for a while. I need to talk to Linc and see if he'd be willing to come back with a group. It could be costly though. So just give me a few days to talk to him and think things through. This isn't urgent. Work on the media campaign, and we'll discuss security later."

"That's fine. So, I suggested to Caleb that we should also do internal party debates along with the interviews. We could do a series of events that showcases all four candidates and you. We could also—"

Samuel raised his hands and shook his head. Ahiable stopped talking immediately.

"I don't have time for this right now. I have things to do. Just sort this out with Caleb, but make sure you don't commit to anything without my consent."

"Of course, sure, I'll leave you then. Thanks again. Let me know if there is anything you need," Ahiable mumbled.

Samuel nodded and gestured impatiently toward his study door. Ahiable said thanks again and left, obviously disappointed he didn't get the time to claim credit for all the ideas he and Caleb had discussed earlier that day, but also relieved that Samuel hadn't exploded at him for discussing Linc with Caleb. He hoped that Caleb wouldn't reach out to Linc directly. He had to try and salvage the situation.

Samuel waited until the door closed behind Ahiable, and then he slapped his desk immediately, cursing. Caleb, Caleb, Caleb! The man was beginning to get on his last nerves. He was annoyingly persistent, and although that attribute had benefited Samuel before, now it was wearing him down.

Samuel knew he didn't have a lot of options.

One, he could ignore this recent development and just wait to see what Caleb was going to do next. Linc could disappear, and Caleb would have nothing to go on. Without the man, there wasn't much he could do. The downside of that option was the deal. Caleb may not have Linc, but he could unravel the deal they were so close to finalizing. All his life, Samuel had never thought he could ever have $150 million. Sure, he'd siphoned some millions during his eight-year term in office, but it wasn't more than $50 million, and he'd spent quite a bit on this home, other properties, cars, family, girlfriends, luxury holidays, and so forth. With $150 million, he would be set for life. SecuriCorp was going to deposit $30 million a year into an offshore account in his name until the $150 million was fully paid. The money was so close, and after working on this deal for years, he could practically taste it. Heck, he'd even mentally spent some of it. So if Samuel did nothing, Caleb could destroy his chances of closing the deal of a lifetime.

The second option was riskier, but had a bigger payout. He could have Linc return and try to finish Caleb off for good. Caleb was a man. That was the bottom line. He could be killed. Sure, Linc's associate Cat had almost executed a near-perfect murder, but Caleb just happened to be at the right place at the right time. He couldn't be lucky twice, three times actually, counting Josh's failed attempt as well. Somehow, Linc was just going to have to get the job done. Unfortunately, if Linc failed again, the consequences would be disastrous on many fronts. First of all, if both Linc and Caleb survived the attempt and Caleb was the victor, he could drag Linc right up to the police or dig the truth out of him somehow. Second, every political pundit out there would be suspicious of all these incidents involving Caleb Osei. They'd question whether the GFP was truly behind it, and they could even start looking into the Justice and his own party. They didn't need any scrutiny when the Justice was clearly in the lead to win the election. Scrutiny could also put the deal in jeopardy.

Samuel sighed. Either way he could be screwed, but he had very little control over the first option. He really couldn't just let Caleb continue on the path he was on. He just couldn't. As risky as the second option was, at least he had some control over that. He just had to emphasize to Linc that this had to be clean and successful. Failure was not an option.

Samuel picked up his cell and dialed. It was answered on the second ring.

"Yes?"

"I need you back."

"I've been expecting you to ask. He's getting closer, isn't he?"

"Very close. I need you to do this right. One last shot, and that's it. You can't fail, do you understand?"

"I won't fail. I'll need his itinerary for the next two weeks and some other information."

"Anything you need you'll get, but two weeks is too long. He could blow this whole thing apart within a week. He already has your name."

"He does?"

"Yes, so do this soon, but do it right. I can't stress that enough. Do it right."

"Just consider it done. End of the week."

Linc hung up, and Samuel made another call.

"It's worse than we thought. He has Linc's name."

"Jesus, are you serious? How did that happen?"

"We knew this day would come. The minute he found out about the affair, it was only a matter of time."

"Then you should have done it right the last time. That's what caused this, the botched attempt by Linc."

Samuel scowled. "I am not in the mood for a lecture today. It doesn't matter what happened then. What matters is what we do next."

"You know where I stand on this. Just get it done."

"Good, consider it done, but I'm going to need his itinerary."

"Not a problem. I can get you that. Just get it done right, Samuel."

Samuel sat in his office for hours after the last call. He couldn't move. He hadn't been this apprehensive since his run for his second term. There was just so much on the line, and he had a very bad feeling about this, but the decision had been made, and he had to trust that he'd made the right one. Now, come what may.

25

'*F*ine, I understand, of course. Just keep me posted."

Caleb cussed out loud and threw his phone right across the living room. It missed the TV by inches and smashed against the wall behind the TV console. The battery, back cover, and other pieces came apart. Abby looked up sharply from her magazine and raised an eyebrow at him.

"Hey, what's going on?" she asked as she lifted herself up from her armchair to go pick up the pieces.

Caleb shook his head and waved her back down. He walked over to the remnants of his phone, picked the pieces up, and started putting them back together. Abby was still staring at him.

"Do you want to tell me what's going on? Who were you talking to?"

"It's nothing important," he mumbled.

"Nothing important? You just threw your phone at my TV."

"I wasn't aiming for your precious TV, Abby," he snapped.

She sighed. "I know, I know, but don't tell me it's nothing. Come on, tell me, what's going on?"

"Someone's been blowing me off for days," he muttered angrily.

"Campaign related, or something else?" Abby asked, concerned that he was back to his "someone tried to kill me and I need to find him" mode. He'd seemed consumed by the campaign for the past few days, and she was grateful for that, but with Caleb she could never tell. She hadn't paid attention to his call even though he was sitting in the sofa right across from her, and now she wished she'd at least tried to eavesdrop.

Caleb knew what she was trying to ask, but he wasn't prepared to answer.

"It's okay, babe, honestly, nothing important. I'm just gonna go make a few more calls in the study, okay?"

He walked over to her, kissed the top of her head in an attempt to reassure her, and then disappeared into her study. Caleb dropped his phone onto the desk and dropped into the chair. This last call with Ahiable was threatening to put him over the edge. The man had been blowing him off for days now, and Caleb knew it was because of Samuel. He couldn't get a straight answer out of Ahiable on anything—Linc, SecuriCorp, or the planned media blitz. Ahiable was in complete shutdown mode, and Caleb suspected it was because Samuel had put the muzzle on him. He'd been to Linc's address a couple of times over the past few days, but there was nothing or no one there. It was sparsely furnished, and there were no personal effects or items, not even a hairbrush or toothbrush. It was obviously not a home, just a place Linc slept in, if he slept at all.

Caleb leaned against the chair and stared at the ceiling. He was at a dead end now. He suspected that Samuel had warned Linc and told him not to come back. If that was the case, what now? He really didn't have enough to shake up Samuel. He was the former president. Caleb couldn't just walk up to him and accuse him of trying to kill him. So what if he had a picture of Linc picking up Cat from the airport? He claimed he couldn't remember anything, and he'd evaded the police each time they tried to question him about the poisoning, so there was nothing documented at the police station that implicated Cat. He really had nothing. No leads, no ideas, nothing. He'd taken a chance by going to Ahiable, and it'd obviously backfired. He had an address that was vacant and would probably be cleared out and sold within the next week. Linc was officially a ghost now. Caleb took a deep breath. He had one last option left. He couldn't go directly to the former president, but there was one person he could call.

"Caleb, I was going to wait till Monday to tell you, but good job on the speech for next week. Were we able to confirm that Bill Gates plans to be at the foundation's gala? Let's get a confirmation as soon as possible. I'd like to invite him and Melissa over to dinner. It would be a good photo op."

"I know about SecuriCorp, Justice. I know all about SecuriCorp."

There was dead silence on the line, and the silence stretched into minutes. Caleb hoped fervently that the Justice wouldn't feign ignorance or lie.

"What you and Samuel have been doing, what you have planned isn't going to work. You know that, don't you?" Caleb continued. He needed some type of confession badly.

The silence on the phone continued again, but Caleb began to feel that he had him. He had the Justice.

"I'd rather not discuss this on the phone. Why don't you come over to the house? I'll tell you everything and then you can decide for yourself what you want to do. Okay? Come by. I'll talk."

"Fine, I'll be there in ten minutes. I don't want any lies or anything, sir. I really don't have the patience for that anymore. I told you before, the next time I point a gun at you, I will pull the trigger. And I will only pull a gun on you if you lie."

"I said I'll talk. No lies. See you in ten."

Back in his study, Justice Annan knew he didn't have much of a choice. What was going to happen next was inevitable. He just had to deal with it.

Caleb got up from the desk and walked back out to the living room. Abby was still curled up in her armchair reading. He picked up his car keys from the center table. She raised an eyebrow at him.

"I thought we were just going to spend today at home," she said quietly, aware that she probably sounded clingy. Besides, it was not exactly his home. Caleb had the right to come and go as he pleased.

"I need to go see your dad now, urgent work stuff. I won't be long, okay? Let's go watch a movie later. Find out what's showing," Caleb said, gathering other stuff from the table and heading toward the door.

Abby jumped up from the chair.

"I'm going with you. I think it would be good for my parents to see us together. Maybe we can stay for lunch."

"Abby—"

"No, no, no arguing. Give me one minute to change. If I go like this, my mother will tell me I look like a homeless person. So one minute, okay?"

Abby scurried off to her bedroom, leaving Caleb speechless in the living room. He didn't know what he would do if the Justice confessed to trying to kill him, but he didn't want Abby anywhere close when that confrontation happened. She appeared five minutes later. The oversized t-shirt and sweatpants were gone, replaced by a pink blouse and dark blue skinny jeans. It amused him that she had no qualms about looking scruffy around him, but for her parents she had to look her best.

"Okay, I'm ready."

"Abby, I'd really prefer to go alone. I have a lot to discuss with your father. There's no telling when we'd be done. It could take a while, and I know you wouldn't want to stay with your parents all day," he said, hoping she would acquiesce and stay home.

"Let's take my car then. If I want to leave, I'll leave and pick you up later for the movie. How's that?"

Caleb sighed. There was no getting rid of her.

"Fine, that's fine. Can you go start the car? I'd like to change my shirt as well. You can't be the only one looking spiffy."

Abby beamed and grabbed her bag from the side table next to the sofa. She reached up and kissed him on the cheek.

"I'll be downstairs."

Caleb walked into the bedroom, but he didn't head for the closet where he had some of his clothes. Instead, he went to the bed, lifted up the mattress, and pulled the gun tucked underneath his shirt out. He dropped it on the platform and then dropped the mattress. If Abby was coming with him, then he didn't want to carry a gun on him. In any case, he had no plans of taking it to that level. The Justice was going to confess, and if he didn't, he would have to coerce him another way. He stared at the bed for a moment, torn between taking the gun and leaving it.

"Shit," he swore, picked the gun back up, and walked away.

"You didn't change," Abby said, squinting at him.

"I figured if it looked good for you, then it should be fine for your parents as well."

"Are you trying to tell me something, Caleb Osei? You think since I had on sweatpants around you I should be okay wearing sweatpants to see my parents?"

"Your words, babe, not mine," Caleb said, smiling at her.

She rolled her eyes at him and pulled away from the apartment garage. She started to talk about how judgmental her mother was and how she needed to look like an adult around her, but Caleb wasn't paying attention. His mind was racing. He was trying to figure out what possibly could have driven the Justice and the former president to try to kill him. What? It couldn't be because he knew about the Justice's affair. That didn't make sense, but Cat came over to poison him after he confronted the Justice about that, so it had to be linked. Was the affair so explosive that the Justice would try to kill him? And why was Samuel involved? Why Linc? Further, Cat was in the country for months before Caleb even found out about Bertha and the Justice. None of it made sense, which was why he was so apprehensive about this discussion.

"Are you listening to me, Caleb?"

Caleb rubbed his eyes and turned to look at her.

"Sorry, I just have a lot on my mind. Please go on, I'm all ears now."

Abby started to talk again, and Caleb tried to listen, but he just couldn't concentrate. His eyes drifted out the window, his eyes absentmindedly scanning cars as they drove along. And that's when he saw it. Caleb sat upright and peered through the side mirror, trying to figure out if he was seeing correctly. It looked like the Ford Explorer two cars behind was following them.

"Can you change lanes, Abby? Move to the right."

"What?" Abby stared quizzically at him.

"Just humor me, okay? Change lanes to the right."

"Caleb, what is going on? The light is about to switch to red. I can't switch now. I just need to slow down and stay here."

"Oh Jesus, Abby, just do what I ask. Please switch lanes!" Caleb snapped.

Abby glanced at her mirrors, indicated, and then moved over into the inner lane. She looked at Caleb, but his eyes were fixed intently on the side mirror. Seconds later, Caleb saw the Ford switch lanes into theirs, ending up directly behind them. As Abby slowed down and stopped at the red light, Caleb swung around from the mirrors and looked through the back window, trying to get a better look at the driver of the Ford. The Ford pulled up to a stop right behind them, and then Caleb saw him. It was Linc. Their eyes met, and Caleb felt a chill down his spine. The man's eyes were completely dead and cold. Caleb gritted his teeth. He wasn't going to let Linc get away this time. Caleb opened the passenger door and stepped out.

"Caleb!" he heard Abby shout, but he ignored her. He started walking toward the Ford, grateful that he'd picked up his gun, because he had no doubt that Linc had one on him. He knew that this was it. If they continued driving, Linc could take a different route and disappear for good. He just couldn't let that happen. He would pull his gun on Linc, force him to let him into the car, and then they would drive off and have a chat. A look of surprise crossed Linc's face for a second as Caleb approached. Linc reached down for something to his right. Caleb slid his hand behind his shirt and quickened his pace. And then Linc did the unexpected. He stepped on the gas and rammed hard into Abby's car.

"Jesus! Abby!" Caleb spun around and screamed as Linc rammed her a second time. The Q7 jolted forward, and Caleb watched in horror as Abby's head hit the steering wheel hard. He turned around and hurried toward her, but Linc had no intention of stopping. The next few seconds happened so fast that Caleb had no opportunity to react. He could feel his feet moving fast toward Abby. He felt his fingers touch the car door, and then he felt the car jerk forward hard and fast—and right into the path of the oncoming cars crossing to turn into the opposite lanes. He saw Abby slumped over the steering wheel, powerless as her car rolled right into the path of a tipper truck. Caleb's mouth fell open as the truck barreling down the road slammed into Abby's car. The Q7 flipped up and over, and then crashed back down onto the road. The sounds of crashing metal and glass, mingled with the bystanders' screams, pierced Caleb's core. His knees buckled, and then he collapsed like a ragdoll onto the street.

"Dr. Anyan, can you come in here? I think he's coming around."

Caleb groaned as pain shot through his neck and down his shoulders. He struggled to sit up, but his head felt like it was on fire. He blinked rapidly and scanned the room, trying to make sense of where he was. It looked and smelled like a hospital room, but he was struggling to see through the pain in his head. Eventually the shapes in the room started to take form, and his eyes fell on the person beside him to his right.

Caleb lunged at the Justice, but hands from the left restrained him. The Justice shook his head at the doctor and waved him back.

"It's okay, doctor, it's okay. Can you please give us a moment?"

The doctor frowned at the Justice.

"I need to check him, sir, and it's obviously not safe for you to be alone with him."

"Anyan, I'm fine, okay. Just give me a few minutes. I'll call you or scream if I need to."

The doctor glanced down at Caleb, but Caleb's eyes were fixed on the Justice. He wasn't going to look away. The doctor slowly walked out of the room and closed the door.

"You son of a bitch! You son of a bitch! What have you done? Jesus Christ, Abby! Where's Abby? Where's Abby, goddamn it!" Caleb screamed, struggling to sit up.

"Abby is in surgery. It's critical, but they're trying their best."

"Jesus Christ!" Caleb cursed again. He felt a lump swell in his throat, and he lunged again at the Justice.

"Caleb! Calm down! I didn't do this!"

"Yes you did! It was Linc! I saw him. Do you hear me? I saw him. You and Samuel hired Linc to kill me. I know it! You tried to poison me, and now this! I saw him, Justice. I saw him today, and I saw him four years ago the morning we found Bertha's body. He was there! I need the truth, and I need it now. You, Samuel, SecuriCorp, Bertha, all of it!" Caleb screamed at the Justice.

Caleb frowned as he saw a look of confusion, surprise, and shock cross the Justice's face. Caleb shook his head rapidly.

"Don't you dare deny this! Don't you dare! Tell me the truth!"

"I swear....I swear it, I don't know about Linc being at Bertha's. I don't know about Linc being in town or trying to kill you. I don't know about any of it! As far as I know, Samuel and I are trying to get a deal with SecuriCorp signed. That's it. I thought that was what you were talking about on the phone. I thought you knew about the deal."

Caleb watched the Justice closely as he dropped into the chair next to the hospital bed. He looked perplexed and confused. Caleb forced himself to sit upright and looked the Justice in the eye.

"I need the truth, sir. I need all of it, right now."

"SecuriCorp made Samuel an offer during his first term. They said they would come in and privatize the Ghana army. They would be responsible for everything: training, accommodations, equipment, weapons, technology, salaries, everything. It made sense to us, it really did, but you came along and you had such a vehement reaction to them being here. I listened to you and asked Samuel to kill the deal."

The Justice paused and stared down at his hands. They were shaking. Caleb had no time for pity.

"Then what happened? I said I need to know everything, so don't stop talking."

"Samuel got Linc back in to the country on the side and worked with him for a couple of years. Linc got Samuel in touch with some of the SecuriCorp bigwigs, and the talks of privatization started again. I did my research. I spoke to the COO myself. I spoke to all their senior leaders. I looked into every single report or investigation that had been conducted against them, and it just seemed like speculation. I started to agree that privatization could be a good deal for the country. The money we spend on the army now can be spent on hospitals and education. They also made Samuel and myself an offer. If we could get the privatization deal passed in parliament, we would get $300 million—$150 million each."

Caleb swore under his breath. This was about money?

"You've never been about money, Justice. It's never been about that for you."

"A hundred and fifty million dollars can make anyone be about the money, but that wasn't really why I wanted this. I felt that Ghana could benefit from the privatization. You and I both know that our army is in shambles. They're glorified watchmen for neighboring countries. They live in slum barracks and get paid less than housemaids. We use weapons from twenty years ago, and we beg for scraps from the west. The west already controls our army. They tell us what to do and where to go. They send us helicopters and tanks every now and then, and if we're lucky, we get some fancy gear, and that's every five years. It's a pathetic army, and if anything ever happened here, we wouldn't be able to defend ourselves. We needed this."

"So you just wanted Ghana to have a better army. You expect me to believe that that's it?"

"It's the truth. It was a ten-year deal, and we would get everything. Upgraded camps, the latest technology, training simulations and facilitations, weapons, the whole nine yards, you name it. For ten years, they would build the army up, instill pride of country and service into the men, and restore us to some glory. So yes, I wanted that for Ghana."

"Where do I fit in? Where does Bertha fit in? Why was Linc there the morning she was found? And why the heck is he trying to kill me? I didn't know anything about the deal. All I knew was that you had an affair with Bertha and Joseph is your son. That's it. How does that warrant a hit?"

"Samuel also had an affair with Bertha," the Justice mumbled.

Caleb frowned. "What are you talking about?"

"I told you that Bertha and I ended our relationship and she started seeing other men. Samuel was one of them. I found out about it, and I spoke to them both. Bertha said it was their business. I left it at that. After Bertha was killed, Samuel was equally devastated. I never thought, or suspected, that he could have done something. He had no reason to. I believe that he loved her. If you saw Linc there, perhaps it was just a coincidence. Perhaps Samuel couldn't come over himself. He was still president. Maybe he sent Linc to check on what was happening."

"And me? I know Linc tried to kill me. He picked up Cat Daly from the airport in JFK. I have a picture of the two of them. Cat Daly is the girl I was seeing who tried to kill me. So how do you explain any of that, huh?"

"The day you confronted me about Bertha, I called Samuel. I told him you knew about my affair and that I had decided to come clean. I also told him that you quit working for me, and then we talked about the deal. We were both concerned that you would find out more about the deal. We knew you were resourceful enough. But I swear to you, I explicitly told him you were off limits. I told him that, but he panicked, which doesn't surprise me because he also had an affair with her, and maybe he was hiding more. I saw him a few days later, and he admitted that he tried to have you killed. I told him again to let it go, to stay away from you and let whatever happen, happen. I told him that! I insisted! I had no idea Linc was back in town, and I had no idea that Samuel planned to try again. No idea. You have to believe me."

"Why did he plan all of this before I even found out about the affair? The attempt on my life wasn't a knee-jerk reaction. It was planned. Cat was in Ghana for months before I found out about your affair, and she had contact with Linc during that time. So why was she here? Why go to all that trouble?"

"Because you're Caleb. From the minute we started working on the deal, we knew you could find out any minute. I had prepared responses for you in case you found out about the affair or the deal, but maybe Samuel took his preparation a little further."

Caleb rubbed his temples and shook his head.

"Stop, stop, stop! None of this makes any sense! None of it!"

"The truth often sounds like fiction," the Justice said quietly.

Caleb got up from the bed and gripped the railing as blackness threatened to engulf him.

"You hit your head very badly, Caleb. You really should be resting."

"I need to know what is going on, and none of what you're saying makes sense! It sounds like a damn story! Linc is at Bertha's, but that's all a coincidence? Just there to check on what happened? Linc plants a girl in my life, and I'm supposed to believe that Samuel did that because he was worried I would find out about the deal and his affair with your sister-in-law? Why go to all that trouble for that? I don't buy it. I don't buy any of it."

The Justice was silent. Caleb walked slowly up and down the room as he tried to digest the Justice's story. It was insane, and it was full of holes. He stood in front of the Justice, leaned forward, and looked into his eyes.

"Are you telling me the truth?" Caleb hissed.

"The truth as I know it. I told Samuel you knew about the affair, and then last week when Abby mentioned that you were investigating SecuriCorp, I told Samuel as well. I told him it was only a matter of time before you found out about the deal, and I would confess to it if you did. Samuel must have panicked."

Caleb maintained his gaze on the Justice.

"So this was all Linc and Samuel."

"I was involved in the deal, and I knew Samuel was involved in the poison attempt, but I told him to stay away from you. I did, I swear it on Adubea's life. I swear it."

Caleb tore his gaze away and looked down at the floor. He believed the Justice. What was in his eyes wasn't deceit, but pain and regret.

"Abby...what are the doctors saying?" Caleb asked.

"It's touch and go. She was badly injured, so I just don't know if she's going to make it," the Justice said softly. He leaned forward in the chair and started sobbing.

Caleb sat on the bed, still and numb. This was his fault. He was so desperate to find out the truth. He shouldn't have gotten out of the car. He put Abby at risk. He just shouldn't have. They sat together for a few minutes as the Justice cried quietly in the chair. Eventually Caleb spoke.

"I had a gun on me. Do you know where it is?"

The Justice pointed to a duffel bag by the bed.

"The doctor was going to hand it in to the police, but I asked for it. He didn't want to, but eventually he gave it to me."

Caleb dug into the bag and pulled out the gun.

"I need to go. Linc and Samuel, I can't just let them get away with this. Do you understand that? I don't know what's going to happen, but I need to go."

The Justice nodded, and Caleb stared at him.

"If I'm not back and Abby wakes up, if she pulls through, tell her that I love her. Do you understand that? Whatever happens, tell her that for me. That I love her more than life," Caleb said, choking back sobs.

Annan stood up from the chair and stretched his hand out to Caleb. Caleb shook it.

"You must do what you must, just as I would," the Justice said.

Caleb nodded and then walked out the door.

.

26

The whole house was bathed in darkness, and there was no sign of life or movement, but Caleb still approached cautiously. Both hands gripped his gun tightly, pointing the silencer downward as Caleb slowly walked up to the front door. He leaned against the wall for a brief moment, trying to still his rapidly beating heart and the pain still sweeping through his head. After a few seconds, he gently turned the door handle. The door opened, and he stepped through.

A light in the corner of the room flickered on, and Caleb instantly raised his gun in that direction. Linc was seated in an armchair propped up against the wall in the corner of the sparse living room. The gun in his hand was trained on Caleb, safety off.

"Four whole hours. I thought you'd be here much sooner than that."

"Concussion. I was unconscious."

"Glad you could make it. I've been waiting for you."

"I actually didn't expect to find you here. I thought you'd be gone by now."

"No, I have very specific orders. This needs to be finished."

"I'm here to talk to you about that. Your orders, and whatever 'this' is that needs to be finished."

Caleb inched forward slowly, but Linc shook his head at him.

"I'd appreciate it if you remain where you are," he said as his grip tightened on the gun pointed at Caleb.

"So what now, Linc?"

Linc rose from the chair and pulled a second gun from the back of his shirt. Without any preamble or warning, he fired both guns. Caleb dropped to the floor instantly as two bullets ripped through his shoulder. He got two shots off, but one grazed past Linc's arm and the other hit the mirror on the wall behind Linc. The mirror shattered, and the spray of glass temporarily blinded Linc, but he didn't lower his guns for even a second as he continued to fire in Caleb's direction. Caleb scrambled across the floor and fired back at Linc wildly as he attempted to crawl behind the armoire plopped in the corner near the door. A bullet grazed his cheek, but knowing that Linc was going to be on him in seconds, he ignored the pain, placed his feet firmly against the armoire, and pushed with all the strength he could muster. The armoire only tipped slightly forward toward Linc, and he lowered his guns for a moment, bracing for impact. When none came, he quickly placed his shoulders against the armoire and pushed it right back at Caleb. Caleb's eyes widened in horror as the massive piece of furniture hurtled back toward him. He dropped his gun and raised his arms to cover his face, but it didn't minimize the impact as the armoire smashed hard on top of him. His screams were interrupted as Linc grabbed his legs and yanked him from underneath the wood and glass. Caleb gritted his teeth as Linc grabbed him again, this time by the neck, lifted him clear off the ground, and slammed him hard against the concrete floor. Caleb felt and heard bones cracking, but his whole body was on fire with pain, and he had no idea which bones just broke. Before he had a chance to react, Linc lifted him up from the floor by his neck again. Caleb tried to loosen Linc's hold and kicked at him, but Linc's grip was like a vice, and his strength and height gave him a clear advantage over Caleb. He dangled Caleb for a moment, choked him, and then slammed him back into the floor, harder than the first time.

Caleb screamed in agony and turned on this side, sputtering and coughing. Even in the haze of pain, he knew that the liquid he was coughing was blood. He also knew that he was seconds away from death. He really couldn't endure any more of this beating. He raised his left hand in defeat as his right dug into his side pockets.

"Stop, please stop. I came to talk. I just want to know," he pled, coughing up more blood.

"This is me talking," Linc grunted as he lifted Caleb up once more.

Caleb's fingers circled his pocketknife, and he yanked it out and flicked it open. Without wasting a moment, he buried it deep into Linc's arm.

The burly man winced, but instead of loosening his hold, he tightened his grip around Caleb's neck and squeezed. Caleb pulled the knife out from Linc's arm and started to slash and dice frantically as he gasped desperately for air. He stabbed repeatedly and blindly, but soon hopelessness and darkness engulfed him. The knife dropped, his body slumped, and the last thing he saw was the concrete floor as his body hit it for the third and final time.

Caleb's eyes fluttered open slowly, and he stared into the darkness. His whole body felt as if it'd been soaked in fuel and lit on fire. He wondered if this was hell—absolute darkness and incomprehensible pain. After a few seconds, his eyes adjusted to the room, and he recognized that he was still in Linc's living room. Caleb struggled to sit up, but his left shoulder refused to cooperate. Eventually, he dragged himself on his side across the room to the wall and propped his body against it. His eyes threatened to close, but he forced them open, scanning the room, trying to make sense of what had happened. Linc's body was spread on the floor a few feet from him, and even in the poor light, Caleb could see that his stabbing had eventually done some damage. Linc's arms, face, and neck were badly slashed. Caleb scanned the room, and his eyes fell on Linc's guns a few meters from his body. Caleb forced himself up, picked up both guns, and checked them. One was empty, but the other had three bullets left. He held onto that one and walked over to Linc's body. He prodded it. There was a slight flutter behind Linc's eyelids. Caleb stepped back, focused the gun properly on Linc, and then prodded him again. Linc's fingers moved slightly, and Caleb breathed a

sigh of relief. He came here for answers, and he was determined to get them.

Ten minutes later, a barely conscious Linc was gagged
and bound to a dining chair placed in the bathroom next
to the bathtub. There was a towel draped across his lap
and a bucket of water next to his feet. Caleb was standing
in front of the bathroom mirror, bare-chested and treating
his wounds. He'd slammed his shoulders against the wall
and managed to pop the dislocation back in place, but not
even the five painkillers he'd downed could stop the pain
from tearing through him. He'd painstakingly dug out
chards of glass and wood from his body, and thankfully the
two bullets that hit him when Linc first started firing had
been through and through. However, there wasn't much
he could do about his broken ribs and the frightening gash
at the back of his head. He needed medical attention, but
that was just going to have to wait. He popped two more
painkillers into his mouth and then turned around to face
Linc, who was staring coldly at him.

"When I was a new recruit, I heard rumors that
SecuriCorp actually invented waterboarding and each
SecuriCorp soldier could endure waterboarding for up to
six hours straight. I don't know if it's true or not, but hey,
if I have a SecuriCorp soldier in front of me and water, I
might as well test the theory, right?"

Linc glowered silently at him.

"I'm going to kill you. I hope you recognize that.
You're a major tough cookie and you've lost a lot of blood
from those cuts I inflicted on you, but you're not going to
die from that. I'm going to put a bullet right between your
eyes. Do you understand that?"

Linc continued to glare at him.

"To be honest, waterboarding you, torturing you, that's going to take up too much time, and I don't have time. I need to get treatment or I could die myself, and what would be the use of all of this then? So here's what we'll do. We're going to have a conversation, and I don't mean the type of conversation where you slam me into a concrete floor and break my ribs. Nope, not that type of conversation. I want us to talk, honestly and truthfully. Can you do that?"

After a few seconds, Linc nodded his head. With the gun trained on Linc, Caleb removed the gag.

"If I talk or don't talk, you're going to kill me anyways," Linc muttered.

Caleb nodded. The two men stared at each other for a moment, and then Linc started.

"What do you want to know?"

"Let's start with today. Abby is in the hospital near death. Why did you do that today?"

"You were walking toward me with a gun. I reached for mine, but it slipped under the seat. I didn't have a lot of options. It was either that or wait for you to shoot me right there."

"I wasn't going to shoot you there. I was going to force you to let me in, go for a drive, and talk."

Linc frowned at Caleb. "That wasn't very smart thinking, was it? You approached me with a gun and you expected that I was just going to sit there and let you in? Is that what the US army taught you?"

Caleb waved the gun threateningly at Linc.

"I'm the one asking the damn questions!" he snapped.

"So go ahead."

"What happened to Bertha four years ago? What were you doing there?"

"I was told to go clean it up."

It was Caleb's turn to frown.

"What were you asked to go clean up? Who asked you? Talk to me, and stop using vague sentences!"

"The president told me to go clean it up. So I went. I shot the security man at the gate, went in, and found the body in the living room. She was already dead. I broke up a few things in the house, took some items, and made it look like a robbery. I left and came back in the morning, just to make sure that nothing else needed to be done."

Caleb let Linc's words sink in for a moment. What Linc said explained why the guard was shot but Bertha was stabbed. Someone else killed Bertha.

"Did Samuel kill her?" Caleb asked pointedly.

"I don't know. He called me and told me she was dead and that he needed me to go fix the situation left behind."

"Was he having an affair with her?"

"Yes, he was."

Then it was more than likely that Samuel killed her, Caleb thought. She must have threatened to expose him or something. It was either about the affair or the SecuriCorp deal, but whatever it was, it got her killed. The security man must have known the killer too, because he let him walk right out. It was someone within her inner circle, and it had to be Samuel—otherwise why would he ask Linc to go clean it up?

"And me? Where do I fit into all of this? Why did you try to kill me? You had Cat here months before I knew anything."

"I've been watching you for years, Caleb, watching you just as you've watched others and built a pile of evidence on the people around you. You won Samuel his reelection, but he's never been comfortable with you. He suspected that eventually you would find out something, so I watched and waited. I saw you with your university girls and realized that was your weakness, so I got Anna, or Cat as you call her, down here. Eventually, I knew we would get the go-ahead to kill you."

"Samuel gave you the go-ahead."

"Yes," Linc said, even though Caleb hadn't directly asked him a question.

Caleb paused. So, the Justice was telling the truth. It all tied back to Samuel. He must have had a lot to lose.

"Why did he want me dead so badly? The day you sent Cat to me, the only thing I knew was that Annan had an affair with his sister-in-law and they had a son. That was it. I knew nothing about Samuel. Why would he consider me a risk?"

"I don't know," Linc said simply.

Caleb stared at him, but his mind was elsewhere. Linc's story made sense, but Caleb still didn't understand why Samuel would consider him a threat. Did he really think that by finding out about Annan, Caleb would automatically find out about Samuel's own affair as well? Why would he risk getting rid of Caleb based on such a far-fetched possibility?

Caleb focused his gaze back on Linc.

"Where is Samuel now?"

"I don't know. If I did, I would tell you."

"And my dear ex-girlfriend? Where is Cat? Who was she?"

Linc shook his head. "I can't tell you that."

Caleb recognized the look in Linc's eyes.

"You can throw Samuel under the bus but not Cat, because she meant something to you, huh?"

Linc maintained Caleb's gaze but didn't say a word, and Caleb knew that Linc was done talking. He stood up and raised the gun at Linc. Linc's eyes didn't waver, and there was no fear in them. Caleb hated him for what he'd done to Abby, but he also recognized that Linc was just a pawn, a soldier who took orders and did as he was told. Like Caleb, Linc was also obviously a man in love with a woman, a woman he'd sent in to do his boss's bidding. They were all pawns. He was the Justice's pawn, and Linc was Samuel's. Even though Caleb felt sorry for him, he knew he had to do what he came to do.

He pulled the trigger twice and watched as Linc's head was flung back by the force of the bullets. Then he walked over to the body and checked his pulse. It was really unnecessary to do that, but this was Linc. Satisfied that the man was dead, Caleb sat at the edge of the bathtub and started thinking. What he was thinking of doing was pure madness and suicide, but he'd come too far to stop now. He couldn't just stop, not right now. There was just one more thing left to do, and then hopefully it would all be over.

༄

Samuel poured himself a glass of cognac and nestled into the cozy sofa in the living room. He'd been on edge all day, but now he could breathe. Linc texted him half an hour ago and said that it was done. Caleb was dead. Samuel texted him back, telling him to get rid of the body and come up to the Shai Hills to his home there. Samuel wanted to talk to Linc about Abby. What he'd done was unnecessary, and it was definitely going to get the Justice riled up. He was surprised Annan hadn't called him, but he suspected it was because he was with his daughter at the hospital. If Annan unwisely decided to retaliate, then he needed Linc with him. That was why he left Accra as soon as he heard about the accident. He needed to put as much distance between himself and the situation as he could. It was such a stupid thing for Linc to do, and it made no sense at all. He hoped that Annan would give him the opportunity to explain first. In all honesty though, what could Annan possibly do? In the end, he was a man of reason and logic. He wouldn't jeopardize his career and his future and do something to Samuel. Annan just wouldn't, especially now that Caleb was gone. All the same, Samuel drove up with a bodyguard, who was stationed outside as they waited for Linc. He would have preferred to have Linc leave the country immediately, but it wouldn't hurt to have him around for a few days.

Samuel stared absentmindedly at the carpet in the room. The things he'd done—for money and for love, they had changed him. He hardly recognized the man he'd become anymore, but what other choice did he have? He just hoped it was all over now.

"Hello, Mr. President."

Samuel jumped up from the sofa and stared dumbfounded at Caleb standing in the doorway of the living room, bloodied and battered like he'd just emerged from an unspeakable battle.

"Linc?" Samuel managed to utter.

"Dead."

Samuel felt his heart skip a beat. This couldn't be happening.

"I have a guard out there. All I have to do is scream and—"

"Oh, he's dead too," Caleb interrupted him.

Samuel felt his heart constrict, and the blood drained from his face. Caleb stepped through the doorway and approached him. Samuel took a step back, but the sofa was right behind him. He glanced around the room, trying to figure out what he could possibly do. Caleb raised the gun he was holding and gestured toward the sofa.

"Sit, please."

Samuel dropped obediently into the sofa. Caleb walked over to a fridge in the corner of the room and took out two bottles of water. He handed one to Samuel.

"Drink up. You look like you're having a heart attack."

"What do you want? What do you plan to do? I'm a former president. If you kill me, you'll never get away with it. The police and the army, they'll hunt you down."

"The pathetic army that you and Annan are trying to fix? That army will hunt me down? Or the police that you and Linc fooled into believing that Bertha was killed by armed robbers? Those police?"

"Please, don't kill me. I can pay you whatever you want. Name your price, and you'll get it. I have a wife, and children and grandchildren. I don't want to die. I don't," Samuel sobbed.

Caleb shook his head, disappointed that Samuel didn't have more balls. He hadn't even laid a finger on Samuel, and he was sobbing like a baby.

Caleb slowly eased into the loveseat opposite Samuel and leaned back. He had to make this quick, or he wouldn't survive the night. He was badly wounded, and he suspected he had other internal injuries.

"I'm here to talk, and what happens to you tonight all depends on whether you tell me the truth."

Samuel nodded through his tears. "I will tell you everything, I swear. Just don't kill me."

Before Caleb could say another word, multiple shots rang out, and Samuel's body jerked repeatedly against the sofa. Despite his weakened body, Caleb sprung up and swung his gun toward the door. His mouth fell open.

"Jesus Christ! Are you crazy? What did you just do? Are you fucking crazy?"

"He killed Bertha. He tried to kill you. He put Abby in a coma. He doesn't deserve to live."

Caleb stared at the Justice. He looked like he'd been in a war of his own. His body was haggard, and his eyes were red and swollen. He looked like he'd aged twenty years since Caleb saw him in the hospital. What he said wasn't lost on Caleb, either. Abby was in a coma. His beloved Abby was in a coma. Caleb turned and looked at Samuel. His dead eyes were open in shock, and his body was riddled with at least five bullets. Caleb groaned out loud. This was such a mess!

"Didn't you come here to kill him?" he heard the Justice mutter.

"No! I wanted him to confess! I can't just walk in here and shoot a former president. I am not that crazy!"

Caleb pulled a recorder from his pants and dropped it onto the floor. The Justice let out a sound, but Caleb wasn't sure if it was a sob or just anguish. Caleb walked over to him and took the gun from his hands. The Justice let it go willingly. He was completely broken. There was no fight left in him. Caleb looked him in the eyes.

"Didn't you want to know? Didn't you want to know why he would kill Bertha? Didn't you want answers?"

"Samuel was my best friend for almost forty years. I loved him like a brother. I made him who he was, and then he slept with Bertha. We talked, and I let it go, but this, what he did today goes beyond talk. He disobeyed me. He was weak and scared, and his actions put my baby in the hospital, and I don't know if she's ever going to wake up."

Caleb nodded and wrapped his functioning arm around the Justice. He saw real pain in the older man's eyes, and they mirrored his own. The last time he saw Annan this devastated and broken was when Bertha died. Back then, he was in complete and utter pain, and no matter what anyone said to him, he decided he wasn't going to run for the presidency. Tonight, he looked worse. He looked like his whole world had come crashing down. Caleb knew that even though Annan and Abby had their issues, she was still the man's daughter, his flesh and blood, and he couldn't fault Annan for doing what he'd done tonight. There was no doubt in his mind that Annan was telling him the truth. Such pain and anguish couldn't be faked. Samuel destroyed the Justice's world four years ago, and today Samuel had come close to doing it again.

"I need you to go home now," Caleb said softly.

"What are you going to do? You can't take the blame for this. I can confess."

"No, that won't be necessary. I just need you to go home and let me handle this. I'll clean it up."

As the words came out of his mouth, Caleb could hear Linc's own voice saying he'd cleaned up the Bertha mess for Samuel. That was just the story of their lives, cleaning up shit that their greedy, imbecile bosses created.

He led the Justice out of the house and out to the S-Class parked in the driveway next to Linc's Ford and Samuel's own Mercedes. Caleb hugged Annan again, overwhelmed by emotions he didn't know he had for the man.

"I'll fix this, I promise. Just get to Abby and stay there. Don't leave her side for a second."

"You're like a son to me, Caleb."

"And you're like a father to me," Caleb replied, meaning every single word he said.

He watched as the Justice's car disappeared down the winding driveway, and then he walked back into the house. His mind was racing. Samuel's house was nestled at the base of a hill, over one hundred kilometers away from the nearest house. He was certain that no one had seen or heard him or the Justice arrive. The one bodyguard who was there when he arrived was dead and lying next to Linc's body in the trunk of the Ford. So thankfully, there were no witnesses, but he had three bodies to deal with. He walked out of the house and down a few meters to the utility shed he'd spotted on his way up. He found what he was looking for—cans of gasoline. Fires were notorious for destroying evidence. He didn't actually expect that the Ghana police would show up here and start fingerprinting the place and collecting DNA, but Samuel was a former president. He couldn't just leave his body lying there riddled with bullets.

Caleb spent the next thirty minutes dousing the place thoroughly. Every inch of the property was drenched in gasoline, and Samuel's body got the most of it. Next, he transferred Linc and the bodyguard's bodies into the house and deposited them in the living room in the chairs. He was in a great deal of pain, and he could barely drag the bodies, but it had to be done. When Caleb was satisfied that he hadn't missed anything, he turned on the gas in the kitchen, left the house, got into the Ford, and drove a few meters down the road. Then he walked back up, stood a few meters away from the kitchen window, and fired a single bullet. The bullet shattered the glass and hit the stove, and then a few seconds later, the kitchen exploded. Caleb was in the Ford, driving down the road when the rest of the house exploded. He didn't need to stay and watch. He knew there would be nothing left. It was done. No one would be able to figure out what had happened there tonight. He needed to take the Ford away though, because he couldn't walk hundreds of miles to civilization on his own. He'd get rid of it later.

As Caleb drove away from the burning house, he felt tired but relieved. He and the Justice had done what they needed to do. They'd avenged their loved ones and protected their own. He didn't understand it all, but still he knew it was over. The only thing left to do was to pray that Abby would wake up so that he could tell her he loved her, and that he would continue to love her until the last breath left in his body. She was everything to him. He had no doubt about that. And if the God the Justice believed in so strongly was real, then that God would let her live so he could tell her and show her how much he loved her. That was all he was asking for. Let her live.

27

Eight months later

"The time is here, the elections are exactly one week away, and this is it. I know this will be one for the history books for sure. So let's lay it all on the table and be one hundred percent honest with your comments and predictions. What is going to happen on Saturday, December 7th?"

"Paul, listen, predictions, numbers, all of that is just useless and unnecessary right now. December 7th is going to be a burial, hands down. I'm just really surprised that President Otoo hasn't pulled out of the elections. That's just beyond me. From cocaine scandals, to murder attempts, to broad daylight robbery of national coffers, how can they possibly expect to win? Sometimes dignity should outweigh ego," Kweku said.

"Honestly, sometimes my friend Kweku here surprises me. The GFP has spent the last six months cleaning the party. Those who committed those acts are in jail or in court. What more can we *expect from the president? This isn't ego at all. He's demonstrated integrity and personal resolve to cleanse the party of the corruption that has plagued it and start from scratch. More than anything, he deserves to be on the ballot next week. And I know the people of Ghana will give him the mandate again. In the face of adversity and criticism, he has excelled."*

"See, this is the problem with Ghana, Paul, this right here, what Kwesi is saying. We take everything lightly. In any other country, the president would be impeached and in jail with the rest of them. Cleansing what? Cleansing filth he orchestrated himself? I mean, we're talking about multiple murder attempts here, and he throws a few people in jail and thinks that's it? As a country, we need to raise our expectations of our leaders. We need to be serious here. What the GFP has done isn't child's play. They tried several times to get rid of an innocent man because of the threat he posed. That's dirty, dirty politics, and Ghanaians need to recognize that and end the party once and for all. We shouldn't continue to tolerate what they represent."

"What the GFP represents? Kweku is obviously desperate and disappointed that the GFP is still a contender. Despite all the hits, and I honestly believe some have been fabricated, the party is still standing. Let's acknowledge that."

"Still standing? The GFP isn't even on its knees. It's over. We all know it's over. The only way, and I am dead serious here, the only way the GFP could win on Saturday is if they literally go to the EC, put a gun to Asamoah-Nti's head, and ask him to declare President Otoo the winner."

Paul laughs. "Okay, okay, let me interrupt here. Kwesi, let's just be plain and honest. In the last ten months since the Justice's announcement, the GFP has practically been sinking into oblivion. FreeDem's latest polls place the GFP at 10 percent and the DNP at 90 percent. 90 percent! No party in this country has ever gotten more than 55 percent, ever. Can we really expect Justice Annan to walk away with the presidency by a 90 percent win margin, or can the GFP or some other party surprise us all? We still have a week to go."

⌒

Caleb's heart was beating fast as he walked down the hall-way. He'd never felt this nervous, scared, and anxious before. He thought his heart was going to explode right within his chest. He couldn't believe this was actually about to happen. If someone told him a year ago that he would be at this point, he would have laughed it off and dismissed the comment. Now here he was, about to ask for something that his whole future depended on. He held onto the handle of the door and paused.

"Everything okay, baby? Did you lose the keycard? We can go back down to the lobby and get another one," Abby said, looking up at him with her endearing face and gentle eyes.

Caleb leaned forward and kissed her softly on the lips.

"I love you," he murmured.

She smiled up at him.

"I love you too."

Her words comforted him a little, but he was still nervous as he slipped the keycard into the lock and opened the door. He pushed the door open and waited for her to walk through.

"Oh my God, Caleb, oh my God, oh my God," Abby repeated over and over again as she drank in the sight before her.

The living room of the hotel suite was bathed in the soft candlelight emanating from small, gold candles nestled in white candleholders placed on every surface of the room. The floor was littered with white rose petals and white orchid floral arrangements positioned around the living room in contrast with the red, plush hotel carpet. The furniture was draped in gold and red covers, sprinkled with the white rose petals. There was a tray in the middle of the center table, with a champagne bottle in an ice bucket, two champagne glasses, and a plate of assorted chocolates and strawberries. Through the open doorway of the living room, Abby could see through to the bedroom, where the rose petals on the floor continued up to the bed. The petals on the bed were red and white, surrounding two simple red rose stems, contrasting against the white sheets. Low, soft music played in the background, and Abby recognized the voice of Whitney Houston singing "I Will Always Love You." It was all incredibly cheesy, but since this was Caleb, cheesy was really sweet and thoughtful. Tears welled up in her eyes, and she turned around to look at him.

Caleb was on his knees, a ring box in his hands.

"Oh my God," Abby choked as the tears started to fall.

"Abby, God, I love you. I love you so much. It's scary, exciting and new. I need you to really believe that. I love you more than I could ever, ever express."

Caleb paused and swallowed hard. He was actually doing this.

"I can't live without you. I almost lost you once, and I knew then that I'd rather die than lose you again. I never, ever want to live without you. I need you. I love you, and I want to spend the rest of my life with you. So, Abiel Annan, will you marry me?"

Caleb popped the ring box open, and Abby stared stunned at the massive rock glistening in the box. If she had to design her dream ring, it would be that exact ring. She lifted it gently from the box and stared at it, soaking in its beauty and brilliance. The massive square-cut diamond rock in the center was propped up by two smaller diamonds on each side, and the entire platinum stem of the ring was embedded with tiny diamonds. It was perfect.

Abby got down on her knees in front of him.

"Yes, Caleb, yes, I want to spend the rest of my life with you too. I love you, and I always will."

Caleb let out the breath he'd been holding in. After everything that had happened that year, he knew a yes wasn't guaranteed. She'd been through a lot, most of it because of him, so he never took it for granted that she would want to do this. Since the accident, he'd tried very hard to make it up to her and show her that it was all over and he was here to stay. It took Abby two weeks to wake up from her coma, and even after that, her recovery was slow and painful. She needed multiple surgeries to fix broken bones and patch up her kidneys and lungs. After two months in Ghana, Caleb and the Justice decided that it would be best for her to continue her recovery in the US. So Caleb took her to Chicago to his parents' home. It wasn't the way he would have liked to introduce his girlfriend to his parents, but his father was one of Chicago's top doctors, and it was the place for her to be. They were there for another two months. It was during that time that he knew without a doubt that he wanted to marry her. His mother helped him design the ring, and he picked it up the day they left. He'd held onto it for months now, scared and worried that she wasn't ready and would say no. Two days ago, he decided he couldn't wait any longer, so he suggested they treat themselves and spend the weekend in a newly opened five-star resort along the Accra coast. And now he couldn't believe she'd actually said yes.

He pulled her into his arms, lifted her clear from the floor, and carried her into the bedroom. He swiped the rose stems from the bed and lay her down gently on the bed of rose petals.

He stared down at her, grateful that she'd survived and was doing so well. He didn't know what he would have done otherwise.

"You take my breath away, do you know that?" he muttered, nuzzling her neck with kisses.

Abby wrapped her arms around his neck and whispered. "Show me."

Since the accident, Caleb had been very gentle with her, conscious of her injuries and her recovery, even after the doctors gave them the go-ahead to have sex. Tonight, however, he was going to show her just how much he loved her.

He stretched his body length-wise over hers, tucked his right arm underneath her waist to bring their bodies even closer, and then kissed her deeply and passionately, trying to convey everything he felt in that one kiss. The kiss deepened and stretched into what felt like forever, but it wasn't long enough for Caleb. Eventually, he pulled away reluctantly from her lips and started to trail kisses down her neck and half-exposed chest. Dissatisfied with planting little kisses on her chest, he reached behind her and pulled down the zipper of her white sundress. As he pulled the straps of her dress down her shoulders and over her body, he leaned in to kiss the faint scar across her upper belly. She had a couple more on her lower stomach and thighs. The scars pained him because of what they represented, but he loved her and her body regardless. She'd lost quite a bit of weight since the accident, but she was still his Abby, flawless and perfect. After the dress came off, her bra and panties followed until she was completely naked and exposed in front of him. He went back up to her lips and kissed her softly. She kissed him back eagerly and reached down to unbuckle his belt, but he stilled her hands and shook his head.

"Not yet," Caleb whispered.

For the next ten minutes, he loved and tortured her at the same time, kissing every single nook and cranny of her delicate body. He touched, stroked, licked, and kissed her all over until she was panting, writhing, and screaming. Even after she came in his mouth, he continued to kiss her deeply below, lapping up her satisfaction and burying his tongue and fingers deeper in her. After she came again, he peeled his clothes off quickly, finally acknowledging his own pent up need. As he slid into her, Caleb was reminded again of how much he loved her, loved this, needed this. He'd slept with more women than he could count, but nothing could compare to how he felt when he was making love to Abby. It was a feeling that had grown since their first night together, and it continued to stun him.

"I love you," he moaned as he slowly and repeatedly pushed himself into her.

"I love you too," Abby murmured, wrapping her legs around him and pulling him in.

Caleb clenched his jaw and wrapped his arms around her tightly, increasing the pace of his thrusts like he just couldn't get enough of her. Her pace and body movements matched his, and he was pleasantly surprised by her ferocity and intensity. He was on the verge of exploding, but he held on, waiting for her to come again, wanting to give her everything he had to give. Thankfully, he didn't have to wait too long. Her fingernails dug into his back, and her teeth gripped his neck as her body convulsed beneath him. The intensity of her orgasm rocked him, and he let go completely, emptying himself into her as his arms gripped her for dear life. God, he loved her.

"Roses, orchids, candles, chocolates, strawberries, the whole nine yards, huh? You're full of surprises, Caleb Osei. Dare I say a changed man?" Abby said ten minutes later, taking a bite of the strawberries she'd fetched from the living room.

Caleb gazed up at her.

"Forever changed," he said, tickling her.

Abby giggled and looked down at him.

"Promise we'll stay this way forever and ever? You'll love me always? You'll be with me always?"

Caleb sat upright and pulled her into his arms, hugging her tight.

"Nothing will ever, ever keep me away from you. You're stuck with me, Abiel soon-to-be Osei, stuck with me for life."

He kissed her, tasting the chocolates and strawberries she'd just eaten. The taste excited him, and within minutes the tray was on the floor and she was back in his arms, underneath him. He hoped each night of their future would be like this. He sincerely hoped so.

"Oh no, no, no!"

Caleb's eyes fluttered open, and he looked frantically around the room.

"What? What happened?"

Abby was sitting in front of the bedroom dresser, staring down at her fingers. He couldn't see what she was looking at.

"The ring doesn't fit," she said dejectedly.

"What?"

"The ring doesn't fit, Caleb. I've lost too much weight. It would have fit six months ago, I'm sure."

Caleb sighed. "Babe, we can get it resized. It's not a big deal, okay?"

"You don't understand. I want to wear it now. Resizing can take weeks!"

Caleb chuckled. He was going to have to get used to her theatrics and drama.

"What do you want us to do, babe? Blow air into your finger?"

Abby rolled her eyes at him.

"No, we're going to get it resized now. I know someone. I think she can get it done in days, but we need to go now."

Caleb glanced at the clock by the bed and groaned.

"It's only 9 a.m. Can we please sleep in? I didn't get any sleep last night."

Abby rolled her eyes at him again.

"Whose fault was that? I don't want to waste a minute, Caleb. I need to wear my ring."

Caleb lay still for a minute, and then he got up from the bed and started picking up his clothes from the floor.

"Okay, Mrs., let's go get your ring fixed."

"You're going to be a very wise husband, Caleb Osei."

Caleb smiled. If getting a ring resized constituted wise, then he was off to a darn good start.

⌒

"It's a beautiful, beautiful ring Abby, just beautiful. He has really good taste, but he should have come to me. I have rings just as nice."

Caleb smiled half-heartedly at the jewelry shop owner that Abby had dragged him to see. She had a nice store with nice pieces, but he was certain that his custom-designed Harry Winston ring was still the right choice for his baby. He leaned against the glass counter as Abby started to chat with the woman.

So this was what married life was going to be about, following the Mrs. to places he had no desire to be and listening to nonsensical female conversations. His mind started to drift to Annan and the campaign. He'd expected that the Justice would drop out of the race after Abby's accident and the tragic demise of Samuel Aryee, but after lengthy discussions with his wife, party officials, and even Abby after she woke up, he'd decided to stay in the race. Caleb told him he had to kill the SecuriCorp deal, and he did. After that, Caleb stuck closely by the Justice, helping him through his campaign and Abby's recovery. It was an incredibly tough time for them all, but they'd pulled through. The elections were about a week away now, and there was no doubt that Annan was going to win. It was a done deal. The GFP didn't stand a chance. After the elections, Caleb wanted to take Abby away on his dream island trip and figure out their future together. She never went back to her job after the accident, and he had no idea if he wanted to stay in politics, so it would be an opportunity for them to figure out their future together.

"I hope you don't plan to lose more weight, my dear. This band is exquisite, but you don't want to get it resized over and over. You know, your mother got her ring resized, too. It was after your aunt Bertha died."

Caleb turned his head slowly at the mention of Bertha's name. The woman continued to talk.

"She lost weight as well, so quickly too. The ring didn't fit at all. So, she came in here a couple of weeks after it happened. She was so distraught. We had to reduce the ring considerably."

He didn't know why his mind went where it went, but it just did. Right there in that store, it all hit him hard. All the pieces came hurtling toward him, and he froze. It really couldn't be. It just couldn't be.

"Yes, I noticed the weight change too. I guess trauma does that to a person. Now, I'm wondering if I shouldn't do anything to this ring, you know. I do plan on putting some of the weight back on. I like my curves," Abby said, winking at Caleb, but even though he was looking at her, he didn't even see her.

"Oh, your mother loved her curves too, although I see that she's decided to stick with the thin look. It does suit her though, makes her look regal, I think. So, do you have any wedding details planned? When? Where?"

"It's only been a day, but I am definitely making all the decisions. I have the final word. He'll do whatever I say,"

Abby said, winking at Caleb again. This time he saw her, but it was her words that got his attention.

"That's the power of women, my dear. These men, no matter how serious and powerful they are, they do what the women say. Trust me, you should ask your mother. She'll tell you. I'm sure she has the Justice wrapped around her finger," the storeowner said.

Caleb stepped away from the counter and bent over, placing his head in between his legs. He couldn't breathe. Abby walked over to him and rubbed his shoulders.

"Hey, what's going on? Are you okay?"

Caleb kept his head lowered as he tried to process what he was thinking and hearing. It just couldn't be.

"Baby, talk to me," Abby pled.

He lifted his head and looked at her, trying to focus. If what he thought, what he suspected was remotely true, what could he possibly do? Everything was going so well. He'd proposed. He was prepared to live happily ever after. And he needed his happily ever, needed his peace. Why did he have to hear this and think what he was thinking now?

"Jesus, Caleb, talk to me. Is this buyer's remorse? Panic attack?"

"Gosh, no, no, definitely not, okay? I think I'm just hungry. I didn't have dinner, and I haven't had breakfast either. I just got a little woozy."

Abby looked relieved.

"Okay, okay, let me just finish this up, and then we'll go back to the hotel and get brunch, okay?"

Caleb nodded.

"I'll go wait in the car."

Caleb felt tortured the entire drive back to the hotel. He was in love, happy, and ready to get married. If he stirred the waters now, it would only bring pain to the one person he loved more than anyone in the world. On the other hand, if he didn't pursue his suspicions, he wouldn't be able to live with the suspicion either. So what could he possibly do?

"Hey, are you coming in?"

Caleb blinked rapidly as his eyes focused on Abby. They were parked in the parking lot of the hotel, and she'd opened the door on her side, ready to get out. She looked worried as she stared at him. Right then and there, he made his decision.

"I just need to go do something really quick, okay? I'll be back in less than an hour."

"I thought you were hungry. And what do you need to go do right now?"

"I really need to go see your dad right now. He has a meeting this afternoon, and something just hit me. I'll get wakye from Auntie Muni. Your dad loves it as well. I'll be back soon, okay? I promise."

Abby stared at him with questions in her eyes. Caleb leaned across the seat and pulled her in for a hug. He squeezed tight and kissed her on the lips.

"I love you. I'll see you soon," he said softly.

"Hurry back," she responded, kissing him back.

Then she stepped out of the car and walked away. Caleb watched her for a minute, debating with himself about what he was about to do. Five minutes later, he drove off.

28

The house was quiet, which was not typical of the Annan household. Over the last few months, there were always people in and out of the house—campaign workers, the media, family members, and other politicians, just a slew of people. Now with a week to elections, the family had some peace and quiet. Earlier that week, Caleb had notified all regular and repeat visitors to give the Justice some space before the elections. There was no need to panic, worry, or discuss the elections at length. The win was guaranteed.

Caleb parked his car next to the Justice's and walked slowly into the house, still debating his decision to show up here today. He checked the Justice's study first, but there was no one there. Next the kitchen, but it was also empty. He suspected that the cook was in her room in the back house listening to her favorite gospel radio show. All the rooms downstairs were empty, so he figured they were both probably upstairs. He headed for the master bedroom first. There was really no need to check the other rooms. People usually built massive houses but ended up using just three rooms—the master bedroom, living room, and kitchen. And for some more affluent ones, the study was included.

Caleb closed his eyes and stood in front of the door. What he was about to do and ask was insane, but he was already here. He had to see it through. He turned the knob and opened the door quietly.

She was standing next to the bed with her back to him, leaning over the side table. He studied her for a second, trying to be certain, but he knew he was right.

"Hello, Bertha."

She turned around instantly. At first, she looked stunned, surprised, and then the look was quickly replaced by irritation. She pursed her lips and then glared at him.

"Are you okay, Caleb? Why are you calling me by my sister's name?" she said, her voice raised above its normal pitch.

The Justice stepped out from the bathroom, a towel in his hand and remnants of shaving foam on his face. He stared at Caleb, a look of complete and utter regret and hopelessness in his eyes. Caleb's heart sank, and he forced back a tear.

"What happened? What happened to Adubea? What happened to Abby's mother?" Caleb's voice was barely a whisper as he addressed the Justice.

"What are you talking about, Caleb? What is this nonsense? This is me, me, Adubea, why are you talking like this?" she said heatedly, ignoring the Justice's defeated look and stance.

"Stop, please stop. He knows. He knows," the Justice said softly to her.

"He knows what? What does he know? You're the one who needs to stop. There's something wrong with him, can't you see? He's seeing things. He's bringing up my dead sister and tormenting me. I am Adubea!" she snapped at him.

"I said stop! Just stop! It's over. It's done. So please just stop!" the Justice snapped back.

She shut up instantly and sat on the bed, glaring at him. Annan turned to Caleb and sighed.

"Four years—I really expected you to figure this out sooner than that. Each day I've waited for you to walk up to me and ask."

"What happened? Tell me everything, and I want the truth, sir. No more lies. You've lied to me enough. So right now, just tell me the truth from the very beginning."

The Justice sat down on the bed next to her and looked forlornly at her.

"It's time to talk, okay?"

She shook her head vehemently. "If you want to bury yourself, I won't dig the grave for you."

Annan shook his head and looked up at Caleb. He gestured to the armchair in the corner of the room opposite the bed. Caleb sat down slowly, mindful of what he had tucked into his pants, underneath his shirt.

"Bertha, please, tell him the truth, the real truth, not the story you told me that night, but the real story you told me later. He needs to know. No more lying."

"Fine, if it's the truth you want, it's the truth you'll get," she finally conceded.

❧

It was almost 10 p.m., and Bertha was sitting in her living room, watching TV, and having a late night snack of mangoes. The knock on the main front door was subtle. She almost didn't hear it, but she had just turned down the volume of the TV to make a call, so she heard it. She frowned, wondering who would be there at that time of the night and why the security man at the gate hadn't called up to the house. What were those phones in the guardhouse for? Feeling curious and irritated, she walked up to the door.

She peered through the curtain and then pulled the door open, surprised by who her visitor was.

"Dubie, come in, what's going on? Is everything okay? Why are you crying? Talk to me."

Adubea stepped past her sister and waited for her to close the main door.

"How could you? How could you do this to me? What have I ever done to you? What would make you do this to me?" Adubea started to cry.

Bertha stood still and feigned confusion. She knew what Adubea was talking about, but she wasn't prepared to admit to anything.

"I don't know what you're talking about. What have I done, Dubie? Come inside, sweetie, let me get you some water," Bertha said, reaching for her sister's hand.

Adubea slapped Bertha's hand away.

"Don't you dare touch me! I don't want your water! I don't want anything from you! All you've ever done is take and take and take! Why? How could you?"

Bertha walked away toward the living room, annoyed by her sister's outbursts.

"You can stand there and scream like a village woman with no decorum, or you can come in here and have a civilized conversation. It's entirely up to you, Dubie."

"What decorum and class did you have when you slept with my husband? What decorum and class did you have when you had an affair with my husband and his best friend! What? Tell me, what decorum?"

There, she'd said it, Bertha thought. It was finally out. She stopped in the middle of the living room and turned around to face her sister. She'd waited for this moment for a long time. She'd wished for it, yearned for it. Each day she'd wanted to flaunt the affair in her sister's face, but she restrained herself, knowing that it would destroy Annan's career if word ever got out. She'd suffered silently because she loved him and wanted him to succeed. Now, she could look her sister in the eye and tell her what she'd always wanted to tell her.

"Look in the mirror, Dubie. We may look the same, but we've never been the same. You don't have what it takes to love and maintain a man like Joseph. You may wear pearls and look like a queen, but you have no clue what someone like Joseph needs. You have no idea about the fire, love, dedication, and strength a man like him needs from a woman! No idea. I gave all of that to him. I have made him who he is! If it wasn't for me and the love and encouragement I have provided him, you wouldn't have the fancy home you have and the status you enjoy. All that you have and own is thanks to me! Me!"

"You're insane and delusional, but then again, you're a slut and a harlot, and people like you always think that it's always about you! Men get bored, men want to try different things, and they want challenges, but it's all fleeting!"

Bertha snorted. "Fleeting? I was in your bed with your husband a month after you got married! Fleeting? I've been more of a wife to him over the last thirty-five years than you were or ever will be! You can never trivialize what he and I have, you stupid snob!"

Adubea stood still in silence and shock as her sister's words sunk in. Bertha could see that she was forcing back tears. Knowing her sister, she probably assumed the affair was a one-time incident. That was typical Adubea, living in a bubble and assuming the world functioned in a predictable and perfect way.

"It's over for you, Bertha. Joseph is done with you, and so is Samuel. I won't let you destroy my family or continue to take from me. You need to find your own life."

"Your family? Are you really that naïve, my dear? I complete your family. My son and I complete your family. Have you ever looked at Joey? Have you ever looked at my son? Are you that blind living in your ivory tower? We are his family too!"

Adubea gripped her stomach as if she'd been punched, and Bertha knew that her words had cut deep into her sister, emotionally and physically. Adubea always assumed the best of everyone, even if she had some airs to her attitude. Bertha also knew that Adubea had welcomed her and Joey into their lives because that's what family did. Adubea and Joseph believed so strongly in family that Adubea accepted that it was the right thing to do. She never questioned Joseph's attention to Bertha, because in Adubea's mind she probably assumed he did it for her. He loved her, so why wouldn't he take care of her sister? It was a bit more surprising that she never picked up on the resemblance between uncle and nephew, but then again, her sister had always been blind, naïve, and stupid. Bertha watched in amusement as rage flashed across Adubea's face. Then her sister reached for the flower vase on the mantle behind her and flung it hard at Bertha.

The vase barely missed Bertha, and she looked up stunned at Adubea.

"Oh I see, the ice queen is finally waking up. It's a little too late, my dear."

"You're never, ever going to have him again. I will go the media and I will destroy his precious career if he ever goes near you again. You're ostracized from my family, *my family*! No phone calls, no emails, no texts, no visits, absolutely no contact with you, or he is done! Done!"

"You're the one who's delusional. Joseph will never leave me. He'll never agree to something like that. He doesn't know how to live without me!"

"He's already agreed. How do you think I found out? I overheard him talking to Samuel earlier this evening. They talked it through, and they both agreed they needed to end things with you. I confronted Joseph, and he promised me that our family was too important to him. He promised me that he's done for good. He swore it! So I'm sorry, dear sister, you're not that irresistible. Leave us alone. Do you understand me? Leave my family alone," Adubea hissed.

Bertha was stunned and surprised. She shook her head.

"He wouldn't," she said, almost under her breath.

"He did," Adubea said, obviously reveling in her sister's change in demeanor. She stepped up to Bertha and pointed a finger at her.

"No matter what you think you had with him, it's over now. You can have this house, you can have your son, but you can't have my husband!"

Within seconds, and with a speed she didn't even know she possessed, Bertha had the kitchen knife she was using to slice the mangoes in her hand. Then she stabbed Adubea and didn't stop stabbing. She could hear her sister's screams. She could hear and feel the blood dripping off her hand and onto the floor, but she didn't stop. Even when her sister's body fell to the floor, she couldn't leave it all alone. She continued to plunge the knife in and out. It was only the knock on the front door that interrupted her madness. She blinked and stared dumbfounded at the bloodied body of her sister lying on the carpet. The knock came again. Bertha dropped the knife and walked over to the door. She pulled the curtain back a little.

It was the security man.

"What is it?" she snapped impatiently.

"I thought I heard some screams, madam. Is everything okay?"

"We're just watching TV. The volume was loud. I've turned it down now, so please return to the gate."

He squinted through the window, trying to get a better look at her. Bertha dropped the curtains closed and stepped away from the door.

"I said we're fine. Just go back to the gate, and don't interrupt us like this again. Do you understand?"

"Yes, madam, please let me know if you need anything."

Bertha waited by the door for a few minutes, and then she returned to the living room. She ignored the body on the floor and picked up her cell phone from the sofa. There was one person she could call who could fix this.

The phone rang ten times, and then the line was cut. She called again repeatedly. Eventually, he answered.

"Bertha, it's late! I can't talk to you right now. I'm home with my wife."

"You won't have a home, a wife, or your presidency if you don't help me out right now."

"What is it now, huh? You need to stop with the threats and the blackmail and the—"

"My sister is dead."

"What? What are you talking about? I spoke to Joseph just a couple of hours ago. She was home with him. She was fine. Why hasn't he called me? What happened to her?"

"She overheard your conversation with Joseph this evening and came over to my house to threaten me. She just went crazy. She attacked me. She grabbed a knife and tried to stab me and we fought. I don't know how it happened, but we struggled for the knife and now she's on the floor, not moving. She's dead, Samuel, she's dead in my house."

"Oh my God! Oh my God! Bertha, what have you done? What in God's name have you done?"

"Did you hear me? She went crazy! She attacked me!" Bertha shouted, pacing up and down the living room, carefully avoiding the body and the blood.

"Why are you calling me? Call Joseph. Call the police. What do you expect me to do?"

"Fix it! I need you to fix it!"

"I'm the president of Ghana, not a magician! What do you want me to do? Raise her from the dead?"

His words struck a chord in Bertha, and her eyes drifted to the body of her sister splayed on the floor. Could she? Could she do what she was thinking?

"I need your help to clean this up, Samuel. Your man Linc, send him here. Tell him to get rid of the security guard and make it all look like a robbery."

"Jesus, Bertha, I can't do this. You need to call Joseph. You need to tell him. I can't do this."

"Then everyone will know! You want me to call the police? Fine, I will call the police, wait here by her body, and then tell them she confronted me over the affairs I had with the chief justice of Ghana and the president! I will tell them about everything! Do you think I can't do that?"

There was silence on the phone, and she could almost hear him thinking, weighing his options.

"I'm serious, Samuel. Help me, or it'll all be over for you, for both of you, and for your party too."

"Linc will be there in twenty minutes, but you need to call Annan. He needs to know. Whatever you're planning, whatever you have going on in your head, talk to him."

Samuel hung up before she could even say another word. Bertha dropped dejectedly into the sofa and stared at her sister's body, dreading what she had to do next, but knowing she had no choice. For the next ten minutes, she stripped Adubea of her clothes and dumped them into a trash bag. Then she got out one of her own dresses, stabbed it randomly with a knife and then carefully dressed Adubea up in it, certain that no police officer in Ghana would double-check to ensure that the cuts on the dress matched the wounds. Next, she started on Adubea's jewelry. Bertha lifted up Adubea's left hand and stared at her sister's wedding and engagement rings, two pieces for which she'd craved and envied her sister. Joseph got Adubea new rings fifteen years ago, and that was one of the darkest moments of Bertha's life. She remembered how saddened and devastated she felt when she saw her sister's new rings for the first time. It should have been her. She meant every single word she said to Adubea—she made Joseph who he was, not her sister. He would be nothing and no one if it wasn't for her perseverance and encouragement. And yet it was her docile sister who basked in the glory. She hadn't planned for this to happen, but what could she do?

Bertha slipped the rings onto her finger, but they were too big. Luxury had made Adubea slightly bigger, but getting the rings resized wouldn't be a problem. The hardest part, the biggest challenge, would be fooling the family. Bertha dropped the rings into her handbag and stripped her sister of all her other jewelry, car keys, and other items in her pockets. When she was done, she went up to her room, grabbed some of her own personal items, and dumped them into her bag, which was getting bigger and bigger.

Twenty minutes later, she was in Adubea's car, driving toward the man and the home she'd craved her entire adult life. She wasn't sure what was going to happen next, nor was she sure if she could really pull this off, but she knew she'd always wanted this, so she had to try. It was crazy and insane, but if it worked, if by God it worked, she would never, ever let anyone come between her and Joseph again. This was her life now.

29

"And you just let her in? You just let her into your lives after what she did? How could you? Why would you?" Caleb shouted angrily at the Justice, ignoring Bertha, who still didn't look remorseful after telling her story. There was a defiant look in her eyes that irked him. He wanted to reach over and snap her scrawny neck in two.

"I didn't have a choice. I recognized her the minute she walked in, but then she started to cry. She said it was an accident. She said Adubea attacked her, they fought, and it just happened. I called Samuel, but Linc had already gone to the house and done what he did. How could we explain any of that? What was I supposed to do? Tell me, what choice did I have?"

"You had choices! Everyone has a choice! If you're so concerned about your career, you could have told a different story. You could have said Adubea went to visit Bertha, surprised the burglars, and got attacked and killed. You could have said her interruption saved Bertha, who was sleeping upstairs, but the men were gone by the time she got down there. You could have said anything! Instead, you let her murder your wife and then slip into her shoes as if nothing happened? How could you?" Caleb could barely control his anger now.

"He could, because he loved me!" Bertha snapped back.

"Don't talk! Don't talk! All of this is because of you! You just don't know when to stop, do you? You lied to me. You're here because you lied to me, and I was too weak and too distraught to do the right thing. So please, don't talk!" the Justice barked at her.

Then he turned to Caleb, his voice and tone softer, more regretful.

"You may never believe me, but you have no idea what I went through. I loved Adubea with all my heart, all my heart. I was devastated. I was broken. The pain you saw me go through then, it wasn't because I'd lost my sister-in-law, it was because I'd lost my wife! I gave up my bid for the presidency to honor her, to show respect. Yes, I went along with the lie of what had happened, but that's because I didn't know what good would come out of telling the truth. Abby's mother was gone, Joseph's mother would be thrown in jail, and my life would be over. I did it to save my family, but there isn't a day that goes by that I don't think about that night she walked in here. Not a single day that I don't wish I had been strong enough to make different choices, but everything, everything I have ever done in my life I have done for my God, my country, and my family. And that is the truth!"

"The truth is you lied, and whatever reasoning you had doesn't make it any less bad. You lied. Jesus, how could you do it? How could you live like that? All for what? To protect what? You didn't think your daughter deserved to know her mother was dead? Geez, and Abby, how could she not tell the difference?" Caleb asked, perplexed.

"She almost did, and maybe she did, but it just didn't seem possible. She came to me a few days after she returned home for the funeral and asked me if I had noticed anything strange with her mother, her behavior, the way she looked, the way she talked, all of it. I told her Adubea had been through a very traumatic experience, and she would never be the same. I also told her that sometimes when a twin dies, the other twin starts to take on characteristics of the other. She accepted it, at least as far as I knew."

"The sickness, the bipolar thing, that was a lie too, wasn't it? You used it to cover up her behavior."

"Yes," the Justice said.

"But you were giving her medicine. What were you were giving her?"

"What medicine?" Bertha asked, staring quizzically at Annan.

"I had mood suppressants mixed into your food," he replied dryly.

"What? You were drugging me? Why would you do that?"

"Because you're crazy! You're insane and you don't even recognize it. You killed my wife! Just because I couldn't turn you in didn't mean I wasn't going to try and control you. I should have just turned you in and let you rot in jail!" the Justice yelled angrily.

Caleb stood up and started pacing the room, cussing repeatedly. This was so messed up it was mind-boggling. He walked away from them and placed his forehead against the wall, shocked by everything they'd just told him. He was thinking about Abby as well. What now? She deserved to know, and there was no way that he was going to help them perpetuate this lie.

"Bertha! Bertha! Put that away!"

Caleb swung around from the wall and shook his head at the sight of Bertha with a gun in her hands.

"Really?"

"I will do everything I can to protect what I have," she hissed through clenched teeth.

"Bertha! Put that away!" Annan bellowed, pointing to the open drawer of the side table. She shook her head and stepped away from the bed and Annan, the gun still trained on Caleb.

"You and Samuel planned the attacks on me, didn't you?" Caleb asked her as everything started to sink in.

"Caleb, please..." Annan started to say.

"Stop, Joseph! Stop being so weak! Yes, I planned it. Joseph was prepared to confess if you ever confronted him, but I wasn't. So four years ago, I told Samuel to keep an eye on you, because you were the one person who could destroy everything. I wanted us to be ready and prepared. Samuel understood what was at stake."

Caleb looked at the Justice. "Did you know about this? Did you lie to me?" He was more hurt than angry.

"I swear, I didn't know. I put it all together after you mentioned Linc's name at the hospital. Then I knew she and Samuel must have decided to disobey me. Samuel always had a weak spot for her."

"You knew she was behind it, but you chose to kill your friend rather than deal with the devil in your own house? You decided to shoot your own best friend dead instead of the woman who killed your wife and put your daughter's life in danger?"

"Samuel was just as guilty! And I did it to protect my family!"

"Then tell her to put that gun away, or I'll drop her like a sack of rice," Caleb said, drawing his gun slowly from his back pocket.

Annan turned frantically to her.

"Bertha, Bertha, listen to me. You don't want to do this with him. You don't. It's over. Put this away and let's talk."

Bertha's hands shook a little, but she didn't lower the gun.

"I put this away and then what? Ask him! Ask him what he intends to do."

"I asked Abby to marry me last night, and she said yes." Caleb paused to let his words sink in, and then he continued, "And I will not let my future wife continue to believe that her mother is alive. That I can't do. What Abby decides to do with that information is up to her."

"Caleb…" Annan pled with him again.

"Don't let him do this, Joseph. Think of your son, of our family, of your presidency! The elections are a week away!"

Annan turned to her.

"Give me the gun, Bertha. This is over. If Abby can't forgive us and she hands us in to the police, then so be it, but this is over!"

Bertha jerked away from him and swung the gun wildly to the right, aiming for Caleb. Caleb caught the crazed look in her eyes, and he knew he had no choice. Without a moment's hesitation, he pulled the trigger just as her finger pulled back on hers.

"No!" Annan and Caleb screamed at the same time, but for different reasons.

Caleb watched in horror as Annan stepped in front of Bertha and the bullets he'd just fired. The force of the bullets pushed them both backward, and they dropped hard onto the floor. Caleb rushed over, dropped to his knees, and lifted Annan from her body, his heart sinking at the sight of the bullet holes in Annan's chest. Caleb pulled him into his arms and cradled him, sobbing hopelessly.

"Please, no, no, no. Please. God damn it! Please!"

Annan's eyes and the pain in them touched Caleb to his very core.

"I'm sorry," Annan murmured, coughing up blood with each word.

"It's okay. It's going to be okay. I'm going to call the commissioner. We'll get you to a hospital," Caleb said, crying.

"I did it for…" Annan coughed up blood again, as he struggled to speak.

"I know, I know, you did it all for your family."

"I love you like my son, Caleb. I love you like my son."

The Justice's words reverberated through Caleb, and he gripped Annan's body tighter against his own as his sobs increased in intensity.

"And I love you like my father."

Annan coughed once more, and then his body was still. The floodgates were open, and Caleb couldn't stop himself. He sat there on the floor with Annan's lifeless body in his arms and cried uncontrollably. He cried for the man he'd truly loved, respected, and admired, despite all his flaws and misplaced sense of purpose. He cried for the great man he knew Annan could have been to both the country he was obsessed with and the family he loved. He cried for all the bad decisions, some his own, that had led to this point. More than anything, he cried because he knew everything was forever changed.

He sat on the floor reeling and in pain as his lack of options hit him hard.

"What have I done? God, what have I done?"

Caleb felt his fingers getting numb, but he held on tight to Annan's body. Out of the corner of his eyes, he could see Bertha's body and knew that she was dead, despite Annan's valiant attempts to save her. The two bullets that pierced the Justice's chest were lodged in her own chest, and from the pool of blood around her body, it was obvious that she was gone.

"Argh!" Caleb screamed, as the enormity of what he'd done assailed him.

He shouldn't have come. He should have gotten out of the car with Abby. He shouldn't have brought his gun either. Nothing good ever came out of carrying his gun around. He shouldn't have fired on Bertha either. He knew she was probably a lousy shot. She was no threat. He wasn't even sure where her bullets ended up. He could have taken her down another way. Bottom line, he shouldn't have come.

The sound of a ringing phone interrupted Caleb's cries, and without reaching for the phone in his back pocket, he knew who it was. She was probably worried sick. Bad decisions had led him to this point, but now he had to make the right decision, the best decision. The cook and the security guard at the gate hadn't heard the shots, the screams, or his crying, but eventually someone would show up to the house and to the bedroom door, and Caleb would have no explanation. What could he possibly say? No defense of his would stick. The truth would sound bizarre, and they would throw him in jail instantly. But what other option did he have? He couldn't burn down this house like he'd done with Samuel's. Sure, the police believed that to be an accident, but twice in one year was too much of a coincidence. In any case, there was a security man at the gate who saw him come in. He couldn't just kill him in cold blood. There was the cook too, wherever she was. There was no covering this up. He either had to stay, call the police, and turn himself in, or...Caleb flinched as he thought through the implications of the second option. Staying meant the certainty of a lifetime behind bars, but leaving also meant the certainty of never seeing Abby again. She would be pained either way, but which would hurt her more?

Caleb lowered Annan's body slowly onto the floor and stood up. He pulled his phone from his back pocket and made one call. In the end, the decision was a no-brainer.

30

One year later

"*Folks, welcome to this morning's edition of* Spotlight. *My name is Paul Ntsiforo, and I have the usual suspects with me this Saturday morning, Kweku Berko and Kwesi Pianim, and we also have a very special guest here this morning, Joseph Amissah, the nephew of the late Chief Justice Joseph Annan. As everyone knows at this point, Chief Justice Annan's memorial is this weekend. The country suffered numerous political blows last year, most notably the accidental death of former President Samuel Yara, and then the tragic and senseless killing of the great Chief Justice Annan. Gentlemen, welcome. How are we feeling today? And Joseph, I will start with you.*"

"*Personally, the tragedy that hit my family last year is just incredibly painful, and I honestly can't begin to express what I feel in my heart. I loved my uncle deeply and sincerely. He was like a father to me, and he was the most important male figure I had in my life. My own father died when I was very young, but Uncle Jay's death has completely rocked me to my very core.*"

"You've experienced a great deal of tragedy then, from your father at an early age as you just said, then the murder of your mother only five years ago, and then your uncle and aunt are killed a year ago. I mean, losing family through natural causes is difficult as it is, but what your family has suffered is beyond that."

"Yes, it is, definitely. And let's not forget that my cousin Abby almost died in her car accident last year. I mean, I hear people refer to us as Ghana's cursed Kennedys, but we're talking about lives here, people who meant the world to me. And the hardest part is it all doesn't make any sense."

"So, Kweku and Kwesi, I'd like you to jump in here. It all doesn't make any sense. We talked about 2012 at length last year, and a year later, I just want to ask you, do we truly know what happened in 2012?"

"We have some facts, but what we don't have are the motives behind the facts. Let's look at the sequence of some of the events. First, there's a hit put on Caleb Osei by the GFP, and there seemed to be irrefutable evidence to support that notion at the time. But those implicated always claimed that it was all Josh, and it must have been Caleb who killed Josh. Something that is now absolutely plausible. And then there's another poisoning attack on Caleb Osei that is attributed as a second attempt by the GFP, something I never understood. Why would the GFP take that risk again? Then the car accident with Abby Annan happens, and the assumption at the time was the GFP had decided to broaden its reach and just aim for the Justice's direct family members. Again, what was the sense of that? And you remember that I questioned all of that. Then President Yara's vacation home explodes, and the police say it was a gas leak. Then just a week before elections last year, the Justice's body and that of his wife are found in his home, shot dead, and the last person who was seen entering and exiting the property is Caleb Osei. Do you remember what I said last year,

Paul? I said that Caleb Osei is not what he appears to be. I said it. And today, for me, I think everything that happened last year is all connected to him. My theory is that he may have had dealings with some people within the DNP who attempted to take him out and blame the GFP. And eventually the Justice must have found out, and so he killed the Justice. That is my assertion. Caleb Osei orchestrated the events of last year and dealt a blow to the country that will take us years to recover from."

"You know, Paul, I agree everything may not be as it seems, but it's so predictable for Kwesi and the GFP to now point fingers at Caleb and the DNP because of what happened before the elections. Did Caleb Osei kill the Justice and his wife? It's possible, yes. I won't deny that. He left the scene and completely disappeared. However, we can't make any conclusive statements. We just can't. We can speculate and make claims as much as we want to, but something happened here in Ghana last year that we will never, ever understand. The bottom line is this: Ghana lost one of the greatest leaders this country has ever known, hands down. I will stand by that any day. And I am not saying this because Joseph is here. I mean it sincerely. Justice Annan would have been a truly great and iconic president. I really wish that he could have died as president. I really wish it. My sincere condolences to Joseph, his daughter, the rest of the family, and the whole country. Our loss is immeasurable."

"I think I agree with Kweku on this one. I mean, I've done my own investigations, and I know others have done the same, but we simply don't have facts and answers. It's all speculations and theories, so we may truly never know. Speaking of his daughter, Joseph, how is your cousin, and where is she? I understand she's not here for the memorial?" Paul said.

"Understandably, my cousin has been deeply been affected by this tragedy. She took it very badly, and she spent some time in a facility in the US to deal with the trauma and just—"

"*Losing both parents on the same day in that manner is hard, but is part of what she's going through because of her relationship with Caleb Osei? There are rumors that they actually got engaged before this happened,*" *Paul interrupted.*

"*Abby and I haven't discussed her relationship with Caleb. To be honest, we haven't really been in touch. I visited her a couple of times when she was getting treatment in Texas, but after that she needed some time on her own. I still felt this memorial was important to do, because as Kweku has said, this loss isn't just our loss, but it's also the country's loss.*"

"*Do you think she's been in touch with Caleb? Do you think she knows where he is?*" *Paul pressed.*

"*I honestly don't know. What I know is Abby is deeply wounded and devastated, and all she's trying to do now is to heal.*"

"*Kwesi and Kweku, I'd like to get your take on the where-abouts of Caleb Osei. According to reports from the Ghana police, there's a warrant out for him here in Ghana, but it's been a bit more challenging getting the US's cooperation because of a lack of evidence, they say. What are your thoughts about that, and do you think Abby Annan is harboring him somewhere?*"

"*I think it's disappointing that the US government has refused to put him on their wanted list when he's a wanted man here. It's very insulting to us as a nation. And this whole lack of evidence thing is outrageous. The security man at the gate saw him enter and leave the house. No one else came in until the cook found the bodies in the bedroom. So what more evidence do they need? And if he was innocent, why would he disappear? Why didn't he stay to explain himself? We really need to press the US to find him and re-turn him. And I also sincerely hope that Abby Annan isn't harbor-ing the man who destroyed her family and our nation,*" *Kwesi said.*

"*You know, I'm always amused by the theatrics and antics of my colleague here, but let's look at the facts. What evidence do we* have besides the word of the security man that he was there? I'm not saying he didn't do this, don't get me wrong, but what do we have? Caleb Osei is also a US citizen and former US military, so trust me, the US will not quickly and eagerly hunt down their own based on one eye witness who didn't even see the killings. I can't fault them for that. And unfortunately, the Ghana police haven't been able to dig up more evidence. No guns, and the only suspect is gone, so then what? And with the Caleb and Abby matter, it's unfortunate and I can't imagine what she's going through, I really can't. I saw her after the incident, and I have never seen pain like that before. I really doubt she's with him."

"So, Joseph, your uncle's funeral was attended by many big-wigs across the world. That guest list was literally a who's who in international politics and business. We had Bill and Melinda Gates, Donald Trump, Rev. Jessie Jackson, IMF Director Christine Lagarde, then-Secretary of State Hilary Clinton, and presidents and prime ministers from Europe, South America, Jamaica, and practically every African country and more European ones. But I understand that the memorial is more low-key?"

"We opened up our hearts to mourn with everyone earlier this year for the funeral, but for this memorial we preferred to do it smaller. The family and the country just need time to reflect on their own."

"That's understandable, of course. Kweku and Kwesi, I'm going to switch gears a little and get your thoughts on some political happenings. President Paa Kwesi Nsiah, almost a year into his presidency. What's the scorecard?"

"Forty percent, and that is my honest opinion. I think Nsiah is acting like someone who hadn't planned to win, and now that he has, he's like an eager beaver trying to change everything," Kwesi said.

"Paul, I hope you never stop doing this show because I don't know what I'll do without Kwesi's completely comical and exaggerated comments. According to FreeDem, President Nsiah's approval *rating is at 70 percent. That's monumental. This is someone who was destined to remain in third place with his little party until tragedy gave him an opportunity. Kwesi and the GFP are just sore losers, really, just angry that even after Annan's death the GFP didn't win the elections. Ghanaians demonstrated great thinking and foresight by voting for President Nsiah and demonstrating that we have options, and we exercised our options. The two-party contests we've endured for decades are over. Both the DNP and the GFP have a lot of work to do and will need to compete with the rest of the underdogs. It's a new era now in Ghana, a new, inspiring, and bright era."*

"Kweku, fantastic last words, thank you. Joseph, my producer tells me you have an announcement."

"Yes, two announcements, in fact. One, in honor of my uncle, I'm adding Annan to my last name, and two, I've joined the DNP and I intend to run for president of Ghana in 2016."

⤻

The light breeze mingled with the warm sunrays felt good against her skin, and she closed her eyes and lifted her head up, relishing the feeling. It was an unusually warm December day in Texas, but the wind was cool, and that made it more bearable. She wrapped the cardigan tighter around her body and leaned against the porch railing, staring out at the beautiful countryside before her. A year ago, she couldn't appreciate the beauty in anything, but she'd come a long way since that day in December. Life was too short and too precious to carry pain, anger, and hurt in her forever. She was better now, but she still preferred to take it one day at a time. Today in Ghana, her cousin was hosting a memorial for her father. She'd thought about going, but she knew she wasn't ready to do that yet. She just couldn't deal with the condolences that were packaged with probing and inappropriate questions. She had nothing to say to anyone, and she didn't owe them any explanations. She'd endured two months in Ghana after the incident, preparing for the funeral and suffering the scrutiny of outsiders with their theories. She couldn't grieve the way she wanted, and that torment had nearly sent her over the edge to insanity. She was better now, and if she was to be truly honest, it was really thanks to him.

Just as the thought of him crept into her head, she felt his arms slip around her shoulders as he pulled her back against him, hugging her.

"Hey," he whispered against her cheek.

Abby turned around and smiled up at him. Thank God for this man.

"Hey back," she said, placing a soft kiss on his lips.

Reyn touched her cheek and stared into her eyes. She was gradually getting life back into them, and that gave him hope. When he got the call from her in February asking for help, the fear and pain in her voice had shaken him to his very core. Without a moment's hesitation, he flew down to Ghana, put her on a plane, and brought her to Texas. He got her checked into one of the best mental rehabilitation clinics in the state and just supported her through the grief process. It was difficult for him to watch her go through what she went through, but he stood by her all the way, even after the two suicide attempts. After two months in the clinic, he put her up in the guesthouse of his vineyard. Nothing romantic or physical happened between them during that time. It was the last thing on his mind. He just wanted her to heal and get better, and he was prepared to be a friend to her for as long as she needed. There were many nights he could hear her from his bedroom in the main house, screaming and crying. And each time, he left his room to go console her. Most of the time, holding her was enough to calm her down. Other times, she screamed and cried till morning.

The sex happened about two months ago, but it wasn't something he pushed or asked for. She came to him and said she wanted him to love her and never leave her. He knew part of why she said that was because she was still hurting and was grateful to him, but he'd told her several times that she owed him nothing. She could up and leave any day, and he would never resent her for it. He never wanted her to feel indebted or obligated to him. And when she said she didn't, he chose to believe her. There were days he wondered if she knew what she wanted, but he just had to trust what they had. He slipped his hands under her cardigan to pull her in closer for a kiss, and then his fingers brushed against the ring.

The ring, the ring, the ring.

The man was no longer in her life, but his ring hung on a chain permanently around her neck and against her heart. Since the day Reyn picked her up in Ghana, he'd never seen her without it. It took months before she opened up about her relationship with Caleb, but he suspected she was holding a lot back. She said she knew in her heart that he'd killed her parents, but what hurt her most was that he left without a word, no call, no email, nothing. She had no idea why he did what he did, and not getting the answers compounded the pain she felt. What Reyn didn't understand was why she continued to wear the ring if she was that hurt. Why carry around the memory of the murderer who took your parents and ended your world? It made him feel like he was in a three-way relationship, and he was always going to be number two. She never said that to him, but he felt it and suspected it was true. Abby could kiss him, tell him she loved him, be with him, and support him, but until she took that ring off and put it away, Caleb would always be between them.

He pulled away a little.

"Are you going to be out here for long? I have to head down to the bar to help with prep for the tasting."

It was subtle, but Abby noticed his withdrawal. She slipped her hands into his hair and brought his head down to hers for a kiss. They kissed for a while, but eventually he pulled away again.

"Let's save some of this for later, okay? I really need to go help out."

"Of course. Give me a few more minutes and I'll be right there, okay?"

He nodded and walked back into the house. Abby turned around and looked out at the vineyards. She pulled her cardigan open and gently fingered the ring hanging around her neck. This was beginning to be a problem for Reyn, she knew that, but she wasn't sure she was ready to let it go either. Caleb had hurt her very badly, more than she could ever express to Reyn, her cousin, or her doctors, but a part of her wondered if he'd had no choice. It just didn't make any sense to her. Something happened that morning that she couldn't put her finger on. He'd proposed, he was happy, and he wasn't faking that. So, what made him go over to her parents' house that morning and shoot them dead? He wouldn't just do that without reason. He loved her, nothing could make her doubt that, but what she needed was answers. After he disappeared and the days dragged into weeks and then months, she'd began to realize that Caleb was truly gone and no answers were going to come. Caleb was gone for good, and right now all she had was Reyn.

Reyn loved her unconditionally. She knew that, and she loved him too. He was a good man. She was proud of him for what he'd done with his life since he left Ghana. He bought a well-established vineyard in Texas Hill Country, which was second only to Napa Valley California in the production of wines. Reyn's vineyard was also less than an hour from Emma and the kids in Austin, and an hour and a half from his parents. His sons came up every other weekend, and Abby adored them. They were a little cautious of her at first, and in the beginning, because of what she was going through, she was wary of getting too close to them too. The relationship between her and the boys was better now, and even with Emma, who was quietly seeing someone else. Everything was working out for Reyn. He was doing what he truly always wanted to do, making wines, and he was successful at it. This place and this life suited him, and she was really happy for him, happy to be there with him. So why was she still wearing Caleb's ring?

Abby's heart jumped as a man stepped out from behind one of the vines, just a few hundred meters from where she stood on the porch.

"Oh my God!" she gasped, startled.

It couldn't be. The man stood still and looked toward the house in her direction. He had a cap on, pulled down low, so she couldn't see his face clearly, but the height and the build were so familiar. Could it possibly be? Even if she couldn't see his eyes, she knew those shoulders, the arms, the waist, and the stance. It had to be! She stepped away from the railing and started to walk slowly down the stairs, her eyes fixed on him. The man remained still, staring in her direction. Abby's heart was pounding furiously as her feet touched the bottom stair.

"Abby? Are you coming? I want to show you something on the way to the bar."

Abby swung around at the sound of Reyn's voice.

"I'm coming, Reyn, just a minute."

She turned back around and her heart plummeted instantly. The man was gone. She scanned the vineyard desperately, but there was no movement anywhere.

"Hey."

She turned around again and looked at Reyn standing at the top of the stairs with his hand stretched out to her.

"Coming?" he asked.

"Yes, yes, I am," Abby responded and walked up to him. She placed her hand in his and squeezed.

"I'm here," she said softly.

Reyn nodded, acknowledging that her response carried greater meaning than just her physical presence. He squeezed her hand back. She was here with him, even if she continued to wear the ring, she was here with him. As she walked into the house with Reyn, Abby was tempted to turn around one last time, but she didn't. She wasn't going to chase ghosts anymore. She had a good life here with Reyn, and if Caleb ever wanted to talk to her, he would have to show up and walk right up to her. Until then, she was here with Reyn.

"Did you see her?" Cavill asked as Caleb slipped into the car next to him.

"Yeah, I saw her."

"Well? Did you talk to her? How did it go?"

"I didn't go up to her."

Cavill frowned.

"I thought that's why we came here."

"I couldn't. I just couldn't. I didn't know how to," Caleb said, his voice somber.

"Maybe another time?"

"Maybe," he responded.

Recognizing that his friend didn't want to talk, Cavill started the car and drove off down the narrow pathway off the Proctor Vineyard and down toward the highway.

Caleb lowered the passenger seat, stretched his body, and closed his eyes. A year ago, he had no choice but to leave. He was a coward, yes. He'd expected the Justice and Bertha to confess their sins to Abby and deal with the consequences, but when the time came, he couldn't do the same. He chose his freedom. He called his partner in crime and ex-marine buddy Amani Cavill to get him out. Cavill booked him on a flight to Nepal, mainly because the country had no extradition treaty with the US. Caleb wasn't sure then how it was all going to play out. He spent three months in Nepal, dealing with his demons and torturing himself over the decisions he'd made. He thought about calling her a few times, but each time he chickened out. What could he say? He could either leave her to hate him, or he could tear her entire world apart and tell her that her aunt had an affair with her father for over thirty years; had a son with him, her dear cousin Joseph; and also had an affair with her father's best friend. And then the finale, the kicker that could literally destroy her—your mother's been dead for four years, killed by your aunt who took your mother's place, and your father knew all about it, and proactively helped sell the lie. But that wouldn't be the end of the story. He could add icing to the cake—your aunt and President Yara put a hit out on me because they were afraid of what I'd do if I found out. But nope, that wouldn't be the end of the story either—after all of this, your father put himself in front of a bullet meant for your psychotic, sociopathic aunt. Yup, your father died for the bitch. How could he possibly tell her all of that? He loved her desperately, but he couldn't tear her life to pieces. It was best for her to hate him alone for now than for her to hate her entire family.

Caleb pulled out the one picture he allowed himself to carry around every day. Abby was lying across his chest, her long hair draped across her naked, smooth back, her twinkling eyes peeking out at the camera he held stretched out in his left hand. His right arm was wrapped around her waist. He was smiling broadly, grinning like he'd won the lottery. It was the night he proposed, the happiest moment of his entire life, a moment he would never forget. A part of him was pleased to see that she was still wearing the ring he gave her. He'd caught a glimpse of it even from where he hid in the vineyards. He'd watched her touch it fondly, and he could have sworn she looked wistful. When he stepped out from behind the vines, he had every intention of walking up to her. The fact that she was wearing the ring had given him some hope that she might still be in love with him, in spite of everything. Then he heard Reyn's voice, saw her turn around to him, and that was when he chickened out. She'd been living with Reyn for a while now, and it pained him deeply that she went back to him. What she felt for this guy was incredibly strong, and Caleb was jealous, even though he knew deep in his heart that what he and Abby had was genuine and real. All the same, it hurt to know that she went back to Reyn. But if he was honest with himself, he knew that it was the best place for her to be. Reyn obviously loved her, and he was single now, so he could give her a good life. Caleb would never be able to do that. Even if she forgave him and took him back, what sort of life could he possibly give her? He wasn't a wanted man in the US, but he still couldn't live an open and ordinary life. They wouldn't be able to get married, buy a house with a picket fence, have kids, and live happily ever after. She would never be able to go back home and see her family there. They would ostracize her. The entire country would shun her. What sort of life would that be?

He was going to love her until the day he died, that was for sure. But right now he had absolutely nothing to offer her. And so, he left her on the porch with Reyn and walked away. He hoped, though, that one day he would have the courage and the nerve to find her and tell her everything, from the very beginning to the end. One day he really hoped he could do that. Even if she never forgave him, he hoped he could at least give her some closure someday. Until then, he had one last thing to do.

The club was packed to the brim, and the music was incredibly deafening. He hadn't been to a place like this in over fifteen years. High, drunk, and crazed students were screaming, shouting, jumping, and hopping around for no logical reason. The music wasn't that good, so what was their excuse? He caught a glimpse of her chatting with a group of girls near the bar, and he clenched his fist. This was one reunion that was long overdue. Despite the crowd of crazies blocking his way, he managed to push through and was by her side within minutes.

"Hello Cat," he whispered softly into her ear.

Even with her back facing him, he felt her body tense, but she bravely turned around to face him.

"Hello Caleb," she said, squaring her shoulders and attempting to look defiant.

She tapped the purse that was slung across her shoulder. "I'm carrying, so in case—"

The syringe was in and out of her arm before she could complete her sentence. Her eyes bulged, and she stared down at her arm, stunned. Her eyes floated up to meet his.

"Caleb, baby…" she mumbled.

He leaned close and kissed her cheek.

"Goodbye, Cat. Don't fight it, and say hello to Linc for me."

And then he turned and walked away. He heard her attempt a scream, but her voice sounded like a faint whimper, and he continued pushing his way through the crowd. He didn't even pause when he heard a thud, likely to be her body hitting the floor, followed by the screams of panicked revelers. He kept pushing his way through, his head down, his cap even lower. Cavill's chemist buddy had upgraded the Strychnine, and this version was guaranteed to work in less than three minutes. Eventually he was out the door and sliding into the car waiting out front.

"You got the bitch?" Cavill asked.

"I got her."

"Alright then, since we have that out of the way, I have some great ideas about what we can do next."

Caleb chuckled. "Okay, I'm listening."

"First, there's Sudan. That shit is seriously getting out of hand, but I think you can do some good damage there. We could get in, deal with the rebels, end the conflict, and be gone in a year. Since you have a fondness for creating chaos in African countries, I figured you could actually do some good in Sudan. Bill Clinton and Kofi Annan would be grateful. What do you say?"

Caleb laughed. "Uh, option two, please."

"Fine, fine, if you need a break before your next mayhem, that's fine. I get you. So option two, Hawaii, where Page Affleck is currently frolicking in the sun."

"What?"

"Remember Page? Cat's friend from the university back in Ghana? I kept tabs on her a little, since she was super hot *and* clean. Tough combo, you know."

"She's in Hawaii?"

"Hawaii, bro, lying in the sun in a bikini, surrounded by equally stunning women. So, what say you?"

"Hawaii," Caleb said as an image of Page flashed through his mind.

Cavill grinned. "That's why we're friends, bro, but when we get there, you gotta promise me, no politicians, or politicians' daughters, or any of that government BS—and most important, absolutely no guns. You got it?"

Caleb laughed out loud and pulled his seatbelt into place. Hawaii wasn't exactly his dream beach location and Page wasn't his dream girl, but both would just have to do...for now.

THE END